LUCINDA'S PAWNSHOP
BOOK ONE

Devil's Daughter

AN URBAN FANTASY BY

Hope Schenk-de Michele and Paul Marquez
with
Maya Kaathryn Bohnhoff

bird
st.
books

ABOUT THE AUTHORS

Hope Schenk-de Michele and Paul Marquez have been best friends for more than four decades. They both grew up in Los Angeles, California, and share a passion for mystery and science fiction. This passion led them to create the forever young and beautiful daughter of darkness, Lucinda.

While creating *Lucinda's Pawnshop*, they co-produced such titles as *Bloody Proof* and *El Grito*, a dual language, straight-to-video detective film shot in English and in Spanish. They also produced the 2001 *Imagine Awards*, 200 episodes of the syndicated home improvement television show *Home Magazine*, *Humphrey the Bear* for Galavision, and others.

Paul and Hope have also created an exceptionally fun board game called *SPIN, SKIN and WIN* for the young adult market, and are currently developing it into a television show.

To assist in bringing Lucinda's story into the literary world, Hope and Paul enlisted the help of Maya Kaathryn Bohnhoff as a collaborator. Maya is a *New York Times* best-selling author of science fiction, fantasy, and alternate history, as well as a performing and recording artist with her husband, Jeff. She is the author of more than a dozen novels, including *The Last Jedi: Star Wars (Star Wars: Coruscant Nights— Legends)* with Michael Reaves (Lucas Books, 2013). Her short fiction has appeared in such magazines as *Analog, Interzone, Baen's Universe* and *Amazing Stories*. Maya was a finalist for the John W. Campbell Best First Novel Award in 1990 and is a founding member of Book View Cafe—a publishing collective of professional authors established in 2008 on the theory that you can never have too many books.

All three authors reside in California: Marquez in West Hollywood, Schenk-de Michele in Toluca Lake with her husband of twenty-two years, and Bohnhoff with her family in San Jose.

DEDICATIONS

Thank you to my life partner of 38 years, William H. Grotticelli, whose passing was too soon and devastating. Thank you for your unconditional love and support throughout the years and for giving me everlasting great memories. It is through those loving memories and dreams that you have shed sunlight on me once again. Love you!

Thank you to my dear and longtime friend, co-author, and producing partner, Hope Schenk-de Michele. Thank you for your unwavering belief in this story because, without you, *Lucinda's Pawnshop* might never have seen the light of day.

—Paul Marquez

Thank you to my dear, loving husband, Richard de Michele, for over 23 years of unwavering support and resounding patience. It is you who makes our life the loving, magnificent adventure it is. Thank you to my dearest friend, co-author, and producing partner, Paul Marquez, who shared the dream.

—Hope Schenk-de Michele

To my oft-time writing partner and Jedi master, Michael Reaves. You are a light and an inspiration in more than a literary sense. And to Marc and Elaine Zicree who have never ceased to give me their faith and support. Thank you from the depths of my soul.

—Maya Kaathryn Bohnhoff

ACKNOWLEDGMENTS

DEVIL'S DAUGHTER: LUCINDA'S PAWNSHOP, Book One is the result of the unwavering belief and determination that paved the road for two longtime, dear friends to share the amazing ride of telling this story.

Thanks to Maya Kaathryn Bohnhoff for loving our story from the very beginning and being part of our team. And thank you to Jay McGraw, Joey Carson, Lisa Clark, and Andrea McKinnon from Bird Street Books for taking Lucinda's story to the public. Thank you to the collective creative team who are bringing our long-awaited dream to reality.

—Hope Schenk-de Michele and
Paul Marquez

I'd also like to acknowledge all of the above folks, especially Hope and Paul, for their patience and willingness to trust, and for their tremendous pioneering spirit in undertaking this foray into the literary world. Thank you for letting me be your Sherpa guide.

—Maya Kaathryn Bohnhoff

CHAPTER ONE

Brittany Anders had grown up watching old Hollywood musicals. She still watched them—still loved them. She watched them in black and white when she could. They were made in black and white, after all, and ought to be watched that way. She often caught herself humming show tunes. Her coworkers at the law firm of Dunfy, Corrigan, and Price thought it was amusing, and occasionally annoying. She made a point of trying not to hum in front of the senior partners.

She was humming now as she made her way up from the car park to her office on the thirty-fourth floor of their Lexington Avenue building. The song was from *Guys and Dolls*—a ditty about racehorses she'd always thought of as the "Can Do" song. Today, Brittany felt that she could do anything. She smiled, raising her eyes to the ceiling of the elevator.

Rising. That was her. A rising star at DC&P.

She had been an associate with the firm for only two years, fresh out of law school, but she had proven herself to be quick, savvy, and reliable. Aaron Price— one of the senior partners—had watched her present evidence in a civil suit mere months ago and had tapped her to move up into the ranks of the junior partners. He said she had *presence*, and had taken a professional interest in her.

She'd come to realize that the interest was a bit more than professional. She'd no sooner been promoted to the rarified precincts of the thirty-fourth floor than Aaron had asked her out. She'd been a bit nervous at first. Afraid that perhaps her new status came with strings, but he had been quite clear that he "didn't work that way." She had made a point of not listening to the gossip about the senior partners that might have hinted otherwise—and Aaron Price generated a lot of gossip.

Aaron was in his forties, divorced, and good-looking in a sleek, athletic way. Her younger sister would have called him a catch. She smiled as the elevator doors opened into the elegant foyer, then switched her tune to "Everything's Coming Up Roses" as she bypassed the secretarial cubicle just outside her own (brand new) office.

Her secretary, Terry Passavoy, rolled his eyes eloquently. "Oh, Lord," he said. "What old favorite of my mother's are you eviscerating now?"

Brittany gave him a mock scowl. "Eviscerating? I beg your pardon. I happen to have a fine voice."

"Hm," said Terry. "Don't quit your day job."

"This, from a man who wears ugly bow ties."

He reached up to touch that accessory lovingly. Today's tie was chartreuse. "Bow ties are not ugly. Bow ties are cool. And fashionable. They have a certain . . . *gravitas.*"

"Not that one," Brittany retorted, and headed into her office.

Quitting her day job was the furthest thing from her mind. She was a junior partner as of last week, and had been assigned lead counsel on a high-profile insider trading case. She had her own office—small, impersonal, but elegant and all *hers.* She'd yet to find time to personalize it. The box of tchotchkes, awards, and family photos she'd brought up from her tenth floor cubicle was still sitting atop the tiny conference table next to her bookshelf; a framed *Phantom of the Opera* poster lay beside it. It seemed out of place in this office. She'd take it home.

She moved to the box, pushed the poster to one side, and removed a framed photo of her entire family—Mom, Dad, older brother Roger, younger sister Stephie, Brittany herself, bracketed by her two siblings. This would go on her desk to remind her of who was really responsible for her having the opportunity to step into a junior partnership at a major New York law firm.

"Oh, by the way, Aaron wants to see you," Terry called.

"That's Mr. Price, to you, Mr. Passavoy. Where is he?"

"His office."

Brittany smiled. He was *not* "Mr. Price" to her. Not anymore. She dropped her briefcase and purse on her desk, set up the photo facing her chair, then hummed herself an entire garden of roses as she made her way down the broad, artfully decorated corridor to Aaron's office.

When she left his office half an hour later, she was silent. Her steps were deliberate, measured. Her thoughts, eddying. She felt disoriented, cold. She rubbed at her arms as if that would raise her internal temperature.

"Brittany? Brit?"

She glanced up. Terry was looking at her with an expression of concern on his handsome face.

"Is something wrong?"

Her head shook automatically. "No. No. I'm just . . . the Redmon case has taken a . . . a turn. Hold my calls, Terry. Okay?"

"As you wish. Can I bring you some coffee?"

"I'd like that. Thanks."

She went into her office, closed the door, and sat down at her desk. She took out her laptop, woke it, logged in, and fired up her e-mail.

There. There it was—the message Aaron had forwarded to her. There was a file attached. She took a deep breath. Opened the file. It was, itself, the contents of an e-mail that had been sent to her newest client—Brant Redmon. It described a merger that was about to happen—something that would cause the stock price of a medical instrumentation manufacturer to soar. The e-mail was dated a day and a half *before* her client had purchased thousands of shares of the stock . . . and a week before he sold just over half of them for millions more than the purchase price.

Terry came in with her coffee. She thanked him automatically. He looked at her strangely, but didn't speak. Thank God for that. He closed the door carefully behind him as he left.

Brittany sat back in her chair, cold to the bone and feeling as if all the air had left the room. Brant Redmon was guilty of the charges she was defending him against. He had been forewarned that the stock in Medivantage Inc. was going to go sky high when its partnership with one of the world's largest pharma companies was unveiled. She had assumed—naively, it now seemed—that he was innocent of the charges.

Aaron still thought of him as innocent. Yes, he had purchased the stock knowing about the merger, but he had been intending to buy it all along. Then, on the eve of the purchase, he'd gotten this e-mail. He'd spent the next day or so agonizing over the decision. In the end, he'd bought the stock anyway. He realized his mistake.

Brittany stared at the screen, her mind automatically going into damage control mode. She wondered if Redmon had deleted the e-mail—*really* deleted it, not just dragged it into his trash. She'd have to ask him. She checked the forwarding address. It was a series of numbers at a popular e-mail service—most likely an anonymous, phantom account. She'd bet if she replied to it, she'd get bounced. She tried anyway.

She saw that Aaron had been copied on the message. So had the other senior partners. Now they were asking her—*Aaron* was asking her—to lose the evidence of their client's mistake.

Which meant, didn't it, that he and his partners had already deleted it from their own machines? Now they were asking her to smother incontrovertible evidence that the client in her first signature case had not only done what she was preparing to insist he had not, but had perjured himself in a series of depositions.

Just now in his office, Aaron had described this as a "bump in the road." If it came to light, this was no bump in the road; it was an IED. And she was being asked to help disarm it. Possibly throw herself on it.

She tried to imagine being Brant Redmon—prepared to buy stock he felt would benefit him, only to have someone place him in the untenable position of having to pass on what he already suspected would be a good purchase. Aaron had described it as a catch-22. Should Redmon have to pass on a stock he wanted simply because someone had shown him evidence that it would be successful?

Aaron was right; that wasn't fair. But would their lie of omission result in fairness?

What was it Aaron had told her just now: "Success comes with a price." It had been a joke between them since their first date a week ago—a wordplay on his last name. As she had achieved success at Dunfy, Corrigan, and Price, so she had attracted Aaron Price. She had been attracted in turn . . . and so had purposefully screened out the office gossip.

How deep did her attraction go? Deep enough for her to do this? She found him charismatic and easy to be with. He certainly seemed to enjoy being with her. She admired him—respected his legal acumen. She didn't need to ask if he admired and respected her. He wouldn't have voted to promote her if he didn't.

Her mouse pointer hovered over the Delete icon in her mail app for a moment. She glanced over at the family portrait she'd placed on her desk—four smiling faces that bore a strong resemblance to her own. For their sake, if not for her own, she needed to think this through.

She logged out, shut the laptop, picked up her purse, and headed for the foyer.

"I have a couple of errands I need to run," she told Terry, and hurried into the elevator before he could ask her any questions.

She needed to walk, because walking—especially in the balmy autumn air with its underlying threat of the chilly days to come—gave her mind a place to run. She let it run. Let it pick and pull at the dilemma she found herself in. If they won this case—and she contributed to winning it—she'd get a bonus to go with the promotion she'd earned. Her family—who had sacrificed so much to send her to law school—would be proud. And Aaron . . .

She shook herself. Aaron's affection for her had nothing to do with how well she handled the Redmon case. It annoyed her that she imagined it did. She wasn't that cynical, was she?

On some level, she knew this was a test. Aaron Price wanted to be sure the firm could trust her loyalty to the company and its clients—sure that she was DC&P material.

Was she?

She was standing on the corner of Twenty-Third and Lexington, contemplating an impulse buy at V23. followed by a latte at Gramercy Star Cafe, when a storefront she'd never noticed before caught her eye.

LUCINDA'S PAWNSHOP & ANTIQUARY the signage said—and it had appeared just to the right of V23, where there had been a jewelry store the last time Brittany had noticed. There had been scaffolding on the facades of these buildings for some months. Apparently some of it had been taken down, revealing the new store— although "new" wasn't exactly the word she'd have used to describe the storefront. It had a distinctly Old World look to it—a dark red door with a multipaned window set in brick, a huge front window to match.

Curious, her dilemma shoved momentarily aside, Brittany crossed Twenty-Third and bypassed both the café and the boutique to stand before the pawnshop. The display in the sunny front window was a mishmash of found objects: an ancient mandolin awash in mother-of-pearl; a gold, pearl, and peridot bracelet; a silver tea set; a doll with posable arms and legs and huge gray eyes; a trio of ceramic Chinese cat teapots; a desk set with a letter opener that looked like Excalibur; a set of blue onion flower dishes.

Funny that she should remember blue onion flower. It was a pattern her grandmother had collected. In fact, the storefront reminded her powerfully of the sort of place Gramma had dragged her into when they visited the little Northern California town where she lived. Brittany had hated it then. Now the memory seemed pleasant and comforting.

She peered through the store window, trying to see past the display of items into the depths of the shop. All she saw was darkness punctuated by glowing pools of amber light. She had the bizarre impression that the place wasn't as empty as it appeared to be—that something moved amid the shadows, just out of reach of the light.

A shiver ran down her spine. Gloomy little cave.

She started to turn away, but was halted by the items in the window. This was exactly the sort of place where she might find a token of her new position at DC&P. Collecting things ran in her blood—at least that's what her mother claimed. She'd taught her from childhood to commemorate major life events with tokens of success or change.

"Keeps you from getting jaded," Mom had said. "Gives you a touchstone— something to remind you of what you can accomplish if you put your mind to it."

The thought drew Brittany through the door of the shop. She was delighted by the soft tinkle of the appropriately old-fashioned bell bolted to the door frame. Her gramma's favorite antique store had had just such a bell. The door closed behind her, cutting off the street noise so completely she reflexively glanced out the window to make sure Twenty-Third Street was still there. It was, but it seemed no more real than a TV show with the sound turned off. The only noises in the shop were tiny, delicate ones: the ticking of a variety of clocks, air sighing through heat registers.

She stepped farther into the room and had the fleeting impression that the shadows pressed toward her as she advanced—that they watched her, whispering beneath counters and in corners.

She stopped in mid-room. Maybe she should just leave.

The impression faded suddenly. The shadows were just shadows, and whatever Brittany imagined had populated them was gone. She blinked. The store no longer seemed dark and gloomy. It felt cozy, in fact. Filtered sunlight fell through the front windows, blending with the golden radiance from a chandelier that hung over the center of the hardwood floor. The glass display cases, which ringed the main room, were softly lit with some sort of clever illumination. The walls seemed to be covered in books.

She reached out a hand to tentatively brush her fingertips across the spine of one leather-bound volume. A feeling of inexplicable dread coursed through her. She pulled her hand back and chided herself for having an overactive imagination. She took a step away from the bookshelf, then jumped and glanced down as something brushed past her ankles.

A sleek ginger cat wound itself about her legs. It looked up at her with huge, amber eyes and opened its pink mouth in a toothy "meow."

"Well, hello there. Aren't you a beauty."

She reached down to pet the cat but it trotted away across the room, where it leapt to the top of one of the display cases. Brittany followed it, peering at the items on display as the cat wove its way down the length of the counter.

These objects were even more varied than the ones in the front window. Besides the inevitable jewelry, there were antique wire-rimmed glasses; an ink pot and quill pen; several tiny leather-bound volumes; a gold watch with diamonds sparkling around its face; a collection of strange glass balls with tiny figures inside; a set of dominoes that looked as if they were made of bone; a chess set that seemed to be carved from ebony and ivory; a trio of see-, hear-, and speak-no-evil monkeys that gleamed in gold, silver, and copper. There were several daggers—or maybe they were just fancy letter openers. There was even a small, pearl-handled revolver with what looked like rubies set into the grip—eyes in a pale, oblong face.

Fascinated, Brittany followed the cat to the case in the farthest corner of the room. There, laid out on a bed of midnight-blue velvet, were a dozen or so pens. They were magnificent, gleaming in a dozen shades, made of wood, of carnelian, of jade, of nacre, of ivory. Of them all, one drew her eye as if it were the only pen in the case. Its body was a lacy filigree of gold—or something that looked like gold. Beneath that, was a deep azure barrel. The nib was silver, as was a little lever in the side of the pen.

"Oh," Brittany breathed, mesmerized.

The cat purred, sat, and began to clean itself.

"Find something you like, dear?"

Brittany gasped in surprise and glanced up. An older woman smiled at her from the opposite side of the display case, where she stood mantled in the light from the chandelier.

Where the heck did she come from?

The woman appeared to be in her fifties, with a round moon face and faded red hair. But there was nothing faded about her eyes. Behind her wire-rimmed glasses, they were the most vivid shade of green Brittany had ever seen. With the exception of those eyes, the woman's resemblance to her grandmother was uncanny.

"Actually, yes," she said. "That pen." She pointed down into the display case.

The proprietress followed the gesture with her peridot eyes. "Ah, yes. That pen. Beautiful, isn't it?"

"Very. Might I see it?"

"Certainly." The woman slid open the back of the case and lifted the pen out, setting it down atop a black velvet pad that accentuated its bright gleam.

Brittany picked it up and turned it in her hands. It was heavy, solid, and felt good in her fingers. As if it just fit there. As if it had been waiting for her to walk into Lucinda's Pawnshop and find it.

She wanted it. No matter what it cost.

"This is a real fountain pen, isn't it?" she asked. "The kind you have to fill from a bottle?" She tapped the little silver lever.

"Exactly. The filigree is fourteen karat gold, too. The barrel is lapis lazuli—which is why it's so heavy—and the nib is sterling silver."

"It must be quite expensive, then."

"I'm asking three hundred for it."

That was a pleasant surprise. She'd expected more. She *loved* how it felt in her hand, the way light raced along the traceries of filigree.

"It still works?"

"Oh, yes. It still works. It's not an antique, though; it was a custom piece made for a local attorney."

Brittany glanced up. "Really? Who?"

"A criminal lawyer named Adam Clinton. Maybe you've heard of him?"

The name surprised Brittany into laughter. "Heard of him? You could say so. He was a hero of mine when I was in law school. I studied the cases he defended like some people study . . . oh, I don't know, history, I guess. Or poetry."

She looked down at the instrument in her hands. Suddenly the whole outing seemed like kismet. She came to a firm decision—glad she could be confident about *something*—and set the pen back on the pad.

"I'll take it. This is just too good to pass up. You accept credit cards?"

"Of course." The proprietress produced a fancy velvet box into which she put the pen, tying it carefully to the inside of the box with a blue ribbon that perfectly matched the lapis barrel. Then she aimed a glance at the ginger cat. "Get down, please, Vorden. You're smudging the glass."

The animal gave a feline snort of umbrage, then stood, stretched, yawned, and leapt from the top of the case to vanish into the darker recesses at the back of the store.

"Beautiful animal," Brittany said.

"Yes, and she knows it."

"Adam Clinton," Brittany repeated as she watched the shopkeeper wrap the little velvet box in paper and tie it with string—something she thought quaint. "I haven't heard that name for ages. He was such a luminary in criminal law. A real success story."

"They say success comes at a price," the older woman said thoughtfully.

Brittany stifled a shiver, covering it with nervous laughter. "Funny. Someone else actually *did* say that to me today. Or something like it."

The woman paused to give her a searching look. "You're not superstitious, are you?"

"No," Brittany assured her, "not at all."

"Well, that's good. Some people might be bothered by—" She cut off and shook her head, then held the wrapped package out to Brittany, who handed over her credit card.

"Bothered by what?"

"The poor fellow who owned this pen died rather tragically."

Brittany felt a moment of shocked embarrassment that she hadn't known Adam Clinton had died at all, much less tragically. "I hadn't heard," she admitted. "How did he die?"

"You know, I don't remember, exactly. Memory gets a bit tattered at my age. I just remember that it was tragic in some way. Shocking, as I recall. Or maybe 'ironic' is the word I'm looking for."

Odd thing to say.

The woman smiled, handed Brittany her receipt and card, and said, "Thank you for coming in. I hope the pen pleases you."

Brittany nodded, feeling suddenly as if she'd just pulled an all-nighter. She was definitely stopping by Gramercy for a latte. She needed to focus.

⁜

The proprietress of Lucinda's Pawnshop watched the young woman leave, then slipped through a curtained doorway into the back of the shop.

"Going out, Lucinda?" The strawberry blonde perched atop a padded stool pretending to read the latest issue of *Elle*. She pronounced the name "Lu-*ceen*-da."

"Of course I'm going out. Due diligence, you know."

"You're leaving the store untended?"

"I don't expect anyone to come in. If they do, you could fill in for me."

The blonde's perfect nose wrinkled. "I think not. If someone comes in, I shall summon Rey."

"As you like." Lucinda turned and headed for the rear door.

"Shall I tell the master you've hooked one?"

Lucinda glanced back over her shoulder, but kept walking. "*May* have hooked one. You can never be sure about people."

The blonde snorted delicately and tossed her long, thick hair over one shoulder. "Tell me what I know not."

"The expression," said Lucinda, "is 'tell me something I don't know.'"

The blonde shrugged and turned her amber eyes back to the magazine.

Lucinda let herself out through the back door of the little shop, stepping out into the alley in a shaft of sunlight. Her features and form faded almost to transparency, then began to blur and morph. Years rolled away from the face, the features sharpened, the skin glowed with youthful vigor. Her body changed as well, growing longer, more slender. Even the clothing crawled into sleeker, more fashionable lines.

In mere moments, the faded fifty-year-old was gone. There was nothing faded about the young, breathtakingly beautiful woman who strode down the alley and out onto Lexington Avenue. From her slender limbs to her vividly auburn hair and creamy complexion—both set off by the vivid green of a dress that clung to every curve—she was a patch of bright color against the shadows and grimy, aging brick and asphalt.

The only thing she had in common with her older version was a pair of strikingly green eyes.

⁜

Brittany left the café nursing a cinnamon latte and feeling . . . she couldn't put what she was feeling into words. She had just spent three hundred dollars on a pen. A *pen*, for the love of God. She felt . . . stupid, numb. What was she doing? She needed to get back to the office. She needed to face the inevitable.

If only she knew what the inevitable was. Duty? Loyalty? To what? To the company, Aaron, the client, to principle . . . to justice? She pulled her scattered thoughts into line. She would go back. She would look over the incriminating document. She would talk to Aaron. She would do what she had to do.

She shouldered her way out the door of the coffee shop and almost bumped into another young woman on the sidewalk. She glanced up into shockingly green eyes. "Excuse me!" Brittany murmured. "I wasn't watching where I was going."

The woman smiled at her. She had a stunning smile, hair the color of polished cedar, and a figure that made Brittany feel inadequate and flabby. She also seemed familiar.

"Are you—" she began, then shook her head and held the door open. "Were you going in?"

"No, I just wandered too close to the door," the woman said. Her voice was warm, with an undercurrent of gentle humor.

The cinnamon scent of Brittany's latte rose up to hijack her other senses. She could *see* the scent, *hear* it, *feel* it on her skin. As peculiar as that was, she wanted nothing more than to stand there on that sun-warmed sidewalk and absorb the moment.

She met the other woman's eyes again, her mouth open to ask if she was related to the owner of the pawnshop next door to V23. Silly, how those green eyes reminded her of the pen in her purse, of papers she needed to sign . . . of a piece of evidence she needed to destroy.

You're stalling, said a small, prickly voice from her rational mind. *You're putting off the inevitable. Just do it. It's pro forma.*

She flashed the other woman an apologetic smile and hurried away up Lexington to the law offices of Dunfy, Corrigan, and Price. She made one more stop on the way there, dropping in at an art store to purchase a bottle of ink.

Back at her desk, Brittany unwrapped the golden pen, filled it, and tried it out on a notepad. Smooth. It was a delight to write with; it had weight and substance, and seemed to fit in her hand as if made for it. Holding it gave her a visceral thrill of pleasure. In her childhood, she might have slept with it under her pillow.

She set it down atop her desk and finished her latte while she scanned her e-mail. She found her thoughts straying to Adam Clinton. Aware that she was still putting off the moment of truth in the Redmon case, she surrendered to her growing curiosity about her law school hero. She googled "Adam Clinton criminal attorney dead" and scored a series of hits.

What she found wasn't just tragic; it was disturbing. Her law school hero had been slain by a man he had successfully defended on a murder charge. He had, according to several reports, gotten the alleged killer off on a technicality having to do with the police search of the man's residence. His one-time client had entered his home—invited, to all appearances—then stabbed Adam Clinton to death with a letter opener. Clinton had bled out from over two dozen stab wounds.

Brittany felt a cold, icy ball of horror form in her heart as she read the description of the crime scene given by the housekeeper—the blood-soaked carpet, the gore-spattered desk. The coroner's statement was equally chilling: there had been very little blood left in the body, which meant his heart had kept beating for some time as he lay, helpless and terrified, on his office floor.

The killer had gone from there to murder several other people connected to the case—two witnesses to his alleged crime and a legal assistant in Clinton's practice. He'd been finally and fatally shot by the police detective who had initially arrested him, and whose family he had been terrorizing.

Murdered. Someone she had known—had admired—had been brutally murdered by a man he had defended. Brittany's stomach lurched. She felt as if a freezing hand had caught her by the throat. The pen lying on her desk suddenly filled her with more dread than satisfaction. How could she use it without thinking of Adam Clinton dying, alone, on the floor of his office, while his heart pumped his life out into the carpet?

Consequences.

The word popped unbidden into her head. Actions have consequences. Adam Clinton's actions—the ones that had gotten a murderer acquitted—had resulted in his own death and the deaths of three other people, plus untold trauma to the detective and his family.

It was like . . . dominoes. A domino is a tiny thing—an inconsequential thing—unless it falls and begins a cascade of consequences. Karma, her mother would call it. As you sow, so shall you reap—there was a scripture that said that, as she recalled. She thought about that when she read the daily news—politicians outed for sex crimes or taking bribes or conflicts of interest. It seemed, sometimes, as if people's sense of propriety or reality or even simple humanity was disintegrating day by day.

Brittany shook herself and tried to keep her mind from drawing a comparison between her own circumstances and what had happened to her one-time hero. This wasn't a murder case. It was about money, not lives. Brant Redmon was not a dangerous man. He was a corporate CEO, an international businessman and entrepreneur—someone who got written about in *Forbes* and *Money*—not a gangster or a career criminal. He'd been a law-abiding citizen until he had acted on financial information provided by that e-mail. Acted *in spite of* that information, according to him.

There was a light tap at the door of her office, and Terry poked his head in. "I've got the Redmon deposition and briefs for you to go over and sign," he said.

Brittany took a deep breath and exhaled, blowing all thoughts of Adam Clinton and dominoes and murderers out of her head. She lifted the fountain pen. "Well, I've got a pen and I'm not afraid to use it."

Terry brought the file to her desk, his eyes on the pen. "Wow, isn't that a pretty thing? Sort of antiquarian, though, isn't it? You know they make cartridge pens now, right? Is that real gold?"

"Yes, it is. And lapis lazuli. I like that it's antiquarian, as you call it."

"Wow," he said again. "I've always wanted an excuse to say 'lapis lazuli.' Can I hold it?"

She handed him the pen. He hefted it, frowned, and handed it back.

"Not my style," he said and headed for the outer office, rubbing his hand on the gray twill of his suit coat. "Are you in or out?"

"I'm out for everyone but one of the senior partners."

"Mmm. Bet I can guess which one."

"I meant . . . Oh, never mind," Brittany said as the door snicked closed.

Her mind was already on the trial briefs and depositional records she had to read over, correct, then sign or initial. She uncapped the pen and began working her way down through the pile. She had almost succeeded in forgetting about the incriminating piece of information in her e-mail box when she got to the last document—a schedule of evidentiary documentation being presented by her legal team.

She looked it over. Everything was there . . . everything but that one damning item. Her pen hovered over the signature line, feeling suddenly heavy in her hand. Her signature on that line would give credence to a bald-faced lie . . .

Which will keep your client from going to jail and potentially destroying his entire professional life. What is the matter with you? You knew the stakes were high at this level.

Yes, but not this high. I'll be lying in a court of law.

Brittany let out a chuff of frustration. *Oh, for the love of God, just sign the damn thing! Get it over with. You know you're going to have to do it eventually.*

She set the pen down, absently massaging the writer's callus on her right ring finger. She needed to talk to Aaron. She had to be sure she was doing the right thing—or at least not the tragically *wrong* thing. A misstep here could ruin her career . . . or worse.

Brittany got up from her desk. Her gaze skated by the photo of her family. What would it do to them if she screwed up this opportunity . . . one way or another? She hadn't exactly sailed through college and law school, but her family had seen her through all of that. The last thing in the world she wanted to do was to disappoint them.

She left the office, giving Terry a hasty "Be right back," and plunged down the hall to Aaron Price's office suite. The doors were slightly ajar. She'd raised her hand to knock when she caught the sound of voices within.

"Redmon's an ass," was the first thing she heard. The voice was Larry Corrigan's.

He was a fiftyish fellow, portly, with watery gray eyes and a friar's fringe of mouse-brown hair. He was avuncular and jovial-looking, which made people want to trust him. Brittany would never have imagined she'd hear him say such a thing about a major client—especially in that scathing tone of voice.

Some perverse imp drove her to lower her hand and lean her head close to the door to catch the conversation.

"An ass who pays us well." That was Aaron.

"Yes. Because he's wealthy enough *not* to have been so desperate to purchase that Medivantage stock that he tempted insider trading charges. What was he thinking? As visible as he is, as high-profile as that merger was, did he imagine the SEC would turn a blind eye to such serendipitous timing?"

"It's 'he said/they said,' Larry," said Aaron. "Without that e-mail, the state doesn't have a case."

"Yes, that e-mail. Where did that come from, do you suppose? I hate anonymous tipsters."

"I suspect I know who it was. He's already been purged from Redmon's organization. In fact, I suspect forwarding the e-mail to us was retaliation."

There was a moment of heavy silence, then Larry said, "If the e-mail doesn't emerge in evidence, is that retaliation going to go further?"

"Not in this case. Not if the tipster is who I think it is. He's got his own secrets to keep. Such as, how he got that e-mail in the first place and who he got it from."

There was a moment of silence, then Larry Corrigan sighed and said, "Then it stops here."

"It stops here. No one outside our offices will know that Redmon got a tip on that stock. It's just some ex-employee's contention that he did."

"Is Brittany on board?"

"Of course," Aaron assured him. "I told her Redmon intended to buy the Medivantage stock before he received the tip."

Was that the truth? Brittany silently begged him to say it, to repeat it so she could sign the evidentiary paperwork with only a small, niggling qualm instead of feeling she ought to confess to the nearest priest—despite not being Catholic.

What he said was, "There's no reason for her to know what a piece of work the guy is."

"He's an ass," said Corrigan again. "I swear he does stuff like this on purpose just to get us to earn our retainer."

"No, he told me he's got some big project he's kicking off in Qatar or Kuwait or someplace. Something that required a massive infusion of capital up front. The Medivantage merger gave him a solid opportunity to acquire those funds."

Corrigan sighed again. Leather creaked as he heaved himself out of a chair. "I just hope this case doesn't blow up in Brittany's face."

She didn't hear what Aaron said in reply; she was already on her way back to her office, trying not to look shaken.

"I'm back," she told Terry unnecessarily, went into her office, and shut the door behind her.

She didn't return to her desk. Instead she stood next to the desk and stared out the window at the Lexington Avenue canyon, the deepest recesses of which had been brought to light by the advancing sun. There was a dove perched on the windowsill—or a pigeon, maybe; she'd never been certain of the difference. It was a large, beautiful bird, gleaming in iridescent shades of blue-gray. It was facing into the office, its head turned slightly to one side as if watching her.

That was absurd. It was probably watching its own reflection in the window and wondering what that other bird was doing in there.

Brittany had no more than had the thought when the bird's piercing gaze met hers. Its eyes were green. She'd never seen a pigeon with green eyes. A thrill ran down between her shoulder blades at the weirdness of it. It was as if the thing was waiting for her to do something. Waiting for her to decide . . .

She took a half step toward the window, caught the movement of her own reflection, and found herself staring into her own eyes. They looked haunted. *She* looked haunted. The injustice of it brought swift anger. She'd done nothing to deserve this. She'd worked hard, she'd put in extra hours, she'd been loyal.

She caught a flicker of movement behind her in the small room just before Aaron Price's voice said, "Daydreaming, Brit?"

Brittany jumped and spun away from the window. "Aaron! You startled me! No, I wasn't daydreaming. I was just—" She gestured toward the window. "That bird. It's got green eyes."

Aaron chuckled. "As fascinating as that may be, do you really have time for zoological pursuits?"

Brittany vacillated, her attention still half on the pigeon. "I suppose not. Aaron, I need to talk to you about this thing with Redmon."

"Yes?" He looked at her expectantly, straightening his tie.

"His story—how sure are you of it? I mean, do you believe him when he says he'd already made plans to buy the stock? Can he prove it?"

"No, he can't *prove* it. All he's got is that handwritten note reminding him to call his broker and have him purchase Medivantage. It's dated, but the prosecution will contend it could have been written after the fact. And yes, I believe him. Absolutely. Which is why we need to make it go away."

Liar. He was lying to her. Anger flared in her breast and she thought she had some idea how he'd answered Larry Corrigan's hope that the case wouldn't blow up in her face. She didn't want to know, she realized.

She let none of what she was feeling reach her eyes. "Aaron . . ."

As if sensing her ambivalence, he said, "Look, sweetheart, he was in a catch-22. I mean honestly, can you imagine how he must have felt? He's getting ready to buy stock in this company and this thing lands in his in-box. What's he supposed to do, Brit? Not buy a stock he already thought would be a good investment? Undermine his own corporate interests? All he did was read his e-mail. He couldn't exactly unread it, could he?"

No. No more than I can unread it. She sat back down behind her desk feeling . . . trapped. She looked at the pen sitting atop the paperwork.

Pick it up and sign the damn papers! she snarled at herself. *This is crazy. This man trusts you to do what's right for the firm. Do it.*

But I can't trust him!

Aaron followed her gaze to the sheaf of papers on her desk—the evidentiary schedule uppermost—then raised his eyes to study her face. "I was thinking," he said as he rounded her desk, "that the time is ripe for a celebration of your new status here. How about dinner tonight? Just the two of us? Your place after?"

She nodded. So, he was escalating the affair. "Dinner. Sure."

"O-okay. I expected a bit more enthusiasm than that."

She looked up at him. He seemed genuinely wounded. All the rumors she'd shut her ears to clamored to be heard. How she'd heard someone mention a Mrs. Price and told herself they were referring to his mother.

Still, she smiled. "I'm sorry. I'm just distracted. Dinner sounds wonderful. I'd like that."

"Great. What if I just drop by your office at around six thirty? We can go over to the Waldorf . . . Peacock Alley?"

She nodded, willing her smile to deepen as he rested his hip against the corner of her desk and leaned in to kiss her, putting out a hand to steady himself. His left hand. There was a band of white skin on the ring finger.

She frowned. That was not the hand of a long-divorced man. Why had she never noticed before?

I didn't want to notice.

He must have brushed her family portrait—the little stand buckled, flipping the photo over onto its back with a clatter of sound that startled both of them.

Brittany stared at the photograph with something like horror, suddenly and strongly feeling her family's presence—their gazes loving, admiring . . . trusting. Their middle child—the one who everyone else had deemed most likely to drop out of high school—had made it to a prestigious Manhattan law firm.

Aaron straightened, glancing down at the picture. "I don't like an audience," he said (Another lie, Brittany thought.) He picked up the photo and set it, face down, on the desk. Then, he kissed her.

It was a teasing kiss—gentle, with a promise of more to come. He straightened, a cockeyed smile on his lips, arousal kindling in his eyes. "Until tonight," he said, then tapped the paperwork. "Get to work, counselor. Don't forget we have a meeting in half an hour . . . and a hot date tonight."

Brittany sat silently for a moment, her fingers pressed to her lips. That kiss—that smile—had once made her feel warm inside, happy, aroused. What she felt now was confused and empty, with a growing anger.

Her gaze fell on the photograph lying facedown on her desk. She had worked every day of her life at DC&P with that portrait where she could see it—where she could look at it throughout the day. Today, she had avoided looking at it because it made her feel wretched.

For a moment, she pictured herself in some dim future, having a drink with her colleagues, bragging about how she'd gotten Brant Redmon off on insider trading charges. It was not a story she could tell her family at Christmas.

Anger swarmed up, hot and insistent, bringing tears to her eyes. Anger that Aaron would ask this of her. That he would manipulate her in this way. Worse than that, she understood, in a blinding flash of clarity, that if the deceit were ever discovered and the case did blow up in her face, she alone would go down for it. Her superiors had set themselves up to have plausible deniability. It would be her word against theirs.

She wondered if any or all of them had ever been put in the position she was in now. Hell, maybe this was a rite of passage at DC&P.

Her eyes went back to the pen sitting atop the signature line of the evidentiary schedule as if poised to sign it. All she needed to do was pick it up . . .

Steeling herself, she pulled the schedule to her, picked up the pen, and wrote a note on the bottom of the last page. Then she signed it, ignoring the shrill voice of reason that told her she was being a wimp and a sap. Then she opened the e-mail she'd received with its incriminating attachment (yes, her reply had bounced from the phantom account), and forwarded it to Terry with a note: "Make sure this file goes into the evidentiary package for the Redmon case."

Brittany set the family photo back to rights and sat gazing at it, turning the pen in her hands. Adam Clinton had signed lies into existence with this pen. Had twisted the truth and inked away four human lives, including his own. She remembered an upperclassman once remarking in a tone of worshipful awe that Adam Clinton could get the Devil off on a technicality. She'd thought it the highest compliment, then. How could she have been so monumentally naive?

Suddenly, the pen made her palms itch. She slid it into a drawer and turned to glance at the windowsill. The green-eyed bird was gone. Only half aware of what she was doing, Brittany slipped her family portrait into her briefcase, picked up the trial briefs, her briefcase, jacket, and purse, and left the office.

No, she was *not* a wimp or a sap. She had a backbone, and it was damned well going to hold her upright as she marched out of here.

"Going to lunch?" Terry asked as she drew level with his desk.

She shook her head, handing the briefs over to him. "Going home early. Things to do."

Good. Her voice had been cool and level—completely at odds with the seething stew of emotion on the inside. She started to walk away, then turned and looked back at her secretary. "Terry, if I were to leave DC&P and go to work somewhere else, would you be willing to come with me?"

His gaze met hers, startled. "Well . . . well, yeah. I mean, I've been working for you since you got here. But why would you leave? You've got everything going for you."

She smiled. "Does seem that way, doesn't it?" She turned on her heel and entered the elevator, humming.

Can do.

CHAPTER TWO

The pewter-gray pigeon alighted on the back doorstep of the pawnshop in a flutter of feathers. Its form faded, drifted, expanded as if molded by invisible hands. In mere moments, Lucinda—a young and vibrant Lucinda—stood in the grimy sunlight of the empty alley.

She shook herself mentally as she always did upon shape-shifting. She had been doing it for millennia, but never without that moment of disorientation as her perspective altered. In this case, she had shifted from a form with monocular vision to one with stereopsis. It took her a second to be able to trust her eyes.

When she saw the world in three dimensions once again, she opened the rear door and stepped into the shop. The back room was empty, but she heard voices from the front of the store. Had someone come in after all?

She extended a tendril of thought ahead and ascertained that this was not the case. There was a human being in the shop, but his was a familiar soul signature—translucent and gray. The other two entities in the room were not human.

Lucinda squared her shoulders and went through into the shop.

Two men stood in the front room, conversing in low tones. One leaned casually against the glass-topped counter, imposingly tall, slender, and stunningly attractive. He wore a beautifully tailored burgundy Gucci suit coat over a saffron silk shirt and form-fitting blue jeans. The shirt was open at the throat, exposing the sculpted column of his neck. His collar-length hair was a wavy chestnut shot through with gold, his cheekbones were high and sharp, his oddly tilted eyes a shade of amber that made Lucinda think of topazes, his skin a flawless, creamy bronze.

The whole effect—the casual sophistication, the aura of barely tamed feline savagery—was mesmerizing. Most people—male or female—would look at Lucien Trompe and believe they might be looking at the most attractive man on the planet. That was exactly what they were supposed to believe; he had designed himself to foster that attraction. He was, quite literally, a self-made man—built to enthrall.

He appeared to be in his early thirties. He was not. He was eons older. He held the ginger cat in his arms, stroking it reflexively. Its purr was loud enough to vibrate the display of tiny teaspoons in the wire rack that sat atop the counter behind him.

Lucien Trompe was not his name, of course. Nor was Satan or Shaitan or Mara or Ahriman or Dan Patch or Old Nick or Loki or Coyote or any of the other monikers humans had bestowed on him over uncounted centuries. His real name— the name given him by his own Father—the All-Father—was Lucifer, Light-bearer.

Ironic, that.

The other man in the room was much less relaxed. In his dapper three-piece suit—which was the same shade of light brown as his hair—he was unremarkable, faded . . . but only in comparison to his companion. In any other company, Rey Granger, with his gray eyes, fair skin, and finely planed features, might have been the most handsome man in the room. In a room with Lucien Trompe, he was barely noticeable.

The conversation stopped. Both men turned to watch Lucinda's entrance. Rey's blue eyes were hungry; they were always hungry when they looked at her, and would remain so, since Lucinda had no intention of inviting his advances. Lucifer's topaz eyes were merely curious.

"Daughter," he said, his beautiful face lighting in a smile, "Vorden tells me you sold the Clinton relic today." His voice was dark, smooth, mellifluous, and wore an accent that suggested Cambridge.

Lucinda raised her eyebrows. "She had to tell you? That surprises me. I thought you would be following that connection. You said it was an important one."

"It *is* important, but I had a number of other things to tend to. And, of course, I knew you'd be personally involved."

"I was." Lucinda grimaced and made an impatient gesture. "Which seems not to have helped. I'm sorry to have to report that the mark turned at the last possible moment."

"What?" Lucifer's amber irises seemed almost to glow. He stopped stroking the cat. The cat stopped purring.

Lucinda shrugged. "What is it humans say these days: she got cold feet? I'm not sure why. Although I suspect she sensed she was being manipulated."

Lucifer cocked his head, frowning. "By the talisman?"

"No, by her senior partner, Aaron Price. He was less than subtle . . . and she overheard a telling bit of conversation."

Lucifer straightened and turned to face her, setting the cat down atop the display case. She felt the tension building in him as static on her skin.

"What conversation might that be?"

"A dialogue between her would-be lover and another of the senior partners. She caught them in a lie." Lucinda smiled wryly. "You should appreciate that, being the Father of Lies."

Rey let out a cough of disbelief. "She's a lawyer defending a corporate CEO. You can't make me believe she isn't used to getting a steady diet of lies."

Lucinda uttered a trill of laughter. "From her clients, certainly, but not from her own senior partners. Not from the man who recruited her—the man who's been wooing her. She was supposed to be on the inside of the lies. I think she found herself on the outside and didn't like it. Then, of course, there's the fact that if the case unraveled, she'd be left holding the suspicious end of the yarn."

Lucifer tapped the top of the glass counter with one long, lean finger, putting a bit more force into each tap. "You're certain she's abdicated her duty to her employer?"

"I'm certain she means to resign."

Again, the whip-sharp glance; the static increased. "Then she didn't sign the documents."

Lucinda shook her head slowly, bright auburn hair sweeping her shoulders. She could feel Rey's gaze following the movement.

The ginger cat chose this moment to rub her cheek against Lucifer's hand. He moved with lightning speed, wrapping his fingers around the cat's neck and jerking it from the countertop to dangle helplessly in the air. Its amber eyes went huge and wild, and it raised its claws to rake at his hand. He shook it, squeezing until its pink mouth opened in a silent yowl of distress.

"Don't. Ever. Distract me."

He flung the cat away. It disappeared in a flash of golden motes before even one paw touched the carpet.

Lucinda smiled. "Temper, temper, Father."

Lucifer flicked cat hair from his suit coat and returned her smile with one that would have curdled milk. "I despise obsequiousness in subordinates."

Lucinda laughed. "Liar! You *love* obsequiousness. You feed on it."

He acknowledged the truth of that with a nod. His smile evaporated. "However, I *do* despise cowardice. I thought Brittany Anders had the courage of her convictions."

"She did. Just not the convictions you expected. At any rate, she's gone now, and the paperwork she left behind may get her erstwhile client convicted of insider trading. This poses a problem. What shall we do?"

Lucifer turned his hot gaze to Rey Granger. "Yes. What shall *we* do? What shall we do with these human beings when they can't even be trusted to yield to temptation?"

Rey shifted restively from one foot to the other. "If she still has the talisman, there's a chance we might yet get to her," he said, his tone hopeful.

Lucinda shook her head. "No. She left it behind."

Her father's gaze speared her, the golden depths suddenly dark. Rage was building in him again; Lucinda felt it as furnace heat—something of fire and brimstone. "She left it *behind*? It was *chosen* for her. *Chosen*. In fact, its *spirit* chose her. How could it not maintain its hold on her?"

"Clearly, something else had a stronger hold. Pride. Fear. Anger. Who knows, really?"

Lucifer turned to Rey with a violence that shone like fire in his eyes, but when he spoke his voice was cold, dry, and very, very soft. "*You* vetted her, Reynard. How did you not see this potential weakness?"

Rey exhaled as if someone had punched him in the stomach. Fear stood out on his face in a sudden dew of perspiration. "Looking at her history—cheating in school, shoplifting, some drug use. She-she cheated with her best friend's fiancé, broke them up, then dumped the guy. She seemed corruptible."

"*Seemed*?" Lucifer's body tensed, ripples of dark emotion radiating from every ersatz pore. Beneath his hand, the glass of the display counter cracked and crazed—fissures running from the tips of his outspread fingers with the sharp snap of splitting ice.

Rey jumped three steps backward, gaze on the riven glass, blinking in fear. He put a trembling hand to his tie.

"You apparently read garden-variety teenage stupidity as something much more useful. This is not the first time," Lucifer added, his voice deepening to a growl, "that you've misjudged a mark. I remind you that you have a body of flesh and blood and bone. It can be broken in so many ways . . . as you well know."

Rey went absolutely still, his only movement a flickering glance into the shadows at the rear of the store. Lucinda could feel his heart beating out his terror from across the room. She had no doubt he'd gladly have followed the cat into the Between, if he'd had the power, but unlike Vorden, Rey couldn't simply fade into the nether dimensions, nor could he die—nor even age. He would remain frozen in his late twenties, suffering whatever Lucifer made him suffer . . . and merely *wishing* he could die.

Lucinda intervened smoothly. "I don't think this was Rey's fault. He couldn't have predicted that the woman would suddenly grow a backbone. I doubt it was some unexpected virtue that caused her to back off. Only that she had a stronger sense of self-preservation—especially once she realized she was going to be the one to take the fall if the truth were known about their prestigious client. Most unfortunate, that bit of eavesdropping."

"That talisman," said Lucifer, "was tailored to her. It was decades in the making."

"What is a decade or three to us?" Lucinda asked, then: "Is she that important to our plans?"

"*She's* not important at all. She's a link in a chain. Redmon is the more important link. Redmon, with his deep Middle Eastern connections." Lucifer made a dismissive gesture with one hand, tossing his anger aside. "Of course, you're right, Daughter—what is a decade or three to us? We have other options. Her senior partner is now facing the lesser of two evils. Does he let the evidence speak against his client, or does he take measures to silence it himself?"

Lucinda was fairly sure she knew what choice Aaron Price would make.

"You say the woman left the pen behind?" Lucifer asked her.

"Yes. It's in her desk drawer."

"Then there is still a chance we can retrieve the situation."

Lucinda nodded. "Of course. I can—"

"No, Rey will take care of it. I have more important work for you, Daughter. There is a particular relic I wish to acquire. If you're impressed with something that was a decade in the making, you'll appreciate this even more."

"A new relic? Delightful. You know how I enjoy treasure hunting."

Acquiring relics was roughly half of Lucinda's job. The other half was placing them. All of them—every one—were like Adam Clinton's pen. They were soul magnets. Or perhaps soul snares or soul tethers were more apt terms. The souls were bound to the relics in a sort of mutual possession. The soul had possessed the object, which now possessed the soul—while both were possessed by the being who called himself Lucien Trompe.

Rey Granger was bound by such an object. What it was, Lucinda didn't know, though she'd admit to some curiosity about it. Were he to die while in thrall to it, he would face judgment by God and banishment to the remoteness men called Hell—something he had entered into a special contract with Lucifer in order to avoid.

Lucifer's interactions with humanity were circumscribed by divine laws that were as unforgiving as any other laws of physics. He could not interfere in the course of human history through direct action, but only through indirect manipulation and the power of the spoken or written word. He could not acquire material objects on his own; hence he employed indentured mortals like Rey Granger, who had served him for nearly half a century, or creatures like Vorden, whose evil was veiled but whose sphere of influence was limited to particular vices. Of all those who worked for the Dark Angel, his most valued asset was his daughter, Lucinda.

Lucinda Trompe was unique in all the world. Half mortal, half immortal, she had been sired by Lucifer on a human mother—THE human mother. The woman the Torah called "Eve."

It was her humanity that made Lucinda so valuable to her father. Unlike him, she could empathize with humans. She could, if she chose, *have* human experiences. She lived among them, worked among them, and understood how they thought in a way her father never could. Hence, it was her task to oversee their brush with the supernatural.

There were limits to that oversight, though, set by God Himself. Lucinda could not directly push or pull a soul into service to her father, but she could offer it opportunities for choice. Here, in this world, on this plane of existence, choice was everything and free will was sacrosanct.

Lucinda flicked another glance at Rey, wondering at the choices he'd made. Choices that had taken him from war-torn Vietnam into the service of Hell.

"What marvelous artifact am I to seek?" she asked her father.

His golden eyes held a spark of impish delight. "A Book of Shadows. A very particular Book of Shadows. It belonged to Morgan le Fay—not the creature of myth and legend, but the real and quite powerful adept. I have every confidence you will find it somewhere . . . some time. *You* have never failed me." The look he sent to Rey made the human shudder visibly.

"Another little piece of Armageddon?" Lucinda asked.

"A potentially important piece, as it happens."

Lucinda smiled and bowed her head deferentially. "Then I shall do my utmost to find it," she told him, and turned to go.

"Daughter, tell Vorden it would please me if she came out of hiding."

"*She* needn't tell me anything." The titian-haired woman stepped out of the shadows at the rear of the shop as if they had given birth to her. "I sense when you desire me . . . as you know. Just as I also sense all desires that come to the souls of mortals."

She glided past Lucinda with an arch expression on her perfect face, looking pointedly between her and Rey.

Lucinda was inwardly amused at the succubus's arrogance. She might be able to answer Lucifer's unspoken summonses or sense Rey's desires—for all Lucifer had granted him immortality, his flunky still had a mortal's weaknesses—but of

Lucinda's emotions she sensed only what Lucinda *allowed* her to sense. Now, for example, Vorden would perceive nothing but wry annoyance.

There were advantages to being the Devil's daughter.

Lucinda couldn't help but notice that Vorden had affected a ring of dark, ugly bruises on her fair neck—a reminder of Lucifer's sudden violence. But a reminder to whom?

Lucinda might have found Vorden's possessiveness and jealousy amusing—as if there could be, in reality, any sort of competition between them for Lucifer's regard—but she was keenly aware of Vorden's nature. The succubus was a creature of instinct, crafted by the Dark Angel for his own purposes. Dark emotions—lust, anger, jealousy, greed, possessiveness—were the only ones she had, and she wore her bruises not so much as a reproach but as a badge of honor.

Lucinda paused in the curtained doorway to look back at the tableau. Vorden, still in her human guise, was incautiously winding herself around her master's physical form, rubbing her ample breasts against his arm and caressing his hair. She knew that he was just as capable of batting her out of the way in this form as in her feline one. Knew it because he had done it . . . many times. Fortunately for her, he was already engaged in a discussion with Rey and ignored her completely.

She was used to that, too.

The Devil's daughter shook her head. Seeing Vorden and others like her groveling and debasing themselves before her father conjured emotions in her own breast. Chief among them was pity. She had her mother to thank for that.

CHAPTER THREE

British nobility was under siege and had been for decades. The enemy was modernity; the siege engines were public utilities and the goods and services necessary for the upkeep of a large, no-longer-productive estate. Naworth Castle—the Cumbrian seat of the Howard family—was such a place. It had been in and out of the family for centuries—a main residence, a monstrous country manor with a twenty-thousand-acre yard, and a school, before the Howards discovered that tours, large important meetings, product launches, and movie productions were lucrative enough to allow them to maintain their ancestral home.

In the long history of the seat of the Howards, however, the date that Lucinda was most interested in was the year that Naworth burned. Hence, she stood now on the castle grounds in the spring of 1844, keeping watch in the gathering dusk among the trees that ringed the great heap of stone—a bailey and keep that had stood since the thirteen hundreds. This was a long time in the lives of men. A long time to Lucinda, as well, though she reckoned time differently than a mortal might.

Lurid light flickered across her vision and washed over her face. Even from her vantage point many yards away from the burning castle, she could feel the heat of the flames. It made her think of those imaginative representations of Hell, which almost made her laugh. Since before Dante Alighieri's time—though more since—humans imagined Hell to be a super-heated prison of fire and brimstone. Those who had visited it knew it was cold. Cold and dark and distant.

She shivered and gave her attention to the blaze. It was only the relatively untouched part of the castle that Lucinda was interested in. Lord William's Tower, built in the fifteen hundreds, was, ironically, one of the oldest parts as well. Three upper rooms—a bedchamber, a private library, and a chapel—somehow managed to survive the fire. The thing that Lucinda sought was somewhere in those rooms—most likely in the library or the chapel. Where might depend upon whether the current owner of the volume believed it sacred or profane.

The west wing of the building was already completely involved, and the fire crew from the village of Brampton had arrived on the scene with two water wagons. They engaged the flames with bravery and pumps completely unequal to the task. Lucinda shook her head. The closest body of water was too far away to be of use; they would try to get a hose to the castle cistern.

As seven or eight local lads rushed past, she leapt to join them—just one more Brampton boy hoping to be of service, or at least hoping for a spectacle to take home to their less courageous comrades. They hollered and waved and begged of the firemen where they might help out. One of the regulars deputized them to enter the main hall, pull down the tapestries and curtains there, and haul them into the central courtyard. To get the furniture out if they could, too.

That was perfect. It meant Lucinda would not have to use supernatural means to be where she needed to be. The chaos caused by the fire would suffice.

"You there! Boy!"

She turned to see a red-faced man bearing down on her. From her altered perspective, he seemed a giant. "Sir?"

"Make sure someone gets to the upstairs rooms. Get the bedding and anything else as might burn. Throw it from the windows."

"Yes, sir!" She doffed her cap, set it back on her riot of short, red curls, and followed the other boys into the central courtyard. Firemen had already flung wide the doors of the main hall and directed the boys through them.

Lucinda took in the situation at a glance—to her right, the hallways were clear of fire; to her left, flames were climbing the tapestries to the second-floor gallery. Men and boys were already at work here in the hall, tearing tapestries and draperies from the walls of the west-leading corridors, hauling furniture out into the courtyard. Straight ahead was the grand staircase, already billowing with smoke.

She grabbed two of the other boys as she cut across the entry hall. "Hey! The constable says we're to go up and get the burnables upstairs as well. C'mon!"

The boys followed her up the staircase to the second-floor gallery and began their work of yanking paintings and hangings from the walls and tossing them down to the growing crew below. After a moment or two of helping them in this, Lucinda turned and sprinted lightly toward the tower. The billowing smoke swallowed her as she crossed the top of the grand stair, but after several strides, she found herself in a corridor in which the smoke was much lighter.

The first room she encountered was the chapel built by Thomas, Lord Dacre, after the Battle of Flodden. Could Morgan le Fay's Book of Shadows be here? She'd hardly call it a religious work; most people of this era (or Thomas's) would consider it blasphemous, but there was no accounting for the pride of ownership that came with such an artifact. It was that pride of ownership that likely had allowed the book to be spared this long.

Lucinda heard the crash of falling beams behind and below. At this rate, the chapel wouldn't last long. She knew it had not survived the fire intact. She took a step toward the chapel doors.

"It's not there."

She whipped around at the sound of the voice, though she knew whose it was. She was not so much startled as surprised. Had her father sent her a helper . . . or a spy?

"Nathaniel, whatever are you doing here?"

Nathaniel—also in the guise of a village youth—gave a very human shrug. "Speeding things along, Shaliah. He is impatient."

She arched an eyebrow. "Is he, indeed? How very human of him."

Nathaniel's facial expression did not change. It never did, though she had tried countless times to surprise him or make him laugh or anger him. Lucifer had a team of mortals like Rey who had "cut deals" with him rather than face judgment, but Nathaniel wasn't mortal. He was a spirit. An angel, to be precise, who had fallen because he had allowed Lucifer's taint to touch him. Even in this disguise, there was something otherworldly about him—a detachment and poise that was both lovely and inhuman.

Lucifer had assigned Nathaniel to "assist" her in her missions—lucky Lucinda, to have such a fond father. The Fallen was more spy than assistant, she was certain, but she made use of him—in more ways than he or his lord suspected. *Shaliah*, he called her—*emissary*. He was a stickler for protocol, but Lucinda was never certain whether he used the archaic Hebrew title to remind her that she was Lucifer's agent or to remind himself that she was his superior.

"Try the library." Nathaniel inclined his head toward the intersection just down the hall. A tendril of smoke wended its way between them.

Lucinda willed herself to the library with a mere thought—most efficient when there were no eyes to see. She stifled a tickle of annoyance when Nathaniel materialized right beside her with barely a half-second's delay.

The library was a huge cube of a room with shelving that covered every wall up to a height of about fifteen feet—including the one bisected by the door. Every inch of every shelf was covered with books of every color and size. Only the hearth broke their march.

Lucinda smiled. "You'd think, being who I am—what I am—I should be able to just"—she reached out a hand toward the shelf—"and the thing would fly to my fingers."

Nathaniel just looked at her, unblinking, through the eyes of a Brampton lad and said, "You should know it when you feel of it. But there is not much time."

As if to punctuate that statement, something heavy fell just beyond the library door, prompting shouts from the village boys down the hall. Smoke scooted under the door and curled across the floor.

"Well, my friend," Lucinda said, eyeing the rows and rows of books, "how may we best divide our effort?"

"If I might recommend—I can direct the fire to bar any interruption while you seek the tome. Or vice versa."

"I'll find the book. You tend to the fire. And Nathaniel—"

"Yes, Shaliah?"

"See that none of the villagers are harmed."

The angel's eyes sparked with mild interest. "You fear for their safety?"

"I fear changing history. No one died when Naworth burned in the nineteenth century."

"Perhaps history is yours to make. If some of them die, history will record it faithfully, will it not?"

"If some of them die, it could impact my father's schemes in centuries to come. He would not like that."

One corner of the angel's mouth twitched. "The Dark One has suffered setbacks before and adapted. He is, I suspect, infinitely adaptable . . . if not infinitely patient. But then, you know this."

He was gone before Lucinda could answer, leaving her to her task. She shook her head. Nathaniel had a rare capacity for speaking in subtext. In this case, she was at a loss to know what that subtext was.

Ignoring the growing smell of burned timbers and the smoke oozing beneath the library door, she moved to the center of the room and held her hands before her at shoulder height, palms facing out, fingers splayed. She coughed once, then quickly pulled a bubble of clean air around her. Then she closed her physical eyes and opened her spiritual senses.

In a darkness like the night sky, points of luminance appeared—bright and dim, translucent and opaque, dark and fair. She began to turn slowly, seeing her own arms as thick cables of gold radiance, her hands as the source of a web of sense that reached out and up, sampling the contents of the shelves. She did not try to condition what she expected to feel from le Fay's Book of Shadows; she merely tasted and tested the spirit of the words contained in each volume.

Humans did not realize that every word had a spirit. Not a literal spirit—as once primitive people had believed djinn or fairies to be—but an intent, a power, an energy. If they knew—if they had known historically—they might have spared themselves much agony. Every tragedy of human kind, every atrocity, every conquest of power, every massacre, began with words that took form in action. Mankind was its own worst enemy. It needed no Satan to send it to Hell; it was perfectly capable of sending itself there.

Century after century, prophets and avatars arose (or descended, depending upon your point of view) and spoke. They pleaded, they exhorted, they illustrated, they illumined. A Krishna, a Moses, a Buddha, a Christ, others—one after the other, they thought and spoke and lived love and oneness and respect for life. They shed their light and they shed their blood. Yet, out of every generation, only a handful of souls listened.

Many of those souls shed their blood, in turn, to spread a message that most people didn't want to hear. The prophets of God wasted their breath on such as these—so her father often said. Mankind was unworthy of God's love and attention. It deserved its ultimate fate—a fate Lucifer had made over into his driving purpose: Armageddon.

Lucinda's father was hell-bent (she loved that expression) on bringing mankind not to its knees, but to its grave. This book she sought was just one more piece of his elaborate plan—one more nail in humanity's coffin.

She had covered perhaps half the shelves when the growing physical heat in the room penetrated her concentration. There was a strange musical sizzle, then a popping sound, and the heat's intensity soared. Lucinda's eyes flicked open reflexively; a long tongue of flame licked its way up the inside of the library door. Once it reached the dry wattle-and-daub ceiling, this place could be an inferno in moments and the book lost. Nathaniel could slow the flames and push them this way or that, but he could not make them disobey the laws of physics.

Lucinda closed her eyes again and pressed on, focusing all of her senses on her search. The heat of the fire was beating relentlessly against her back when a dark, freezing thrill assaulted her palms and ran, like liquid nitrogen, up her arms to her core. She stopped turning.

There, framed in the void between her outspread hands, was a hole in the fabric of reality. Unlike the other objects in the room, this one did not give off light or heat or even cold. It sucked light, color, and warmth from the atmosphere, and the spirits of the words in it were foul beyond description.

Lucinda opened her eyes. She faced a corner in which stood one of four cabinets—tall, heavy, mahogany. It was windowless and its thick doors were shut and locked.

The tower shuddered as something below in the main residence gave way with an explosive roar. This was followed by shouts below and away, and the sound of falling beams, crumbling masonry, and shattering glass. A scorching draft rolled down the upstairs corridor and blew in the weakened library door, sending shards of burning wood in all directions.

Lucinda could not die in this fire, but her human body could suffer damage. She crossed the room to the cabinet in three long strides, ignoring the oven-like heat, the encroaching flames, the shouts calling on those in the house to flee. Locks were no obstacle to the Devil's daughter. She set her hand upon the mechanism and caused the simple tumblers within to simply fail. The door swung open and there it was, on a shelf with several other volumes—Morgan le Fay's Book of Shadows.

It was not much to look at—its leather cover discolored and worn, the metal bands and locks of newer vintage than the book itself, as if someone, understanding the dire reality of the thing, had sought to chain it. It was bound in beaten bands of gold, silver, and copper. Ah, and there were wards on it, too, no doubt placed there by well-meaning witches or wizards or holy men. That explained the muted "voice" of the presence that permeated the book. The wards and metal bindings served to muffle le Fay's dark spirit, but once unchained, it would reach out, seeking living souls that would resonate with it.

Lucinda pulled the book from the shelf and, in so doing, touched the volume next to it. Her hand—chill where it touched the Book of Shadows—caught a flush of warmth from the book to its left. She turned her full attention to it. It was a holy book—a Qur'án, to be exact—and it was immensely old, by human reckoning. She moved the Book of Shadows to her right hand and placed the palm of her left on the Qur'án. It gave off extraordinary energies, nearly as much from the marginal annotations of a single commentator as from the original text.

She pulled it from the shelf and opened it, ever aware of the chaos stalking her. The Qur'án was illuminated with illustrations that were still amazingly vivid, but it was the annotations that drew her. They were also in Arabic, and covered the margins of some pages with tiny, densely packed, but elegant script in a hand she knew. These notes were the work of the great Muslim scholar, 'Abū l-Walīd Muḥammad ibn 'Aḥmad ibn Rušd, known more commonly by his Latinized moniker, Averroes.

Renaissance man, indeed. Lucinda would not have been surprised if the twelfth-century philosopher, scientist, and polymath wasn't the very person for whom the term was coined.

Flames shot across the ceiling of the room with a sound like the tearing of fabric. Searing chunks of plaster rained down on Lucinda's head. One large piece struck her hand and knocked the Qur'án from it. She bent to reach for it but, overhead, a beam sagged toward her with a groan like the death cry of a huge beast.

She felt Nathaniel before she heard his voice this time.

"Shaliah!"

He caught her shoulder, hauling her physically out of the path of the beam. It came down between her and the fallen Qur'án. Sparks flew past her face, brushing her cheeks with tiny, hot kisses.

She thrust the Book of Shadows into Nathaniel's arms. "Take this and go!"

She didn't wait to see if he went. She made a sweeping gesture at the flaming beam and sent it in chaotic flight toward the library windows. They shattered and blew outward, splinters of glass riding the fire's winds. She reached for the Qur'án where it lay on the floor and set her palm atop it. In a heartbeat, she knew the book's future as she had read its past. Unlike the Book of Shadows, this book would survive into the twenty-first century. She saw its trail as a pathway of light weaving through the centuries to . . .

"We must hurry," Nathaniel said softly. That he was still here was unsurprising. He was diligent to a fault when it came to minding his master's assets.

A thick braid of water arced through the broken window to fall, hissing, onto the flames about them. They must have gotten the hose to the cistern. Soon firemen would be beating their way up the stairs.

Lucinda picked up the Qur'án and slid it back into place, then shut the cabinet firmly. She glanced at Nathaniel, still standing patiently amid the flames, and the two evaporated from nineteenth-century England to reappear nearly two centuries later on a New York City street.

⚜

Rey Granger was used to being in the right place at the right time. It was something his long association with Lucifer accorded him. The Dark Angel had directed his gaze toward the offices of Dunfy, Corrigan, and Price and knew from the "heady taste of strong negative emotions" that chaos had followed in the steps of Brittany Anders' unexpected abdication.

Rey, therefore, was in a position to answer the summons for a maintenance underling to accompany a Mr. Salazar from DC&P's security department and remove the turncoat lawyer's belongings from her office. Dressed in vivid blue coveralls with a MONROE'S MAINTENANCE logo on the breast pocket, unassembled cardboard boxes tucked under his arms, and Lucifer looking out through his eyes, Rey found Ms. Anders' office peopled by her ex-senior associate, Aaron Price, and her secretary, Terry Passavoy.

Passavoy was anxious; Price was angry and embarrassed, and Rey knew (because Lucifer knew) that he had caught the two men in the midst of an argument. Price had a laptop computer tucked under one arm. As Rey and the security officer entered the office, the lawyer shoved the machine into Passavoy's arms and pointed at the door.

"Take this to my office and leave it there. Then I want you to scour your own hard drive and transfer everything Ms. Anders was working on to the company server and delete it from your computer. Do it now."

"Mr. Price," Passavoy objected, "her last instructions to me were to file the Redmon evidentiary briefs—"

"And I'm telling you that it would be ill-advised of you to do so. Ms. Anders clearly didn't have her mind on her client's case. I'm going to need to go over everything she did in the weeks leading up to this." Price jerked his head at the door through which Rey and Salazar had just entered.

Passavoy let himself out, looking as if he'd swallowed a lemon.

"I've already accounted for all of Ms. Anders' case files," Price told the security officer. "I want you to oversee the removal of Ms. Anders' personal items from her desk and closet."

"Yes, sir." Salazar glanced at Rey. "Go to it."

Rey nodded and moved quickly around the desk. Of paramount importance was getting that pen into the hands of someone here who might better respond to its allure—or, barring that, to simply get it back. Aaron Price, he figured, was a good bet. It occurred to him to wonder why Lucifer would not have gone after Price in the first place. The answer came in an icy flash of epiphany. Price was practically assured of a place in Hell already. Winning his allegiance was not as much a victory as seducing a young woman like Brittany Anders, whose soul was threaded with Light.

Rey pulled open the top middle drawer and let out a sigh of relief. Couldn't have been easier—the pen was sitting right there in the pencil tray. She hadn't even bothered to put it back in its box or hide it. Rey glanced up at Price, who was having a very quiet conversation with Salazar in the middle of the room. He let out a soft whistle—just loud enough to catch the other men's attention.

"What is it?" Price asked, frowning.

"Oh, nothing, sir," Rey said. "Just this pen. It's . . . well . . . wow!" He held the pen up where the light from lamp and window caught it and made the golden barrel flash and gleam. "Do you think that's real gold?"

Price held out his hand and Rey put the pen into it.

"Huh," said the lawyer, looking bemused. "Heavy."

He started to hand the pen back, but Rey had turned to assemble a box and was carefully not looking at him.

Give it just a moment, Lucifer's voice whispered in Rey's head. *Just a moment.*

Price moved to set the thing on the desk, then hesitated. He gave the pen a second look, turning it in his hands, then opening it. He looked momentarily mesmerized by the thing.

That's it. Feel how well it fits your hand?

Rey grimaced. Brittany Anders had no doubt looked like that, too, for a moment. Somehow she had been able to leave the pen behind. Rey was willing to bet this guy wouldn't.

He was rewarded for his jaded view of human nature when Aaron Price tucked the pen into his breast pocket.

"Well, I doubt it's real gold, but it's a damn nice pen, and if Ms. Anders doesn't want it, I'll take it. Box this stuff up and get it out of here. Mr. Salazar, give Ms. Anders a call and let her know she can pick up her belongings downstairs at the receptionist's desk. If she doesn't come get them within a week, you're free to dispose of them as you see fit."

He exited the room then, leaving Rey and Salazar to box up the few personal belongings that Brittany Anders had left behind.

As Rey bent to put the first handful of odds and ends into the box, he felt Lucifer's presence ooze from his mind like water draining from a swimmer's ear. It was a strange sensation. He had gotten used to it in the decades since he had pledged himself to Lucifer's service, but he still marked it every time. It left him with the most curious combination of relief and loss.

✠

Lucinda put Nathaniel to the task of locating Brittany Anders. She was curious, she told him, about how the young lawyer had managed to escape the thrall of Adam Clinton's pen. That talisman, after all, had attached to it what amounted to a distilled essence of greed, ambition, and corruption—powerful incentives, all. Perhaps if she understood why it had failed, it would aid Lucifer in building a better soul trap.

"Do you know," the Fallen asked her as they stood together on a busy New York street, "why your father singled the Anders woman out for his attention?"

"Do you?"

"He shares none of his deepest reasoning with me."

Lucinda regarded him with sincere curiosity. He was once again wearing his customary human persona—a tall, handsome, dark-haired man with artistically even features and a swimmer's physique which he held uncompromisingly erect. He carried a briefcase that housed le Fay's book. He was, Lucinda told anyone who saw them together, a buyer of antiquities and art for her shop and an old family friend.

"Wouldn't you like to know?" she asked him.

"I have no burning desire. Obviously, it serves our lord's ultimate purpose. I am merely curious."

Burning desire? Was that a pun? "She was a means to an end," Lucinda suggested.

One sleek brow rose minutely. "Aren't we all?"

"You're jaded," she teased him. "Find the woman."

"What will you do," he asked her, "when I have found her?"

"I'm not sure. But right now . . ." She raised her head and looked down Madison Avenue toward her target. "Right now, I'm going to go shopping."

"Shopping?"

"Yes. For a very special book."

"The Qur'án from the Naworth library?"

"My father mentioned that Brant Redmon had deep Middle Eastern connections. I thought perhaps a very valuable Qur'án might be . . . an asset."

She left him with a peck on the cheek and he—looking like a well-dressed young businessman—walked through the doors of a café and disappeared.

Bauman's Rare Books was possibly one of Lucinda's favorite places on Earth. It was a sanctum—quiet and filled with the scents of leather, polished wood, paper, and binding glue. It smelled of books and history, both of which she loved. It looked, appropriately, like the formal library in some English great house or estate. Its hardwood floors were covered with Persian carpets upon which sat heavy mahogany tables and leather-upholstered chairs, at which patrons could sit and peruse the rare volumes the store obtained.

Lucinda went directly to the first clerk whose attention she drew and stated her request. There was a Qur'án, she said, that she had just missed at an estate sale not two years past. She had reason to believe it might have ended up here. The clerk deferred to the store manager, who confirmed the existence of the volume but said that it was in less than good condition, having spent decades in a moldering box after heat and water damage from a fire. It was being carefully restored . . .

"I have a book restoration expert on staff for my private collection," she said. "I would like to purchase the book immediately. How much are you asking?"

The manager named a sum, Lucinda paid it, and instructed that the book—stored in a special preservative box—be delivered to her Seventy-Second Street flat.

In the end, it took her all of an hour to make the arrangements. When she left the bookstore, Nathaniel was waiting for her on the sidewalk, still wearing his human skin. He was pretending to be unremarkable in every way; his entire persona invited people not to look at him or even notice that he was there.

She greeted him with a smile. "Well?"

"Our friend is currently in a restaurant on Lexington Avenue, in deep discussion with a young man."

"A friend?"

"A journalist."

Interesting. Lucinda wondered if perhaps Brittany Anders was not done trying to undermine her colleagues at DC&P.

"I do believe I'll go join them," Lucinda said and strode off down the street, high heels tapping out a confident cadence on the sidewalk.

"Is this the type of story you're interested in, Mr. Amado?" The young lawyer leaned toward him across the table, hands clasped around her coffee cup.

"Interested in, yes, but . . ." Nick searched for the right words. "But the problem is, I'd have to have some credible, documented evidence of wrongdoing, or anything I write would be mere muckraking and could result in a libel suit, as you know. Do you have anything to prove—"

She shook her head in obvious frustration. "No. No, damn it. I wasn't thinking of anything but getting the information to the court and getting out. But when I called my secretary—I mean, my *ex*-secretary—this morning to find out what had happened with the evidentiary documents, he told me he'd been stopped before he could file them. That means the real information will never make it to the judge. Like I said, I was focused on getting out of there. It . . . it wasn't until I had a chance to calm down and think straight that I realized I had to do more than that. That I couldn't just stick Terry with the responsibility when he didn't even know what he had. "

That sounded hopeful. "Your secretary is still there?"

She nodded.

"You don't think he knows what's going on?"

"He suspects something, I'm sure, but I didn't share what I knew with him, no. Although, if he looked over the evidentiary manifest, he'd see the smoking gun. He's smart. I'm pretty sure he'd know what it meant."

"But you're not sure he's done that, nor have you discussed it openly."

"No. Not yet. He was still at the office when I called. A senior partner was in my office clearing out my belongings."

"Might he be able to get some evidence?"

She shook her head. "I would never ask it of him. I don't have a new position yet. Although I do have an interview lined up already." She smiled momentarily, then sobered again. "I couldn't ask Terry to risk his job yet. If he *hasn't* looked at the materials—if he doesn't know what's there—well, I'd hate to put him in that position."

Nick shrugged. "Then there's really nothing I can print, Ms. Anders. I'm sorry, but I can only work from credible sources. It's not that I don't believe you . . ."

It really wasn't that—he *did* believe her. Or perhaps it was only that he *wanted* to believe her. He had been watching Dunfy, Corrigan, and Price for several years now, had been suspicious of their seemingly miraculous record of establishing the innocence of clients whose guilt looked like a slam dunk. He had even written a couple of articles on previous court cases but had only been able to call attention to their courtroom dramatics. Nothing illegal about emotional manipulation or sleight of hand.

It had been those articles that had prompted Brittany Anders to call him. He'd thought, at first, this just might be the break he'd been hoping for—a DC&P junior partner with a tale of corruption—but as much as he believed her allegations to be true, he knew he couldn't write a word without evidence. He had colleagues who would—for the right amount of money, page space, eyeballs, or airtime.

He raised his gaze to the TV over the coffee bar, where a group of well-groomed pundits were batting around the proposition that a national leader had falsified his educational records. Five minutes ago, they'd been clucking over the antics and foibles of a celebrity and opining about what was wrong with her.

That wasn't journalism, damn it. It was theater.

"I'm sorry," he said again.

Brittany sighed, then rose to leave. "Yes, of course. Well, thank you for taking the time to talk to me, Mr. Amado."

He stood with her, reaching across the table to shake her hand. "If you or your secretary manage to come up with anything . . ."

"I'll call you right away, I promise." She smiled ruefully; he smiled back encouragingly, then she was gone, wending her way through the noisy room to the door.

Nick drank the dregs of his latte and decided he'd grab another to go. Shouldering his camera bag, he swung out of the booth, heading for the counter. He'd gone no more than three strides when he collided with a young woman who seemed to have appeared out of nowhere. He dropped his camera bag. It hit the floor with a thud.

"Oh, good Lord! I'm so sorry!" the woman exclaimed as he snatched it up again. "Your camera . . . is it all right?"

Nick flipped open the bag and glanced in; the Nikon was in one piece. He brought his eyes back to the woman and felt his breath stop in his throat. She was . . .

vivid—huge, remarkably green eyes in a creamy, heart-shaped face, full lips just now curved into a surprised "O," a mane of wavy auburn hair. She was wearing a turquoise dress of some fabric that seemed to float around her as if in a perpetual breeze.

She was stunning; he was stunned.

"I-I-I . . . I'm sure it's fine." Damn, he was stammering for God's sake!

"Yes, but there's no way to tell until you use it again."

"I could take a picture of you. It's digital—"

She demurred, glancing away and holding up her hands as if embarrassed by the thought of someone snapping her picture. "But, here." She offered him a business card, seeming to produce it from thin air. "If there's anything wrong with the camera, call me or drop by my shop. It's just up the street."

He glanced at the card. "Lucinda's Pawnshop and Antiquary?"

She nodded, smiling wryly. "We're a specialty store. Though, I may wish it was a camera store before too long."

"What? Oh, yes. Of course. My . . ." He patted the camera bag absently, though he was sure he'd forgotten what it was for. "I'm sure it's fine. Really."

"Let me know. I'd hate to be the one to ruin your week. "

"Oh, I doubt you could do that . . . Lucinda? Is that really your name?"

She nodded. "Lucinda Trompe."

"That's nice. Sort of old-fashioned. Nice meeting you, Lucinda." *Nice meeting you. Lame. Completely and totally lame.*

Nick pocketed her card and held out his hand. She took it. She had a firm, confident handshake that made him feel as if he'd just thrust his hand into a beam of sunlight. He shivered at the touch.

"Dominic," he said. "Dominic Amado."

He smiled. She smiled. They did the narrow aisle two-step, laughed, and then moved in unison toward the door. Out on the sidewalk, she turned to him and smiled again. Her smile was like sunlight, too. He wanted to bathe in it.

"You're a professional photographer?" she asked.

"Journalist, actually. I do some photojournalism, but mostly print and online media. It's a living—sometimes barely. My parents still nag me to get a real job."

A flicker of darkness crossed her face. "You're lucky to have parents to nag you. My parents were never together in any real sense, and Mom died when I was a little girl."

"You still have your dad, though?" he prompted, hoping the sun would break again from behind her clouds.

It didn't. She made a face. "Or he has me."

Strange thing to say. He shivered again, though for a different reason.

She laughed then, but there wasn't anything joyful in it. "Just listen to me. I'm a hop, skip, and a jump away from maudlin." She glanced at his camera bag. "Let me know about the camera, okay?"

"Sure," he agreed, and found himself wishing it would turn out to be broken. Then he'd have a ready excuse to see her again. "It was nice running into you," he added, smiling. Then, before he could say anything more ridiculous, he turned and headed up Lexington.

⬧

Lucinda watched Dominic Amado stride away from her—his thick, longish, burgundy-black hair gleaming in the morning sunlight—and felt . . . perplexed. Her mind was exploding with sense information that she was unaccustomed to receiving. It tempted her to stand on the sun-washed street wallowing in sensory input—to admire the sheen of the young man's hair, the animal grace of his stride. She wished she might have spent a few more moments in his company, and was seized by the pleasant but absurd hope that his camera would be broken so that he'd seek her out and ask her to make good on her promise to get it fixed. She supposed she could *arrange* for it to be broken . . .

She shook herself. What was the matter with her? She'd met thousands of beautiful men in her time on Earth. She had resolutely ignored them. He was just one more.

Yet, it was undeniable that when she had looked into *this* man's eyes, intent on taking his measure, she was seized by breathless and alien emotions—uncertainty, loneliness, a visceral pull . . . something beyond any of those things. His were bottomless eyes—so deep a brown they were almost black, and set in a strong-featured, angular face the color of old gold. His eyes were all she'd noticed of him until he'd smiled.

Dominic Amado might be one of the most beautiful men she had ever met, but it was not mere beauty that had arrested her. Deep in the young eyes was an old anguish, something that had spoken to her in a wordless undercurrent when they'd shaken hands. Dominic Amado was as much a victim of torture as any prisoner of war. It was the sort of thing that could be useful if it fell into the wrong hands—which made her question the wisdom of giving him that business card.

Focus, Lucinda, she told herself, and turned her mind to the matter at hand—Brittany Anders' crusade against DC&P. A crusade that suffered from a lack of evidence. Now, even though there was a journalist involved, and a potential scandal in the offing, there was little chance of Brittany's crusade going anywhere without divine intervention.

Lucifer would be pleased to hear that.

CHAPTER FOUR

Lucinda set the Book of Shadows on the black altar and stepped back. "I brought you le Fay's Book of Shadows. May I ask why you want it?"

The seemingly infinite chamber was silent and dark but for the shaft of pure blue-white light that fell on the book and the sculpted chunk of gleaming obsidian beneath it. Light chased around the fractured planes of the rock in traceries of twilight silver. The book opened of its own accord and the pages riffled as if in a breeze. Lucifer solidified out of the shadows—a scintillating cloud of smoke that coalesced to become the beautiful, gleaming man. One golden hand brushed the pages, then lingered caressingly over the book.

Lucinda shook her head. Why her father so loved grand gestures that he performed them even for her benefit, she had no idea. She had asked him often enough, but his answer was different every time.

"Why do I want it?" he repeated now. "To make trouble, of course. To weave another thread of my grand tapestry."

"I gathered that much. You ought to be able to make a great deal of trouble with that. If someone should actually purchase it, that is. It radiates cold and darkness. Have you targeted a book collector? Someone with wealth and power?" She raised her eyes to his and knew hers mirrored his mischievous glow.

"No, actually, I've targeted a group of idiotic young girls with too much wealth, and very little power . . . at the moment. The book . . ." He stroked the pages. "The book will change that."

Lucinda folded her arms across her chest. "Girls," she repeated skeptically. "A group of idiotic young girls is going to somehow help you bring about the ruin of mankind. Really."

Lucifer smiled. It was not a warm expression. "Oh, they will purchase the book because they think it will solve all their First World problems. That it will enable them to foil the enemies and win the friends and date the young men they want. I expect they will do more than that. *Much* more. I'm nothing if not inventive—but then I've had to be."

That was true enough. The Father of Lies had spent millennia in search of clever ways to sidestep the limitations the All-Father had placed on him. He had gotten very good at it. Lucinda recalled an evening more than 160 years ago, when Lucifer had attended a lecture given by Thomas Huxley—widely referred to as "Darwin's Bulldog." The Dark Angel had sat, that evening, beside Darwin's cousin, Francis, to hear Huxley speak about natural selection.

At the conclusion of the lecture, Lucifer turned to the cousin and asked a profound question: "But what does this mean to the world? A theory is all very well and good, but I fail to see the practical application."

Francis—to whom his cousin's theory of evolution was a holy grail—was quite taken aback. "Truly, sir?" he replied. "Imagine, if you can, the ramifications for farmers alone. Armed with this knowledge, they would be able to breed a superior form of livestock with much less trial and error."

"Ah! Of course! I see." Lucifer saw more than Francis Galton could possibly imagine. He then opened his mouth and uttered fourteen words that would change the world: "It's too bad it cannot be employed to breed a superior form of men."

Fourteen words and, over a century later, the world was still not cleansed of their bloody stain, for Francis Galton would become the father of Social Darwinism and the eugenics movement . . . and the grandfather of a racist ideology that would result in the agonies of the Holocaust and countless other offenses. The blood of millions of Jews, Catholics, Romany, and those who had the temerity to sympathize with them was shed horribly because of those fourteen words.

Lucifer had meant for those words to spark Armageddon, but they had not. Now, Lucinda had brought him an entire book full of words. Powerful, dark words. What might he do with those? *Sticks and stones will break my bones, but words will never harm me.* That was perhaps the stupidest aphorism humanity had ever devised. Words were far more powerful than most humans realized.

Lucifer picked up the Book of Shadows, smiled at the open page, then closed the volume and handed it back to Lucinda. "Of all my inventions, this is one of my finest. See that this is displayed prominently in the shop—on that gilded bookstand, I think." He hesitated then asked, "Have you heard of the Nihilim?"

"The Nihilim? An obscure pseudo-Christian sect, aren't they?"

"Obscure? I doubt they would be flattered by that description. They consider themselves to be the only true Christians on the planet. They fancy themselves descendants of the biblical Nephilim with a dash of nihilism tossed in. They believe human values such as kindness and love are baseless; what God really wants is a good, old-fashioned, no-holds-barred melee in which those left standing will have proven their spiritual worth simply because they're still on their feet and in possession of their life's blood. They're local—to New York, I mean. They have a colony along the Hudson. I think they have . . . potential."

He shrugged as if it were of no moment. "Don't mind me—just fantasizing."

Lucinda returned herself to the realm of Form with a thought, materializing in the back room of the pawnshop. She went through into the storefront, Book of Shadows in hand. The gilt bookstand stood at the end of the glass-topped counter closest to the door. Currently, it had a volume of poetry on it that had belonged to a serial arsonist.

Lucinda glanced at the front door of the shop, wondering who would walk through it to claim the Book of Shadows and how soon. She hesitated before she put the book in the stand. It was still cold to the touch. Still carried an almost magnetic pull to her dark blood.

Like likes like, she thought, grimacing.

"He has found a worthy target, then?" Nathaniel asked from the shadows behind the counter.

"Apparently. Idiotic young girls, he said."

"You seem . . . troubled."

She turned to glance sharply in his direction. He had made himself part of the shadows so she could not read him clearly.

"Troubled? Not at all. I am merely fascinated by the way his mind works. Millennia we have been at this, and he still surprises me. I want to understand him."

"To emulate him?"

"Should I not wish to emulate him? I am his heir."

"You are also *her* heir," the angel said.

He meant Eve, of course. Lucinda set the Book of Shadows down on the stand and picked up the poetry book to return it to the bookshelf. "*She* is dead these countless centuries."

"And still you mourn."

She glanced at him again, struggling to gauge his intent, but he was gone—back to the realm of the Formless. A chill ran up her spine. Of all the beings who populated the in-between realm she and her father inhabited, Nathaniel was the one she understood least. She did not like that. If knowledge was power, lack of knowledge was weakness.

In her position, she could not afford to be weak.

⊹

Terry met Brittany in the elegant lobby of Dunfy, Corrigan, and Price. She had called him directly on his cell phone to arrange picking up the boxes the security department had packed and taped for her. She didn't want to see Aaron Price again—ever.

43

Terry looked stricken. He handed over the two boxes and the rolled-up theatre poster. "What happened, Brit?" he asked in a whisper. "They said you just quit."

"I did." She glanced at the guy sitting behind the security desk. "Do you think you might know why?"

Terry followed her gaze, then took back one of the boxes. "Why don't I carry this out for you. You have a cab?"

She nodded, then turned and led the way out to the sidewalk, where a shiny yellow Prius covered with advertising awaited her.

"It had something to do with the Redmon case, didn't it?" Terry asked as they stepped out onto the glittering concrete.

She hesitated a moment, then said, "He's guilty, Terry. He's guilty and they all know it, and they tried to fix it so that if someone found out he was guilty, I'd be the only one blamed for hiding the evidence of it."

His eyes narrowed and his nostrils flared. She knew that expression; Terry Passavoy was going into *Die Hard* mode. "Are you going to blow the whistle on them?"

"You really think I could make that stick? I have no evidence. They have it all."

Terry got it immediately. "So, that's what you wanted me to get off to the DA. I thought Price was a little too eager to get his hands on it." He shook his head. "I'm sorry, Brit. This is a crappy thing to have happened to you. And to add insult to injury, Price took your new pen."

"He's welcome to it. I think the bloody thing is cursed."

"Cursed? Really?"

She laughed. "I was kidding. Although, it did make me feel weird. Like I said, Price is welcome to it."

She moved to the cab, opened the rear door, and set the box on the seat. Terry handed her the second box.

"I couldn't find that picture of your family you put on your desk," he said.

"It's okay. I took it with me when I left. It's going into my new office next Monday."

"You've got a new job already? Brit, you're magical! You've only been out of work for three days."

She smiled. "It's a nonprofit. Salary's not nearly what I was making at DC&P, but it's enough." She met his eyes. "You want to come work for me? I could really use an assistant."

"Seriously? Tell me where to be Monday morning and I'll be there. In fact, I'll go back in and quit right this minute."

Brittany laughed. "You might as well finish out the week here and get your paycheck. I'll text you the address. Come see me Monday morning."

She left feeling curiously light. She'd called her parents the evening she'd gotten the job at the nonprofit and knew they were proud of her decision to work there, though they were disappointed that her previous position had turned out not to be as wonderful as she'd first thought. All she'd told them of the situation at DC&P was that the firm had some ethically questionable practices that she took exception to. Her parents respected that and didn't pressure her for more information than she was willing to give, though she suspected her brother was going to be deputized to grill her at some future date. She'd cross that bridge when she came to it.

Her only real regret—besides not being able to blow the whistle on her ex-law firm—was that she had spent three hundred dollars on that damned pen.

✤

The bell over the door tinkled cheerfully, causing Lucinda to glance up from the Book of Shadows on its stand. She had spent the past several days scanning its pages. It was full of potential trouble. Spells and incantations and rites that would invoke myriad hazards and poke holes in the barrier between the realms of the Formed and the Formless, loosing a million trickles of entropy and evil. She had been wondering when the target for this particular artifact would put in an appearance, when she felt a presence at the front door. She turned, knowing already that it wasn't her father's idiot girls.

Dominic Amado stood in the open doorway, looking around the shop with obvious curiosity. She felt his pull immediately, as if she were an ocean and he a moon. She closed the Book of Shadows and smiled at him.

"Oh dear. I take it this means your camera is deceased."

"The camera is fine," he hastened to assure her. "I was just . . . curious. About your shop." He hesitated, looking a bit uncomfortable. "Also, I just accepted a commission to do a piece on poverty in America. I thought perhaps I could interview you."

"Interview *me*? Why?"

He came farther into the shop. "I was thinking you might be able to provide some insights into why people pawn things. What sort of circumstances force them to part with objects that are valuable to them, sometimes for deeply personal reasons."

Lucinda glanced around the shop. "To be honest, most of our stock comes from . . . estate sales and auctions. Collectors of one sort or another." She saw the disappointment in his dark eyes and hastened to add, "Though we do occasionally acquire objects from . . . well, from people in dire need of quick cash."

He flashed a smile. "Are you . . . I mean, is this a bad time?"

"Not at all. As you can see, I'm not exactly run off my feet. It's pretty quiet around here early in the week at this time of year."

She gestured at the little reading table that sat in an alcove among the bookshelves beneath a chandelier that had not been there when Dominic Amado had arrived. She regarded it with interest to see what it told her about her visitor. It was Moorish in style—looking like something she'd seen in numerous cathedrals, only much smaller.

He was looking up at it as well, a surprised expression on his face. "Huh. That's interesting. That light fixture reminds me of one Father Francis had in the rectory office when I was a boy. Where did you find something like that?"

"It came with the building," she lied easily. "Would you like some tea?"

"Oh . . . I—" He chuckled softly. "I was going to say 'no,' but I just realized that a cup of tea would be really nice. Seems to suit the place."

"Great, I'll be right back." She paused in the curtained doorway to the back rooms. "Did you have any trouble finding the place?"

"No, though I was surprised to see it here. I'm in this part of town fairly regularly and I've never seen this shop before."

"We've been under wraps for a while. The renovations . . ." She tilted her head toward the sidewalk, then went through into the back rooms, feeling a vague sense of . . . disappointment. She had somehow hoped that even with the card she'd given him, Dominic Amado might not have found the store. She knew what it meant that he had. Darkness had touched him.

She was back in just the amount of time it took to put water in a ceramic teapot, plop in bags, put the pot and cups on a tray, and heat the water with a spark of thought.

"That was quick," Dominic said when she came to the table with the tea tray.

"Magic," she said, smiling. Then, when he quirked a dark eyebrow, she laughed and said, "We have one of those hot water dispensers."

"Do you mind if I record the interview?" he asked as she poured tea.

She grimaced. "My voice sounds awful in recordings, but sure."

It sounded worse than awful, actually; it sounded a bit inhuman unless she rearranged the sound waves a bit. Her father's voice didn't even register as a voice on man-made machinery. It sounded like the distant roar of a tornado.

"I don't see how that could be," Dominic was saying. "You have a very pleasant voice—very warm."

He set up a tiny voice-activated digital recorder, then accepted a cup of tea from Lucinda. The questions he asked were thoughtful and searching. He wanted to know if anyone had ever changed their mind after they'd accepted the money for their item. (Yes, they had.) Had other family members come in and tried to get the item back? (Yes, that too.) Had any argued with her about the value of the object? (A handful. She didn't tell him that she paid what she must to get particular items because money was literally no object.) Had any of them told her their stories? (Most often not, but some certainly had.)

"Why do you think they do that?" he asked. "Do you think maybe they're hoping you'll just lend them the money or give it to them without them having to part with a beloved keepsake?"

She thought about that. In fact, she'd thought about it often over the years. "I think they just want me to understand how important this all is to them. Both the object they're pawning and the situation they're in. I think they want to not feel as if they're betraying something or someone. I think they just want another person to know that they've had to do this thing. Someone who doesn't judge them for it."

"And you don't—judge them?"

"I'm in no position to judge them, Mr. Amado. It's quite simply not my job."

He smiled at that, no doubt taking it differently than she had meant it. "Please, call me Dominic—or Nick. Tell me, how does it feel when someone bares their soul to you like that?"

She stared at him. Why had she not anticipated that question? She should have seen it coming. "How does it feel?" she repeated, as if she were contemplating the question. "I . . . I'm not sure I have words for it. It depends on the story, I suppose, and how the person pawning the object feels about what they're doing. It feels . . ."

She looked up into his eyes then, and met something there she could not have described if she had tried. For someone who'd lived as long as she had, it was a most peculiar sensation.

Truth or lie?

"Sometimes it feels as if I'm being turned inside out," she said. "At other times, I feel a sense of overwhelming relief."

He sat back in his chair, his expression puzzled, and whisked a thick curl of dark hair back behind his ear. "Relief? Really? Why is that?"

"Because I know that in some cases, that person's life will be better without the object than with it."

He gazed around the store as if seeing it for the first time. "You mean . . . like something that depresses them because it belonged to a lost loved one—that sort of thing?"

She shrugged. "Sometimes. More often, I sense that the object—whatever it is—is something they're obsessed with. Or it represents something they're obsessed with. Sometimes inanimate objects can exert . . . a powerful influence on people. Many of the items here are like that, I think, for whatever reason."

His eyes were suddenly hooded, as if he didn't know how to respond to what she was saying. "If you really believe that, aren't you a bit concerned about selling them to someone else?"

She smiled again, crookedly. "Oh, yes. I am certainly concerned about that."

"You believe in that, do you? Magic. Curses. That sort of thing."

She checked his eyes again. They were watchful without being wary, curious without being judgmental. She realized she was testing him—probing to see how he regarded the arcane.

"I'm sure it seems silly—" she began.

"No. Not really. Unusual, maybe. Do you ever just want to give them the money and let them keep the thing they want to pawn?"

She laughed. "If I did that, Mr. Amado—Dominic—I wouldn't have a business."

He smiled brilliantly; she felt the smile as a sharp contraction of her heart.

"I understand," he said, "but don't you just sometimes want to? I think I'd want to."

Of course you would.

"I do sometimes want a person to keep the item, yes. I sometimes feel badly about taking it from them."

He asked if she had any memorable stories that she could share. She did. She told him about a woman who pawned a pocket watch that had belonged to her ex-husband. It was, she told him, one of those cases in which she and the seller had both been relieved to have the watch change hands.

"Her ex was abusive. Came close to killing her and her daughter and ended up in jail. He'd inherited the watch from his own father who had also been abusive. He'd talked for years about getting rid of it, but never did. She got rid of it for him, finally, while he was in jail. She didn't really want it back. She pawned it for enough money to take her daughter and move on to a new life."

Now Dominic leaned toward her, his eyes intently on her face. "Do you know what happened to them? Did they manage to start a new life?"

She did know what happened to them, and sensed that the knowledge was important to Dominic Amado. "They did. And when her husband got out of prison, he tracked them down and went to find them."

The blood drained from Dominic's face. Fear at what he expected her to tell him burned deep in his eyes—in his soul.

Intriguing.

"What happened?" he asked.

"He threw himself on their mercy, apologized for everything he'd done, and begged for a second chance. They remarried last year. He's a changed man."

Dominic took a long, deep breath and let it out. "That's an amazing story. Can I use that one? It's . . . heartening to hear that sometimes people can change."

Mixed messages. That's what she was getting from him. Relief that the story had a happy ending, and yet . . . "Of course you can use it," she said.

"So, did they ever redeem the watch?"

Lucinda looked away. "Oh, there was no redeeming that watch. It was gone. Came back though, about three weeks ago, as part of an estate sale. Life can be strange that way."

His eyes kindled. "So, it's here, in the shop—the watch?"

The front door swung open just then, with a sharp shrilling of the little bell. Lucinda jerked and glanced up. A trio of girls of about sixteen came tentatively into the shop, eyes wide and trying to take in everything at once. Lucinda was a bit chagrined that she hadn't sensed them when they reached the doorstep. Somewhere in the back of her mind an awareness piqued. She knew what they were here for.

She rose and looked down at Dominic. "I'm sorry, Nick, I . . ."

"Oh, sure." He shut off the recorder and popped it into the pocket of the plaid flannel shirt he was wearing—red and green; quite a fashion statement. "Can I go take a look at the watch?"

Lucinda gestured toward the glass display case. "It's at the end there, right next to the cash register." To the girls, she said, "I'll be with you in just a moment."

"Oh, no problem," said one of them—a pretty platinum blonde. Her gaze was riveted on Dominic as if she were memorizing his every feature. She dragged her attention reluctantly back to Lucinda. "We're looking for books . . . about magic."

"Most of those would be in the next room." Lucinda waved a hand at a door toward the rear of the shop where the bookshelves in the front room ended.

The girls made a beeline for it, but not without backward glances at the tall, beautiful young man who was even now crossing the room to the display case at its far end. They disappeared into the adjoining room.

When Lucinda reached him, Dominic Amado was gazing after the teenagers with a puzzled look on his face. "I didn't even notice that there was another room to the storefront." He gave her a lopsided smile. "And I call myself a journalist."

He looked down into the case then, his attention arrested by the collection of timepieces there. Lucinda slipped the magnetic catch on the display case and slid back the lid, then watched her companion closely, wondering if he would sense which watch she had described so vaguely and what he would make of it if he did.

She found herself studying his strong profile, the way the thick waves of dark hair fell around his face.

"Which one . . ." Dominic's voice trailed off as he reached down into the case. His hand paused above a sterling silver watch that sat in a row of four similar time-pieces. "Is that it?"

Lucinda nodded.

Dominic picked up the watch. He didn't hold it long. With a furrowed brow, he put it back on its bed of velvet, then stuck his hands in the back pockets of his jeans.

"You know, I'm sure this is just the power of suggestion, but it feels . . . weird. Negative." He chuckled and glanced at Lucinda from the tail of his dark eyes. "I wonder if it would have creeped me out if you hadn't told me anything about it."

"Me too," Lucinda said smiling. "So it felt . . . evil, did it?"

"It was disturbing. Though, as I said, its story is disturbing—so, no surprise there."

"Ooo!" cooed a female voice from the other end of the counter. "What's this?"

Lucinda turned. The girls had returned to the front of the shop and found Morgan le Fay's Book of Shadows—or, rather, it had found them. She took a deep breath. So be it. She turned her attention back to Dominic.

"I'm sorry, I . . ." She gestured at the girls.

"Of course, I completely understand. Here, let me leave this with you. In case you think of any more stories that might invoke some thought in our readers." He pulled out his wallet, extracted a business card, and handed it to her.

Lucinda looked down at it. "Dominic A. Amado, freelance journalist," she read aloud. She wrinkled her nose and glanced up at him from under her lashes. "Pardon my insatiable curiosity, but what does the 'A' stand for?"

He blushed. He actually blushed. Lucinda was fascinated in spite of herself at the discovery of an adult American male who could still blush.

"I don't spell it out for a reason," he said.

"Ah. Meaning, the 'A' stands for Abusive Parents?"

She did not imagine the momentary shift in his expression before he laughed. "Ah, no. Just a mother with a sense of the absurd and the overly dramatic."

He turned and moved to retrieve his camera bag from the reading table, while the girls followed his every move. He didn't even notice them, but he smiled at Lucinda.

"Let me know when you've got time to finish the interview and tell me some more stories." He sketched tipping an invisible hat and headed for the door.

That was it? No flirting? No come-hither looks?

"So, you're really not going to tell me what the 'A' stands for?" Lucinda asked.

He looked back at her from the sunny doorway, his smile slipping toward a lopsided grin. "I'm really not." The door closed quietly behind him, the little bell offering no more than a breathless shimmer of sound.

Lucinda put on a smile and moved on to her next customers. Lucifer had been right about them, of course—too much money and too little sense. She doubted they could have mustered a rational thought between the three of them, but one of the trio—a dark-eyed girl with flawless peach skin—examined the le Fay volume thoroughly, at least pretending to know what she was doing.

"This is a Book of Shadows," Lucinda told them. "Very old. Early sixth century. It's been rebound at least once since then, most certainly. The pages are a mixture of rag paper, parchment, and fiber—mostly parchment."

"You mean," the girl said, pausing to look up at Lucinda, "that this is actually a *real* Book of Shadows?" She caressed the leather cover with something like reverence.

"Yes. It's a very special one, too. It alleges to have belonged to Morgan le Fay."

"Book of Shadows," repeated the blonde, glancing from Lucinda to her mesmerized friend. "What the hell is Book of Shadows, Janine?"

The third girl—whose original hair color was a mystery beneath shades of blue that ran from periwinkle to darkest midnight—answered for her companion, after a fashion. Rolling her eyes, she drawled, "Earth to Stevie! A book of spells?"

Stevie snorted. "Why didn't you just say so?"

"You never listen to me," said Janine. "The BOS is like a witch's recipe book. It contains all of the witch's spells, rituals, incantations, and herbals."

"Freaking marvelous," said Stevie. "Does it have anything epically dire in it?"

Janine leafed through the book to about its halfway point, then let it fall open. It was the same page that Lucifer had opened it to. Lucinda felt the tug of the book's dark spirit.

"Wow, I guess," she breathed. "This is a ritual that's supposed to stop a river from flowing or make it run backwards . . . or turn to blood." She looked up at Lucinda, who stood silently by, watching. "Did this really belong to Morgan le Fay?"

"Yes," said Lucinda just as the girl with spiky azure hair said, "Don't be stupid."

Lucinda met her gaze. "I can assure you, miss, it did."

"Morgan le Fay wasn't even a real person," objected Azure Hair. "She's part of a fairy tale or something."

"She was a real person," said Janine absently as she paged reverently through the book. "She wasn't exactly the way they portray her in movies, but then neither were Arthur and Guinevere. Le Fay was a powerful practitioner of the Art."

Lucinda smiled. "You know your history."

Stevie stepped forward and touched one of the pages. She pulled her hand back with a frown. "How come it's in such good condition? Shouldn't it be falling apart after so long?"

"It's a book of magic," said Lucinda wryly. "It's had a little extra help staying in good condition." She didn't add that she was part of that extra help.

"We'll take it," said Stevie. "How much?"

Lucinda named a five-figure sum that would have caused most teenaged girls of this ilk to implode as they tried to calculate the loss in terms of clothing, shoes, and trips to the hair salon. Stevie didn't bat an eyelash. She whipped out her credit card and paid for the book.

"I'm curious," said Lucinda as she rang up the sale. "Why would you girls want a thing like this? I rather expected to sell it to a collector."

Janine looked scandalized. "This doesn't belong in the hands of some stupid collector. It's a witch's book; it should be used by witches."

Lucinda hesitated as she handed over the receipt and the package with the book inside. "Are you girls witches?" she asked, trying to sound skeptical and surprised.

"Yes, we are," said Janine with conviction, then marched out of the store with her friends trailing her.

"Nosy old bat," muttered Azure Hair as the door closed behind them.

Lucinda watched them go, then took Nick Amado's card out of her pants pocket and considered what sort of stories she might tell him that would make him come back and talk to her again.

CHAPTER FIVE

"Will you pursue him? *I* would pursue him."

Lucinda was well used to Vorden's comings and goings. They no longer startled or ruffled her—notwithstanding that the succubus had materialized not two feet away bathed in the light from the pawnshop's wide front window. Lucinda ignored the frisson of sexuality that accompanied her like a veil of scent.

"I'm sure you would. I haven't yet decided."

The titian-haired demon pouted prettily. "He is lovely, is he not? He wears darkness. I could taste it." She licked her full lips and smiled. Her human mouth sported catlike incisors.

Lucinda considered Vorden's words for a moment. Yes. That's the way she would have described it as well—Dominic Amado *wore* the darkness; he did not embody it or radiate it or hold it within. What did that mean?

"Our lord would want you to pursue him. He is special, that one. He found the shop, after all. He would make a mighty lieutenant for our lord."

Lucinda felt her own perverse demons rise. If "our lord" wanted her to do something, perhaps that was reason enough not to do it. She shook herself. She could not afford to succumb to emotional impulses. Not now.

Her father had spent millennia setting up his games, positioning his pieces and sowing the seeds of hatred, disunity, and deceit by any and all means open to him. Of course, God had been at work throughout that time as well, sowing His own seeds age after age. The world was in a particularly ripe condition for the sowing to bear fruit for both sides.

The industrial revolution, the growing interdependence of the human community, scientific discoveries and religious revelations, the advent of the Internet and instantaneous worldwide communication—all this had brought mankind to a precipitous stage in its development. It was possible, now, for the diverse kindred of the Earth to integrate—or to disintegrate and destroy much of what God had spent uncounted ages building. Mankind was primed to either leap forward or slide back into a time darker than any imaginable by zealots, fantasists, or science fiction writers.

Lucinda could not now lose her balance. She glanced up from the display case she was rearranging and slid the glass lid shut with a click.

"Unlike you," she told the succubus, "I have a mortal body that must be fed and rested. I'm going home."

"Home? To the Dark Realm? Or to that tiny human box you insist upon keeping?"

"Home," repeated Lucinda. "To my flat."

It wasn't a box, of course. It took up the entire top floor of a venerable building overlooking Central Park. Her "human box" was exactly as she wished it to be, which meant that there were parts of it that changed constantly, and parts that never changed. Most of the unchanging parts were the rooms she showed to human acquaintances and friends (of which she had but few).

Oddly, the room that formed the heart of the place, insofar as Lucinda was concerned, was also unchanging, except as dictated by the hand of God, by way of Nature. It was a rooftop garden that mimicked the place she had known the first five years of her mortal life. Not Eden, certainly—but then, Eden was more a state of being than a place. Lucinda's garden was nearly one-third of an acre of tree-lined paths, waterfalls, koi ponds, and grassy areas bordered with flowering shrubs and fruit trees. It was a blooming glory in spring, a paradise in summer, a maze of flame in fall, and a pristine, glittering wonderland in winter.

None of her human friends had ever seen it. Nor her father or any of his cadre. It was hers and hers alone. She went there almost every evening when she arrived home. It was a place to think. A place warded so powerfully that no one—not even Lucifer himself—could surprise her there. Her home read the energies of the supernal realms and warned her when someone drew near through the Between—or from the street.

So it was that she knew Rey was entering the building before he had so much as passed through the revolving doors at street level. The trees told her as she sat beside a gurgling stream, trailing her fingers in the chill, crystalline water. They announced his arrival with a shimmer of sound that was ever so slightly discordant. Interesting. That hinted that Rey was disturbed by something.

Lucinda sighed and lifted her hand from the water. Her fingers were dry before she rose to answer the summons of the elevator bell that she knew would come. She waited, though, until Rey had physically rung the bell before answering. No sense in letting him know she was forewarned of his approach. Secrets were necessary to her existence. Her father's secrets were legion. She felt compelled to keep up.

"May I come up?" Rey asked through the intercom.

"If you please. Is something amiss?"

"No, I just . . . needed a change of scenery, if you catch my drift."

Lucinda considered sending him away, but thought better of it. She did not dislike Rey—might have liked him a great deal had she been able to trust him. She pitied him, if truth be told, and knew what he meant about a change of scenery. For anyone with an ounce of human blood, being in Lucifer's company (or Vorden's or any other of the demonic tribe) was wearing and disorienting. One was never truly alone, and Rey, lacking the special powers granted Lucinda by her mixed lineage, had no means of creating even a tiny bubble of privacy. He was under constant surveillance, like a high-security prisoner, with no escape possible. Even his thoughts were not his own.

Except when he was here, in Lucinda's "human box," shielded by her complicated system of wards.

"Come on up," she told him, and triggered the elevator's lock.

She flipped on the flat screen TV that pretended at being a photo of whatever she felt like seeing at any given moment. There was news. There was always news—death and destruction in the Middle East, suicide bombings, embassies being shut down under threat of same, wars still rolling along in some countries, rumors of war in others. The Western world was not proofed against these pathetic results of her father's earnest work. There was rampant distrust in Washington, DC, and national capitals abroad, racial unrest in the US and Europe, people so focused on their own selfish and mundane wants that the lines of who was "them" and who was "us" were drawn in closer every day.

She flicked past several channels. A group of protestors proclaimed with brightly colored placards that "God Hates America." (Possibly He did, though not for the reasons the protestors supposed.) She paused to watch a member of Congress make jaw-dropping statements about climate change science being the "Devil's work."

"Satan's hope is to deceive us such that we no longer trust that God's creation is tailor-made for our survival," the congressman told the anchor of a network commentary show. "The Devil is at work here."

Oh yes, he was. She wondered how many ears he had whispered his sweet, slithering words into to turn the truth on its head; the idea that a conspiracy of scientists and liberals existed was some of his best work. Work she didn't share in. Lucifer's hands and feet and mouths and ears were legion. She was only one operative among many, but she was the most powerful of them, and the only one with free will. She held out hope that those two things would trump their sheer numbers.

She changed channels again: a televangelist ranted about the end of the world. That brought a wry smile to her lips. If only he knew how close that eventuality hovered. If only he was half as certain as he pretended to be that Lucifer was busily plotting mankind's downfall. If only he knew that when it happened—if it happened—it would come from numerous unexpected directions simultaneously. Some of them much closer to his own domain than the poor preacher had any notion.

Lucinda returned to the comment her father had made earlier about the fundamentalist doomsday cult of Nihilim—a braiding of the words "Nephilim" and "nihilism." The Nephilim were mythical giants, supposedly the children of angels and human females. In a sense, that was what she was—child of the first fallen angel and a mortal mother. Is that why he had mentioned the group to her? He had some reason, of course. Lucinda decided it was worth her while to follow up on that one; Lucifer never spoke carelessly, and his words never had but one meaning.

She knew it was not so, but sometimes she felt as if she were the only being of power standing between Lucifer and his end game. One single, solitary, lonely mole embedded with the Enemy. Had God even marked her efforts over the millennia? Was He even aware of how many times she had forced Lucifer to adapt, as Nathaniel had put it? Did He know how she had skated the thin ice of discovery century after century; how she risked all to be her mother's daughter? Surely He must, though she'd seen no sign of it.

She brought her thoughts up short, chiding herself for the momentary lapse into self-pity, and glanced at the elevator's display. Rey was halfway to the top floor.

Rey was an enigma to Lucinda in some ways. She did not know his entire story—only that he had made a literal deal with the Devil. She knew the substance of his arrangement with Lucifer—immortality in return for complete submission and a supernatural enhancement of whatever native talents had made him of such interest to her father that he would keep him close.

Rey was cagey, certainly, and bright and acquisitive. He was also a chameleon, capable of blending into any group, capable of being persuasive and personable, suave and funny. None of those things should have made him indispensable, but asking Lucifer why the human was so favored had only ever netted her an elegant shrug, a knowing smile, or a glib comment about having odd tastes in pets.

"To what do I owe the pleasure?" Lucinda asked when Rey stepped off the elevator into her foyer.

He stopped at the top of the short, wide flight of red granite steps that flowed down into her living room. "I wish it were a pleasure, Lucinda. But you're your father's daughter. I'd be stupid to take you at face value, wouldn't I?"

Lucinda frowned. What had brought this on? "I beg your pardon?"

He came down into the living room and sauntered across the vivid Persian carpet toward where Lucinda stood near the gleaming black hearth. She waved a hand and a fire sprang up in the grate; she was silent, waiting for him to make himself clear.

"Vorden says you have a new boy toy."

"Rey, I have never in my incredibly long and complicated life had a boy toy. What are you talking about?"

"The journalist. Vorden says you 'favor' him. Which I guess is her way of saying, you think he's hot."

She cocked her head to one side. Jealousy? "I barely know him. I came across him meeting with the young lawyer that Father was so interested in. I eavesdropped on their conversation. He . . . had a certain darkness about him, so I gave him a card."

"Vorden said that, too, that he had an interesting layer of darkness. I think she's hoping you'll recruit him so she can get her claws into him, give him crazy fantasies, then feed on them. What's your interest in him?"

She didn't know, honestly, but wasn't about to tell Rey that. "Why is that your business?"

"Because it's your father's."

She shrugged. "Then let him ask me. Indeed, he would ask me, if he half cared. Apparently, he doesn't. Which begs the question: Why do you?"

Rey was apparently no more willing to answer her questions than she was to answer his. "Do you like Amado's darkness, Lucinda? Does it taste like chocolate on your tongue? Does it make you quake with lust?"

"I don't honestly know what his darkness is." True enough.

"Would you like to know mine?"

She stared at him. "Did Father send you?"

"Can you imagine that he would?"

"Then why—"

"You didn't recruit this guy." It was a statement of fact.

"I'm not certain I will. He may be unsuitable. He failed one test already." Lucinda turned to face Rey fully, bringing flame to her eyes. "Is that what this is about—the fact that I didn't recruit him this afternoon? What—you think I didn't recruit him because I'm getting soft? Or being mutinous? Or perhaps setting up my own little realm within my father's domain?"

"None of those things. I think you didn't recruit him because of what you said: he may not fit, or he's not ready yet."

"So?" She spread her hands askance. "Have I disappointed you, Rey?"

He flashed a wide, white, unexpected grin, suddenly boyish. "Hell, I'm not disappointed. I'm relieved. The way Vorden described this guy, he was God's gift to succubi. I figured if she was ready to eat him up and ask for seconds, maybe he had a similar effect on you."

Lucinda flung back her bright hair, kicked off her shoes, and moved to curl up on one end of her cream-colored sofa, feet tucked beneath her. "I am not Vorden," she said deliberately. "Vorden is a one-dimensional construct, not a person. What-ever my lineage and whatever my predisposition to faults both human and inhu-man, I am, above all things, a real person."

Rey seemed to relax down to his soul. He flopped comfortably at the other end of the sofa, crossing his legs with studied ease. "Vorden thinks *she's* a real person."

Lucinda arched her brows. "Vorden is also delusional. It's not unlike my father to surround himself with delusional creatures—present company excepted, of course."

"Of course." He gave her a sly glance. "I was serious about sharing my dark-ness with you. I'm sure you've wondered."

She did not answer that charge. "Why now?"

Rey moved his gaze to the TV, where a congressman gesticulated wildly from a podium, face red with outrage—from there to the flames leaping in the great, black fireplace. Chips of mica glittered, mimicking stars in a dark sky. His handsome face, flooded with firelight, was uncharacteristically solemn.

"Now . . . I sense a sort of impatience in you. An edginess. A restlessness."

She didn't answer, but simply watched him.

"Maybe you're bored," he went on. "Maybe you're tired of being his . . . his second. I don't know, but I feel *something*."

"Did Father send you here to 'feel me out' as the humans say? Does he think I'm chafing under his command?"

Again the grin. "I imagine he expects that. Goes with your territory."

She made a questioning gesture. "Then what, Rey? Does he think I need a distraction?"

Rey looked away again—back at the fire. "How do I know what he thinks? I'm just a human flunky. A pet. I don't even fully understand what I am to him." He turned to face her, suddenly, his pale eyes intense. "This isn't about him. It's about *me*. It's about what I think, and what I think is that I . . . I can't say I love you. That would be stupid. I'm not sure I'm capable of love, or ever was. I'm pretty sure I have no idea what it is. But I know I want you, and that hearing Vorden talk about this guy—this Amado . . ."

He shifted a bit closer to her on the sofa. "Here's the thing, Lucinda. If you need a distraction, I'm good with that. I can be that. If you'll let me. If you need it. Want it."

Lucinda simply stared at him, repelled. Her first impulse was to tell him that she had no desire for him at all, not even as a distraction. He had been a pleas-ant enough associate (she could not call him a friend), until she had begun to sense his attraction to her. He had been unwittingly helpful to her on a number of occasions. But she had never felt any but the most passing attraction to him. Now, she felt none. Now, she felt repulsed.

She let none of this show in her expression, of course. Being on less-than-friendly terms with her father's most oft-used human operative would be unfortunate.

She chose her words with care. "Yes, I am impatient. I'm impatient to see my father's plans come to fruition. I'm restless because he doesn't always 'keep me in the loop,' as they say. He loves keeping his secrets. I'm restless because I'm bored with the human condition."

Rey snorted. "Welcome to my world."

"Rey, I'm not hungering for a human toy. And if I were . . ." She reached out a hand and gently touched his sleeve. "I respect you and value you far too much to make a toy of you—regardless of what my father might think. We are both human, you and I, to one degree or another. That is a rather important thing to hold in common, don't you think?"

Lucinda could see his pleasure at hearing this in his eyes, feel it radiating from him in waves. He covered her hand with his, momentarily stunning her with the solid human warmth . . . until she felt the void where his soul was, and knew that it cowered from the darkness with which he had surrounded it.

She withdrew her hand, still smiling, still offering him their common humanity, but she was now certain of one thing: she did not want to know any more about Rey Granger's personal darkness. Whatever he had done that caused him to choose servitude to Lucifer over God's judgment and a chance of redemption, Lucinda was content to let it remain his secret.

Rey opened his mouth as if he had more to say, but no words emerged. He shook his head and rose.

"I'll go now, I guess." He looked at her hopefully. "Although, if you wanted—"

She smiled, but didn't move. "Now, Rey, what would my father think?"

He opened his mouth again; no words tumbled out this time either. Then he smiled crookedly. "Your father would most likely hate the idea. Which might be enough of a reason to do it."

Lucinda pretended to consider that. "I'm certain I would survive his displeasure, but I doubt you would. I would hate for you to be destroyed on my account. I'm enough my mother's daughter to dread being the cause of a friend's annihilation."

He frowned, turning inward for a moment. She felt his perplexity before he grinned again. "Friend, huh? Well, that's something, I suppose."

He leaned down to kiss her on the cheek, then turned and trotted up the steps to the foyer. He pushed the elevator button, then turned to face her. "So, if the Old Man doesn't have a problem with us being an item . . ."

She gave his implied question no answer, but merely tsked at him. "Never let him hear you call him that."

The elevator opened and he was gone.

Lucinda took a deep breath and tilted her head back against the sofa cushions. What was it that Rey had left unsaid? Why the evasions?

Of course she had been evasive, too, but she knew why. His evasions, like his jealousy of Dominic Amado (real or pretended), were harder to fathom. She decided she must fathom them, one way or another. They could be important.

⊹

Across Central Park in a pinnacle of glass and steel, Brant Redmon picked up a prepaid cell phone and dialed an international number. To the man who answered, he said four words: "Things are in motion."

"And the funds?"

"Will be in place in a week's time."

"We are pleased."

Redmon chuckled genially. "Of course you're pleased. Now you can afford your little coup."

"I assure you, my friend," said the other man's faintly accented voice, "it will not be little."

Redmon hung up the phone and sat back in the tatty, overstuffed leather chair that was his favorite, though it stuck out among his other designer furniture like a goose at a swan convention. He called it his "thinking chair" and he had held out for years against his wife's terrier attempts to get rid of it. He reached out a hand to caress the gilded statuette that sat on the corner of his desk. It was a Hindu deity with multiple arms that his grandfather had picked up in a little curio shop in Mumbai. It had a particularly shiny spot on its crowned head where three generations of Redmons had stroked it for luck.

Nathaniel, from his vantage point in the Between, knew all of this about Brant Redmon and, having followed the electronic impulses through the ether, knew the location his contact occupied in space and time and ideology. The full shape of Redmon's scheme was not discernible at this point, but it was formed enough for the Fallen to know that his master's plans were, as his human tool had said, in motion.

CHAPTER SIX

His report complete, Nathaniel watched Lucifer pace his dark sanctum, Satan's eyes following his own reflection in the glistening black walls. The Lord of Demons glowed as if from within, the light reflecting back from the glassy surface to glide across his hair. It was as if he bent all light and drew it to him. Which, of course, he did. He devoured light and put it out again as raw heat.

"So," Lucifer said, "that's another countdown begun."

"Yes," Nathaniel told him. "Redmon has set things in motion. Soon the money will be in the hands of Ibrahim Darzi; he will execute his plans, and Saudi Arabia and Kuwait will explode with sectarian violence."

Lucifer gave the angel a sidewise glance from the tail of his burning eyes. He would see only a pillar of light. The Fallen did not bother to wear a physical garment in the Between. He wondered, from time to time, why Lucifer did. Perhaps he envied mortals. Nathaniel doubted he'd admit it.

"They are not Darzi's plans and never have been," Lucifer said. "But he and his American associates will be blamed for them no matter how well he covers his tracks. Now, tell me about the Book of Shadows. Have our young witches begun working with it in earnest? I felt their magic as a flutter in the ether. What did they do?"

"They used it to roil the waters of a Sleepy Hollow millstream."

Lucifer's sleek brows rose. "Disappointing. I expected more of the little bitches. I far prefer the sorcery of an earlier age." He smiled darkly. "Salem. Now that was witchcraft."

Nathaniel stirred. "But, there were no witches at Salem, Lord."

The smile became brighter and more chilling. "No, but I made them believe there were. It took so little, Nathaniel. A simple fungus in their rye, a simple word in the ear of the parish pastor delivered by a terrified little boy . . . and where was our absentee landlord of a God while I performed that little bit of playacting?"

Nathaniel did not answer the rhetorical question, though he suspected that God had done what was needful to limit the effects of Salem. "God's behavior is no longer my concern."

"Well, *these* pretend witches will do far more when I'm done with them. It will be a magnificent and deadly chain reaction."

"What have you planned, Lord?"

Lucifer shook his head. "I am a skilled writer of history, Nathaniel. A skilled writer doesn't tell, he *shows*. Go, now. Return to my daughter."

Nathaniel did as ordered (he always did as ordered), finding Lucinda in the pawnshop. He appeared to her in the human form she was accustomed to—tall and elegant, with dark hair, eyes that changed color, a face with strong features that she had once told him were "eerily perfect." He wasn't certain that was a good thing, but he kept those features nonetheless.

She glanced up at him when he materialized in the middle of the shop. She had been studying the items at the far end of the glass case.

"Do you have a sense about any of them?" he asked.

"Yes. The watch. The one that . . . that Dominic was so repulsed by."

He marked her casual use of the mortal's name, though her voice held only a certain bemusement. They both knew the provenance of that watch. Its original owner had died in 1902 by his own hand . . . after torturing and slaying his young wife. No reason for the murder-suicide was ever uncovered by the horrified New York City constables, though certainly Lucinda knew why it had happened. As did Nathaniel. The man who had imbued the watch with its initial charge of evil had been deceitful, cruel, and patient. Sterling Vincent had wooed his bride over a period of months, even as he planned her torture and death. His own death had been an afterthought, an escape hatch when he was found out too soon by his neighbors and the authorities.

He had not escaped, of course. No one did. Not even in death. Or perhaps especially not in death.

"The Redmon plan has gone to the next stage," Nathaniel said. "The Arabian connection is engaged."

"Ah. Good," she said, but she sounded distracted.

"Your father plans to do something significant with the little witches."

"Of course he does."

"Do you know what it is?"

Lucinda shook her head, doodling absently on the glass with the tip of a finger. "I sometimes wonder what would happen if he ever broke the Law, if he ever did more than urge the wrong people to be in the wrong place at the wrong time." She turned to look at him and, for just a moment, Nathaniel thought he saw almost to her soul. "You know God better than I do, Nathaniel. Do you think He would do anything if my father broke the Law?"

Nathaniel considered that. Yes, of course, God would do something, if He needed to. "I think the Law is so binding as to be unbreakable, and Lucifer knows it."

She tilted her head to one side, sending a cascade of auburn waves tumbling across her shoulder. "You called him 'Lucifer.' I can't remember the last time you called him by name. It's always 'master' this and 'my lord' that. What's gotten into you, Nathaniel? Feeling rebellious today?"

He couldn't read her smile. He never could. "No, Shaliah. Never that."

The corner of her mouth twitched and he thought she would ask him, for the thousandth time, to call her Lucinda. She didn't. She asked, "Why, though? What did he ever do for you?"

He didn't answer, and before she could prompt him, he felt a mortal presence cross the threshold into their pocket of reality. Nathaniel's movement—from where he stood to the reading table among the bookshelves—happened faster than any mortal eye could track. He sat down to play the part of a customer poring over the literary wares. He shifted his appearance, too, adopting a plaid shirt, longer, curlier hair, darker skin.

A second later, the bell tinkled and the door opened, revealing a pretty but weary-looking woman perhaps in her mid- to late thirties with ash-brown hair, and watery blue eyes. She wore jeans and a gray peacoat, with a bright red scarf wound round her neck and tucked beneath the lapels. All of her clothing had seen better days. She was smiling, but Nathaniel could tell the smile didn't reach to her soul. She was jittery and anxious beneath the sunny exterior. He sensed she was also ill.

"Hi," she greeted Lucinda. "Are you the owner?"

"My father is, actually, but I manage the place for him."

At the altered sound of her voice, Nathaniel looked up to see that Lucinda had also changed her appearance. She was now a fresh-faced young man, with light chestnut hair.

"I've never seen your shop before. Is it new?" the woman asked.

"Yes, ma'am. We sort of came in with the latest renovations on the block. Can I help you find something?"

"Well . . ."

Uncertainty warred with anxiety in the woman's heart—was she doing the right thing? Both uncertainty and anxiety lost to resolve and an upwelling of love for someone. Nathaniel was sometimes surprised he still recognized the emotion.

"I'm looking for a gift for my husband's birthday. I saw that sign in your window—'for the man who has everything'? Dan doesn't. Have everything, I mean. But he's hard to buy for."

"I hear you. Sounds like me trying to find stuff for my dad. He's the ultimate man who has everything."

"With a shop like this, I don't wonder."

Lucinda moved to the far side of the glass counter and made a showman's gesture along its length. "I have all sorts of unique gifts for men. Pens, cuff links, rings, tie tacks, watches."

The woman was approaching the glass cabinet, gazing down into it. "Oh! Pocket watches. My husband's father had a pocket watch. Dan always talks about it. Says he asked his dad what time it was ten times a day just to get him to take out that wonderful watch. It was a game they played . . ."

Her voice trailed off as she scanned the items in the case. Her eyes caught on something and, for a moment, she was frozen, staring. Nathaniel was almost certain he knew what had literally caught her attention. Lucinda's instincts, he had come to know, were rarely wrong.

"How much is that watch?" the woman asked.

"The silver one? It's one-twenty."

"Oh." The woman's disappointment had the tang of cold copper. "Would you . . . could you take less?"

The young man shrugged—a youthful gesture. "Make me an offer."

"Really? I can bargain?" the woman laughed. "Used to do that at flea markets all the time when we lived out in the 'burbs." Sadness. "I . . . Can I see it?"

Lucinda nodded and lifted the watch out of the case, laying it on a velvet mat.

"Oh, wow. Would you take eighty for it?"

"I'm not sure I can go that low. One hundred even?"

"Ninety?"

"Ninety-five."

The woman hesitated; clearly even that was too much. She ran a thumb across the watch's etched cover, then picked it up, pressing the winding wand as she did. The cover flipped open, revealing a pristine crystal and polished brass face with Roman numerals and elegantly turned hands of gleaming blue-black.

"It's beautiful! So beautiful. Dan would love it, but—oh, my God—if I spent ninety-five dollars . . ." She held it, stared at it, turned it in her hands, then—coming to a sudden decision—snapped it shut and started to hand it back to Lucinda. "I'm sorry, it's too much . . . I mean, Dan would . . ." Just shy of putting it into Lucinda's hands, she stopped, peering at the back of the watch. "Oh! It's engraved already! I guess that's it, then. I couldn't give my husband a watch with—" She cut off, her eyes widening, then read: "'To Daniel, with love.' That's—that's amazing. Daniel is my husband's name."

She was silent for a beat, then said, "I'll take it."

Lucinda smiled. "Wonderful. Would you like it gift wrapped?"

"Please."

While Lucinda boxed and wrapped the watch, the woman dug into her purse, coming up with a neat packet of bills. She laid them out on the glass counter one by one, as if parting with them were difficult. Nathaniel had no doubt it was.

"I just had a thought," the woman said as she pushed the pile of bills across the counter. "Is this watch pawned? I mean, is someone hoping to get it back? I'd hate to buy it if . . ."

"That's kind of you, Mrs. . . ." Lucinda gave the woman a questioning look.

"Oh, Collins. Mona Collins."

"That's kind of you, Mrs. Collins. It was pawned, yes. But I don't think the previous owner wants it anymore. Her circumstances have changed."

"Oh, that's all right, then." Relief. She hesitated for a moment, then said, "You know you remind me an awful lot of my son, Rowdy. He . . . he's coming home today on leave before he ships out for Kuwait. He's in the Marines. You just . . . look so much like him."

As if embarrassed by having confided all that in a complete stranger, she took the wrapped box, thanked Lucinda again, and left the shop.

Lucinda leaned her forearms on the countertop and watched Mona go. Nathaniel watched Lucinda watching Lucifer's latest victim and said nothing. After a moment of this, Lucinda seemed to shake herself, then straightened, resuming her natural human form.

"I should follow up on her," she said, turning as she spoke to face Nathaniel. Her eyes widened in surprise. "Why . . . why do you look like that?"

Look like Dominic Amado, she meant. The Fallen returned to his usual material form, but for a moment, he had read her reaction through her unguarded eyes and felt the depth of her attraction to the mortal. He was surprised as much by his own emotions as by hers. He had no time to sort them out, but he recognized one of them as unease.

"I thought it might please you," he said now. That was true enough.

"It doesn't please me. I don't like being manipulated, Nathaniel. Not by you. Not by *anyone.*"

She turned on her heel and headed for the back of the shop, leaving Nathaniel to contemplate her words and his reaction to them. Unease, yes. Possibly even dread. The question was why? It was true that in their immensely long acquaintance, he had never known her to show the least attachment to any mortal save her mother. She seemed to regard even Lucifer with cool detachment, but the emotions he'd read in her eyes just now were neither cool nor detached.

The Fallen was certain nothing good could come of that. He contemplated the idea that Dominic Amado might be a danger to Lucinda in some way. That he might compromise her. If that was the case, what could or should Nathaniel do about it?

⛭

Janine Sorentino loved the library. Loved being there, surrounded by books. Loved working there among them, inhaling their perfume. The library was housed in a huge colonial-style building that had become a second home to her during her sophomore year of high school. It was here Stevie and Mags had come across her, poring over some book about the Salem witch trials. They'd teased her at first, but she'd impressed them with her knowledge of witchcraft and they'd soon stopped teasing and started listening.

She was still agog over Stevie's purchase of the le Fay BOS. Not agog that she'd done it, but that she could *afford* to do it. The amount of money that Stephanie Halleck had forked over for that book was more than both of Janine's parents made in an entire month.

She was so caught up in her own thoughts as she trundled her book cart down the 130–139 aisle that she didn't see the man until she all but ran him down. In fact, if she didn't know better she would have sworn that he was simply not there one moment and there the next.

She hauled up her cart just short of hitting him and gasped. "I'm sorry! I didn't see you there."

He turned and she realized he was a pastor or priest. He wore a dark suit and a clerical collar, but—*holy shit*—he was too young and good-looking to be wasted on some priesthood. His tilted eyes were a shade of hazel she'd never seen before and seemed to be lit from inside his head. She hoped he was an Episcopalian or a Lutheran or something and not Catholic and celibate.

He started to smile at her and opened his mouth to say something. Then he frowned and closed it. "You," he said quietly, though she felt his voice vibrating in her head and heart. "I saw you at the mill Thursday night. With those other girls."

Uh-oh. Janine scrambled for something to say. Did she fib and deny being there, or—

"I know what you were doing."

"Wha-what do you mean?"

66

"I know a satanic ritual when I see it, child. What did you do to the millstream?"

Janine felt an absurd flush of pleasure beneath the flutter of panic. This guy had seen her do witchcraft. He had seen her do *real* witchcraft. "I . . . we . . . What did it look like?" Somehow, that came out sounding more flippant than curious.

"It looked as if you troubled the waters."

Now, that was a real biblical way of putting it. "I reversed the flow of the stream, that's all," she said, not without pride.

The pastor's eyes seemed to glow with a dark intensity that Janine took for religious zeal. "Sorceress."

"I'm not a sorceress. I'm a witch. There's a difference."

"Oh, you are more than a witch, young woman. I see a halo of darkness around you. You are a minion of Satan. It is *he* who gives you the power."

Now *that* made her mad. She hated it when people made that ignorant assumption, which was categorically wrong. "Satan-shmatan. Let me tell you something about witches, Reverend. We don't worship Satan. We worship the same God you do."

"Lies. You worship Satan and some heathen earth goddess."

"Bullshit. *I'm* the witch." She tapped her chest with one fist. "I think I know who I worship. And since when does God have male hormones? God's a spirit, remember?"

She thought for just a moment that she saw a corner of the pastor's mouth twitch upward before he crossed himself and began backing way from her, his mouth drawn in a grim line. There was something odd about the way he crossed himself, but Janine couldn't say what it was.

"You know nothing about God," he told her, his voice harsh. "Nothing."

"Look, *Reverend*," she began, but he continued to back away from her toward the end of the shelves. He gave her one last, penetrating glance, then turned away and disappeared behind the rows of books.

She stood, frozen, for a second, then rounded her cart and hurried after him. She reached the end of the stacks and looked both ways, but the pastor was nowhere to be found—the jerk. She blanched at her own thoughts. Was it blasphemous to think of a man of God as a jerk, even if he acted like one?

Janine was rattled and angry and a little scared at first—what if this guy found out her name and went to her parents, or her school? She left her cart untended long enough to make a quick search of the library. The weird pastor was nowhere in the main room—nowhere in the meeting or study rooms. He'd effectively vanished. Probably thought the whole place was possessed or something. She wondered if she should track him down and apologize. Sleepy Hollow was a small enough town that finding out which church had a drop-dead gorgeous pastor couldn't be *that* hard.

She made her way to the head librarian's desk near the main entrance. "Excuse me, Mrs. Martin, but do you know which church the pastor who just left belongs to?"

Mrs. Martin, silver-haired and bifocaled, blinked up at Janine. "Pastor?"

"Or priest. I couldn't tell which on sight. He had a collar?" She gestured at her own neck.

Mrs. Martin shook her head. "Sorry, dear. I didn't see him."

"But he must've gone right past—" Janine stopped herself. Mrs. Martin was very sensitive about her age and her eyesight. "I guess he must've gone into one of the study rooms."

He hadn't, though; she'd checked them all. Mrs. Martin had probably just fallen into one of her Jane Austen novels and disconnected from reality long enough for Reverend Smart-Ass to slip past her.

Janine went back to her job shelving books, considering whether she should try to find Mr. Holier-than-thou. Maybe the le Fay Book of Shadows had a spell in it that would help her find him. By the time she was done for the day, she was more amused by the whole thing than rattled. In fact, the more she thought about what the pastor had said, the better she felt.

Hot damn! She had the power. Wait till she told Stevie and Mags.

CHAPTER SEVEN

With Dan's birthday present tucked deep into her tote, Mona went home to her third-floor walk-up on Third Avenue. The foyer, hallway, and stairwell were dark and dingy, but she was proud of what she'd been able to do with their two-bedroom apartment every time she stepped through the door. This time was no exception. It was tiny, but Mona was good with fabrics and considered herself the Queen of Rummage Sales. She had managed to furnish the place from secondhand stores and other people's castoffs, which she'd refinished with Rowdy's help in the basement of the apartment building.

It hadn't always been like this. Not that long ago—had it only been four years?—she and her husband, Dan, and her son had lived on a quiet, tree-lined street in a quaint suburb. She'd been happy there. Their current situation had come at the end of a long downward slide that had begun when Dan had injured himself at work. He'd recovered, but the injury had left him unable to do the brute force manipulation of machinery that his job required. He hadn't the education necessary for administrative work, was a miserable salesman, and couldn't manage other workers without losing his temper.

Mona's job as a home care nurse simply hadn't paid enough to allow them to keep their house. They were underwater on the mortgage, couldn't keep up the payments, and couldn't refinance. So, they'd lost the house, sold most of their furniture, and moved into the city where—theoretically—Dan would be able to find work more readily. In practice, few businesses wanted a forty-year-old guy with a bad back, a hot temper, and a high school diploma. So, he spent his days looking for work, keeping up the apartment, and, lately, hanging out at a tavern on the corner, using money he got from doing odd jobs in their building. His unemployment insurance had run out long ago.

Mona took the gift-wrapped watch out of her tote and placed it in the middle of the kitchen table. She realized, as she did, that there were dishes in the sink from this morning. Dan hadn't done them before he went out for the day. That was happening more and more lately. When they'd first moved in, he'd been pretty good about keeping the place up, but things had been sliding for a while now.

Mona sighed and began clearing away clutter. She wanted the place to look nice for tonight. Tonight, Rowdy would be home on leave before shipping out on a tour of duty to Kuwait. Worried, she prayed silently that Rowdy and Dan would get along with each other for the few days that her son was home. Watching their relationship fall apart while she could do nothing but stand impotently on the sidelines had been the most painful experience in Mona's thirty-six years of life.

Once, she thought they'd be okay together—back when Rowdy was a little boy and Dan seemed happy to take him to Little League games and buy him ice cream and pretend to be his dad. That had lasted into Rowdy's early teen years, but the happy family portrait had begun to fade even before Dan lost his job. Mona suspected that something about Rowdy reminded Dan of his own youth, a part of his life he never discussed with her. Their relationship had deteriorated with every passing day, and Mona had been at a complete loss to know how to fix things. She'd settled for trying to run interference or play peacemaker, which had only made Dan angry. Things had gotten worse after he lost his job.

She understood that. She'd tried to show Dan that she *did* understand. She knew how hard this was for him, got how useless he felt, how frustrated he was. But her attempts to comfort him had ended in him shouting at her that she wasn't his mother. He'd blamed her nurturing ways on turning her son into a momma's boy.

Rowdy wasn't a momma's boy. He was quiet, considerate, and gentle, but strong-willed. The problem was that he wasn't Dan's son—wasn't his blood—and maybe that had been why Dan had driven him away to join the Marines. That had hurt deeply—to see her son take up a career that was so against his gentle nature—but Rowdy had felt he had something to prove. Mona had never aspired to a military career for her son. She'd thought he'd be a teacher, maybe, or a scientist. He loved science; Dan had teased him for that unmercifully when he'd gone into high school.

Standing at the sink, sorting dishes into the dishwasher, Mona looked out the kitchen window at the fire escape to see if at least Dan had hung out the towels she'd washed before she went downtown. He hadn't. The only thing on the fire escape besides a few potted plants was a cat.

Mona was familiar with the neighborhood cats; this was one she'd never seen before. It was a peculiar color, too, a sort of red-gold brown with darker tips on the hairs that ran down its back. It looked a lot like the cat figurines she'd seen in the museum—the ones from Egypt. What were they? Abyssinian, that was it. It was an Abyssinian cat. Pretty thing. And it was looking right at her, its big green eyes unblinking.

She flipped the locks on the window and slid it upward, then cranked out the screen. "Here, kitty, kitty," she coaxed. "Come in and I'll give you some milk."

The cat hesitated for a moment, then came in through the open screen. Tickled at how easy that had been, Mona went to the refrigerator to get the animal some milk. When she turned around with the bowl in her hand, the cat was sitting next to Dan's birthday present on the kitchen table.

Laughing, Mona picked up the cat and put it on the floor with the bowl of milk. "Sorry, kitty," she told it. "My husband would lose it if he saw a cat on his kitchen table. He doesn't like cats. If he saw you up there walking around, I don't know what he'd do." That was a fact; Mona was a bit afraid of what Dan might do if he saw a cat anywhere in the apartment.

A spark of rebellion flared in Mona's heart. "Hey, I'm paying for this place, after all, right?" she asked the cat. "If I want to invite in a furry little friend, that's within my rights. Dan can just . . . get used to it."

He wouldn't get used to it, she was pretty sure. She knelt to pet the cat, telling herself it was nothing to worry about. Dan yelled a lot, but he'd never really threatened to hit her.

Mona had the table set and an early dinner nearly ready when Rowdy arrived at about three. She was overjoyed to see him, thrilled to have him home, but also aware that he was different than her memories of him. She could barely see her little boy in the solemn young man at her door. With his buzz cut and broad shoulders, he seemed—no, he *was*—a grown man.

Mona paused long enough to take in how mature he looked, then threw her arms around him and let her tears go. "Oh, honey, look at you! You're so grown up!" She held him at arm's length and studied him. "I guess my little boy is gone."

Rowdy smiled at her and the little boy was back. Then he made a mock sad face. "Momma, you told me I'd *always* be your little boy. I'm gonna hold you to it."

She hugged him again and had him put his duffel in the spare room she'd made up for him. Then he sat at the kitchen table petting the cat while she put the finishing touches on the custard she'd made for dessert.

"So, where's Dan?" he asked after a bit.

It still hurt that he'd stopped calling Dan "Daddy," but Mona smiled and said, "I expect he's down at the corner pub. He often goes there after he's done, y'know, looking for work."

"Still nothing? Jeez. Mom, it's been several years."

"He gets piecework sometimes, but it doesn't last. He's signed up as a temp, but the kind of work he's done doesn't usually go to temporary employees. It's just so hard for him. He went back to school for a while and learned some bookkeeping skills, but people seem to want someone who's been doing books for a while, not a guy who just learned. He was always good at math . . ." she finished lamely.

"Well," said Rowdy, "I hope he finds something permanent soon. I really do. It's not fair for you to have to carry the load yourself."

"It's no hardship. I'd work, in any case."

The front door rattled, then opened. Dan appeared in the doorway. Mona's heart fell. She could tell from the way he teetered when he closed the door that he'd been drinking. Not drunk maybe, but he for sure had a buzz on.

Rowdy rose. The cat leapt to the floor and disappeared under the table. "Hello, sir," the boy said, his voice resonant and deep.

Dan stopped halfway across the living room and blinked at the younger man, his face expressionless. "So, you made it home," he said. "Good. Your mom was missing you."

"I know, sir. It's why I'm here. My tour of duty is two years, and I'm not sure if I'll get leave long enough to come home once I'm over there."

Dan nodded absently. "Kuwait, huh?"

"Yes, sir."

Dan nodded again, then focused on Mona. "Smells good, hon. I'll just go wash up." He turned and headed unsteadily down the hall toward the bathroom.

Mona felt herself unclench. She'd been so afraid that Rowdy and Dan would just pick up where they left off, but her son's quiet respect seemed to have short-circuited Dan's anger. To say they hadn't parted on the best of terms was an understatement. Dan had practically driven Rowdy out, laying into him for being "another mouth to feed."

Rowdy helped Mona serve up the food and they sat down to eat as soon as Dan returned. He'd scraped away his five o'clock shadow and put on a fresh shirt, something that made Mona relax even more. He seemed to be trying as hard as her boy to be civil.

He noticed the small box between his plate and water glass immediately. "What's this?"

"It's your birthday, honey," Mona said. "Did you think I'd forgotten?"

He stared at her across the table for a moment and she thought she saw his eyes glisten with tears. "Hell, Mona, I'd forgotten. Other things on my mind. Should I open it now?"

"Please," she said.

He did open it, becoming very still when he saw the watch lying on its bed of fake velvet.

"I remembered what you told me about your dad's watch," Mona said quickly to cover the awkward silence. "How much you loved it when he'd take it out of his pocket so you could see it."

Dan glanced at her, then took the watch out and set the box aside. "It's—uh—it's really nice. A lot like my dad's."

"It's engraved," she said. "Look at the back."

He did, staring at the words, *To Daniel, with love.* He blinked several times, then cleared his throat.

"Do you like it?" Mona asked softly.

"Yes. Yes, I do. I like it." He stroked the watch's crystal. "I hate to think what you must've paid for it."

"It wasn't that much. And it was worth it if you like it." She reached across the table and touched his hand.

Rowdy took that moment to say, "Happy birthday, sir."

Dan seemed to tremble for a moment, then cleared his throat again and set the watch down beside his plate. "Food's getting cold."

As they ate, Mona kept up a conversation with her son, asking him about his time in boot camp and training. He seemed happy to talk about military life and seemed to take special pride in the fact that he'd won several marksman's awards that had contributed to him being selected for a special ops team.

This seemed to perk Dan up. "You're good with a gun, are you? Good to hear. Hard to believe, considering how soft you were before you went in."

Mona saw a flash of anger in Rowdy's eyes, but he didn't rise to the bait. He only said, "Yes, sir. I've gotten to be real good with guns. Especially long guns. I find target practice . . . sort of meditative. I'm good with language, too. I've been learning Arabic. Top of my class."

Dan laughed at that. "They pay you more for being a good shot and yakking in Arabic?"

Rowdy smiled. "No, sir. I wish they did. Funny thing, though. Last week, this guy came to see me—retired colonel—offered me a civilian job doing special ops stuff for one of those military contractors. Blackpool, he said. You know, a mercenary crew that signs on to do dangerous assignments, guard duty, extractions, that sort of thing. He told me that both my firearms expertise and my language skills were a big plus. Offered me a shitload of money to prove it."

"Really?" asked Mona uncertainly. "You mean for when you're done with the service?"

"No. He wanted to swing a special discharge for me so I could do it now."

"So, you're going to work for this Blackpool bunch, then," Dan said.

Rowdy shook his head. "No, *sir*. I've read all about how bad they were during the Iraqi conflict. Government wasted millions on them, and they did really crazy stuff. Acted like they owned the place. Hurt people. That's not what I signed up for. I want to serve my country, not some for-profit outfit."

Dan put his knife and fork down. "You mean to tell me that someone offered you a big salary for doing the same sort of thing the government's paying you peanuts for and you turned them down?"

Mona knew that look, knew what the slow reddening of Dan's ears meant.

"I'm serving my country, sir," Rowdy answered carefully. "Something you said you thought I should do because it would make a man of me. It did. Which is how I know that serving my country is a more manly thing than making a bundle as a hired gun for some outfit with a closet full of secrets."

"Throw my words back in my face, huh? Is that what you just did? Well, let me tell you this, kid—your mom works her fingers to the bone putting food on the table, keeping a roof over our heads. These little luxuries, we really can't afford." He laid a hand over the watch. "I wish to God I could get a job and take on my proper role as head of this household, but I haven't found a damn thing."

"Dan," said Mona quietly. "It's all right. I'm proud he turned down a job like that. God knows what a company like that would ask him to do."

Dan made a shushing gesture at Mona, his eyes focused on Rowdy. "Your mom is sick, Rowdy. Did you know that?"

"Dan!" Mona exclaimed. "It's not that big a deal."

"What is it, Mom?" Rowdy asked, worry leaping to his eyes.

"I have a little tendonitis in one hip, that's all, really. From lifting patients into wheelchairs and helping them in and out of bed. My doctor's given me medication for it."

Rowdy wasn't convinced. "Is that all, Mom? Really?"

"No, it's not all, you stupid shit!" Dan snapped. He clenched his fist around the pocket watch. "Can't you tell when she's shining you on? You didn't tell him about your blood pressure, did you?"

Rowdy looked at her. "Mom . . ."

"It's only a little high and the doctor says it's just stress." Mona was starting to get a little angry now herself. Didn't Dan realize that scenes like these weren't helping her blood pressure? "I need to be able to *relax* more," she added, looking meaningfully at Dan.

He didn't take the hint. "What you need is a son who cares more about you than he does about his own delicate feelings. With the money you got from a job like that, Rowdy, you could probably make sure your mom never had to work again."

"It's not my *work* that stresses me," Mona said, but Dan was already past hearing her.

He raised his fist and shook the watch in Rowdy's face. "She's a generous woman, your mom. More generous than *you* deserve. She and I have worked your whole damn life to make sure you got opportunities to do the stuff you wanted to do—playing baseball, martial arts, and all that. This is what it gets us—a squeamish little girl? And now you stroll in here and tell us you're going to go work for nothing in the military when you could be making enough to pay us back?"

"I didn't know parenthood was about getting paid back," Rowdy said, the scalp beneath his buzz cut going bright red. His jaw bunched with the effort of controlling his temper. "I thought it was about loving someone. When I was a kid and you were taking me to Little League games and karate class, I thought you were doing it because you loved me, not because you expected me to pay you back."

"Rowdy!" Mona scooted back her chair. "You know I love you! Just having you was the best thing that ever happened to me." She saw the tightening around Dan's mouth and regretted the words immediately.

"I know you love me, Mom," Rowdy said, glaring at Dan. "I'm not talking *about* you or *to* you. I'm talking to my so-called stepfather."

Dan shot out of his chair. "You ungrateful little bastard! How dare you talk to me that way! You sucked up all we had to give you, then took off like an unwelcome guest when we couldn't support you in the manner to which you'd become accustomed."

"It wasn't like that," Rowdy growled, rising slowly. "It wasn't like that and you damn well know it! You *drove* me out, you sad son of a bitch."

Mona clapped her hands over her ears, tears welling in her eyes. How in God's name had things gone south so quickly? "Don't call your father that!"

"He's not my father!" Rowdy snarled. "He was *never* my father!"

That was too much. Just too much. Mona shot out of her chair so violently that she flipped it backwards onto the floor. "Both of you stop it!" she shrieked. "Just stop! You're hurting me! Can't you see you're hurting me?"

Dan turned on her, a look in his eye she swore she'd never seen before—something hot and dark and violent. "*Hurt* you? You think *this* is hurting? I'll show you hurting."

He cocked his arm and, for a moment, Mona thought he meant to throw her gift back in her face, or punch her. Before she or Rowdy could react, the Abyssinian cat, which had been hiding under the table, leapt to the tabletop with a wild screech, sending glassware every which way. Water shot across the table and soaked the front of Dan's shirt. The cat followed it, springing from the table to Dan's shoulder. He yelled and tried to step backward, but his chair caught him behind the knees and he toppled to the floor. The cat jumped to the sink and then to the windowsill. It disappeared into the darkness of the fire escape.

Mona could see Rowdy's anger leave his eyes like an ebbing tide. He righted Dan's chair, then reached down to help his stepdad up, but Dan was having none of it. He batted his stepson's hands away.

"Leave me alone, damn it! D'you bring that damned animal with you?"

"*I* let it in," said Mona, and was surprised at the anger in her own voice. "Let Rowdy help you up."

"Hell, no! I can get up on my own." Dan suited action to word and used the chair to drag himself to his feet. Upright, he turned to face Mona, the hot, dark, scary fire still leaping in his eyes. "You got a choice to make, woman. You can have your pansy-ass brat here for two days or you can have me. He stays, I'm gone. You got that? I've got friends down at the pub who'll take me in. Hell, I got *enemies* who treat me better than you do. Now, I'm gonna go get out of this wet shirt. You let me know whether you want him or me." He swung around, almost falling again before aiming himself at the bedroom.

Rowdy moved swiftly to block his path, fists clenching and unclenching. "You can call me names till Hell freezes over, asshole, but don't you *dare* talk to Mom that way."

Dan blinked, his ears going red again, his jaw tightening. "What? You—what? You little bastard! You little cowardly pissant *bastard!*" He cocked a fist, aiming it at Rowdy's jaw.

Mona acted before she thought. "Damn you, Daniel Collins!" she shouted, thrusting herself between her husband and her son. "Damn you to Hell! You. Don't. Call. My. Son. Names!" She put both hands in the middle of Dan's chest and shoved. Hard.

He reeled back a couple of steps, caught himself, and raised his fists. He seemed uncertain for a second about who he should attack, then he hurled himself at Rowdy, arms flailing.

He was no match for Rowdy's disciplined strength. Rowdy caught one fist and twisted, pinioning his stepfather's arm behind his back. Dan roared in pain, loosing a stream of obscenities. They were gibberish to Mona; she was yelling as well—words she didn't know she knew flying from her lips.

Rowdy frog-marched his stepdad across the living room to the front door and flung it open. "Get the hell out, you stupid, washed-up drunk!" he snarled in Dan's ear. "And don't come back till you dry out!" He gave Dan a shove, sending him careening against the wall across the corridor. "Go! I mean it! Go, or so help me God, I'll break you in two!"

Dan pulled himself upright and staggered down the hall toward the stairwell. His breathing was so harsh it sounded as if he was sobbing. Maybe he was. Mona decided that, right now, she didn't care. Didn't. Care.

That scared her. She'd cared for Dan from the moment she'd met him. She turned and buried her face in her hands, weeping in earnest now. She heard Rowdy close the apartment door and throw the dead bolt and the security chain. She felt a gentle hand on her shoulder and turned to look into her son's grim face, distorted by her tears.

"It's okay, Mom," he said. "I'll stay if you need me. Or I can go if . . . you know, if you want Dan to come back sooner. I've got a platoon mate in town. He offered to have me stay with him this weekend. I can give him a call and go on over."

Mona felt her eyes filling with fresh tears. She shook her head. "No. I'd rather you stayed."

"Are you sure? I mean, I feel like this was my fault. I shouldn't have told you guys about that mercenary outfit. I should've kept it to myself."

"You had no way of knowing it'd set him off. I . . . I thought it was going so well. I'm an idiot."

"No, you're not. I thought it was gonna be okay, too."

He put his arms around her and just held her in silence while she cried herself out. Then he released her and wiped his hands on his jeans, as if that would get rid of the stain of the ugly scene they'd just participated in. "I'll help you clean up, okay?"

"I'd like that, thanks."

They went to the kitchen, together, and began to clear the dishes and clean up. They didn't talk much.

Mona found the gift box the watch had come in under the kitchen table and picked it up. The watch itself was nowhere in sight. Dan must've stuck it in his pocket. She found herself wondering, ironically, if he'd pawn it to pay for booze or a place to stay. Or if maybe he really did have friends who'd take him in. Now that she was a bit cooler-headed, she hoped that was the case.

That watch—what had possessed her to get it for him? Had she really thought that buying him expensive reminders of fonder times would bring back the man she'd married? She was a fool.

"Momma? You okay?"

She glanced up, realizing that she was just standing there, staring at the empty gift box. She set it on the table. "I'm fine, honey. Really. Just fine."

CHAPTER EIGHT

Lucinda leapt from Mona Collins' kitchen window thinking that mortals who complained about hating their jobs had no idea what they were talking about. She had just left a malevolent ticking time bomb in the home of an innocent family whose only real fault was that they had allowed guilt to divide and conquer them. Dan's guilt at not being able to keep his old job or find a new one; Mona's guilt that she had been unable to heal the rift between her husband and her son; Rowdy's guilt at being unable to stay in his mother's home and buffer her from his stepfather's temper.

None of it—*none* of it—was necessary or rational, but that was mortal life. It was a jumble of conflicting impulses and warring ideals. The brain craved what the soul knew was dangerous or wrong or just plain evil. Thus had begun humanity's struggle with the knowledge of good and evil—a simple choice between the desires of the body and the soul.

What was it about this particular dysfunctional family that engaged Lucifer? How did he plan to use them? Was Dan Collins the targeted tool, or Mona, or was it the boy, Rowdy? Why had that particular demon been drawn to Mona?

Well, yes, Lucinda knew in general terms that the watch—the watch to which Sterling Vincent's soul was tethered like a captive beast seeking escape—had a penchant for turning the merely angry into abusive tyrants. But she did not know what the watch was supposed to accomplish.

Her father's schemes came in two "sizes." There were schemes intended only to wreak as much random havoc as possible and generally make human beings miserable, and there were schemes that were part of his overarching goal of uprooting humanity—of proving to the All-Father with finality that His cherished human beings would never outgrow their animal roots. That they were unworthy of His love and impervious to His attempts to educate them.

Which type of scheme the Lord of Demons was constructing was never clear at the very beginning. Only once the dots began to connect would the outline emerge. Lucifer, being Lucifer, did not like to divulge which were which.

It had been almost a game between them over the centuries—or perhaps it was a test; Lucifer would set things in motion, then wait for Lucinda to grasp what he was doing. She had long ago realized that she was less a daughter than a student. Her father was most pleased with her when he thought she had figured out what he was doing and stepped in to help. She was most pleased with herself when she figured out what he was doing and was able to spoil his plans while making him *believe* she was helping.

Lucinda was her father's daughter in one regard—she had gotten very good at deception. She also knew when to follow her human instincts. She had done both when she purchased the Qur'án. Her father's interest in the Middle East was not only obvious, it was inevitable. He was following a script written for him in the pages of scripture, and she knew that scripture just as well as he did.

She would prod Nathaniel to see if he might have some more pieces of the puzzle, and if those pieces might connect the Collins family with a larger plot. Likewise, the young would-be witches; what part would they play, and in what scenario? Her father's plans, she knew from experience, were never simple or transparent. They were layer upon layer, thread upon thread, of deceit and seduction, and he enjoyed constructing them immensely.

In the courtyard outside the Collins' apartment, in the lee of a fire escape, Lucinda resumed her usual human form, but had taken only a step or two before she realized something rather disconcerting: she took no enjoyment from the prospect of walking back downtown today. Normally, she reveled in the tactile, visual, visceral joy of being in human form. But not now.

She looked up toward Third Avenue. The sun had already disappeared behind the rooftops, and the streets—in which she usually enjoyed the sheer frenetic energy of the mass of humanity that lived in New York—seemed like cold, dim canyons peopled by scurrying, ratlike predators. She could well imagine that it might always be that way—that Manhattan would remain locked in some perpetual gray twilight. Frozen between the time the sun set and the time the rats put on their nighttime finery and went out to frolic in the pretend illumination of neon.

She delved into the internal cityscape of her own soul and felt a strange unease—an odd, almost frantic desire to be somewhere else. No, to be *someone* else. Someone mortal and mundane. She breathed in, hyperaware of the sensation of her lungs expanding, taking in scents from the scattered restaurants along the avenue. It only made her more twitchy. She looped a strand of hair behind one ear and stepped into the Between, coming out again in the confines of her shop.

Rey looked up from behind the counter where he was playing with a clock—a small, jeweled replica of Cinderella's pumpkin coach, complete with golden horses wearing diamond-studded harnesses. It held in its grasp the spirit of a ballerina so jealous of a rival dancer that she had murdered the woman by arranging for her to receive a gift—a poisoned gift that killed through the simple act of setting the time.

This wasn't the first time Lucinda had found Rey studying the timepiece. She often wondered at his attraction to it. What drew him to it—the use of poison, the betrayal of a rival who thought her murderer was a friend, or something not immediately apparent?

Rey blinked at Lucinda as if waking from a reverie, then shook his head and laughed. "I swear to God, I'll never get used to you doing that. It's been, like, fifty years and it still makes me jump."

"It's been forty-four years," she told him, "and you really should be used to it by now."

"I don't have your radar, Lucinda. I can't tell when one of you demons is coming until the 'door' opens."

She cocked her head and looked at him curiously. "What *do* you feel when one of us *demons* steps out of the Between?"

He pointed at the back of his neck. "Static electricity. Like little ants dancing along my spine. Of course, when it's you, there's another kind of electricity that goes with it. A very *sexy* kind." He gave her a crooked smile.

"I'm flattered," she said, without inflection.

He made a face. "I wish you were more than flattered. I wish . . ."

"I know. I'm sorry."

He stood, his expression saying clearly that "sorry" was not good enough. "Since you're back, I guess I'll go see if His Highness needs me for something."

Any reply Lucinda might have made was lost in the tingling awareness that someone was at their threshold. No, not just someone—Dominic Amado. Something in her expression must have alerted Rey, because he hesitated, turning to look at the door.

The little bell sounded, the door opened, and Dominic stepped into the shop. He was dressed in a deep red shirt, black leather jacket, and jeans that looked brand new. His hair was curried and shining, and he was freshly shaven. Lucinda caught the scent of his cologne—something with bergamot.

She smiled. "Nick! What a pleasant surprise. Did you think of some more questions, or did your poor camera finally give up the ghost?"

He returned the smile; it lit up his face. "Camera's still good. I, uh . . . I did have some more questions, but I was wondering if . . ." His gaze made a circuit of the room. "I was wondering if maybe we could go get a coffee or something. In a more . . . relaxed atmosphere?"

Lucinda scented more than his cologne now; she caught his energy—wary, uneasy. It was the shop, she realized. The shop made him nervous. Her realization brought with it a relief that she didn't want to feel. She wasn't supposed to care how he felt.

"I think I can manage that," she said, and turned to Rey, who was watching the other man with dark interest. "Rey, could you get Vorden to keep an eye on the place until closing time?"

Rey scratched his cheek. "Vorden is out doing an errand for your old man. But I'd be happy to close up for you, if you like. Uh, you gonna introduce me to your friend?"

"Of course. Rey, this is Dominic Amado. He's a journalist and he's been interviewing me for a piece he's doing. Dominic, this is Rey Granger."

The two men shook hands, taking the opportunity to size each other up. They were a picture of contrasts. Rey, in his sharp gray suit, was immaculately groomed with not a hair out of place; even with his hair brushed to gleaming waves, Nick looked as if he were standing in a perpetual breeze. Notwithstanding, there was about him an aura of vitality—of *presence*—that Rey lacked. Perhaps the difference was that Dominic Amado was still master of his own soul.

Lucinda chided herself for drawing the comparison. Whatever did it matter which she thought more attractive? It shouldn't matter—*couldn't* matter. Attraction to Dominic was a nonstarter. Any relationship she might have with a mortal would be doomed from its inception. A mortal would die; she couldn't—at least not by any normal means. A mortal would age and sicken; she would do neither. Best get this interview over with and let it be the last time she saw Dominic A. Amado.

"I'll go get a jacket," she said and hurried to the back of the shop.

There was an actual coat stand there with a jacket on it that Lucinda had bought at a boutique down the street. She might just as easily have fabricated it out of the atoms in the ether, but there was something deeply satisfying about owning things made by human hands. The feel of physical material against her skin made her feel grounded in the here and now—reminded her of her own humanity. She was pleased that Vorden was not around to taunt her about it. The succubus felt it was beneath a scion of the Devil to wear garments manufactured by mere mortals. Vorden "made" all her own clothes—if you could consider the scantily clad succubus clothed.

When Lucinda came back out into the shop, Rey was pretending to organize a bookshelf. What he was really doing was watching Nick survey the objects in the counter-cum-display case. The dark, naked emotion in Rey's eyes made Lucinda glad he possessed no supernatural powers. He did, however, possess real human strength and cleverness. She found herself as eager as Nick seemed to get out of the shop.

"Ready to go?" she asked.

Dominic looked up and smiled, but she caught the frown the smile had displaced. He was bothered by something—Rey's regard? Or something in the display case?

Out on the street, they headed up to the corner bistro as if by mutual consent. She could tell there was something he wanted to say to her. She couldn't read what it was. They entered the Gramercy Star, ordered a couple of lattes, and sat down near a window.

"So," she asked after a sip of her drink, "what did you want to ask me?"

There was that intriguing blush again. "I was curious about . . . well, a number of things, actually, but . . . that watch—the one whose story you told me last time. I noticed it was gone just now."

Lucinda nodded, studying what was left of the heart-shaped pattern in the foam on her latte. "Someone purchased it as a birthday gift."

"How did you feel about that? Did it . . . do you ever think that pieces like that watch might be cursed?"

She was startled into looking up at him. She could count on the fingers of one hand the number of times someone or something had caught her so unawares. She knew the watch had made him uneasy—had stirred up ghosts—but had he sensed something otherworldly about it? Or was he merely superstitious?

"Cursed?" she repeated and laughed. "I wouldn't have pegged you as the superstitious type."

"I'm not. Not normally, anyway. I do think, sometimes, that people can . . . I don't know . . . endow places or objects with their energy—positive or negative. It would explain some things I've experienced. That watch just seemed to have . . ." He hesitated and looked upward as if seeking heavenly advice. "I guess I'd call it 'presence' or 'baggage' maybe."

It was eerie how close he'd come to speaking the reality of the watch. He'd have no way of knowing that its original owner had endowed it with more than mere energy—that there was a malevolent spirit tethered to that watch who would never gain release from it until it was destroyed. It had, in effect, become a prison . . . and a lure.

"It certainly has that. How do I feel about selling it to someone?" She studied him for a moment, making the mistake of looking into his dark eyes, and opted for honesty. Or at least as much honesty as she could safely allow. "It made me uneasy. That watch has always made me uneasy. I'm pretty sure it had the same effect on you."

"I can't deny it. It disturbed me."

"Why?"

He didn't answer right away, instead taking a long sip of his latte.

"The story seemed to have special significance for you," she prodded.

"It did. My father . . . had a violent temper. He made my mother's life—and mine—a living Hell. Things didn't turn out as well for us as they did for the family you told me about. My father never conquered his temper. Eventually, they divorced."

"Did you ever reconcile with your dad?"

Dominic shook his head, dislodging a dark curl that fell over one brow. "No. He . . . he died. Mom remarried when I was fourteen. Wonderful guy. Polar opposite of my dad." He took another thoughtful sip of his latte, then added, "If I thought Dad's problem was as simple as a cursed object, I would have found it and smashed it to pieces. Hell, I would've burned it and buried the ashes in a salted grave."

Caught off guard again, Lucinda said, "None of that works, you know."

He laughed, but his look was questioning. "What?"

"I mean, according to the books of folklore I've read."

"Really? You mean Sister Maria Theresa had it all wrong? She was sure burning and salt would do the trick. At least that was what she prescribed for the comic books I read when I was in her seventh-grade class."

"You're Catholic?"

"Orthodox, actually. I attend a little church in the East Village."

Lucinda decided to let the subject of his faith lie. She picked a story out of the hundreds that went with the objects in the shop and was on the verge of sharing it with him, when he came up with another question—one that had nothing to do with the pawnshop's artifacts.

"So, Rey . . . he works at the pawnshop?"

Lucinda felt a frisson of warning. He was probing to find out if she were attached to Rey. It was an opportunity she knew she should take. She didn't.

"Yes. My father hired him some years back to help me out. We have several associates. Buyers, salespeople, accountants."

"Does your father come in often?"

She understood the intent of the question; his relationship with his own father having been so fraught, of course he'd be interested in hers. She thought of Lucifer and Dominic in the same room; a shiver coursed down her spine. A glance into Nick's eyes made it clear he hadn't missed the reaction.

She laughed. "Not if he can help it. Lucinda's Pawnshop isn't his only venture. He's quite the jet-setting adventurer, my dad. Loves to rub elbows with the makers and shakers. We don't see him all that often down at the shop. It bores him, I'm afraid."

"It doesn't bore you?"

There. She had successfully steered him away from the subject of Lucifer. "Not at all. I love it. I can have adventures if I want—finding items for the store. I can have solitude if I please, and time in which to study and appreciate the things I purchase. I can spend time with interesting people—and the people who come into Lucinda's Pawnshop are *always* interesting."

"But you don't get to keep any of it," Nick said. "Don't you ever get attached to things that you'll just have to give up?"

That simple, casual question did more than startle her. It stunned her all the way to the depths of her soul. She felt weak mortal tears leap to her eyes. Her entire existence had been about giving up things—and people. Beginning with her mother. She tried to pull the tears back—tried to school her face.

"I'm sorry," he said, putting a hand over hers on the table. "Did I say something . . . ?"

"No. It's all right. I just . . . yes. The answer to your question is 'yes.' I have occasionally had to . . . to give up things I'd grown attached to."

She saw the dawn of realization in his face. He squeezed her hand.

"Lucinda, I'm so sorry. You told me your mom died. I should have chosen my words more carefully."

The gentleness in his voice and his eyes set off every warning bell in Lucinda's psyche. The busy bistro suddenly seemed overwhelmingly close and loud.

How to get out of this moment? How to get beyond it? She withdrew her hand and made a dismissive gesture. "Don't be silly. You can't be expected to edit everything you say to make sure nothing reminds me of Mom. I . . . I *want* to remember her. She was unique."

He cleared his throat, straightened, and took another sip of his latte. "That seems like a healthy attitude to have."

"I like to think so."

"You like finding and buying articles for the store, you said. D'you have any favorites?"

The noise and bustle in the bistro faded into the background as she told him about the ibn Rušd–annotated Qur'án, allowing her very genuine joy at having found it to sweep her into an animated—if highly edited—version of the story. She explained how she'd tracked it from the Naworth library to a bookstore in New York and had it restored. She enthused about the significance of having notations from a luminary like ibn Rušd in the text.

It was not lost on her how her story made her companion smile or how his eyes sparkled with interest and pleasure and how his gaze never left her face.

"Lucinda, the mighty hunter of books and antiquities," he proclaimed her when she'd finished. "But an annotated Qur'án? I imagine you'll have that around for a while. I mean, where would you find a buyer for something like that?"

Lucinda smiled. "Oh, I think I know just the place."

"That tells me you're good at your job."

"I hope so. Though, sometimes, I'm not sure what my job is."

They chatted for some time after that—Nick really did have things he wanted to ask for his article—but Lucinda could feel his attraction to her as something alive and magnetic. She waited uneasily for him to ask her out. He didn't, though, and she wondered why. She was bemused . . . and she was relieved. If he had asked, she would only have had to say no. Dominic Amado, whatever her reaction to him or his to her, was just one more thing she would ultimately have to give up.

He walked her back up to the store a little past closing time and said his good-byes on the threshold. She had her hand on the doorknob when he spoke from behind her.

"This is going to sound impossibly weird, but . . . do you believe in God?"

She turned and looked back at him where he stood in the middle of the sidewalk. Nick's face tried to tell her that it was a casual question. The tension radiating from him told her it wasn't at all casual, and a passerby thought it sounded weird enough to shoot the two of them an eye-rolling glance.

"Yes," she said. "I believe."

He nodded, smiled fleetingly, and strode away toward Lexington.

"'The devils also believe, and tremble,'" Lucinda quoted softly from an ancient epistle. She watched Dominic until he turned the corner onto Lex, then let herself into the shop.

She pondered the connections between Dominic Amado, Brittany Anders, DC&P, Brant Redmon, and Lucifer's Middle Eastern plans. The law firm was clearly the hub of that particular set of devilish dominoes. It had its fingers in a lot of pies. Or perhaps irons in the fire was a more apt metaphor. Lucinda wondered what it would take to break that connection. She knew that without a suitable weapon—without material evidence—Brittany Anders' crusade was doomed to futility. The weapon existed. The problem was getting it into the crusader's hands.

CHAPTER NINE

Peter of Holyhaven murmured prayers under his breath as he made his way home from Sleepy Hollow along Riverside Drive. In the frigid air, the pea gravel and grass alike seemed to crackle under the soles of his boots. He trod the verge of the road, carefully avoiding patches of shadow painted vividly by the full moon. Demons and ghosts inhabited shadows, his father said. His father understood these things. As Chief Elder of Holyhaven, Brother Samuel had to understand them. Peter wondered if understanding put an end to fear and if, when he grew up and joined his father in leading the Nihilim, he would no longer be afraid of the shadows.

At fourteen, they terrified him.

A crow let loose a raucous cry as the boy leapt over the elongated shadow of a dead tree. He landed awkwardly and nearly pitched, headfirst, into a pile of leaves on the berm beside the road. He caught himself and rushed on, thrusting his hands into his jacket pockets. Peter hated crows; they were harbingers of evil. Demon birds. He kept one eye on the crow as he hurried up the road, his breath coming out in long streamers.

Why had he stayed so late at the bookstore? There had been almost no one there to witness to today, but he'd had a feeling all day that something important was going to happen, so he had stayed until closing time, waiting for the appearance of a lost soul. No one had come anywhere near the religion section all afternoon.

The crow had spooked him because it seemed to be following him—flitting from branch to branch in his back trail. He put his head down and walked as fast as he could without running. He almost didn't see the girl until he was practically on top of her.

She staggered out of the shoreward woods, scattering leaves every which way and splashing through a rivulet of icy water that ran along the Hudson side of the road. She was sobbing, her face wet with tears, her long hair streaming in the wind. When she saw Peter she held out her hands and cried out, "Stop them! You've got to stop them!"

Peter halted, glancing around to see if anyone else was in sight. There was no one—no cars, no people. It occurred to him that perhaps *this* was the lost soul he'd been meant to meet and save today.

"What is it?" he asked. "What's wrong?" He'd started to add "little girl," then realized, as she crossed the road to his side, that she wasn't as young as he'd first thought. She was close to his age, in fact. She was pretty, too. *Really* pretty—with huge, light brown eyes and hair the color of powdered ginger. He could make out the color even by the moonlight that poured over her like gleaming milk.

"It's awful!" the girl gasped, grasping his arms and clinging to him. "There are these girls in Peabody Field—three of them, I think—over by the old abandoned boathouse. That one, right over there." She pointed over her shoulder toward the Hudson.

"What's happened to them?"

The girl frowned. "No, it's not that—it's what they're *doing*! Awful things! *Horrible* things! They're witching, I think. Casting spells and—and God knows what else! They've got a fire going and I think maybe they're making sacrifices, and—" She dissolved into tears.

Peter scowled in the direction of Peabody Field. He couldn't see the field or the boathouse from where they stood, but he could make out a flicker of light through the skeleton trees.

He covered the sobbing girl's hands with his own. "Do you live around here?"

She nodded, her ginger hair floating silkily in the chill breeze, whispering over the backs of Peter's hands and sending little shivers up his arms and down his spine.

"Yes. Just over there." She nodded over his shoulder toward the landward side of the road.

"Fine. Are you afraid to go on by yourself? Do you need me to take you?"

She seemed indecisive about that, glancing back toward the field. Peter hoped she'd say no so he could get on about checking out the alleged witches . . . and he hoped she'd say yes so he could be with her for just a bit longer. She was that pretty, and her hands were warm beneath his.

She raised her eyes to his face and he felt something he swore he'd never felt before. Somewhere deep in his psyche a door opened to visceral emotions he'd never suspected he contained. It made him feel hot and cold and powerful and weak in the knees all at once. There was a strange quivering in his groin that made him want to kiss the unknown girl's sweet rosy lips, to touch her silken hair, to hold her against him.

I don't even know her name.

Was this what Saint Paul meant when he spoke of burning? He looked deep into those moonlit eyes and wanted her to say she needed to have him escort her home.

"Will there be someone home when you get there?" he asked. *Say 'no,'* he prayed her. *Please say you'll be alone.*

She glanced down, still frowning, and nodded. "My mom and dad are home. I'll be fine. You—you need to go see . . ."

Peter shook himself. Of course he needed to go see. He let go of the girl's hands and she let go of his arms. He felt oddly bereft. Empty. The quivering he'd felt in his groin and his heart eased.

"I should go home," she said, and Peter could hear the regret in her voice. "Be brave."

He swallowed. "I will."

She nodded and moved past him, her feet cat-silent on the gravel of the shoulder. Peter set his jaw and his resolve. He'd read about witches, heard sermons about witches, but he'd never in his life met one face to face.

First time for everything.

He turned to look back at the girl. She was gone. Peter frowned. Something moved low in the shadowing grasses at the edge of the landward wood, drawing his gaze. It was a cat. He couldn't make out the exact color in the moonlight, but it had a pale, mottled coat. Even as his eyes caught it, it disappeared into the brush.

God. Crows and cats and strange, frightened girls and *witches*. He'd sensed today would be special, but he'd had no idea. Gathering all of his courage into a tight little ball, Peter of Holyhaven strode across Riverside Drive and into the woods on the other side. He wended his way through the near-naked trees, working closer and closer to the field. His lips moved in prayer, but now the prayer was for divine assistance and wisdom.

"Help me, Lord. Help me to know what to do."

It occurred to him, as he approached the verge of the wood and heard the unfiltered sounds of the river and saw the ever-brightening flames of the fire on its shore, that perhaps the girl had been confused, or mistaken, or was hoaxing him. His elders in the Nihilim community had taught about witches and demons and such, but he'd never actually seen one—unless you counted crows and cats.

By the time he broke from the wood, Peter was half expecting to find a bunch of kids sitting around a bonfire toasting marshmallows. He stepped past the last tree and dropped down behind a mulberry bush. There were no marshmallows being toasted on Peabody Field. In fact, there was no one at the fire at all. He swept his gaze up river toward the abandoned boathouse. It hunched over the waterline like a huge, thirsty beast, but there was no light in its windows.

Peter extended his gaze past the fire and found them—three girls dressed in flowing white robes or coats. He moved to the other side of the bush to get a better look at them. They were older girls—high school age at least. They were facing the river more or less, so he couldn't see their faces clearly, but he thought he'd seen the one with the weird spiky blue hair in town at the bookstore. In the occult section.

The two girls on each end had raised both hands and were waving them back and forth like people did in Worship sometimes. The one in the middle had a book cradled in the crook of one arm and was making a series of graceful but emphatic gestures toward the Hudson River. Peter held his breath. There was light dancing around them like the Saint Elmo's fire he'd read about that haloed the masts of tall ships, or like the northern lights. He told himself it was just the glow from the fire, but the color was wrong. The firelight was a warm, pale gold. The girls' forms were wreathed in a pale, translucent blue with flashes of green.

Can't be real.

Peter rubbed his eyes and looked again. The light was still there.

If he listened closely, he could hear them intoning. That's what they called it during Worship, anyway. In Worship sometimes people said actual words, sometimes they just made sounds. If what these girls were intoning were words, they were in a language Peter didn't know.

The wind shifted, coming to him off the river. He caught the scent of wet earth and vegetation. Now he could hear the words distinctly, though only one or two of them made any sort of sense. The girls chanted the same phrases over and over, in ragged unison, their voices spiraling into the moonlit sky.

Gif ye lest, Lord, creantor me poeir ofer waeter.
Gif ye lest, Weard, creantor me maistry ofer they riparius.
Thy noma ist caellian; Thy noma ist caellian.
Thy noma beon He That Pars they Waeter.

What were they doing? Surely they couldn't really *do* anything. They were girls, first of all, and power was given only to men. They were just saying these funny old words again and again as if they were cheerleaders at some weird football game.

Peter's concept of power got turned on its head as, beyond the weaving, white forms of the girls, the Hudson began to churn and eddy. Whitecaps appeared to mar its smooth surface, the moon throwing them into stark relief against the surrounding darkness. He began to feel it then—a strange pulsing in the air, like a silent heartbeat—and he began to see it, too, as moonlit threads spun from the fingertips of the girl who held the book. She had stopped chanting now, while the others kept on. Instead of words, she was uttering a series of high, warbling notes as if in some sort of trance or seizure.

Peter had seen such displays at Worship, but not like this. This was no sacred calling-down of grace and mercy from the Lord of All, no speaking in the divine tongue. This was blasphemy. This was sacrilege. This was *evil*.

Peter stood and backed silently toward the wood. He had not quite reached the trees when the Hudson River pulled back on itself and reared up like a fractious gray pony, its crest shimmering and sparkling in the moonlight like a wind-tossed mane. Above the thundering of his own heart, he heard the witches' wild, riotous laughter.

Fear pounding in his head, Peter turned and bolted for Holyhaven.

✝

Janine stared at the great crest of river water with horror and excitement warring in her breast. She had done it. She—Janine Sorentino, teenaged nobody—had made the Hudson River dance at her command. Morgan le Fay's words had come to life again in her mouth and electricity had flowed from her fingertips and she had been granted power over the water of a major American river. More than that, it seemed that the spirit of Morgan le Fay had come to life in her as well. The wild thought struck her that maybe she *was* Morgan le Fay, reincarnated. Or at least a descendant of that potent sorceress, whose book she cradled in her arms.

"Guide me, Mistress," she murmured. "Let me feel your power."

She swept her hand from left to right, watching streamers of light leap from her fingers to send the river up into a mighty plume of water, steam, and ice. The droplets caught the light of the moon and glittered like diamonds in the night sky. It reminded her of wind blowing ice and snow off the top of a glacier.

She'd no more than had the thought when the whole magical display slowed to glacial pace, seeming to freeze in the act of cresting. She became aware that the girls on either side of her had stopped chanting and were making other sounds. Stevie was laughing crazily and swearing in turns.

"Sonuvabitch! I don't freakin' *believe* this! I mean, *damn!* Freakin' *awesome!*"

Mags was silent, her eyes fixed on the river, her mouth half open, her breath coming out in little puffs of steam.

Janine took a deep breath of damp, frigid night air and lowered her hand. The water didn't cascade immediately into its bed, but flowed back down at the speed Janine had set for it, as if the spell had some sort of residual effect. She watched it for a moment, then turned to Stevie.

"Hold the book."

The other girl stopped laughing, wiped tears from her eyes, and said, "What?"

"I said hold the book. I want to try something."

Stevie took the BOS, shaking her head. "Janni-girl, after that, you can try anything you damn well please. You are the *bomb*. What are you going to do?"

"I want to see what happens if I free up both hands. If . . . if maybe I can channel more power that way."

"*More* power?" asked Mags incredulously. "Janine, I'm not sure you *should* do more. Haven't you already done enough?"

Janine turned to stare at the other girl. If someone had told her that Mags Stuyvesant—blue-haired, hard-assed Goth-ghoul of Sleepy Hollow High School—would be the one to get cold feet, she would've called them a liar.

"Scared, Margaret?" Stevie asked. "Wanna go home and curl up with your teddy bear?"

"Of course I'm scared, you moron. She just freakin' stopped the freakin' *river*! That's not supposed to happen, damn it!"

Stevie laughed again; Janine thought there was an edge of hysteria to it. "What's the matter, Mags? Didn't you believe Janine was the real deal?"

"Like you *did*? Admit it, Stevie. You thought this was all a crock, didn't you?"

Janine gaped at Stevie, her breath stopping in her throat. Had this all been a colossal taunt? "Is that was this was all about?" she asked. "You wanting for me to—what—make an ass of myself out here? Were there, like, cameras and-and a bunch of people about to jump out of the woods to laugh at me if I couldn't pull something off?"

Stevie stared back at her, clutching the Book of Shadows to her chest as if it were trying to escape. "Are you crazy? Do you think I would have spent over ten grand on this little recipe book of yours if I'd thought you weren't the real thing? I figured it was an investment. Besides, we already knew you had something going on after the other night at the millpond. So, no, there's no cameras or people lurking in the woods waiting to jump out and say 'boo'! There's just us."

She reached out a hand and grasped Janine's shoulder, giving her a mild shake. "Snap out of it, Janni! You're a real witch! You made the river—" She glanced toward where the Hudson was settling back into its banks and giggled. "Holy shit, Janine! You're, like, a *goddess* or something."

Janine grinned fiercely. Or something. "Yeah, I'm something, all right. I'm Morgan freakin' le Fay!"

She turned back to the water, which had calmed and commenced to flow normally again. The water spell was still bright and blazing in her mind. Having read the way le Fay's spell-casting worked, she understood how the form of the spell could be altered by choosing different words during the invocation of the power through whom the spell was cast. She understood, too, without knowing how she understood, that the language in which the spell was cast wasn't as important as the meaning of the words.

She was eager to experiment now—eager to make the BOS her own. She was more than half-convinced that she was—if not Morgan le Fay, herself—a spiritual descendant with both the capacity and the authority to make changes to existing spells and to create new ones. For now, she'd start with the Hudson River.

She turned toward the water, raising her hands so that the sleeves of the thick robe she was wearing slid up her arms. Her flesh tingled with the cold, though she could feel the heat of the fire at her back. It seemed to her that she had never been so alive. So *present*. She had certainly never been this powerful.

She began the chant again, this time in modern English. After a moment of hesitation, Stevie fell into rhythm with her.

If you wish, Lord, grant me power over water.
If you wish, Master, grant me mastery over the river.
Your name is called; Your name is called.
Your name is He That Molds the Water.

She'd felt Stevie's sideways glance at the change she'd made in the invocation, but she finished the chant in perfect rhythm with Janine. Mags was still silent. Janine felt a stab of irritation. Damn Mags, anyway. What if she messed up the spell? Well, she just couldn't be allowed to.

Janine put all of herself into the spell work, feeling the electricity gather in her heart and head and hands. She thrust the energy out and toward the water, saw it leap from her fingertips in a sizzling, rainbow arc, watched it dive into the Hudson's current and light it up as if fireworks were exploding beneath the surface. Up out of the dark flow rose a rippling tower of water. Black as the night sky, threaded through with ribbons of magical light and capped with moon-washed foam, it blotted out the lights on the far shore, extinguished the stars near the horizon and, finally, obscured the moon itself. It danced and wove and spiraled higher, higher, while Stevie laughed and Mags cowered, and Janine rode a wave of exultation.

She began to mold the water into fantastical shapes. She remembered reading about water horses—kelpies—when she was in grade school. They were magical, dangerous creatures that lived in rivers and lakes, that stole children and laid curses on villages. She made her tower into a huge water horse, all the while imagining what other elements she might master—fire, perhaps, or air, or metal or . . . just anything! She was more than a witch—she was an elemental god.

She felt a tug on her consciousness, followed by a hand encircling her arm, fingers digging in. She broke concentration and turned her head. Stevie was practically in her face, her eyes huge. She shook Janine's arm.

"We've got company," she said tersely.

"What?"

Stevie jerked her chin toward the woods. A handful of men stood there in the moonlight. They carried axes, guns, flashlights, and lanterns. Even as she watched, Janine saw the handful become a dozen, then more. A couple of them carried torches—*actual torches*. A hysterical giggle tried to force its way through her suddenly dry throat. Where were the pitchforks? It wouldn't be a real witch hunt without pitchforks.

The men were not yet close enough to be lit by the fire; she couldn't see the expressions on their faces, but she could guess. They were staring up at her giant water horse with evident disbelief, even as it began to sink back into the river stream. Time seemed to slow to a crawl, the tension in the air something that Janine could feel crawling on her skin.

Then a single voice roared above the thrashing of the river: "Thou shalt not allow a witch to live!"

There was a moment of stunned, breathless silence, then the men were pouring across the grass and sand of Peabody Field toward the fire, mouths open in wordless rage, weapons ready and torches lifted above their heads.

Janine pushed Stevie toward the old boathouse. "Take the book and run! I got this!"

Stevie ran.

Janine whirled back toward the river, vaguely registering that Mags had backed into the glare of the fire and was trying to pull her robe off over her head. Janine ignored her. She reached out both hands to the Hudson, the spell already tumbling from her lips. She'd show them, whoever the hell they were.

She took hold of the water, this time feeling the connection running through the bright strands of magic that leapt from her hands as something alive. She remade the water horse, huge, towering, this time with gleaming eyes. She flung it at the first wave of men, twisting it until it looked less like a horse and more like a horrific, gleaming tornado with a wide, open vortex.

Then, Janine turned to the fire.

⚜

Peter wanted, more than anything, to fight next to his father against the evil on the beach, but he had been ordered to stay back and he was honor-bound to obey.

Instead, he sought the man who had started the rush on the witches with his commanding battle cry. To Peter's surprise, he was standing, tall, erect, and unmoving, at the verge of the wood, watching the others attack the shore.

Peter started to call out to him, then realized he didn't know him—and he knew every man, woman, and child in Holyhaven. The tall man was smiling, and his beautiful face seemed to glow with golden light, though he was not anywhere near the witches' fire. Peter was awestruck—surely, this was an angel of the Lord.

Remembering the story of Jacob mistaking the angel Gabriel for an enemy and struggling against him in the night, Peter was determined not to be so stupid as Jacob. He turned and took a step toward the magnificent gleaming man.

"Lord!" he said. "Are you . . . the angel Gabriel?"

The man turned his head. His eyes seemed to blaze like hot golden orbs. "That is not my name," he said, and his voice sounded deep and sweet and made Peter shiver just as he had shivered at the touch of the nameless girl. "I would give you a *new* name. You are Peter the Summoner. The man who first warned the world of evil."

Then he was gone, seeming to melt into the forest along Riverside Drive.

A cry of terror made Peter whirl toward the beach. What he saw froze his heart in his breast. His father and the other men faced the most horrifying monster Peter could have imagined—a monster against which their human weapons would be useless. It was like a great, towering waterspout with gleaming eyes and flesh made of river water. It tilted its horribly malformed head toward the men on the beach, its maw open and gaping and black as the mouth of Hell. In moments, it would devour them.

Peter forgot his father's instructions and raced, shouting, for the beach armed only with prayer.

The men caught beneath the monstrous vortex tried to retreat, but the witch made the flames of her fire race across the dry grasses to block their path. Peter changed course, circling around the fire on the side toward the boathouse. He thought he saw a flutter of white in the shadows of the derelict building, but he ignored it; he had an opportunity to change the balance of power and was determined to take it.

The blue-haired girl was struggling near the fire to pull off her robe. He came up behind her and wrapped his arms around her, shouting at the top of his lungs.

"Stop! In the name of the Lord, stop, damned witch! Stop, or your sister goes into the fire!"

He wouldn't really do such a thing, of course—not even to a witch—but she couldn't know that. He pretended he *would* do it, though, dragging his captive closer to the flames.

The dark-haired witch took her evil attentions from her water creature and focused her wild eyes on him. While the grass still blazed, the river monster rippled, then stilled, then seemed to slide back toward the Hudson. The girl in his arms struggled, sobbed, and swore, her voice muffled by the fabric covering her head.

"Let her go!" the DarkWitch cried. She clenched her fists and stepped toward him. Her eyes were losing their wildness and he could see fear in them.

Good. Peter wanted her to be afraid. And distracted. He wanted the men of Holyhaven to have a chance to subdue her.

His father and Elder Morris had almost reached them when the girl he held caught his shin with a flailing foot, and he lost his grip on her. His father cried out and dashed forward, an axe held loosely in one hand, while he reached toward his son with the other.

Things happened so fast after that, it was hard for Peter to track, but as he grappled with the girl, she tore her robe off at last. A trailing sleeve dragged through the fire and burst into flame. The girl shrieked and hurled the burning rag into the face of the man closest to her—Peter's father. The leader of Holyhaven fell back with a roar of terror and deflected the flaming robe with his axe.

Peter felt the warm spatter of blood on his face, saw it soaking into his jacket. The girl in his arms was suddenly limp, her head flopping to one side at an unnatural angle. He let go of her, letting her fall to the sand. Her throat was a mass of red, the last futile beats of her heart pumping her blood out through the wound that had nearly severed her neck.

Peter backed away from her body, away from the pale, accusing eyes. He couldn't look at his father. He was afraid of what he might see. Instead, he glanced up at the Dark Witch. She was frozen, her gaze on the horrid red tide creeping up into her friend's shockingly blue hair. Peter heard a deep sob break from her lips only seconds before the sounds of sirens reached his ears.

It was only his stunned imagination, of course, but Peter of Holyhaven thought he heard sweet, deep, shivery laughter.

CHAPTER TEN

Today was the day Rowdy shipped out for Kuwait. Mona wished, with all her heart, that he wasn't going—wasn't going to be leaving her alone in New York with Dan. It was traitorous to feel that way about being with her own husband, and she wouldn't—in a million years—let on to her son that she felt that way. Rowdy had a commitment to his unit, to his country, she told herself. It would be selfish of her to use his love for her to make him break faith with either.

"Look, Mom," he told her as they said good-bye at the bus station, "when I'm stateside, I'll be assigned to Camp Lejeune in North Carolina. You could move there. You'd like the Jacksonville area. And Emerald Isle is really beautiful. It's right by the ocean. I know how much you love the ocean."

"I don't know that Dan would—"

Rowdy's face darkened. "I'm not talking about Dan moving, Mom. Just you. I think you need to get away from him."

"I can't do that, honey. I-I *love* Dan. Sure, he's having a hard time, but he—"

"Mom, he's not just having a hard time—he *is* a hard time. He's his own worst enemy."

"He's got a temper . . ."

He put a hand on her shoulder and gave her a gentle shake. "Momma, it's more than that. He drinks. And he's a weepy, mean drunk. I've seen that look on guys before, Momma. He was gonna hit you the other night."

Mona shook her head. "No."

"*Yes!* I'm not kidding about this. I want to know you're safe if I'm not around to protect you."

"Sweetheart, if Dan is his own worst enemy, then he needs someone to be his best friend. That someone is me. I'm his wife."

"Momma!"

Mona covered his hand with her own. "Your bus is here, honey, and you've gotta go. Look, I promise if anything bad happens, I'll do what you say—I'll go to Camp Lejeune. I'll wait for you to come home. I'll be fine."

He threw his arms around her and squeezed her tightly and kissed her fore-head, while she remembered when he'd had to stand on Dan's easy chair to do that. When he let her go, there were tears in both their eyes.

"I just don't want to let you down, Momma," he told her. "Dan's done it over and over again, and I don't want to be like Dan."

She smiled. "You could never let me down, Rowdy Collins. Not ever."

He was gone then, off to North Carolina and thence to the Middle East. Mona watched the bus out of sight, and it seemed to her that her courage drained away with every bit of distance between her and her son. She went home, wondering when or if Dan would come back, and which Dan he would be if and when he did.

The thought was unsettling, not in the least because she was so ambivalent about it. What sort of mood would he be in? From past experience she knew it was a crapshoot. He might be sulky and silent, sober and penitent, or angry. He might growl and grumble until he got over it, beg her forgiveness, or snap and snarl at her until she placated him.

That was the unsettling thing, of course; Mona never knew which Dan Collins she was going to get. Usually, it was the sulky, silent one. She could deal with that, she decided, and determined that when he got home, Dan would have nothing to complain about. The apartment would be shiny clean and the fridge stocked with his favorite food. His laundry would be done, his favorite magazine set out, the place would smell like his favorite cookies.

Mona had learned through experience how to work around Dan's moods. Sometimes she failed and he wouldn't talk to her for days, or he'd yell and go away again . . . which, right now, with her being so mad at him for treating Rowdy the way he had, wouldn't be a bad thing.

As it happened, he called before he came home. It was about 7:00 P.M. and Mona had a chicken in the oven with potatoes and broccoli when her cell phone buzzed. The sight of Dan's name and face in the incoming call window made her heart do backflips. Answering, she reflected wryly that her heart had once leapt like that because she so much wanted to hear his voice, not because she was afraid of what he might say.

"The kid gone?" were his first words.

She tried to read his voice. It was low, curt, surly.

"Yes, Dan. Rowdy's on his way to North Carolina. I've got dinner in. One of your favorites: roast chicken."

He was silent for a long moment, just breathing into the phone. "I'll see you," he said, and hung up.

He was home only minutes later, smelling like a brewery and looking the worse for wear. His clothes were dirty and stained, his hair greasy, his eyes red. Mona was torn between disgust and pity. She let pity win.

"Oh, sweetie, you look awful. Why don't you go shower and change and I'll get dinner on the table."

He didn't move. He just stood in the middle of the living room and glared at her, clenching and unclenching his fists. Mona remembered what Rowdy had said about seeing that look on other guys. Guys who got violent.

She smiled as winsomely as she knew how. "You'll feel a lot better once you're yourself again."

"Yeah? That what you want, Mona—for me to be myself?"

"I love you," she said simply.

He seemed to battle with himself a moment, then turned and stalked back to their bedroom. She heard the shower running shortly after, and breathed a sigh of relief. One hurdle jumped.

When Dan came out of the bedroom, he really did look more like his old self. He cleaned up well, and Mona thought he looked handsome, notwithstanding the dark look on his face. He was mostly silent during dinner, sometimes answering her questions and comments with grunts or growls, but Mona was heartened when she realized he had the watch she'd gotten him in the breast pocket of his shirt. That was a good sign.

They made love that night for the first time in a while and, though Dan was a little rough, the fact that he wanted her at all after the big fight they'd had made her feel better about the whole situation.

They could get through this. She was sure of it.

The Souq al-Mubarakiya was one of the oldest continually operated market-places in Kuwait City. It was a bright warren of cobbled pedestrian ways bordered with kiosks, food stalls, and storefronts—some of which had been operated by the same families for generations. Lucinda chose it because it was a place frequented by merchants and government functionaries. Specifically, one Ibrahim Darzi, a mid-level administrator whose family and tribe had been on the short end of the dip-stick with the discovery of oil in the 1960s.

Darzi had striven, all his adult life, to become one of the movers and shakers whose opinions influenced policy both in Kuwait and abroad. It was not his lot to do such a thing publicly—his clan affiliations did not lend themselves to either open influence or a rapid rise to power—so he remained behind the scenes and largely off the radar of Westerners as one member of a minority party in Kuwait's parliamentary assembly.

It was to Ibrahim Darzi that Brant Redmon's resources had flowed and, while Lucinda did not have all of the particulars (there were only so many questions she could ask without tipping her hand), she knew that Darzi—a member of the thirty-five or so percent of Kuwaiti Muslims who were Shi'a—had long been frustrated by Western policies where they encountered the incomprehensible (to them) divide between the Sunni and Shi'a branches of Islam.

That such resources had been given Darzi, considering his views on the way the Sunni majority wielded power in the region, was a recipe for disaster. In other words, it was something that would serve Lucifer's purpose and push humanity one step closer to world conflagration.

So, on this balmy-cool autumn eve, as the souq's lights came up and tourists and locals thronged the avenues, a new storefront appeared on Oman Street between a frozen yogurt shop and a florist. Gazing out the front window of the shop, which looked toward the heart of the city, Lucinda had a commanding view of a portion of the stunning, modern skyline. She could just see the Rashed Ibrahim Ismael Mosque and the Mubarak al-Kabir Tower, and appreciated the melding of past and present they represented.

"This is an interesting choice of venues," said her father's voice from behind her.

She had felt him, of course, but only moments before he stepped through from the Between. He could not surprise her. Or perhaps he simply didn't try. If he ever did, it would mean he no longer trusted her. The thought raised a shiver more of spirit than body.

"Interesting?" she repeated. "How so?"

He moved toward her, spreading his hands in a questioning gesture. "Darling daughter, I know you. You do nothing without some scheming behind it." He smiled. "They say the apple doesn't fall far from the tree."

She didn't react to his stress of the word "apple" and returned the smile. "Thank you, Father. I appreciate the compliment."

"Well, what intrigue have you got planned?"

She shrugged, a gesture that rippled down the length of the *jellaba* she wore as part of her disguise. "I knew this to be an area of intense interest for you, so I thought perhaps I might . . . stir the pot. Ibrahim Darzi frequents this avenue. Since he is a Shi'a Muslim, I thought he might be interested in a very special Qur'án. One annotated by ibn Rušd."

Lucifer looked at her inquiringly. "Ibn Rušd was a Sunni."

"Exactly. I theorized that the annotations in his holy book from a member of a rival sect might—how shall I put it—inflame Darzi's sectarian sensibilities. That could only help our cause."

Her father came to stand before her, took her head between his hands, and kissed her forehead. She only imagined that his lips burned.

"You are everything I could ask for in a daughter, Lucinda . . . or, given your current form, should I say you're everything I could ask for in a son?"

Her current form was that of a bearded, young Kuwaiti man wearing the traditional *taqiyah* and *jellaba*—cap and robe. She pressed her hands together and bowed slightly. "Again, thank you."

Lucifer's eyes brightened. "I sense that your quarry is approaching. I leave you to your business. When you return to New York, I will have a special surprise for you." He took several steps backward and vanished as if he had stepped through a porous membrane into another room—which was essentially what he had done.

Lucinda had no time to wonder what Lucifer's "special surprise" was. He'd no more than disappeared than the door of the shop opened, admitting a tall, handsome man in a sleek, gray business suit and a turquoise *taqiyah* that precisely matched his tie.

Lucinda bowed deferentially and greeted Ibrahim Darzi. "As-salamu alaykum, sir. Welcome to our humble shop. How may I serve you?"

"And unto you, peace. Now, please, explain to me how I have never seen your shop before."

"We are new here as of this week. As you see, we do not even have proper signage." She gestured toward the front window, through which could be seen a sign that merely said AL-KITAB—BOOKS in Arabic script.

Darzi glanced around the room. "You have religious texts, I see."

"Yes, sir. Some of our volumes are quite rare. We have, for example, a fine illuminated volume of Rumi, also a marvelous twelfth-century Qur'án annotated by ibn Rušd—"

Darzi raised his eyebrows and his hand. "Annotated by ibn Rušd, you say? Extraordinary. Can you show me this book?"

Lucinda moved to gesture at a glass-covered stand set apart from the main display case in a pool of light. The book within was opened to a page that Lucinda had chosen with care.

"Here, sir."

Darzi's eyes focused on the book and did not leave it as he crossed the room to Lucinda's side. He peered down at the graceful text of one of the verses that ibn Rušd had annotated. It was the *surah* entitled *Al-Mâ'ûn*—Small Kindnesses.

"'Do you see the one who belies religion?'" he read softly. "Such is the one who harshly repulses the orphan, and encourages not the feeding of the indigent. So, woe to the worshippers who neglect their prayers, those who wish to be seen of men, but refuse to do small kindnesses.'"

Darzi tilted his head to one side that he might read the philosopher's annotation, which he also read aloud. "'So, concisely, is stated the essence of Islam.'" He was silent and still for a moment, as if digesting this, then raised his eyes to Lucinda's face. "Where did you find this?"

"In my travels," she told him. "I visited a bookstore in New York City, of all places. And there it was. It seemed somehow inappropriate that it should be in such a place or that someone should purchase it who was not a believer."

"May I . . . ?" Darzi indicated that he wished to hold the book. "I will be most careful."

Lucinda nodded, then opened the case and lifted the book out to set it in Ibrahim Darzi's hands. Darzi held it as one might hold a newborn child—with love, reverence, and care. He held it close to his face that he might smell the leather binding, touched a page gently with a fingertip.

"It is beautiful. Precious beyond price."

"Yes. Notwithstanding the commentary is by a Sunni." She said the last word as if it were distasteful.

Darzi did not take his eyes from the pages he was studying. "The Sunni have also produced great minds. Ibn Rušd is, possibly, the greatest of them. I have a copy of his defense of Aristotle. It is brilliant. I had no idea he had annotated the Holy Qur'án."

"Please forgive me if I have offended," Lucinda said.

"No matter," murmured Darzi absently. He had turned to another page and was perusing another verse and another of the great polymath's observations with a frown knitting his brow.

After a moment, he looked up at Lucinda. "How much are you asking?"

Lucinda named a sum that was enough to speak to the book's value, but not so much that a man of Darzi's means would not consider it.

Darzi nodded, his lips pursed, then closed the Qur'án. "Your price is a fair one. I would like to purchase the book. Do you have a means by which I can transport it safely?"

Lucinda bowed, smiling. "I do, sir. We have special cases for such rare volumes—and instructions for their care."

Fifteen minutes later, Lucinda watched Ibrahim Darzi walk away with the Qur'án concealed in an aluminum carrying case. She could not read the man's soul—that power belonged only to God—so she had no way of knowing, at this juncture, where her meddling would lead.

Stirring the pot, indeed, she thought, and wondered if her scheming would bear thistles or figs.

✥

The conversations were brief and somewhat terse, the silences were strained, but Mona was hopeful that once she and Dan got back into a regular routine, things would settle down and slide back to normal. They always had before, more or less. Still, it was a relief to get up the next morning and get ready for work in the quiet apartment while Dan snored away in bed.

Mona was getting a carton of yogurt out of the fridge when she realized the snoring had stopped. She froze for a moment, then went to the kitchen table and stuck the yogurt into her tote bag. She'd made it almost to the door when Dan's voice stopped her.

"Where're you going?"

She pasted a smile to her face and turned to face him. "I'm off to work. I've got three home visits to make this morning before I go to the clinic."

Dan stood in the mouth of the hallway, dressed in his pajama bottoms. He glowered at her. "It's not right for you to work, Mona. You should be at home, taking care of things here."

She stared at him, open-mouthed. "Dan, if I didn't work—" She stopped, realizing that there was no safe way to finish that sentence.

Dan was nodding. "Yeah, that's what you think, isn't it? If you didn't work, we'd starve."

"That wasn't—"

"We'd lose the apartment," he went on relentlessly. "We'd end up in the street—you and your useless husband."

Mona put her hands out entreating him to stop. She hated it when he got down on himself. "Dan, stop it! You're not useless. You've just been unlucky. Things will change. The economy is picking up. People are hiring all the time now—especially temps."

"I am not going to be some sort of damn Kelly Girl!" He moved toward her now, pointing at her. "You don't even think of me as a man anymore, do you? You think I'm a loser, cuz you wear the pants in the family!"

"Wear the—Dan, where are you getting this stuff?"

"What stuff?"

"I've never heard you talk like this. Never."

103

"Well, maybe that's because I've never been honest until now. Here's what I think: I think that a man should work, and a wife—a *proper* wife—should stay home and take care of his house."

Mona shook her head. She was beginning to be annoyed with this sudden return to 1950s gender dynamics, not to mention the uncalled-for belligerence. What the heck did he expect of her?

"I *have* to work, Dan. In fact, I *like* to work. I have to go to work right now, or I'll be late."

She turned back toward the door, heart heavy. Her hand was on the knob when Dan threw himself at her, grabbed a handful of her hair, and yanked her head back. She shrieked in pain and surprise, and swung her tote, dealing her husband a weak blow on one hip. That was enough.

Dan grasped the handle of the tote and flung it across the room. "Damn it, woman! Don't you *dare* turn your back on me while I'm talking to you! I'm your husband! Show me some respect!"

"You're hurting me!" Mona shrilled.

"You haven't *seen* hurt yet, you holier-than-thou bitch!" He shook her head for emphasis.

She screamed louder. Bent backwards and off balance, she flailed, trying to make him let go. She only succeeded in hitting him a couple of times, which made him even madder.

He shook her harder, his voice rising to a roar. "Shut up! Shut up! *Shut! Up!*"

But she couldn't shut up. He was hurting her, terrifying her—and when she wouldn't shut up, he yanked her upright and backhanded her across the face. She tumbled away from him, a handful of her hair pulling out by the roots. She fell heavily against the little table by his favorite chair. The table tipped over, dumping a small reading lamp and Dan's new pocket watch onto the floor.

Mona tried to rise, but she was dizzy, disoriented. Her eyes fixed on the watch—a symbol of her love for the man who was currently spewing hatred at her. It had fallen face down with the engraved *To Daniel, with love* staring back at her. The words—the watch itself—seemed to taunt her. At that moment—the moment before he reached down and pulled her from the floor—Mona could not remember what loving Dan had felt like.

He got her by the collar of her scrubs this time, ripping the fabric as he pulled her upright only to knock her down again ... and again. She tasted blood, the room swam in and out of focus, she hurt everywhere, but mostly inside, in the empty space where her heart had been.

Mona wondered idly how Dan's beating her could sound so much like some-one pounding on wood, or how her thin screams could mimic sirens so perfectly.

Through it all, the watch lay on the carpet beside her, a small, ticking observer of the destruction of her life. The silver casing gleamed so brightly, it seemed to glow. In the moments before its ticking ushered her into darkness, she thought she saw a face in the reflective surface. Her last conscious thought was that somehow Dan was trapped inside the watch.

CHAPTER ELEVEN

Back in Manhattan, Lucinda's first instinct was to seek out her father to find out what his great surprise was. Her father's surprises were never pleasant, but they often illuminated the purpose behind his manipulations. She could only hope that would be the case this time.

Her second instinct was to avoid him and to seek, instead, some moments of respite. Some moments in which to plan—among other things—what she would say if Dominic Amado contacted her again. She regretted leaving that connection open-ended . . . on one level. On another level entirely, she was pleased that she'd left it open. Which was stupid. Her whole attraction to the mortal was stupid.

She returned the pawnshop to Manhattan—something that wasn't a "return" at all, in any real sense. It was always there and always elsewhere. It was simply—to outward appearances—either open or closed. After that, she went to her penthouse flat, intending to meditate on her own folly. Instead, she procrastinated by turning on the big screen TV over her hearth, with the rationale that she should keep up on what was happening in the world.

It was no normal TV, of course—at least, not when she operated it "manually." She could literally bring in any channel from anywhere in the world. Theoretically, if she tried, she could even monitor artifacts from here. That was tempting sometimes. She liked the thought of sitting up here in her penthouse, watching what was happening in the world and never going out in physical form.

There was danger in that, as she knew from experience. She had yielded to the temptation a few times—holing up in her sanctum, looking into televisions, or mirrors or even pools of still water to see what there was to be seen. Isolation was like a drug: the more she experienced it, the more comfortable she became with it, and things slipped past her.

That had happened during the early years of the twentieth century. She had blinked—turned her attention inward—and Lucifer had lit the spark that ignited Adolf Hitler. It had started with a father violently opposed to his son's desire to study art, but the disparaging words from an admired mentor, whispered in the ear of a young, would-be artist, sealed Hitler's fate. He already doubted his abilities and feared the people around him were laughing behind his back. He had reacted to that by convincing himself (with some encouragement from a religious relic) that he had a far greater destiny than to paint pictures. He was destined to mold a people, to shape a nation . . . to save the world.

Lucinda turned on the TV to a local station, contemplating how much damage had been done in the world by people who were convinced they were the only one among billions who could save it. How many of them had been subjected to satanic whispers or possessed objects? For as long as she could remember, Lucifer had been enamored with the idea of permanently attaching his captive souls to articles they had imbued with the raw energy of their vices. It was the difference, he'd said, between a millstone on which one stubbed one's toe and one that hung around one's neck . . . with focused and malign intelligence.

Lucinda curled up on one end of the sofa, noticing that, out in her garden, a light and early snow had begun to fall in tiny, feather-light flakes that danced and played in the rooftop breezes. Her eyes were on the TV, but the picture was not what she saw. What she saw, in her very vivid and accurate memory, was Fifth Avenue in Manhattan at a time long before the trees were twined with tiny sparkling lights and the late evening storefronts and apartment buildings bathed in radiance from energy-saving LEDs.

Nineteen thirty-one. December 13. The man Lucinda had followed from a speaking engagement at the Waldorf Astoria stepped from a taxi onto the sidewalk that bordered Central Park and frowned across the street at the row of upscale Fifth Avenue apartments. He had come to the unwelcome realization that he'd forgotten the address of his friend, Bernard Baruch. He was weary from the exertions of his lecture tour, and angry because he was late. Perhaps this was what caused him to forget momentarily that, in America, cars drive on the right.

Lucinda, just one more Manhattan pigeon perched on a Central Park wall, watched as Winston Churchill stepped to the curb and looked the wrong way.

Even in physical form, Lucinda's reflexes were supernally quick. In a split second, she'd taken to the air, calling every pigeon within twenty yards to flock to her. They mobbed Churchill, fluttering around him, beating their wings against his face. He hesitated in confusion and waved his arms to drive them away.

The moment of hesitation saved his life.

The car that should have hit him head-on only sideswiped him, snagged his coat, and dragged him several yards down Fifth before dumping him in an awkward heap. He went to the hospital with bruises, sprains, and a gash in his forehead, but his injuries were not life-threatening. He did not die as Lucifer had intended him to.

Lucinda brought herself back from reverie and drew her knees to her chest, contemplating current circumstance. Now, as then, she played a game of point-counterpoint with Lucifer, and she couldn't help but hear echoes of the past in the situation in the Middle East. Back then, in the string of manipulations leading up to two world wars, she had withdrawn somewhat from the "battlefield." So, she had realized his designs on young Adolf Hitler too late, but had marked an equivalent but far more malevolent interest in Winston Churchill. Her only option was to emerge from solitude and take an active role in her father's work. Lucifer had been pleased to have her join in his careful preparations for war. Winston Churchill had become her pet "project."

By 1931, when both Churchill and Hitler were middle-aged, she'd seen the lines that connected them tightening and knew they were on a collision course.

Enter Mario Contasino. The poor, out-of-work immigrant had come into the pawnshop to hock a collection of rare books, and had gone away again with a small Saint Christopher medal which he hung on the rearview mirror of his automobile, praying it would bring him blessings. Entwined with the soul of the perpetrator of a murder-suicide, the medal would bring him anything but that. Lucinda, ironically, had the cursed artifact to thank for the fact that she recognized the threat to Churchill's life, and saw the horrific shape of Lucifer's plan for Europe. She had sensed its presence on Fifth Avenue that December night.

Ironically, Hitler was also in an accident later that same month in Berlin. Lucinda had been there, too. She recalled, as if it were yesterday, standing among the crowd that had come to celebrate Herr Goebbels' wedding, wearing the guise of a young soldier.

Lucinda shouldered her way through the crowd, drawing closer and closer to the pathway down which Herr Goebbels and his bride would come on their way to their motorcade. She knew by now that Churchill and Hitler were two poles of a spectrum, knew that the death of one and the life of the other would spell disaster for a free Europe. She had decided that what she needed was a way to remove Hitler and Goebbels from the world, and here, she had them both together.

The doors of the church opened, and a great cheer went up from the crowd as the head of the Reich Minister of Propaganda and his new wife exited the church and waved to their well-wishers as they walked from the sanctuary to their car. Adolf Hitler was directly behind them in the company of General von Epp.

How could she accomplish it? She was armed. If she assassinated these men herself, she could literally disappear from sight and no one would know.

No human *would know.*

She felt the magnetic pull of her father's presence. She looked up. He was holding the car door open for the newlyweds—a tall, Aryan youth with the bearing of royalty. He turned his head and their eyes met.

Lucinda smiled.

Lucifer inclined his head slightly before shutting the car door behind the Goebbels and his new wife. He moved to the next car in line to open the door for Hitler and von Epp. Lucinda wanted to scream in frustration, but all she could do was stand on the sidewalk and smile vacuously.

The autos drove off, but they hadn't gotten far when the lead car stopped abruptly. The vehicle carrying Hitler and von Epp, which had been accelerating, plowed into the back of it with the shriek of rending metal. The crowd gasped.

Lucinda gasped right along with them, seeking Lucifer in the sudden rush of bodies. He was shouting orders to the men pouring down the street to the wreck. Moments later, he stood at her side.

"Did you do that?" she asked.

He tilted his head in that way that said maybe *and meant* yes.

"Why?"

"Perhaps to bring a certain player in this scene a sense of his own mortality . . . or his invincibility. Or to begin an internal war between the two extremes."

She looked at him sharply, and extended all her senses to him, to be sure he didn't mean her— that he had not discovered her insidious, silent, centuries-long string of treacheries—but his gaze was on the motorcade, where rescuers were now helping the injured from their cars.

"Hitler," she said.

He looked down at her, his smile deepening. "Wise child," he said. "You see it, too—the sheer magnificence of his evil."

She wished to God she was a wise child. Had she been wise not to take matters into her own hands? Yes, she would have revealed herself and been forced to fight Lucifer openly . . . and alone. And she would have had to do it with no guarantee that the absence of Goebbels, Hitler, and von Epp would not have produced a greater horror than what was already happening to European Jews and other disenfranchised peoples.

Later events had proven that her dread of Hitler and his politics was well placed, but after all was said and done, she had wondered what it would have meant to give into that impulse to pull him and his cohorts from the pages of history. In the end, would such an act not have meant that she was truly her father's daughter?

A face on the television caught Lucinda's eye. It was a face she knew because she had seen it in her own shop just weeks ago. It was one of the teenaged girls who had taken Morgan le Fay's Book of Shadows—the blue-haired one. She didn't have blue hair in the picture they showed on the news, but Lucinda did not (indeed, could not) forget faces.

Reflexively, without bothering with the remote control, Lucinda raised the volume on the television.

"Authorities are still trying to make sense of the situation," the female anchor was saying. "All that is currently known is that Margaret Stuyvesant—the youngest daughter of Assemblyman Walden Stuyvesant—was killed with a single blow from an axe. Her two closest friends—whose names are being withheld to protect their privacy—survived the attack, which took place near an abandoned building on Peabody Field just north of Sleepy Hollow. Under arrest are twenty members of a religious sect that call themselves the Nihilim. This includes Samuel Reitman and Morris Bayer, the leaders of the group. A minor male was also detained as a person of interest. His name has not been released due to his age."

The camera panned back to reveal a male anchor to the woman's left. "What's truly extraordinary about this case, Helen," the man said, "is the accounts given by the members of the Nihilim about the events leading up to Margaret Stuyvesant's death. A number of them claim that the girls are witches and that they were on the beach doing what they term the 'Devil's work.' The members of the religious sect—which has a small enclave near Ossining—believe that the world will end in the next several decades." He turned to the camera. "As of this hour, Samuel Reitman—also known as Elder Samuel of Holyhaven—has confessed to having killed the girl, but claims he did it in self-defense. None of the girls involved were armed."

Lucinda felt as if she were a pillar of ice. The Nihilim. That was the cult her father had asked her about. What was he doing with them, and why? It was a connection she needed to understand before it was too late. She flipped the TV off with a flicker of thought and stepped into the Between.

Peter had waited for what seemed like hours when the police sergeant came to his tiny holding room and told him that the man from child protective services was here to take him to a shelter. He'd told the police when they put him in the room that he wanted to go home, but they had said that wasn't possible. The enclave was being investigated, the public defender had told him. He would be released to his mother if things checked out. So, Peter had paced, he had prayed, he had come close to falling asleep with his head on the hard Formica of the tabletop. He was no closer to understanding what had happened.

He asked again, "Where's my father?"

The sergeant was about his father's age—maybe older—and Asian. He seemed sympathetic, but was unable to tell Peter anything. He beckoned Peter out of the room and led him down a long hallway to a waiting area.

"Have a seat, kid," the officer told him, then gestured at the counter across the room where a man in a long trench coat was signing papers. "That's the guy from CPS. He's signing you out; he'll get any belongings you had on you when they brought you in."

"Just my clothes and boots," Peter said, seating himself in the row of chairs facing the window. "And my New Testament."

"Yeah, about that. You'll get the Bible back, but your clothes and shoes are in the evidence lockup. I'm sorry about that." The officer touched his shoulder. "Take care, kid. Peter. That's your name, right? Peter Reitman?"

"Peter of Holyhaven," Peter said firmly. "To be of the Nihilim, you must renounce your worldly name."

The man's sleek black brows rose. "D'you even know what 'renounce' means?"

"It means I gave up that name. I'm just Peter."

"Whatever. Take care of yourself." The cop turned and strode off down the hall, snapping his fingers in time to music only he could hear.

"Peter the Summoner," said a deep, warm, resonant voice so near Peter's ear, he nearly leapt out of his skin.

He turned to see, sitting one chair away, the gleaming man he had met on the shore of the Hudson on the Night of the Witches. The man who had given him a new name. The man who had called the Nihilim to act.

"That is your name: Peter the Summoner," the man repeated.

"Who are you?" Peter asked him. "Where are you from?"

He shook his head. "My name is not important. Nor where I'm from. What is important, Peter, is that you not let your fears get the better of you. Your fears are unworthy of you. Unworthy of God. I am here to remind you that you are Peter—a rock—and that upon this rock of faith, God will build His temple. I am here . . ." The radiant being hesitated, made a strange, wry face, then said, "I am here to ask you a question. Think of the things that are coming to pass in these days. Do these not seem like portents of the End of Times?"

Peter opened his mouth to answer, because this was something he'd given much thought to, but the strange man put a finger to his own lips.

"Do not answer me. Only ask yourself the question and seek the answer within yourself and within the Book. Here is another question: Did not Christ say that a house divided against itself cannot stand? The Nihilim are not alone. There are hundreds of enclaves like Holyhaven. Thousands of people like you. People of the Lord, all. They are scattered. Rudderless. Purposeless. They wait and know not what they're waiting for. Is it possible, Peter, that they're waiting only for someone to summon them to serve the Lord in this time of the End?"

"Do you . . . you can't mean *me*."

"Can't I?" The strange, tilted eyes seemed to be laughing at him. "Are you not Peter the Summoner? If you are not, who will gather the lost sheep?"

"Okay, Peter. Let's get going."

Peter's head whipped around so fast he nearly made himself dizzy. The CPS guy was right in front of him, looking down at him with sympathy in his dark eyes.

"What?"

"Let's get out of here, okay? I've got your Bible." He held out Peter's New Testament.

The boy took it, sticking it into the breast pocket of his state-issued coveralls. "Thanks," he said, then: "What about my dad? What's going to happen with my dad?"

The social worker's face was sober. "I'm sorry, Peter, but your father is under arrest for killing that girl. The detectives and lawyers are going to have to figure it out now."

"He didn't mean to hurt anyone, sir," Peter said, holding back sudden tears. This wasn't his father's fault. How could he make the police understand that? "It was an accident." He turned to beg the gleaming man's help. He'd been there, he might have seen—

But the man was gone, leaving Peter to stare at an empty chair.

"If that's true," the CPS guy was saying, "then it'll come out in court. You'll be able to talk to the lawyers, too, I'm sure. You can tell them what happened."

Peter turned back to him. "I will. I *will* tell them what happened, because it's important that they understand."

It was his job now, Peter realized. To make people understand. First, he had to find the people the gleaming man had spoken of—the People of God.

Nathaniel manifested the very moment Lucinda entered the Between. That did not surprise her. What surprised her was the part of her that wanted to find it comforting, as she had when she was a child.

Nathaniel had been with her almost from the moment Lucifer had brought her into the Between at the mortal age of five. She had known nothing, then, of the circumstances of her conception and birth. She had known only that this tall, beautiful man had come to her and held out his hand and asked if she would like to see a magical place. She had left the stick she had been using to etch pictures of animals in the dirt and gone to him.

It had been like walking into a gigantic soap bubble at first—like stepping through a shimmering membrane that muted the sound and scents and sights of the world she had left and made them seem faded. What she remembered most—millennia later—was turning from the shining Between to see her mother running from their clever house of wood and mud to the place where she had been playing. To hear her mother's voice sharp with terror and despair, calling her name again and again.

Her name had not been Lucinda then—Lucifer had given her that name because it echoed his own. It meant "illumination." The name Eve gave her was Mariel. She never spoke the name to anyone, but held it in the silence of her soul. She later had come to know that Mariel meant "rebellion," but it was not until she had grown almost to adulthood that she thought she understood why her mother had given her a name with such a strange meaning. She came to believe her mother had hoped she might one day rebel against her father . . . her real father, Lucifer, not her earthly father, Adam—the man she had thought of as her father every day of her young life.

She had been with Lucifer for only a small while when she asked to go back to her parents. That was when he had told her that she was not "Adam's get," as he had put it, but his and Eve's. She was half-mortal—a "changeling" in the parlance of those who believed in such things. If he allowed her to go back to the mortal world, Lucifer told her, she would age physically until she was an adult and then stop. She would never sicken and never die, while everyone around her—everyone she loved—withered and went to dust.

Innocence was a terrible thing if one was destined to lose it. How could Eve have betrayed Adam so? Lucinda's sense of outrage had extended beyond Eve and Lucifer to include God Himself. How had He allowed such a thing to happen?

Lucinda had grown to adulthood and beyond in the Between, serving as her father's protégé in testing the obedience of men. After a while she had come to think of it as home and was no longer inclined to try to escape. There was, after all, nowhere for her to escape to that held any meaning. Adam and Eve were long dead, and their spirits cut off from her by the dictates of divine physics.

It was Nathaniel—her constant companion—who had brought the question of Lucinda's parentage out into the open by asking, simply, if Lucifer had ever told her how she came to be born. Just that. Lucifer had often explained to her the fickleness of human character—their complete lack of constancy. That was, after all, why Lucifer existed—he was the Tester of Souls, the being taxed with trying the intentions of mankind. He had portrayed the All-Father as both naive and petty and told her that her parents had been ejected from paradise because of some token disobedience that, in her young mind, she somehow imagined must have led to Eve's seduction by Lucifer. Nathaniel's simple question hinted that there was something more to be told. It had piqued Lucinda's natural curiosity, and she had asked.

Lucifer had answered with dark enjoyment. "I'm sure you recall what I told you of the tree of the knowledge of good and evil."

"Yes, of course. They ate the forbidden fruit and it changed them—or so I gather."

"I lied," he had told her. "The tree was not forbidden them. That was a fairy tale made up for a fretful child. God gave Adam and Eve the knowledge of good and evil, along with a human spirit and free will—gifts that separate them and their progeny from the animals. I decided to take advantage of those gifts. I took Adam's form and went to your mother beneath the tree of the knowledge of good and evil, and she, believing I was Adam, let me lie with her."

Lucinda had felt a lightning jolt of icy betrayal course through her—body and soul. In that moment, she began to understand why her mother had named her "Rebellion" and why this demon who had styled himself her "real father" could never be either friend or ally.

"Do you want to know what happened next?" Lucifer had asked, seeming to enjoy whatever emotions he read in her face. "Your surrogate father, with his perfect sense of timing, appeared almost at the moment you were conceived. You can imagine what he thought—what *she* thought when she realized that it was not Adam she held in her arms, but a snake—figuratively speaking. I made a discreet exit, of course, while perfect Adam, flushed with rage and jealousy, stood over his weeping, humiliated wife, pointed at her, and roared, 'Woman, what have you done?'"

"But she'd done nothing," Lucinda had observed mildly. Even that early in her life, she had enough guile to know better than to let Lucifer see what he had just done to her soul.

"No. And God, seeing the ruination of His best creatures, condemned Adam for his rage and judgment and exiled him from paradise and me from Heaven. Your mother, being what she was—softhearted, naive, and loyal to a fault—went with her mate into the greater world."

"She loved him," Lucinda had murmured so quietly she doubted Lucifer had heard her.

Many times since that day Lucinda had contemplated asking Nathaniel why he had suggested asking about her birth. She had never done it. She now knew that questions could be dangerous.

She thought about that now, as Nathaniel assembled himself out of the ether, first resembling a cascade of embers, then a cloud of scintillating smoke, then a mist composed of rainbows, and finally, a man. He appeared as a man because she wished it, she knew. She had told him once that it disconcerted her to speak to a being who had no eyes for her to read expression in. So, for Lucinda, he was a perfect man. Ironically, even with eyes—eyes that could be gray one moment and green or blue or even lavender the next—he was still unreadable.

"Nathaniel, I was seeking you," she told him when he had materialized before her.

"Which is why I am here," he said.

"Here" was Lucinda's Between—a place that looked like a farm garden except for the fact that every color in it was surreally saturated. The grasses looked like green velvet, and the water in the endless stream had the blues of glacial ice and spun rainbows into the ether. The corn was golden and ready to be picked and the silvery tassels whispered in a nonexistent breeze. The light was Lucinda's favorite light—the light of an October evening just at sunset—and every tree spilled leaves of copper and gold onto the vibrant grass. The ether pretended at being air and was balmy with just a hint of autumn cool to it. Everywhere were jack o' lanterns simply because Lucinda loved them—and a scarecrow, because she felt every cornfield should have one. Her scarecrow stood right next to her—a smiling man of straw and rags.

"I had a question for you," Lucinda told the angel, "about the little witches from Sleepy Hollow. Father said he had a surprise for me. Is it about what happened to them the other night?"

The Fallen tilted his handsome head to one size and gazed at her expressionlessly. "I believe that to be the case."

"He brought them into contact with the Nihilim. A doomsday cult, he said."

"Yes."

She gave the Fallen an arch look. "I do hope this is part of a long-term plan and not some silly side game he finds entertaining."

"Do you find it entertaining?"

"Not as such. As I said, I hope it's part of a larger plan."

"I believe it is, though I couldn't tell you what plan, exactly. As you know, he is fond of his secrets . . . and quite taken with millennialism."

"Of course he is. The Book of Revelation is his script."

"The end of the world," Nathaniel murmured.

Lucinda made an impatient gesture. "Christ said 'end of the *age*,' not 'end of the world.' Irrelevant, I suppose. Lucifer's convinced half of Christendom that it's the world that's coming to an end in fire and brimstone and not the age of human folly—potentially, at least. So how do these Nihilim figure into it? They seem particularly useless now."

Lucinda felt another energy enter her pocket of the Between and knew that her private discussion with Nathaniel was over. She turned to look at the scarecrow.

"Hello, Father. As you've no doubt gathered, I've discovered your surprise."

The scarecrow gazed down at her questioningly through painted eyes. "You always were a clever girl. You take after me, in that way. Yet, you say the Nihilim are useless?"

"Father, they're in jail. And, unless I'm very much mistaken, they will go to prison for murder. Or at least their leaders will."

Lucifer abandoned the scarecrow and materialized on the grass next to his daughter—a towering figure of amorphous black, amid which floated a gleaming face with eyes like flames. "Have you never observed," he asked, "what happens to a group of zealots when their leaders have fallen? They become something quite terrifying . . . and majestic."

Ah. Now that made some sense. He meant to use the fallen zealots to rally his "troops."

"Point taken," she said. "Do you expect the witches will continue on now that one of their number is dead?"

"Janine Sorentino and Stephanie Halleck have tasted a power unknown to most human beings. What do you think?"

"I think you are brilliant and evil. It was a worthy surprise."

"Oh, you know only a bit of it. Come," he said, and quite suddenly they were in *his* sanctum of obsidian black and oily anthracite rainbows, and he was wearing Lucien Trompe like a soul-fitting suit.

He showed her and Nathaniel the events that had taken place in Peabody Field on the Hudson, and the part he had played in them. She saw Margaret Stuyvesant die by the light of the witches' fire, and read the look of sheer horror in the eyes of the youth who had held her at the instant of her death. He must have been the minor mentioned in the news report. The one whose name the police would not reveal. She would find out his name and where he had gone. She knew better than to lose sight of souls her father had touched.

"Now do you see how the tapestry is to be woven, child?" Lucifer asked her. "Do you see how these seemingly marginalized people will play on the loom of their own destruction? Those around them imagine that they are tinfoil-wearing, fringe-walking fools who are mad as hatters and just as powerless. But they are soldiers in a great, dark army, needing only to be galvanized and guided. They are waiting and watching for the end of the world. Waiting and watching for someone to lead them in the battle against the great Satan." He bowed slightly and laid a hand on his chest.

Lucinda shook her head. "You make me feel inadequate, Father. All I've done is hand a book off to some witches and introduce a Shi'a zealot to a Sunni philosopher. I've played so little a part in this."

He gazed at her through his burning eyes and chilled her to the soul. "Nonsense. You have played a very important part in getting us to this point in time, Lucinda. All these centuries of herding these stupid, unworthy creatures and we are finally—*finally*—to the point where they are capable of forging a global civilization . . . or destroying themselves utterly. With those two books—le Fay's Book of Shadows and ibn Rušd's Qur'án—we have created the very atmosphere that will make Armageddon a reality. Giving Darzi that book, my dear, was a stroke of sheer brilliance. You and I will make certain that they destroy themselves—or sin so egregiously that God will finally destroy them Himself out of disgust. You will play a prime role in that, too, I promise."

"What role is that, Father?" she asked, trying to sound interested and not uneasy.

He reached out with one graceful hand, smiled, and touched her cheek. "That is also a surprise."

With all the drama of a bubble bursting, Lucinda found herself facing Nathaniel in her own domain. They were alone. The scarecrow was just a scarecrow again. She felt a tug on her consciousness.

Rey. He felt . . . angry.

"I should get back to the shop," she said.

"Yes, Shaliah." Nathaniel bowed his head.

She started to step into the Real, then hesitated, looking back over her shoulder. "Nathaniel, you asked once, if Lucifer had told me how I was conceived. Why?"

"Did you ask him?"

"Yes. Why did you prompt me to do it?"

The angel's face showed no expression. "This is neither the time nor the place, Shaliah. You are wanted at the shop."

Odd. She had never known the Fallen to avoid a subject. He was often cryptic and opaque, but she had rarely known him to be cagey.

"Fine. Let me know when it's the time and the place. It can wait. It's hardly important information."

She stepped through into the Real and heard voices in the front of the shop. One of them was Dominic Amado's. Her response to his voice disturbed her. She might look like a mortal woman; she might even feel like a mortal woman in moments like these. But she was not. She tried to remind herself of this as she put a smile on her lips and headed to the front of the store.

CHAPTER TWELVE

The shop was a stew of emotions and energies as Lucinda emerged from the back rooms. Rey was seething with distrust and jealousy. Dominic was awash in wary confusion. Vorden . . . was just Vorden. She had contrived to be as close to Dominic as she possibly could without occupying the same space. She had him cornered behind the reading table where two bookshelves met, her larger-than-usual breasts nearly brushing his arm. If Vorden had been a mortal woman and not a succubus, Lucinda would have laughed.

Rey watched Vorden and Nick, narrow-eyed, from behind the counter. Lucinda could feel the gears in his head grinding, squeezing ever more hostility into the atmosphere.

"Nick!" she said brightly. "I didn't expect to see you back so soon."

Vorden pulled back, her voluptuous mouth set in a pretty pout. "Killjoy," she mouthed at Lucinda, then added, aloud, "Your timing is atrocious. I almost had him convinced to ask me out. You must have cast a spell on him to make him so impervious to me." Her grin was wicked and taunting at once.

Damn Vorden. She loved to tread the thin edge of propriety when it came to both her sexuality and her true nature. Her theory was that it mattered little what she said, no mortals would ever take it seriously. They would either think she was joking or eccentric or even a bit insane, but they would never imagine she was really a demon in the service of Satan, even if she were to tell them so point-blank.

Nick slid out of the succubus's entrapment zone and moved with swift grace to join Lucinda at the end of the display counter. Sensing movement to her right, Lucinda glanced over at Rey. He had straightened, his pale eyes never leaving Dominic's face. She recoiled from the violence in those eyes.

"Got a minute?" Dominic asked her.

"Sure. Why?"

"I've got some people I'd like you to meet. And, well . . . actually they asked to meet you."

"Really? Why would they do that?"

"They're a family that was living in our church shelter. People who had to pawn a lot of . . . of memories. Things that meant a lot to them. Some, they got back—most, they didn't. They're part of the piece I'm writing, too. I told them about you and how you felt about taking things from people you knew were precious to them. They wanted to meet you. And I . . . I thought you might appreciate that."

"Watch out for this guy, Lucinda," Rey said. His voice, like his face, was tight and hard. "I think he's on a fund-raising expedition."

Lucinda turned to look at him, making no attempt to hide her anger. "Rey . . ." There were about a thousand things she wanted to say. What she elected to say was, "Watch the store."

Rey's expression did a lightning change. His jealousy was swamped with sudden fear. Sometimes Rey seemed to forget that she wasn't a mortal woman; it was good policy to remind him. That he needed the reminders made her wonder what his relations with mortal women had been like.

Next to her, Nick shifted uneasily. "Lucinda, I hope you don't think—"

"I don't. Ignore Rey. He's . . ." She almost said, *He's a soulless idiot.* She didn't. ". . . under a lot of stress," she finished.

Dominic's car was an aged Volvo hatchback that seemed to be in mint condition. It was low-slung, painted a gorgeous shade of metallic forest green, and had elegantly understated fins.

"Do you do your own mechanical work on this thing?" Lucinda asked him as they navigated to the East Village where his church was located.

"Uh . . . yeah. I started doing it out of thrift and found out that I really enjoy it. It's very . . . meditative." He frowned at the road ahead of them. "You don't have to answer this, but what's with Rey? He acts like . . . I'm not sure what he acts like. A protective older brother, maybe."

Again, he'd surprised Lucinda into laughter. Older brother—that was rich. There was no one on the planet who was older than Lucinda. No one with any human blood in their veins, anyway. As for those who had no blood and no flesh at all—Vorden, Nathaniel, and the various demons who served satanic purpose—age didn't really mean anything.

She readied a lie and brought it to her lips, then looked sidewise at him. What was it about this man that made it next to impossible for her to deceive him? "Rey . . . has bit of a problem with jealousy."

Nick nodded. "Ah. That makes sense. I gather, then, that Vorden—that's an unusual name—is his girlfriend? She was sort of . . ." The blush. "Aggressive."

Well, that was a relief. She wouldn't have to lie about the fact that Rey's jealousy was directed at *her*, not Vorden. "She knows how to push his buttons," she said mildly, which was true. Vorden knew how to push all men's buttons. The pushing just didn't always have predictable results.

"Why is that funny?" Nick asked, catching the humorous twist of her lips.

"You blush," she replied before she could think better of it.

Surprise. He laughed. "I . . . I *blush?*"

"When Vorden was coming onto you. You blushed. You also blushed when I asked about your middle name."

He kept his eyes forward. "Yeah, well, there's a reason for that."

"You're still not going to tell me?"

"Not . . . not yet. Maybe later. Maybe . . . if it feels right."

"I hope I earn that trust," Lucinda said, in all honesty. The words were no sooner out of her mouth than she regretted them. She'd as much as said that she wanted to prolong her time in Dominic A. Amado's company.

She did, she realized, very much.

San Ysidro y San Leandro Orthodox Catholic Church of the Hispanic Rite was a remarkable edifice despite its relatively small size. It stood out among the surrounding brick buildings like a queen among commoners. Its facade was white-washed to blinding brilliance that contrasted sharply with the dark brown in the ranks of arched windows, the eaves, and the door lintels. A spire with a golden cross sat atop the roof like a crown, deepening the regal impression.

"Quite a mouthful," Lucinda commented, nodding at the church's signage.

Dominic laughed. "It is, isn't it? My mom used to joke that the church's name was bigger than the church itself. I think the Spanish have a knack for long names and titles."

They parked on the church's side of the one-way street and entered the sanctuary through whitewashed wrought iron gates. Lucinda shivered as she stepped across the threshold. What would her various observers make of her coming here?

For all that it was a Christian church, the sanctuary reminded Lucinda of a Hindu temple, so brilliant were the colors, and so gleaming the baroque touches of gold. At the far end of the long, narrow, and dark nave, the apse was a festival of bright hues and gold ornamentation. On each side of the altar was a brace of votive candles in bright glass holders; flames flickered in about half of them. Every inch of wall space overlooking both the nave and the altar was covered with paintings of the Holy Family and saints. Some were prints from museum galleries, others were hand-painted and had a distinctly Iberian style.

Lucinda had never admitted to anyone that entering houses of worship—churches, mosques, synagogues, ashrams, all—affected her deeply. In this case, it was not the crosses or crucifixes or other symbols of devotion, or the staring eyes of the painted saints, or the long-suffering patience in the face of Christ, or the prescient sorrow of his Mother. It was the sense that in a house of worship, more than anywhere else, God watched her, judged her, and condemned her just for being who and what she was.

Yes, the message of Christ was that the All-Father did not condemn the innocent for the acts of the sinful, but Lucifer had countered that message by insisting that scripture lied. She was his daughter; she carried his stain. Nonetheless, she sometimes prayed in the darkness of her sanctum—and her soul—and waited for signs that God had heard her. She occasionally thought that she'd received such a sign, but she had not been taught how to see or hear or feel it, so how was she to know?

She had never prayed in a house of worship—she avoided them for the most part—but she had given God sidewise mental glances there, and she'd looked for signs in them as well. She prayed only in the warded privacy of her rooftop sanctum.

"They're downstairs," Dominic said, gesturing at a narrow wooden door to the left of the apse.

Lucinda came back to the physical world with a start, only just realizing that she'd been elsewhere mentally.

"The Rendóns. They're working in the social hall downstairs."

The social hall echoed the dimensions of the sanctuary—a long, narrow room with a kitchen at one end and a doorway that opened into a tiny parking lot in the rear. The black and white tile floors were aging, but spotlessly clean. Parishioners worked at long trestle tables preparing care packages for the homeless and jobless of the neighborhood.

Among them were Alberto and Isolde Rendón—the parents of a school-aged son and daughter, Aurelio and Trina. Their story was a common one: both parents had been well-employed until several cycles of sickness and job loss had led to the sacrifice of their apartment and their car. They had pawned or sold almost everything they owned in an attempt to feed their kids. The church had taken them in, then installed them in a group home co-run by a collective of religious and community organizations.

Alberto had found work again, finally, Isolde had a job interview lined up, and the family was saving money toward first and last month's rent on an apartment in a building just down the street from Nick's place on East Fourth.

"We're here to pay it back," Alberto said. "Because the goodness of the people in the Village meant so much to us."

The Rendóns chatted with Lucinda and Nick for some time about the nature of their recent troubles and how it intersected her business, but Lucinda knew that no artifact from this family would have ever ended up in her shop. At least not at her father's bidding.

When Nick ducked into the kitchen for a moment to help move a box of supplies, Isolde leaned close to Lucinda and said softly, "Nick would be embarrassed if he knew I told you this, but he's the one who arranged for my job interview with a lawyer friend of his. It's for an administrative job at a nonprofit. I wanted you to know what a good man he is."

Lucinda did not miss the twinkle in Isolde's eye. Neither did Alberto.

"Isolde," he said with mock severity, "you are incorrigible. Forgive my wife, Lucinda, she is a compulsive matchmaker."

"She's right, though," Lucinda said. "Nick *is* a good man." *Which is why I should get as far away from him as I can.*

Nick returned from his chore, smiling, and looking back and forth between the Rendóns and Lucinda. "Should my ears be burning?"

"Absolutely," said Isolde.

"I should get back to the pawnshop," Lucinda said, rising from the table.

She and Nick went back upstairs, where he paused to genuflect toward the altar. There was no cross there, Lucinda noticed, but rather a painting of the Last Supper.

"Can I show you something else?" Nick asked when they'd returned to his car.

Lucinda hesitated. "I . . . I need to be back by closing time to do inventory."

Nick raised his right hand in a Boy Scout salute. "I promise. Come on." He held out his arm as if he were going to escort her to a prom.

"Where are we going?"

He walked her down the street half a block to a tiny, pocket paradise with arbors, vegetable gardens, chickens, and a miniature forest dominated by a turtle pond and a weeping willow encircled by an elevated tree-house walkway. The vegetable gardens had mostly been harvested, but the foliage was still clad in its autumn brilliance. The park—El Jardin del Paraiso—took up the width of the city block and was populated by villagers who gardened, tended their chickens, or sat at bistro tables watching their children play among the fall leaves.

Nick led Lucinda to the willow walk, where they stood, leaning against the thick wooden railing and watching the turtles among the reeds in the pond.

"Those animals can't survive winter in there can they?" Lucinda asked. "The pond will freeze."

"Microclimate," Nick said. "Caused by the sea air. The water gets cold, but not so cold that the critters in it can't survive. Some of the plots back there"—he gestured over his shoulder toward the vegetable gardens—"are experiments in cold climate farming. I love this place. When I was a kid, I used to come here to escape when my father was in one of his moods. It took me a while to figure out that when I did that, Mom bore the brunt of my cowardice."

Lucinda turned to look at him. "Somehow I have trouble seeing you as a coward."

"I was."

"You were a child. You probably didn't realize what was happening." *I didn't realize what was happening to me, either.*

He looked down at his hands. "I did, actually, but I was afraid. Afraid of him beating me up. Of watching him beat Mom up. She did a good job of hiding her black eyes and bruises. For a while. I was eleven when I realized I couldn't hide out down here any more. That was a bad year, but at the end of it, Mom divorced him and took out a restraining order. Then, she met Joe. I thank God for that every day."

Lucinda doubted he was exaggerating. She studied his profile—the strong jaw, the aquiline nose, the high cheekbones, the large, deep-set, dark eyes—and marveled that as beautiful as this man was, the greater beauty was invisible to the human eye. She considered her own internal struggle.

"It must have been hard," she said, "not to be relieved when he died."

She felt as much as saw him stiffen, felt, again, the darkness she'd sensed in him when they'd first met.

"Yeah," he said. "It was . . . hard. You think you want something, and when it happens, you wonder . . ."

"If you caused it by just thinking about it?" She watched him for a moment. "You didn't, in case you wondered. Human beings don't have that ability."

He met her gaze. "You talk as if you understand what it's like to . . . to want something you shouldn't."

In the moment their eyes met, she realized that she *did* want something she shouldn't. Very much. She also knew that wasn't what he was talking about. She looked out toward the pond, watched the sun ripple on the water.

"You're very perceptive. Yes. I think most people have something they'd like to escape from."

"Your father?" When she didn't answer, he asked, "Can't you just leave? Work somewhere else? You clearly have marketable expertise. I'm willing to bet some gallery or auction house would pay top dollar for someone with your background."

Someone with my background. There is no one on the whole planet with my background, she thought. Aloud, she said, "It's complicated."

He smiled ruefully. "Isn't it always? I guess we have that in common—complicated families."

You have no idea . . . and never can. Lucinda stifled a shiver—or rather, tried to stifle it. Dominic, ever perceptive, caught it.

"It's all right," he said. "We have each other, right? I understand your complications; you understand mine. Maybe we're a match made in heaven."

Her laughter caught both of them unawares. He stared at her, bemused, maybe a little embarrassed, and she, knowing he could have no conception of why she was really laughing, could not stop.

He was suddenly ill at ease. "I'm sorry, that was a stupid thing to say. I'm assuming a lot."

Lucinda reined in her dark mirth. "No. No, you're not. Really, you're not. It's just—you're Orthodox Christian and I'm . . ." There was no good way to finish that sentence.

"Jewish?"

She grimaced and shook her head. "I'm not *anything*, Dominic. I'm not anything at all."

He frowned. "You said you believed—"

"I *do* believe in God. I'm just not sure I—" How could she even come close to describing her relationship with the God of the Universe? She opted for a wry smile. "I'm not sure He believes in me."

He turned to face her. She felt his urgent need to assure her that she was wrong—that of course God believed in her. But that wasn't what he said. What he said was, "I know that feeling."

She was surprised at the genuineness and depth of emotion behind the words. "I can tell," she told him. "I just can't imagine why. Isolde told me you were a good man. I'd say she's got that right."

His dark, intense gaze held her motionless against the railing of the tree house. "You can't know," he said softly.

They were less than an arm's length apart. Lucinda could feel the warmth of his body and the keenness of his longing. Her own desire to kiss him almost overwhelmed her. She quivered, hovering on the verge of giving in to human need and sheer amazement that this man had breached her millennia-old defenses. She, who had been alive from the dawn of humanity, had never felt what she was feeling at this moment. Her peculiar upbringing—conducted mostly in the Between—had not offered the opportunities that young human girls had to try on relationships with boys. At the point she might have followed Lucifer's urging to take a lover—either human or inhuman—she had discovered his deception and understood, for the first time, that her abduction was not about saving her, but about hurting Eve. At wounding God's beloved child.

Now, her heart was open and alive and she had to find a way to close it and send it back into dormancy. There was no other path open to her.

Still, she leaned into him. He lowered his head; she lifted hers. A hand's breadth lay between them, then the width of a finger. She felt the warmth of his breath on her cheek . . . and pulled back from the abyss. She stepped away from him abruptly, shaking her head.

"I'm sorry, I can't."

"No, *I'm* sorry. I was rushing you, I know." He was embarrassed again.

"You weren't. It's not that I don't want . . . I just can't."

He was silent for a moment, then said, "Lucinda, there's something here. Between us. I think you feel it, too. It's been there from the moment we met. From the very instant I looked into your eyes. Tell me you don't feel it and I'll take you back to your shop and never try to see you again."

She gazed up at him, desperately wishing that she could tell him exactly that. But that was a lie too big even for the Devil's daughter.

"I can't tell you that. I'd be lying. I find it damned hard to lie to you, Dominic A. Amado. *Damned* hard."

He relaxed back a step. "Then what do we do?"

"I don't know, but right now, I think I should go back to the shop. And maybe you should—I don't know—go to confession or something."

"Don't laugh. I probably will." He was smiling, and the smile healed at least a few of her self-inflicted wounds. He held his arm out to her again. "Come on."

He escorted her down off the tree-walk onto one of the paths that ran across the pocket park from Fourth Street to Fifth. Before they headed back to the car, he turned her toward Fifth and pointed.

"See that building right there? The tan one with the black door—you can just see it through the trees."

She nodded.

"That's where I live. Third floor on this side. I can look down on paradise every morning while I eat my oatmeal. I'd invite you over, but perhaps that's not such a good idea right now. For either of us."

"Agreed."

They came out on the Fourth Street side of the park and walked across the street to Nick's Volvo. He got out his keys and moved to unlock the driver's side door; Lucinda rounded the rear of the car toward the passenger side. She'd almost reached the sidewalk when she felt a stab of unadulterated malevolence so strong, it made her stumble. The roar of a car engine spun her toward Avenue C. A red

Mercedes accelerated down the street toward them, riding so close to the parked cars that it was nearly clipping them.

Dominic!

She spared him a glance and caught him in the split second that he looked up and recognized the danger. He froze.

Lucinda was not in avian form today, and no flock of flushed pigeons was going to deflect a hurtling car. She had no choice and no time. She grasped the speeding vehicle with her will and flipped it onto its side—her hands pantomiming the physical act. It plowed down the center of the street in a spray of sparks and safety glass, accompanied by the shriek of tortured metal.

It came to a stop yards away and fell back onto its tires with a groan. People from the neighborhood were already running toward it. A woman on the sidewalk in front of the church was calling 911 on her cell phone.

Lucinda rounded the side of the Volvo to where Dominic leaned against the driver's side door, eyes closed, head tilted back. She thought he was praying. She put her hands against his chest, seeking assurance that he was unharmed.

"Are you all right?"

He nodded. "Just . . . really wound up. That was an *epic* adrenaline rush."

"No wonder. You were nearly killed." The thought stunned her. That this man—this beautiful, so alive man—had come *that close* to passing through the Veil into a place Lucinda was not permitted to go. A place she would *never* be permitted to go.

She thought about the malevolence she'd felt just before the murderous car had appeared. It had been muddy, confused, and incredibly strong. Almost supernaturally strong. She turned and started down Fourth toward where the car had already been surrounded by East Villagers.

Dominic caught her arm. "Where are you going?"

"Stay here. I need to go check on the driver."

"Stay here?" he repeated as she jogged down the street.

She reached the car just in time to see a couple of men help the driver out onto the asphalt. The sight of the man drew Lucinda up short. He was young, blond, well-dressed, well-curried. She'd never seen him before. She extended her senses—tendrils of questing thought probing his mind. She didn't know him, and there was nothing about him of one of Lucifer's cursed objects.

"What happened?" someone asked him.

"He doesn't seem drunk," someone else said.

The driver was holding a hand to his forehead. A slow trickle of blood oozed between his fingers. "I-I-I haven't been drinking. I don't know what happened. I was—I was driving up Avenue C and I . . ." He turned and caught sight of the ruined side of his car. "Oh my God, what did I *do*?"

A siren whooped once out on Avenue D and an emergency vehicle pulled around the corner coming the wrong way up Fourth, lights flashing. Frustrated, Lucinda turned away, to find Dominic standing beside her.

"You don't take orders very well, do you?" she asked him as she took his hand and walked with him back to the car.

"I never have."

He drove them back to the pawnshop and walked her the half block up the street from where he'd parked.

"Why the solicitude?" she asked him. "I'm not the one who was nearly killed."

"I'm just soaking up as much time with you as I can get. Almost dying . . . has a strange way of adjusting your priorities. Which brings me to this point. I need to tell you something."

Lucinda regarded him warily. "What might that be?"

"Adeodatus."

"Excuse me? What?"

"The 'A' stands for Adeodatus."

Lucinda felt as if the Universe were holding its breath. She knew she was holding hers. "Dominic Adeodatus Amado," she murmured, her voice husky and airless.

"Well, when you say it like that, it almost sounds indecent. It means—"

"I know what it means. It means whoever named you was either tragically romantic, or passionately religious, or both." She tried to be flippant, but couldn't quite carry it off. "It's beautiful."

"So, now I've confessed my dark secret, after nearly being killed. Which means there's only one more thing I need to accomplish tonight."

"Which is?"

He put his hands on either side of her face and kissed her very gently. Then he turned on his heel and strode back up the street to his car, leaving her standing as if lightning-struck on the sidewalk outside Lucinda's Pawnshop.

Her mind, her heart, her soul, felt disconnected and weightless, her body, as if fire and ice battled up and down her spine. Beneath it all, she grasped one immense reality. This man the Universe—no, *God*—had forced into her life bore a name that, when its component parts were assembled, meant "Gift of a Loving God."

The Universe, Lucinda knew as few others did, operated on symbols and metaphors that revealed ever deeper levels of existence and meaning. Was that name such a metaphor? Was Dominic Adeodatus Amado a message from the Divine? Was he *the* message Lucinda had been waiting for her entire life? Or was he something else—a Trojan horse?

For a horrific moment, she entertained the idea that Nick might be one of her father's games—a means of testing her, of torturing her, of breaking her. She found comfort, oddly, in a passage of Christian scripture.

Every kingdom divided against itself is brought to desolation, Christ had said, *and a house divided against a house falls. If Satan also is divided against himself, how will his kingdom stand?*

Satan would have no means of manipulating Nick without corrupting him, and if there was one thing Lucinda knew, it was that Nick's heart was clean of her father's taint. The thought of him being corrupted by Lucifer filled her with a horror so deep and wide that it threatened to swallow her. She would rather, she realized, see him dead than subservient to her father's will.

He honked his horn as he drove past her up the street toward Lex. She turned and waved . . . and warded him against attack. She may not have known the human driver of that red Mercedes, but she was certain she must know whoever . . . or whatever . . . had possessed him.

The question was—which of several suspects was it?

CHAPTER THIRTEEN

Dan Collins was numb inside. Sitting in the NYPD cruiser with a blanket covering his shoulders, he'd tried to go back through the morning in his mind—tried to decipher the mystery of what had happened, but it was hard, like wading through molasses. He remembered the sound of Mona's weakening cries, the sound of the apartment door slamming open, the sound of policemen's voices. The swelling in his jaw reminded him painfully of being thrown to the floor, hands that grappled with him. He remembered Mona, lying on the floor next to him, a policeman already on his knees beside her.

He remembered the watch.

It was weird, but one moment Mona lying there like that had filled him with a huge, intense ache, a feeling of devastation, a desire to cradle her in his arms and murmur endless apologies. The next moment, all he could see was the watch she had given him. Rage welled up inside him, swamping the ache, the devastation, the regret, the love. Rage at the humiliation of not finding work, at not being able to support his family, of endless lines at the unemployment office, at the HHS office, at job fairs, at temp agencies. Rage at the way Mona silently did her better-than-you number on him.

She had work. For her getting work was easy. And she'd lord it over him in that smarmy, pious way of hers. Pretending she was putting him first, when it was ever only about letting him know that he wasn't man enough for her. That he was a failure as a husband and a father and a provider.

The rage had possessed him then, until it was all he could feel. Everything he'd ever felt for Mona, for Rowdy, for anyone else died with a whimper and Dan had fought. Everything had been taken from him—*every damn thing.* These thugs were not going to get his watch, too. He'd bucked, flailing with his legs, throwing the cops standing over him just long enough to grab the watch and shove it into the waistband of his briefs.

He'd let them cuff him after that, aware only of the strange chill of the watch pressed against his abdomen and the black, oily chaos in his head. He wasn't even sure who he was anymore. Somehow that had been taken away from him, too.

The cruiser came to a stop. Dan glanced up. They were in some sort of parking garage. An armed officer opened the door of the car and pulled him out. The guy was about his age, maybe a bit younger; his face was grim and his eyes were cold. Dan shivered; this cop had been the one who read him his Miranda rights. His partner—a woman with tightly braided blonde hair—came around the rear of the cruiser to grasp Dan's right arm. Her grip was like steel. Her eyes were even chillier than her partner's.

They hated him, he realized. Why did they hate him? He hadn't done anything wrong. He'd only been trying to make Mona realize . . . something. What was it? He couldn't remember now. Sorrow struggled beneath the numbness; he crushed it with a fist of anger. How dare they? Mona was his wife. *His* wife. She'd been disobedient; that's why he'd been disciplining her in the privacy of his own home. They had no right to stop him.

The watch tucked into the waistband of his briefs burned with an icy fire. He wanted to reach down and pull it out, but his hands were in cuffs and the officers to either side had hold of his arms as they marched him into the precinct and he couldn't reach it. It hurt.

Dan whimpered.

"What're you whining about, you dickwad?" muttered the male officer to his left.

"Hurts," he mumbled.

"Bet your wife hurts a lot more, you stupid SOB."

They took him to the booking room and all but threw him into a chair. The man—Officer Dobrovny, his name tag said—stood over him while his partner spoke to the booking officer and started his processing. He lost track of time—of everything—until they dragged him upright and took him to a counter where he was issued an orange coverall and told to hand all of his belongings over to the desk sergeant. They pulled the blanket from his shoulders and uncuffed one of his hands.

"All I got is my wedding ring," he said. His lips and tongue felt heavy, as if the muscles didn't work right.

"Take it off and give it to the sergeant," the woman said. "It's not like it means shit to you."

Dan peered at the nameplate over her badge. *Johansson.*

"You're hard," he told her.

"And you're a dirt bag . . . sir," she replied.

He took off his ring and set it on the counter, then dropped his hands to his sides and waited. Would they check him for the watch?

They didn't. They took him to a locker room. The male officer entered with him and watched as he changed into the coverall. Dan focused his entire attention on the watch. It had stopped burning so badly, but now his entire consciousness was bent on keeping it hidden. He palmed it when he removed his pajama bottoms and felt a flash of exultation as he reached for the orange coverall. These cops were stupid; they hadn't even noticed the damn watch.

"What's that?" Officer Dobrovny stepped forward and pointed at Dan's right hand.

His fingers had parted slightly and the watch chain glittered under the locker room's fluorescent lights. Dan hesitated.

"Open your hand, sir." The cop had his hand on his billy club.

Dan opened his hand. "It's . . . it's a watch." He stared at it. *To Daniel, with love.* "It was . . . it was my dad's."

Officer Dobrovny held out his hand, palm up. "Hand it over."

"I . . . I can't. I can't lose this. I have to keep it with me."

"Yeah. I can tell it's real special to you. Hand it over."

Dan glanced into the younger man's face. He was going to destroy it; Dan could read it in his eyes. Because he hated Dan and Dan valued the watch, the cop would destroy it. His fingers tightened around the silver case.

The officer's hand moved to his gun. "Hand. It. Over."

Given no choice, Dan did, and felt instantly bereft and angry. He wanted to call down the hosts of vengeance on this stupid cop for daring to take that watch from him. He wanted to jump him and take the watch back.

What happened next defied imagination. As his hand closed around the watch, a strange, blankness of expression rolled over Officer Dobrovny's face like an oil slick on a troubled pond. He frowned and lowered his gaze to the watch's gleaming case, going still as a statue. He cocked his head as if he were listening to something Dan couldn't hear.

Dan carefully climbed into his coveralls and zipped them up, his eyes never leaving the cop's face. Then he stood there, waiting for Dobrovny to do something. Say something.

The cop's jaw worked. Then, almost in slow motion, he unclipped the chain and fob from the watch and handed the watch back to Dan.

"Why?" Dan asked, savoring the cold rush of sensation that moved up his hand to his arm, to his heart, to his head. He put the watch into the breast pocket of his coveralls.

"Man should have something of his father's," the younger man said. He swallowed convulsively, and Dan knew there was a personal story behind that assertion.

"But I can't let you have the chain," Dobrovny went on. "Choking hazard."

He instructed Dan to hold out his hands and cuffed him again, adding a second set of restraints to his ankles. Then he escorted him to a jail cell.

Dan was okay with that. He had no place else to be, he supposed, and he could feel the chill of the watch over his heart, even through the fabric of his coverall.

⁕

Mona Collins regained consciousness in the ICU at Beth Israel Medical Center. Light flickered beneath her eyelashes. She heard the soft, familiar beep of a heart monitor, smelled the crisp, warm scent of pristine sheets. She opened her eyes slowly, letting in the filtered light from the room's single window a bit at a time.

How had she gotten here? Had she been in an accident of some kind? Fallen down the stairs? She'd caught her toe in the carpet at the top once or twice.

Eyes open as wide as she could get them (why didn't they want to open all the way?), she glanced around the small room. She was alone, but noticed there was a video camera in one corner of the ceiling. It hurt to move her eyes. When she closed them, her mind replayed her final conscious memory—Dan's face in the watch.

No, that had been a weird dream—a nightmare. Dan's face couldn't have been in the watch.

The memory cleared and became more urgent. No, his face hadn't been *in* the watch, it had been reflected in the watch's case as he stood over her in their living room. Her heart rate spiked at the memory; a light began flashing on the heart monitor to the left of her bed. Moments later, alerted by the monitor, a nurse and a doctor—both female—entered the room. The nurse was about Mona's age and wore a sympathetic smile; the young doctor was kind but businesslike.

"Glad to see you're back with us, Mrs. Collins," she said. "I'm Dr. Evelyn Chao. I'll be your attending physician while you're at Beth Israel."

"I wondered where I was," Mona whispered, her voice dry and weak.

The nurse left off checking her IV feeds and offered her a sip of water, which Mona accepted gratefully.

"Do you remember what happened?" Dr. Chao asked gently.

Mona tried to nod, but her neck felt stiff. She was wearing a neck brace, she realized. Oh, God, had he broken her neck? She fluttered her fingers and wiggled her toes.

The doctor seemed to read her sudden agitation, and laid a calming hand on one shoulder. "You're badly bruised and have a couple of dislocated and cracked ribs, some contusions and lacerations, a black eye, and a concussion. You'll be with

134

us for at least the rest of the week. We need to make sure the concussion isn't exacerbated. Jackie will be your nurse until around midnight."

The doctor checked her vital signs, had the nurse remove several of the IV stents and the oxygen tube, and ordered her some clear broth. Then she asked, "Do you have any questions?"

"What time is it?" Mona asked.

Dr. Chao checked her watch. "It's 11:30 A.M. You were unconscious for about twenty-eight hours. Now, I need to ask you a question: Is there someone we can contact for you? A family member, a friend? We've already advised your employer."

Mona thought of Rowdy. He might still be at Camp Lejeune, or he might be on his way to Kuwait. No, she couldn't do that. If Rowdy knew she was in the hospital, he'd want to come to her right away. That might end his career in the military before it had really begun. That left only one option, unsettling as it was.

"My husband . . ."

"I'm sorry, Mrs. Collins, but your husband is in jail and I think he's going to stay there for a while."

"Are you praying, son?"

Dan glanced up at the sound of the voice. The speaker was in the cell next to his—one he shared with another man of about the same age—maybe fifties or sixties. He wasn't sure what they were in for. Didn't much care.

He hadn't been praying; he'd been contemplating the watch. He lied. It became easier with practice. "Yes, sir. I was."

"That's good. Prayer will sustain you in this awful place."

"Yes, sir. I imagine it will."

"What's that, son?" the older fellow asked next, nodding at the watch that Dan was turning in his fingers. "A religious relic?"

"My father's watch." It became a game—a game you won by convincing the target that you were something you were not and hiding what you were really about.

The other man rose from his bunk and came to stand at the bars between the two cells. "May I ask your name, son?"

"Dan. My name is Dan."

"Why are you in jail, Daniel?"

Truth or lie? Which would be more satisfying? "I beat up my wife." There, it felt good to say it. Powerful.

The man seemed taken a bit aback by that. "May I ask why you did this thing?" he asked. His voice was gentle, sympathetic.

"I . . . I don't recall, to be honest. She did something I didn't like." He struggled to remember what that was. Why was remembering so hard? He dug into the memory. "Oh, she . . . was going to work and I didn't want her to. I was sick of her working. She just kept saying that she had to work—that she *wanted* to work. *I'm supposed to be the breadwinner, the head of the family. I'm supposed to be the one who decides who stays under our roof. She was supposed to stay home and take care of things.*"

The man was nodding. "That's God's plan. The woman is the helpmeet, not the master of the household. So, you asked your wife to stop working and she disobeyed you and you punished her? Is that right?"

"Hell, yeah."

"She committed the original sin, Daniel. She disobeyed her husband and thereby disobeyed God. Eve also disobeyed God and damned all mankind. It is not a sin that should go unpunished."

"Kind of ironic," Dan said. "She was the religious one. You'd think she'd get that. The police didn't get it either. They broke into our apartment and arrested me." (*The door slamming open. Shouting. Mona lying on the floor, bleeding . . .*)

"How long have you been here?"

"Days," Dan said. "I think."

"Days, and your wife still hasn't come to bail you out?"

"I'm still here, aren't I?"

Why hadn't Mona come to bail him out and tell the cops it was all just a big mistake? He thought he knew, but it was hard to remember. He put a hand to his head. Raked his fingers through his hair, clawed the memory out of hiding.

"They said I put her in the hospital." Dan's hand worked, squeezing the watch, turning it end over end. *She deserved it, too, the stupid bitch. Bringing her dumb brat into our house, throwing me out into the street. She chose her punishment when she chose her son over her husband.*

"How do you feel about that?" the man asked. He was damn nosy.

Dan turned his full gaze on him. "Like it was God's will."

The man smiled at him. "That is a refreshing thing to hear. Isn't it, Brother Samuel?"

He glanced back at his cell mate, who was still seated on his bed. The man nodded, though he didn't smile. He looked worn and weary—wrung out.

"Far too few people these days concern themselves with God's will. I'm Brother Morris, by the way. We—Brother Samuel and I—are elders of a religious community here in New York. The Nihilim."

Dan vaguely remembered hearing about the Nihilim on the news recently—some wild-ass story about witchcraft.

"So, you're both men of God, then. Pastors."

"We are men of God, but we don't believe in ordination by human authority. Our calling comes directly from our heavenly Father." His eyes rolled toward the stained ceiling of his cell. "We are ordained of God to prepare mankind for the end of the world."

Dan turned sideways on his bed to see Brother Morris's face better. "Pardon me for putting it this way, but if you're men of God, what the hell are you doing in jail?"

"We are accused of murder. But all we did was serve the Lord by removing evil from the world."

Dan's curiosity was piqued. "Yeah? What sort of evil?"

Brother Morris glanced pointedly at the security cameras in the outer corridor, then actually raised his voice to say, "A coven of witches was working its sorcery on the banks of the Hudson just south of our faith community. As I think of it now, I am certain that their spells were directed as much at us as they were at the city of New York. Brother Samuel's son saw them and warned his father. Together, we led a small army of the righteous to confront the witches. They tried to kill us first, but did not prevail. Brother Samuel smote one of them with an axe and ended their reign of terror. Now, the State of New York intends to prosecute *us* for protecting its citizens from Devil worshippers." He shrugged, managing to make it look like a ritual gesture of piety.

Dan rose and turned to face the zealot through the bars of their cells. He couldn't help but notice that Brother Samuel, still slumped on his bed, had buried his face in his hands and seemed to be crying silently. He ignored the coward.

"Then, you guys are just like me. You're under arrest for doing the will of God."

"Yes. That is correct."

"You're martyrs."

"Indeed."

Dan liked the idea of being a martyr, of being part of an army of the righteous, falsely arrested for doing the will of the Lord.

"You said something about the end of the world," he said. "Tell me about that. Tell me about the end of the world."

Brother Morris's eyes lit with zeal. "Have you ever heard of Armageddon, Daniel? It is the war to end all wars . . ."

CHAPTER FOURTEEN

"'And you will hear of wars and rumors of wars. All these things must come to pass, but the end is not yet. For nation will rise against nation, and kingdom against kingdom. And there will be famines, pestilences, and earthquakes in various places. All these things are but the *beginning* of sorrows.'"

Lucifer quoted the words slowly, as if savoring them. He was in what Rey thought of as his "war room," looking down through a huge round window onto the "map" of the world. The room wasn't really a room, of course; it was a place-less place in the Between. The window wasn't really a window; it was a shimmering portal through which the Devil could watch over his various plots. Nor was the map a map. It was the world itself, seemingly framed in Lucifer's portal.

Rey didn't like it here. Like its master, it refused to obey natural laws. Things here refused to be solid. They shifted and morphed in an endless train of forms in a space that changed imperceptibly in size and shape until you suddenly realized that you were looking at something that wasn't there a moment ago. That included the other beings. They were flickers, vapors; the sounds they made were whispers. Rey had the impression that they were in constant motion, but once in a while, they would suddenly assume some form—never even remotely human—then go to vapor again. Why they did this, Rey was never sure. All he knew was that if he tried to look right at them, they simply were not there. It was as if his eyes refused to see them. At this point in his insane existence he had simply given up trying.

The Devil himself was enveloped in a cloak of shifting darkness, from which his beautiful face gleamed, golden. No other human shape or features could be seen. It was a form that Rey found particularly unsettling. Knowing how Lucifer worked, Rey suspected that was probably why he'd chosen it for this interview.

Lucifer's radiant face turned toward Rey where he stood—or hovered, or just *existed*—as if in a willful mist, on the far side of Lucifer's window on the world. He shifted restlessly under the Devil's scrutiny, feeling as if ghost cats threaded them-selves around and between his legs and other *things* slithered or oozed or drifted by him. It was a creepy sensation that made him want to wriggle out of his skin.

He hated this no-place—hated the way that Lucifer summoned him here, just snatching him away from whatever he was doing in the real world. It gave him the willies . . . and worse. At least this was an audience he had requested—something he wouldn't have done if he hadn't felt it necessary.

Lucifer raised a smoky (or was it liquid?) appendage and gestured at the globe spinning silently below them. Wisps of night-black shadow tore away from him as he moved, to melt into the darkness of the ambiguous space.

"Do you have any idea of what's happening on the surface of that rat-infested planet? Don't you want to gloat just a little bit? You always were a man who enjoyed a good gloat."

Rey nodded. "Wars and rumors of wars. Famine. Pestilence. Yeah, I get it. We human beings are pretty worthless. God doesn't need to curse us; we're too bloody good at cursing ourselves."

"You *are* worthless. And stupid. And easily manipulated by your own animal desires. *You*, my friend, are the damned—*literally* damned—poster boy for human weakness. Men like you make my job easy."

As you take pains to remind me at every opportunity. "Can I ask you something? It's something I've been wondering since you—"

"Since I rescued you, Rey. You were moments from death. Moments from enlightenment. Moments from your karmic debt coming due."

Rey raised his hands. "I'd never deny that, Lord, and I'm grateful. Which is why I want to warn you that you may need to pay more attention to your little girl."

"Why should I need to, when you pay such excellent attention to her for me? Between you and Nathaniel, Lucinda is quite well watched. What is it you think I need to pay attention to?"

Rey dropped the idea of asking the Devil his question—which, in his fight-or-flight response, he'd forgotten. "In two words? Dominic Amado."

"The photojournalist. Yes, he's been swimming closer and closer to my banquet of bait. He seems not to have settled on a lure. Or perhaps the lure hasn't settled on him."

"I don't think his lure is in Lucinda's display cases, Lord."

The looming black presence rippled and its face turned toward Rey. "I know you've always fancied your tongue to be both glib and clever. You like to let your clever, glib tongue walk around things. Where it concerns Lucinda, I think it would be best for your tongue's continued existence if you'd arrive quickly at the point."

That was not a bluff. Rey knew, to his abject horror, that Hell was what you made of it and that the only thing worse than Hell was the enlightenment a soul must face on its way to Heaven. He remembered his crimes and his sins, and he had no desire to be held accountable for them. He told himself, again, that his subservience to Lucifer and his occasional "timeouts" in Hell—such as he conceived it—were a good bargain considering the alternative.

"Okay. In plain speak: Amado wants your girl. He had a thing for that watch that went to the Collins clan, but it's gone and he keeps coming back. He wants *her*."

"Why wouldn't he? My daughter is a supernaturally beautiful woman. He'd have to be blind or dead not to want her."

"It's not *his* wanting *her* that worries me, Lord."

Lucifer finally looked at Rey as if he actually saw him. "She wants him?"

"Praise the Lord, I got your attention."

Rey immediately regretted the words and the flippant tone. He took a step backward, knowing there was nowhere to go. Impatience with authority had been one of his failings in the army, as well. It had gotten him disciplinary action numerous times. If the war in Vietnam hadn't required so much cannon fodder, he'd probably have been drummed out of the corps long before the events that nearly cost him his life. Lucifer's disciplinary action made the US Army's look like a vacation in Tahiti.

Lucifer's smile was blinding, savage and terrifying. "There goes that glib tongue again. What do I have to do to make it stop?"

Rey held up both hands. "Okay, okay. I'll be plain. Lucinda's the ice queen when it comes to men. Even me—and you know better than anyone what sort of chops I have when it comes to persuading women I'm whatever they want in man. None of that's worked with Lucinda."

"Of course it hasn't. Lucinda's not like any of the women you've seduced. She's not like any woman on the planet—nor in the entire Universe. She can see almost entirely through you. What she can't see, she can't see because it's also hidden from you."

Rey forgot what he'd been going to say next. Something cold had slithered to attention in the back of his mind. "What? What do you mean—hidden from me?"

Lucifer's looming form rippled again, shedding more bits of itself into the gloom around them. They became part of the darkness, reminding Rey forcibly that—in some sense—he was standing in the mind of an unimaginably powerful being.

"Part of our deal, Rey. You serve me with all your chameleon guile and cleverness and I keep your soul and its inconvenient conscience in a bottle . . . as it were. Now, you were coming to a point."

Rey pushed past his sudden dread at the thought of his conscience being in a "bottle" in Lucifer's keeping (as opposed to simply *gone*). "My point is, she wants this guy. And as long as I've been around, she has never wanted anybody."

To Rey's surprise, Lucifer seemed pleased. He smiled and his golden eyes kindled. "I've waited millennia for her to show some spark of real human passion. As you said, she's an ice queen and she's been that way since she attained physical adulthood. Unexpected, but there it is. Now that she's experiencing desires she's willing to pursue . . ."

His smile deepened and the atmosphere around him suddenly teemed with strange, sentient shadows, as if someone had opened an invisible door and let in a bunch of see-through cats. Rey thought of them as Hellcats. He hated it when Lucifer brought them into the picture. He wasn't sure if they were real or just special effects. He didn't want to know.

Lucifer returned his attention to the shivering, amorphous portal, through which Rey could see the Earth. The planet was awash in the fiery hues the Devil used to mark his workings, simply because he enjoyed parodying human imagery. There was nothing of fire and brimstone in the real Hell. It was far more horrific than that.

"She feels it, Rey. She knows the Time is coming. Soon. Very soon."

"The Time," Rey echoed. "Are you talking about Armageddon? That whole millennial end of the world thing?"

What will happen to me when the world ends? That was the question he'd wanted to ask. Now he had another: *Why are you telling me this?*

"Look at the map. Do you see the small, bright white spots all over America, Australia, Europe, the Middle East, Asia?"

He did see them, though they were hard to pick out in some of the larger hotspots. "Yeah. I see them. What are they?"

"Those mark the highest concentration of millennial zealots, Rey. They are people whose belief in a coming global conflict between the forces of good and evil is as certain as my own. Their definition of 'good' is delightfully perverse and, unlike their more rational brethren, they are prepared to help the conflagration along. They come from every race, nation, and creed. There are few religious movements that have not been infested with them. And they are legion."

"Yeah. The lunatic fringe. They think science crawled out of Hell and that all the crap the world is going through is just signs from a wrathful God."

"All the 'crap' the world is going through—the Palestinian debacle, partisan politics, Sunni versus Shi'a violence, refugee crises, xenophobia, misogyny, climate change, general perversion—serves to convince those end of the world true-believers that they must be ready to move at the first appearance of a target worthy of their attention.

To put it in fundamentalist Christian terms, an Antichrist who will perform the great evil of doing angelic miracles and attempting to unite the people of the world in common cause. When they see that prophesied figure, they will be moved to act. And when they act, I win."

Lucifer was on fire with zeal now; more and more of the dark bits and pieces and shreds of himself tore away from his massive presence and cloaked the place in ever more shifting gloom. Rey felt as if a million slugs were crawling over his exposed skin, as if the atmosphere were pressing in on him, suffocating him. He tried to concentrate on what Lucifer had just told him.

"Wait a minute . . . are you saying . . . you're not saying that all this other stuff—climate change, for the love of— You're not saying that's just the *setup* for a bunch of tinfoil-wearing nut bars?"

Dark mirth rippled over Lucifer's face; lightning shafts of lurid red arced through his dark form. The shadows around him danced and writhed. "I'm oddly pleased at your complete surprise. 'All this other stuff,' as you put it, is the setup for Armageddon. A setup for the end of your unworthy species. Those tinfoil-wearing nut bars, Rey, are my army. My berserkers, my kamikazes, my cavalry, and my foot soldiers. Would you like to see them?"

Rey didn't, but that hardly mattered to Lucifer. In less time than it took Rey to blink, the portal showed a dizzying array of people from all over the globe. Some marched with placards proclaiming that God hated any number of things or people; some prayed—swaying in darkened sanctuaries; many wore face-covering masks and carried huge weapons that made Rey's old Vietnam-era M16 look like a popgun; some lived among other people; some lived apart in communes, in covens, in solitary fortresses. He was amazed at the sheer number of them and their diversity. They came in every color, spoke diverse languages, represented numerous different faiths and philosophies.

"Aren't they going to find it hard to work together? I mean, they're all so different."

"They have one great thing in common: their hatred of the concept of human unity. I once witnessed a race unity parade in a city in the deep South of the United States that had the most amazing effect on the Ku Klux Klan and a Pan-African group that was every bit as determined that the races—or at least those with dark and light skin—should be separate. It unified them in the face of the unifiers."

"The enemy of my enemy is my friend?"

"Exactly," Lucifer agreed. "Even now, the leadership of these doomsday groups is emerging all around the globe. All that remains is to turn up the heat and, when the time is right, produce the prophesied Enemy."

Despite his growing fear of what the end of the world might mean to him, personally, Rey was intrigued. "What does this have to do with Lucinda's love life?"

"I once thought that she might be the One herself. I raised her with that intention, but the problem with zealots is that they tend to be very dogmatic and literal in their thinking. It had somehow become the prevailing opinion that the Antichrist would be male. I spent centuries trying to identify the spirit of Antichrist with the Whore of Babylon, but the idea never really took hold. So be it."

For a moment, Rey thought Lucifer meant for *him* to be the Antichrist. It would be, he supposed, a promotion of sorts. His lord's next words burst his bubble.

"If Lucinda cannot be the Antichrist, then she shall be the mother of the Antichrist."

Rey felt a ripple of heat up the back of his neck. "With this Amado character as the father?"

"Don't be stupid. The father will be a human, but a human that I control." Lucifer smiled. "You."

Rey Granger felt as if he had just won the lottery.

※

Rowdy Collins had been in Kuwait for barely two days when his commanding officer called him into his office at the embassy and told him that his mother was in the hospital and his stepdad was in jail. The doctors at Beth Israel had hoped to release his mother after about a week in the hospital, but there had been complications arising from her concussion—some swelling of the brain. Not life-threatening, but needing extra care.

Rowdy's first impulse was to apply for a return to the States on hardship leave. His commander offered that to him, but he realized that if he went home on leave, he would always be short of either time or money for his mother's medical and other needs. Even at best, she wouldn't be able to return to her job for some time—what was she to do for housing and food? If he wasn't actively working, he had nothing to offer. He was committed—at least for the foreseeable future—to staying in Kuwait and doing what the US government was paying him to do.

Rowdy's commander helped him arrange for the bulk of his pay to go into his mother's bank account, but he knew that wasn't enough. His guilt at having left her alone with Dan settled in around him like a lead blanket. He should have heeded his instincts about his stepfather. He hadn't been kidding when he told his mom he knew the look of an abuser. He'd seen enough of them go through the post brig at Camp Lejeune.

Damn it, I should have taken her to Lejeune with me.

Shoulda, woulda, coulda. Mom had always said that when he was a kid regretting some stupid decision—or indecision. Besides, who was he kidding—she'd never have been willing to leave Dan. Not while there was a chance he was redeemable. Well, that ship had sailed. Dan had proven to be a different person than they'd thought he was.

Rowdy violently suppressed both the sting of betrayal and the urge to remember the Dan Collins of his childhood. He focused his full attention on his mother. She deserved the world and, stranded in Kuwait on a lance corporal's pay, Rowdy could not give it to her.

He called the hospital she was in and was allowed to talk to her. He could tell she was doped up, but she assured him she was in no pain. Just tired and dizzy.

"The doctor's hopeful I might be out in another week," she told him, "but I know I won't be able to go back to work for a while. I can go on disability, though."

"But Momma, that's only about two-thirds of your salary. Can you get by on that with the apartment and all?"

"Don't worry about that, Rowdy. My landlord's a great guy; he'll cut me some slack if I need it."

"At least you'll have one less mouth to feed," Rowdy said. "Do you know what's happening with Dan?"

She was quiet for a moment, then said softly, "I don't want to think about that. I don't want to think of Dan in jail—in prison."

He bit back what he wanted to say and told her about the arrangement he'd made for his pay. Of course, she tried to talk him out of it, but he told her it was done and done. She tired quickly, and he let her go with a feeling that he'd let her down. Maybe Dan was right about him. Maybe he was a failure.

Anxiety over his mother's condition affected Rowdy's ability to concentrate on his duties, and he began to feel as if he were failing his mother and his unit. Sometimes it was all he could do not to buy one too many beers when he went to the embassy's tiny NCO club. But the last thing in the world he wanted was to become like Dan. He stayed away from the club and beer, seeing both as too great a temptation, and counted it as a blessing that he was in a place where alcohol was off the menu pretty much everywhere else.

He was off duty, sitting in a Starbucks nursing a cappuccino early one evening, when he became suddenly hyperaware that someone was watching him. He brought his coffee cup up to his mouth and cast around over the rim to see if he could locate the watcher. He found the guy, at last, sitting alone at a table near the front window. The ruddy brightness of the setting sun completely obscured the man's features. Instinct told Rowdy that was intentional.

He lowered the coffee cup and stared right at the guy, expecting him to look away or get up and leave. He got up, but came right over to Rowdy's table and sat down across from him.

Now Rowdy recognized him—it was the recruiter from the Blackpool group, McLeod. He was in civvies, though Rowdy could see that he still wore dog tags—three of them. That was nonstandard. Rowdy wondered if he really was or had ever been military.

"Your sixth sense seems to be pretty well-developed, Corporal," the guy said.

"You were staring right at me, sir," Rowdy replied.

"You'd be surprised how many people don't notice that. A highly developed sense like that is worth a lot in our line of work. Our offer of employment is still open."

"I told you—"

"Yes, I know what you told me, Corporal. But I also know that your situation has changed somewhat. Your need is greater now, isn't it, son? Now that your mother is relying on you."

Rowdy stared at him. "How did you know about my mother?"

The question seemed to amuse McLeod. "It's the nature of our business to know things. Intelligence work is part of what we do. What *you* could do, if you'd sign on with us."

"I'm a Marine," Rowdy said. "I'm duty-bound to serve my country. I can't just quit like it was a nine-to-five job."

McLeod leaned toward him, elbows on the table. "You'd still be serving your country, Rowdy. In fact, you'd be serving in a capacity that stands a hell of a lot better chance of affecting change in this region than the status quo-keeping you're doing here just running embassy missions. Have you thought about what your job here entails? Being a messenger boy who takes 'packages' to warlords and corrupt officials and guards people whose personal politics and beliefs go against everything you believe in? You could be serving in a way that produces real results. You could change the world—not just for your mom, but for every person these eternal Middle East crises touch."

Rowdy had to own that some of his tasks seemed onerous. He'd already been assigned to a security detail for a Sunni official—a cabinet-level minister—who'd called for the violent crushing of recent Bidoon protests aimed at obtaining Kuwaiti citizenship. Rowdy had a natural affinity for the underdog and, in Kuwaiti culture—as cosmopolitan as it was—the Bidoon were definitely an underdog. They were considered *jinsaya*—"without nationality"—because they lacked any legal means of proving they belonged to the land or that it belonged to them. They weren't allowed to work at any but the most menial jobs and were forced to live in crowded, under-resourced housing projects.

Rowdy didn't see much difference between the attitudes of some Kuwaitis toward the Bidoon and the attitudes of the Nazis toward the Romany or of the KKK toward blacks. It had rubbed him the wrong way to have to be in service to Sheikh Malik al-Salim knowing what he did of the man's social views.

He realized he'd hesitated too long in responding to McLeod's last statement. It made it look like he might actually consider taking his offer. That was plainly impossible.

"I'm a Marine," Rowdy repeated firmly.

"And you'd stay a Marine. You'd retain your position in the embassy corps, but you'd be working undercover for Blackpool."

"Doing what?"

"Passing important intel to the people who need it—the people who need to make decisions."

"Intel about US operations?"

"No, about the foreign nationals you encounter. You might also receive special assignments where they're concerned."

Rowdy was confused and let it show in his face. "My commanding officer—"

"The commander of your unit will know in broad strokes what you're doing, but the specifics need to be relayed to me or to other assigned operatives in the organization. We can't afford to have intel breaches in these situations. The more people that know the details of an assignment, the more chance that there'll be a leak. Your commander's a good guy, as I'm sure you've already figured out. He won't ask you to reveal any specifics about your work for us."

It didn't pass Rowdy's notice that McLeod was talking as if he'd agreed to take the job with Blackpool. He thought back to his first night home—of Dan's blowing up at him for being a coward, for thinking small, for not taking good enough care of his mom. He shook the thoughts out of his head. Dan didn't matter anymore. He'd betrayed his trust to his family . . . but that didn't mean there wasn't a grain of truth to what he said.

It still felt weird to pledge allegiance to the Marines and then moonlight for this black ops group, but McLeod was right—Captain Russell was a good guy. He'd been incredibly supportive in the situation with Rowdy's mom.

It was his thoughts turning back to his mother that decided him. With the money he earned on Blackpool's payroll, he could take care of anything she needed.

When he came home to the States, he'd set her up in a nice house wherever he was stationed.

"Okay," he told McLeod. "I'll sign on. Where do we go from here?"

"I'll send you further instructions through another operative in your unit. He'll make himself known by showing you one of these." He held the odd dog tag on his chain between thumb and forefinger and turned it so it caught the light from the fixture over the table.

Rowdy realized it was set in a brass bezel.

"I've never seen a dog tag like that—in a frame."

"Blackpool ID. The brass frames are from melted-down bullet casings, each with its own story. You'll earn one of these yourself one day." McLeod rose and held out his hand.

"Welcome aboard, Rowdy. Happy to be serving with you."

They shook hands, then McLeod wended his way through the tables to the door and out into the fiery gleam of sunlight, where he put on a pair of shades and walked out of sight.

Rowdy watched him go, wondering what the hell he'd gotten himself into.

✦

About fifteen feet from his car, Anderson McLeod pulled out his cell phone and tapped an icon on its startup screen that activated a security scanner. He smiled wryly; yes, there was an app for that, though it was used by a very narrow demographic.

Satisfied that no one had bugged or booby-trapped his car in his absence, McLeod got in and closed the door. Then he tapped a number into the phone's keypad and waited.

The recipient picked up on the third ring. "Darzi."

"McLeod," he identified himself. "Good news. We've got the last man."

148

"What's this?" Brittany Anders peered at the thumb drive her assistant, Terry, held out to her.

"A backup of my laptop the day all hell broke loose at DC&P," he told her. "I found it at the bottom of that last box I unpacked."

Brittany folded her hands under her chin and looked up at him from beneath her lashes. "Forget for a moment that I'm the all-seeing, all-knowing woman behind the curtain and explain—as if to a small child—why this is significant."

Terry sat down in the blocky oak 1980s side chair next to Brittany's equally outdated desk and set the thumb drive down next to her computer. "Okay. Here's the deal: the last thing you did before you checked out of DC&P was to send me the Redmon case files with attachments. So far so good?"

Brittany nodded.

"I back up my e-mail several times a day onto that little, inconspicuous thumb drive just in case the office burns down—which seems a lot more likely to happen here than at our previous digs."

That, Brittany thought, was demonstrably true. The offices of the nonprofit she and Terry had come to roost in were in an aging six-story brick building in Queens. Legal Outreach's digs took up a quarter of a city block, but were a far cry from the opulent offices of their previous employer. She picked up the thumb drive, slowly disengaging from the case file she'd been working on as she realized the significance of what he was saying.

"You've got the attachment on here?" She didn't have to say which attachment she meant. There was only one that mattered: the red flag e-mail that implicated Brant Redmon in insider trading . . . and thereby implicated DC&P in a cover-up. Her heart kicked into overdrive as she pulled the cap off the drive and plugged it into her laptop's USB port.

Terry smiled. "She catches on fast, she does."

"But I thought you didn't have time to—"

"Neither did I. I mean, in all the hullabaloo, I just dumped my stuff into boxes and bugged out. I remembered the flash drive, but honestly, I thought I'd left it behind on my desk. I must've knocked it into the box I was packing."

"Just accidentally knocked it in there, huh?"

"I'm serious, Brit. Trust me—if I'd known I had that piece of evidence, I'd've given it to you before you met with that journalist."

Brittany opened the thumb drive, found the mail archive, and unpacked it. Her heart was racing as she scanned the e-mails . . . and found it. It was there. It was really there, in black and white pixels. She held up her right hand palm out and Terry gave her a high five.

It was time to make another appointment with Dominic Amado.

⬧

Janine wiped the mascara from her cheeks and wondered if she should even bother putting her eye makeup back on. The interview with the DA had been exhausting. There was so much to say and so much she *couldn't* say because nobody would believe her. Not her parents, not the district attorney, not the police—nobody.

She and Stevie had, at first, said they were just on the beach having a girls' night out, but the presence of the white robes complicated things. So, they'd been forced to admit that they were "playing" at being witches and that the folks from upriver took exception to that and thought they were real witches. After that admission, it wasn't necessary to say anything about the river rising from its banks or turning into a voracious vortex. Janine and Stevie had both, by tacit agreement, described only what they'd seen and heard from human agencies.

The men had shown up looking like something out of a bad Frankenstein movie and scared the bejeezus out of the girls. Stevie had run off to call for help. Mags and Janine had been unable to get away before they were surrounded.

Then it was all on Janine to describe how one of the cultists—a kid younger than she—had grabbed Mags and wouldn't let her go, and how Mags had tried to fight him and how some guy with an axe had—

She never could get past that part without breaking down in incoherent sobs. It was so fresh in her mind. She couldn't close her eyes without seeing the kid and Mags and the guy with the axe silhouetted against the fire. The axe head gleaming in the firelight and Mags going down in a spray of blood. Some of the blood had gotten on Janine's robe and on her face and in her hair. She'd showered for an hour as soon as they let her.

She sat in her room now, feeling bruised inside, and not sure what to do next. Mags Stuyvesant wasn't a bosom buddy—Janine had damn few of those—but she was a friend of sorts, and Janine had liked her for her prickliness and her blue hair and the way she bucked authority. And for sticking up for her occasionally.

Now she was dead. Horribly, wrongly, dead.

The Book of Shadows sat on the chair by Janine's bed, underneath a paisley wool shawl she had tossed there to cover it. She could just see one corner of the binding from where she sat on the bed. No one knew about it except for her and Stevie.

It had all started with the book, she realized. Her ability to do real magic, her sense of power and destiny. Without the book, she and Stevie and Mags would still be doing parlor tricks in Stevie's basement "girl cave." They would still be just *playing* at being witches.

Maybe, if she got rid of the BOS . . .

Sudden voices filled her head. Insistent whispers that were wordless, but urgent, telling her to protect the book at all costs. She'd heard the voices ever since that night at the river. They scared her, because they made her feel as if she were connected to the book in ways she didn't understand. As if it called to her blood—not her father's blood, which had come from his Mediterranean ancestors, but her mother's, which was English-Irish. She had once reveled in the idea that she might actually be related to Morgan le Fay; now the idea terrified her.

She stood, impulsively resolute. She had to get rid of it. That was the only way to be safe.

The whispers grew more insistent, hissing gibberish in her mind. She rubbed at her ears as if that could make the voices stop. It didn't. She tried a remembered snatch of scripture: *Yea, though I walk through the valley of the shadow of death, I will fear no evil, for thou art with me.*

That was it. That was all she could remember. So she repeated it, over and over. "Yea, though I walk through the valley of the shadow of death, I will fear no evil . . ."

Janine moved to the chair. The voices shrieked at her.

She said the verse louder: "Yea, though I walk . . ."

She mustered every scrap of herself that she could, then reached down, hastily wrapped the book in the shawl, and bundled it into her arms, careful to let no part of it touch her flesh. She wasn't sure why that was important, but she knew it was.

She slipped out of her room and stood on the upstairs gallery, listening to the murmur of voices from downstairs. Her mom and dad were still talking to the district attorney in the living room. If she were very quiet, she could reach the foyer and slip into the kitchen and out the back door without anyone being the wiser.

She made it to the bottom of the staircase without incident, hyperaware of the dialogue going on in the living room just to the right of the front hallway. She was about to turn the corner to head back to the kitchen when she looked up and saw her little sister standing on the upstairs landing. Janine's heart rate skyrocketed.

"Go back to bed, Judy, or I'll tell Mom," she whispered, making a shooing motion.

Judy stared at her bug-eyed, then scurried back to her room.

Janine held absolutely still for a moment, not even daring to breathe, but realized that there'd been no change in the cadence of conversation from the living room. Then she headed for the kitchen, as swiftly as possible.

She didn't realize how cold it was until she opened the back door and the wind hit her. She hesitated, but told herself this had to be done. She had to get rid of the book. The question was, where? That was when she remembered the mill. If she could throw the book into the waterwheel, it would be crushed.

She began to walk. She'd gotten to the end of her street when her cell phone went off in her pocket, scaring her nearly out of her skin. She checked the number, then answered.

Stevie started talking before Janine could even get a word out. "How'd the thing with the DA go?"

"Okay, I guess. They made me go over it again." Janine turned and headed down the hill toward Broadway.

"It's freaky," Stevie said. "Those religious whack-jobs are actually telling the truth, but no one in the freaking DA's office will believe a word of it. The book is still safe, right?"

Janine's steps faltered. Why'd she have to ask about the damned book?

"It's—it's right here," she said.

"I was thinking maybe I should keep it at my place. I mean, I bought it, after all, and I wasn't a firsthand witness to . . . you know, so they're not on top of me like they are you."

Janine stopped at Broadway to consider which direction to go. To her left was the parking lot of the historical Philipsburg Manor—still lit, but empty of cars. If she went that way, she'd have to cross the causeway to get to the mill. To her right was Pierson Avenue and a back entry to the property. If she went that way she'd have to make her way past the manor and the other outbuildings . . . but she'd be shielded from the street.

She looked both ways and crossed at the crosswalk, briskly, as if the swirls of wind nipping at her feet were tiny, invisible demons.

"Janine? Are you still there?"

"Uh. Uh, yeah. I'm here. Look, Stevie, I've been thinking. About the book. I think it's dangerous. It got Mags killed and it—I mean, the stuff I was doing . . ."

"You weren't the only one doing stuff, Janine."

That was bogus, but now wasn't the time to argue about who had the power. "No, I know, but . . . Here's the thing. I really think we should get rid of the book—"

"What do you mean get rid of it?" Stevie's voice rose nearly to a shriek. "You can't freaking get rid of it! I *bought* that book, damn it! It cost me over ten grand. D'you have any idea what would happen if my parents found out I blew my college spending money on a witch's manual that I didn't even have to show for it?"

Janine stopped walking and felt the cold wind catch up with her and wrap around her like a shroud. She shivered convulsively. "Stevie, Margaret is dead. *Dead* because of this thing."

"No, she's dead because of a bunch of religious weirdos who damn well deserve whatever happens to them. I'll take the book. I'm almost to your place now."

"You're not home?" That was a relief. It meant there was no one to overhear their conversation from Stevie's end.

"No, I . . . felt like a caged animal. Felt like something bad was about to happen. Which I guess wasn't too far off if you're talking about getting rid of the BOS. I'm just out driving around. I'm on DeVries."

DeVries? Janine panicked anew. Stevie was coming toward the old manor from the opposite direction. If she didn't hurry, she'd be caught out in the open. She started to run now, irrational terror making her heart beat faster than she thought possible. She hit the corner and turned left onto Pierson. There were a couple of old farm roads—blocked against cars—that led into the manor grounds. One went past the barn right to the old mill.

Stevie said, "Tell you what—stick the BOS in a bag with some other books. We can say I need them for a school assignment or something. I'll drop by and pick it up."

It was Janine's turn to feel like a caged animal—caught in a snare of her own making. If Stevie showed up at her house, her parents would realize she'd gone out. But if she told Stevie where she was headed . . .

"I'm not at home. I'm . . . I'm out walking. Trying to think."

"Where's the book? Tell me and I'll go to your place and get it."

"No! My parents are, like, wigging out right now. The DA was still there when I left. You don't want to walk into that."

"Then meet me somewhere. We'll figure it out."

"There's nothing to figure out, Stevie. No one's going to believe I really did witchcraft, okay? No one is going to be looking at us. We're the victims. That gives us a chance to get rid of this damned thing—"

"You *bitch*! You've got it with you! Where are you? *Tell me where you are!*" Stevie's voice was raw with rage and fear.

Janine hung up on her, then stared at her cell phone as if her "friend" might leap from it to throttle her. She shoved it into the pocket of her jeans. She needed to get off the road. She ran four or five more yards along Pierson and saw the reflectors on the gate that blocked the gravel road leading into the manor. Every car that passed by made her cringe and pull farther onto the shoulder of the road, glad she was wearing a dark sweater.

Just another couple of yards and she reached the gate. She tossed the book over onto the mill road, then climbed the gate and dropped to the other side. She allowed herself one darting glance back at the headlights on Pierson before she snatched up the Book of Shadows and ran toward the dark, looming rooftops of the estate outbuildings.

The last time she'd taken this path, Stevie and Mags had been with her, and they had all but tiptoed along the narrow road, trying not to giggle. They'd carried the book wrapped in a piece of silk, and a carved wooden box filled with the implements of witchcraft—quarter candles, feathers, salt, cups (chalices, they called them), even holy water that Mags had snatched from her church. They'd talked about making wands.

Things had been so different then. Janine had felt happy and purposeful and certain that her future would be brilliant. Now . . . now everything seemed dark and horrible and she wanted to cry.

From across the manor's vegetable gardens, she saw the profile of the mill in silhouette against the lights of the empty tourist parking lot on the other side of the millstream. She ran past the barn and gardens, cut behind the old manor house, and darted across the yard between it and the mill. She was panting by the time she stumbled into the deep shadows in the lee of the two-story structure, her breath coming in steaming little puffs. She leaned heavily on the wooden railing that overlooked the millpond and waterwheel.

The wheel was dormant now, with most of the milldam's gates closed. For a moment, Janine despaired. She'd been hoping to throw the book into the wheel's gears. She sagged against the causeway railing in defeat. What had she been thinking? This whole effort was useless, senseless. She couldn't destroy such a valuable artifact. It wasn't hers to destroy. It belonged to Stevie. Maybe she should just call the other girl and have her come get it.

No, she couldn't just give up. The book was dangerous. It had gotten Mags *killed*, for God's sake. She peered down at the dark water. She could just throw it in. It would sink like a stone, it was so heavy.

She lifted it to the railing, her heart beating so hard it sounded like someone pounding on wood.

"Janine, you *bitch!* Don't you *dare* destroy that book! It's *mine!*"

Janine spun toward the causeway. Stevie was racing toward her across the wooden bridge, her face contorted with rage, her long blonde hair flying like a banner behind her.

Janine froze, her mind spinning frantically. She froze just long enough to allow Stevie to reach her, to lay hands on the book and try to pry it from her grasp. Janine came to herself on a tide of cold adrenaline. She gripped the book tighter, wrapping her arms around it.

"Let go! *Let go!* Let. Go! " Stevie shrieked at her—pushing, tugging.

She fought back. "Stevie, listen! *Listen!* This thing is evil! That's not what witchcraft is about! It's not about doing evil!"

"Shut up, you stupid twit! This is *mine!* It's mine! Give it to me, or so help me God, I'll kill you!"

Stevie let go of the Book of Shadows and lunged at Janine, digging her fingers into Janine's throat. Off balance, Janine fell heavily against the railing of the causeway. Fear exploded in her head as her wind was cut off. She did the only thing she could think of—she cast a spell.

If you will, Lord, give me mastery over air!
I call Your Name! I call Your Name!
Your Name is He Who Hurls—

"The Wind!" she gasped aloud, and let go of the book with her right hand long enough to hit Stevie with the full force of her will.

Janine's wind roared, lifting the other girl and flinging her backward as if pulled by a wire. The causeway railing caught her just below the knees and flipped her, end over end, into the upper millpond. She landed with a splash that cut short her scream of rage.

Janine was struck by a one-two punch of guilt and relief. She had no time for either; no time to see if Stevie was okay. The water where she'd fallen was shallow—she'd be fine. The water on the other side of the causeway into which Janine threw Morgan le Fay's Book of Shadows was much deeper. She hung over the railing, watching the BOS sink into the weedy water, its passing illuminated by the lamp at the corner of the mill house.

To Janine's astonishment and fear, the water boiled where the book had disappeared, whipped to frothy whitecaps.

I didn't do that, she thought. *I did not do that.*

She heard the sound of Stevie splashing her way out of the upper millpond behind her. It galvanized her. She ignored the boiling water and ran—across the causeway, toward the well-lit parking lot and home.

She got home without further incident and spent several moments silencing her wracking sobs and regaining control over her ragged breathing. She let herself in the back door and into the dimly lit kitchen as silently as she could. Her throat hurt. She pulled the collar of her sweater up around her neck and went to the fridge to get something to drink. Her face felt overheated; the cold air from the refrigerator cooled and calmed. She relaxed a bit.

"Janni?"

Janine let out a startled yip and turned to see her mother standing in the kitchen doorway. "Mom! You scared me." Her voice sounded raspy and weird.

"Are you all right? I thought you'd gone to bed."

"I . . . my throat was dry from all the talking. I wanted something to drink. I'll go to bed after that."

"Good. You look so worn out, you poor thing. I hope this is the last visit we'll have from the DA's office for a while. At least until the hearings get underway."

She watched Janine get out a carton of orange juice and fetch down a cup to pour it in, then crossed the room to put an arm around her, resting her cheek against Janine's hair.

"I know this is horribly selfish of me, but I thank God every day it wasn't you that was killed by those . . . those monsters. I don't care what you were doing out there. It didn't deserve what they did." She hesitated, looking down into Janine's face. "Oh, honey, you're shivering!"

Janine realized the truth of that. Her hands were shaking. She put down the orange juice. Her mom picked it up and poured some into her cup.

"It's just—" Janine began, feeling tears begin to come. "This whole thing . . . Mom, it's so awful." *You can't even imagine how awful.*

Her mom put the orange juice into her hands, then stood and watched her drink it, stroking her hair. When she was done, her mother took the cup from her hands and put it into the dishwasher, then walked her up to bed just like she'd done when Janine was Judy's age. As she hugged her Mom good-night and got into bed, she began to believe that maybe, now, things would be all right.

In the morning, they learned that Stevie Halleck had drowned in the Philipsburg millpond.

CHAPTER SIXTEEN

Peter the Summoner of Holyhaven spent late nights at his laptop and had located a number of other groups of believers using social media. He was surprised at how many there were. Surprised and grateful. True, some of the groups had truly bizarre beliefs—a couple were convinced that aliens would play some part in the End Times, perhaps joining the Battle of Armageddon in their spaceships. Some believed that Jesus had not really been human in any sense of the word, but rather an angel made to seem like a man. Others believed that Jesus was God Himself, rather than the Son of God, while others differed only in which other religious groups or countries or organizations currently on Earth represented the evil figures in the Revelation of Saint John.

It didn't matter, Peter told himself. It had bothered him at first, and he had subjected each group he found to a sort of purity test. He no longer did that for several reasons. For one thing, the gleaming angel had not told him to insist on doctrinal purity. He had only said Peter should summon other groups—but there were no other groups entirely like the Nihilim.

Then, too, the situation for the men of Holyhaven was dire. The district attorney and the witches' parents had gone on the warpath against them and undertook to persecute them through the court system. It was strange, Peter thought, because when his father and the other elders of the Nihilim had talked about the coming persecutions and the inevitable war against the Righteous, they had preached a material, physical war—a war with weapons of men and demons pitted against the weapons of angels and the Nihilim.

Peter had imagined it as a glorious battle with rank upon rank of angels marching down out of Heaven along ladders of light and driving golden chariots drawn by winged horses. The handful of faithful Righteous would be drawn up to Heaven and granted their full invincibility so they could smite the faithless people of the Earth.

Never in a million years would Peter have suspected that the demons of Hell would attack God's people through the Westchester County District Attorney's office. They had been zealous before about convicting the Nihilim Elders of murder, but since a second witch had died (Peter suspected the hand of God in that), they were ready to destroy everything that the Elders had built up. They were even now investigating the Holyhaven charter school, and he feared they would take all of the children and put them into the public school system—and worse, foster care. None of the women of Holyhaven worked at a trade, and the farming and crafts they did only provided the community with a small portion of its annual income. The bulk of the community's revenue had disappeared along with the majority of its men.

There were a couple of wealthy contributors to the community coffers—older believers who had large fortunes and little use for them except to expend them in the service of the Lord. Peter had to marshal those resources, too. He *would* marshal them. If the witches could call down demons and sorceries and criminal judgment, Peter the Summoner could call down angels and miracles and divine retribution.

Peter put the finishing touches on a message he'd written for a sovereign citizen Facebook page and posted it. Then he closed his laptop and knelt in prayer.

✦

Ibrahim Darzi had risen with the sun, performed his ablutions, and done his morning prayers. He looked forward, this day, to reading and meditating upon the verses of the Qur'án, which he would read from what he had come to think of as the ibn Rušd Qur'án. Before he could allow himself that pleasure, however, he had a more worldly duty to perform—a meeting with an operative that could be put off no longer.

He received Kalim al-Maroc in his private home office. He had been picked up and brought there by a cab driver—also one of Darzi's operatives—and he had an official reason for his visit. He was petitioning Darzi for support for the inclusion of the Bidoon in general society and the acknowledgement of their rights to be Kuwaiti citizens. This reason was not merely official, it also had the benefit of being true.

The two men exchanged greetings. Darzi had mint tea served in graceful glasses, then spoke of the mission.

"I received word from my American contact," Darzi said. "We will proceed."

Maroc's gaze flickered and he blinked several times before nodding solemnly. "I understand. Do we know when?"

"Not yet. I am waiting for confirmation from an associate as to the date and time. But the place, we know. It will send a strong message."

Maroc nodded again, and Darzi could see the zeal rising in his eyes. "Yes. A strong message—that we Bidoon will no longer be treated like animals, denied even the dignity of citizenship. Decades, we have waited to be heard. We have spoken out;

they have ignored us. We have petitioned; they have ignored us. We have protested; they have ignored us. After this, they will ignore us no longer. They will listen."

Darzi's smile was grim. "Indeed, they will have no choice. Now, let us go over the plan. Step through it for me."

Kalim al-Maroc set down his tea glass and leaned forward in the ornately carved chair. "When I get the call, I am to drive my vehicle to Seif Ad Dawlah Street and await the motorcade. As it passes, I am to pull in front of the hind-most car, which will extinguish its lights and withdraw. I will, in this way, enter the grounds of the National Assembly . . ."

Darzi listened as Maroc walked through the entire scenario . . . as he knew it. He recited it without error. He left then, his step confident, his eyes still alight with the zeal of the righteous.

"Forgive me, my friend," Darzi murmured at the closed door Maroc had just exited. "Your reward will be in Heaven."

He shook his head. Would that this whole scheme were not necessary. Would that he did not have to have secrets upon secrets or to use Kalim al-Maroc and his cause so. He told himself that what was good for the Shi'a would be also good for the Bidoon, in the long term. A stronger Shi'a presence and voice in government would grant the Bidoon allies that would not forget al-Maroc. More than that, the treacherous sheikh would be gone, and his anti-Bidoon, anti-Shi'a policies and programs with him. That blame would fall on the Bidoon was inevitable, but Darzi would make the case that an entire people should not be punished for one man's sin. If ridding the world of such a man as Sheikh Malik al-Salim led to a wider sectarian conflict, then so be it.

Ibrahim Darzi took a deep breath, whispered a brief prayer, then went to the glass case in the corner of the office in which he had placed the ibn Rušd Qur'án. He reached into the pocket of his suit and fished out a set of prayer beads attached to which was a small silver key. He used it to open the case, and removed the closed book, which he lifted to his lips to kiss the cover.

He moved to a small reading table next to the case across which fell the muted light of dawn, filtered through a long, narrow stained glass window. He seated himself at the table, laid the book upon it, and opened it randomly and with great care. He smiled in anticipation of the verse he would read and the great philosopher's commentary upon it.

It opened to a verse in the *surah* of The Cow that Ibrahim Darzi knew well. The heart of it was invoked by both Muslim and infidel—invoked to defend and to attack al-Islam. The verse read: *And slay them wherever you find them, and drive them out from where they have driven you out, for persecution and oppression are worse than slaughter.*

Yes, he thought, *better to kill one man than to suffer thousands or even millions to be oppressed.*

Now, he was moved to read the passage in context with what came before and after it, so as to get a more nuanced understanding. He read:

Fight in the cause of God against those who fight you, but do not begin hostilities; for God does not love aggressors. And slay them wherever you find them, and drive them out from where they have driven you out; for persecution and oppression are worse than slaughter; but fight them not at the Sacred Mosque, unless they first attack you there; but if they attack you, slay them. Such is the reward of those who suppress faith. But if they cease, God is Oft-forgiving, Most Merciful. And fight them on until there is no more persecution or oppression, and justice and faith in God prevail. But if they cease, let there be no hostility except against those who practice oppression.

Darzi pondered the words of the Prophet for a moment. Pondered what it might be like when there was no more persecution or oppression of the Shi'a minority in Kuwait and Saudi Arabia. Men like Sheikh Malik al-Salim would not rise to such positions of power. Would not be in a position to wreak horrific damage on that minority. Darzi had, for many years, trusted in democracy to bring about justice for the religious and ethnic minorities in Kuwait. He trusted in it no longer, for democracy had brought Salim to power and kept him there.

He brought himself back from the verge of arousing his hatred of Salim—a futile indulgence now and, soon, an unnecessary one—to read ibn Rušd's fine, tight script in the margins of the illuminated page. So beautiful was the calligraphy that it brought tears to Ibrahim Darzi's eyes. It looked ornamental, but he anticipated that the words would be more than that.

"*God does not love the aggressor,*" ibn Rušd had written. *How simple the words, and yet so difficult to fit into the world of men. For we see oppression at every turn and lose track of who or what is the enemy of our faith.*

He had underscored the word "faith" with a flourish, which set Darzi to pondering why he might have done so. Perhaps the next words would be illuminating.

Is the infidel to be found among the People of the Book—among Jews and Christians? Perhaps, but so are the brother and sister. (Here, the philosopher included a reference to another verse in the same *surah,* which Darzi noted.) *And what is our faith? Is it not summed up in this verse?*

Here was another reference—one that Darzi knew, for it had been the first passage he had ever read from this Qur'án when he was in the nameless bookshop on Oman Street. It was *Al-Mâ'ûn*—Small Kindnesses.

Do you see the one who belies religion? Such is the one who harshly repulses the orphan, and encourages not the feeding of the indigent. So, woe to the worshippers who neglect their prayers, those who wish to be seen of men, but refuse to do small kindnesses.

Darzi read the last of ibn Rušd's annotation, wondering at the philosopher's placement of that reference.

Ibn Rušd wrote: *If this care for the orphan and the indigent, this observance of our prayers, this performance of kindness, is the heart of Islam, is this not what we slay—along with our perceived enemies—when we fail to reckon ourselves the aggressors? When this aggression is against our brethren in the Faith of God, can it be said that justice and faith prevail?*

Darzi sat back from the Qur'án in astonishment. Here was a Sunni who doubted the actions of the leaders of his own faith. One who considered the deaths of Shi'as a breach of that faith. No, more than that—a *slaying* of faith. The thought was . . . well, gratifying. Darzi wondered if Minister Salim was aware of the sentiments of this great Sunni scholar. He wished there were some way he might share this with his enemy before he sent him to Hell.

Smothering, again, the smoldering embers of rage, Ibrahim Darzi looked up the first referenced verse in ibn Rušd's notes. It was also in the second *surah*. He read:

Those who believe in your revelation, Muhammad, and those who are Jews, and Christians, and Sabaeans—any who believe in Allah and the Last Day, and work righteousness, shall have their reward with their Lord; they shall not fear, nor shall they grieve.

Darzi felt a small, burning sensation in his heart of hearts. Was this Sunni philosopher speaking to him across the centuries? Were these notes from a long-dead academician *censuring* him? The message seemed clear: to his Sunni coreligionists ibn Rušd was saying that those they perceived as enemies were, in reality, their brothers and sisters in the faith, and that when they slew them, they slew the faith of God and belied His cause.

He shut the book. It was foolishness. He was being fanciful. Worse, he was allowing some deep reluctance to do what must be done to whisper uncertainties to his soul.

It must be a test. Allah was testing him to see if he had the courage of his convictions. To see if he could be dissuaded by fancy. Sheikh Malik al-Salim must be dealt with before he could turn his attention from the Bidoon and focus it on the more populous Shi'a minority.

Darzi told himself those things, but his hands shook when he put the Qur'án back into its glass case.

CHAPTER SEVENTEEN

Many people since the dawn of human consciousness had wished they could be the fly on the wall during a particularly interesting meeting. Lucinda actually *could* be a fly on the wall if she so desired, but flies had a negative connotation in her mind. They were, after all, associated with a biblical plague that—when all was said and done—showed more the hallmarks of her father's handiwork than God's.

She was a moth. A tiny, almost invisible, white moth perched in a pool of light in the Gramercy Star Cafe. She was scheduled to meet Nick there in roughly half an hour, but—thanks to Nathaniel—she had gotten wind of an earlier meeting he was having with Brittany Anders. This was interesting, because it hinted that Brittany had found that telltale bit of evidence against Brant Redmon and her former employer . . . or that she just wanted to see Nick again. That wasn't hard to imagine. Lucinda found the unfamiliar tickle of jealousy bemusing. If this was part of the human experience, she did not much care for it.

Brittany, however, was completely focused on the evidence her assistant had uncovered. She set the thumb drive on the table in front of Dominic and then told him, in a low voice, what was on it.

He started to pick it up, then paused and looked up at the lawyer. "Shouldn't you be showing this to the DA's office?"

"I should, and I will. But I know for a fact that the partners have friendlies in the DA's office. I don't want it to get buried. So, what I'd like to do is give you full access to it. In fact, I want you to have a copy. I want you to write an exposé. That way, if the DA's office doesn't want to pursue it—or even if they do . . ."

Dominic nodded. "Plan B."

"Exactly. I've made a copy of it, of course. This one is for you. There's also this—something one of the partners said: that Redmon wanted the money from the investments for some sort of project in the Middle East. Qatar or Kuwait, Aaron said, though he didn't sound completely sure. There's a personal statement from me on the drive, too. And of course, I'm available if you need more detail before you decide to get involved with this."

Dominic nodded again. "I'll look at it first thing in the morning. I . . . uh . . . I have a date in about half an hour."

Brittany laughed. "A date? I haven't been on one of those in a while. My last almost-relationship ended rather badly." She tapped the thumb drive with a fingernail.

"You were close to someone at DC&P?"

"Close, but no cigar," she said. "For which I thank God every day. Turns out, he was married." She smiled ruefully, then got up, shouldered her purse, and left.

Lucinda flitted away into the night, then came through the front door dressed in slim black pants and a cream cable-knit sweater nearly the color of her moth wings. She felt only as much cold or heat as she wanted to, so a coat was only necessary for appearances. She doubted Dominic would notice.

But he did.

"Lucinda!" He rose as she slid into the seat across from him. "You're early. You didn't go out without a coat, did you?"

"I'm just down the block."

"You came straight from the shop?"

"No, from my apartment. It's over on Seventy-Second. About two and a half blocks from Central Park."

"Wow, I'm impressed. An almost–Central Park address."

She shrugged. "It's an older building. Kind of art deco. I like it. I have a garden. It's . . . my sanctum."

They talked for a while about Nick's church and the Rendóns, about the progress of the community garden. They talked about books.

"What's your favorite thing you've ever read?" he asked.

"*Something Wicked This Way Comes*," she answered without hesitation or irony. "I love the opening paragraphs. The evocative language about October and witches and bedsheets. Halloween has always been my favorite holiday. What about you? What's your favorite read?"

"*The Haunting of Hill House*. I think the first paragraph is amazing. Funny, I would've thought you'd read old-world fantasy. King Arthur, Morgan le Fay—that sort of thing."

She glanced at him, a shiver building between her shoulder blades. What had made him mention Morgan le Fay?

"No, actually. I love old Mary Stewart mysteries, but I've never been able to make myself read her Arthurian novels. Weird, I guess. I prefer contemporary fantasy."

They ordered pizza and salad, talked about some of her newer acquisitions for the shop. He was curious about them, but she managed to distract him by asking about the stories he was working on. He was doing one on the turtle pond and park, another on the church-run group home, a couple of exposés—one of a local politician, the other of a law firm.

Here Lucinda showed immediate interest, wondering if Dominic would talk to her about Brittany's case. He did, but carefully edited her name and the name of the law firm out of the conversation. Clearly, he was a man of principle . . . from which Lucinda ought to walk away, though she already knew she would not. She found herself loving the sound of his voice—rich, dark, expressive—delighting in the animation in his eyes, and the spirit that shone in them. She admired the curve of his lips, the sharp angles of his cheekbones. She appreciated, too, the texture of his thoughts and emotions. She did not pry into either, but let them ripple across her own web of sense like rain on a still pond. It was fascinating to watch her words register and spark reaction that blossomed in his dark eyes to wash back over her.

They were eating dessert—he had a cannoli; she had cream caramel—when she realized, in a moment of genuine laughter and real joy, that she had begun to love him. At least, it seemed to her that she had felt this warmth for the only other people in her long life that she had loved—her mother and the man she still, in her heart of hearts, thought of as her father: Adam.

Dominic Adeodatus Amado had captured her attention, her emotion, her awareness of her own fragile humanity, and he had done it unconsciously and naturally.

She was slipping past the point of no return and knew it. As she should have known it when they stood on the willow walk in his community garden. As she should have known it the first time she looked into his eyes.

Did he feel the same way? She could feel his attraction to her—his desire. And she felt something more than that—a fascination, a quivering awareness, a *focus*. In her whole life, she had never experienced having someone so entirely focused on her—at least, not in any positive way. Lucifer studied her; Nathaniel watched her every move (at least the ones she allowed him to see); Rey lusted for her; Vorden lusted for something she had or *was*—something Lucinda was convinced the succubus hadn't the ability to articulate. Perhaps it was her autonomy.

She could know that Dominic Amado loved her with certainty if she wanted to. She could dip below the surface of his regard and catch his innermost feelings like fireflies in a jar. She couldn't bring herself to do it, though. If she was going to experience this potentially disastrous thing, she wanted to do it in the fullness of her human naïveté.

They finished their coffee and he insisted on paying.

"I invited you out, so I'll pay," he said. "Next time, if you invite me, you can pay. Fair?"

"Fair," she agreed, though she knew that in his line of work finance was either feast or famine; in hers, money was literally no object. He had to be good with his money—frugal in times of plenty, so that when work fell off, he didn't need to resort to austerity measures. He'd had several photo spreads in major magazines recently, and had been nominated for a couple of journalistic awards.

"I'm pretty flush right now," he told her as they made their way out to the street, "so you don't need to worry about me living on rice cakes and peanut butter for the rest of the month just because I treated you to dinner."

They stood on the sidewalk outside the restaurant, the silence between them sudden and awkward.

"Walk me home?" she asked.

"You don't have a coat."

She smiled wryly. "I walked over. I can make it back without risking hypothermia, I'm pretty sure."

They turned and walked along Lexington toward Seventy-Second Street. After they'd established a mutually comfortable pace, he asked, "That Qur'án you bought—did you find a buyer for it?"

"I did. A collector in Kuwait. Well, a bit more than a collector, actually. He's a devoted Muslim and was thrilled to have ibn Rušd's commentary on the scripture."

"Kuwait? How did you manage to find someone like that?"

There was a question she should have anticipated. "He came to New York a while back. Found his way into the shop." She didn't mention that the two events were separated by both time and space. "I think it was love at first sight."

He smiled, looking straight ahead. "I get that."

"Oh, now you're speaking in code. That's not fair." *Did I just do that? Did I just try to flush him out? Am I flirting?*

His smile deepened and he offered her his arm. She took it, and they continued toward Seventy-Second, their steps slowing to a meander.

"Do you believe in that?" he asked after several paces. "Love at first sight? You seem . . . a bit too levelheaded for that sort of thing. Too sophisticated."

She gave him a sidewise glance, understanding immediately that he was talking almost to himself—warning himself not to believe that she might return . . . whatever he was feeling.

"I've never thought about it much," she said. "It seems to me it's not something you *think* about, but something you just feel. When it happens. If it happens."

They reached the corner of Lexington and Seventy-Second and turned right. Halfway down the block, she drew him to a stop in front of her building.

"This is it, my art deco palace."

Dominic looked up the high-rise toward the distant roofline. To him, it would seem as if it was haloed in an aura of moonlit mist. That was its glamour—a ward that Lucinda had placed on it to make it impermeable to both humans and beings of power. Neither angels nor demons could surprise her there—not even Lucifer. Only God had the power to breach Lucinda's wards, but out here on the street, she felt suddenly vulnerable.

Lucinda tugged on Dominic's arm. "Come on up. You showed me your garden. I'd like to show you mine. I don't have turtles, though."

She felt a subtle shift in his energy—was unsure what to make of it—but his words were casual and light. "No turtles? Really. I don't know. A garden without turtles . . ."

"I have koi."

"Koi," he sighed. "I suppose koi will have to do."

He was overwhelmed by the apartment with its high ceilings and sleek, art deco lines. On the way up in the elevator, Lucinda had considered altering it to make it less splendid, then laughed at herself. For millennia men and women had exaggerated their assets to make an impression on potential mates and competitors and here she was, considering editing her sanctum to downplay its quiet beauty. She didn't want to pretend at anything with Dominic—a sentiment she knew was dangerous and absurd. She was nothing *but* pretense—a millennia-old spirit in a perpetually young body. But it was *her* body in which she interacted with Nick, not one of her projected guises.

"Wow," he said, stepping slowly down from the open foyer into her living room. "This is spectacular."

"I'm very lucky to have found this place," she said quietly. "It was a bit of a wreck when I first saw it. I did a lot of work." It went without saying that she'd done it without lifting a finger. "Come on through to the garden."

She moved past him down the steps and across the living room to the French doors that gave out on to the terrace. As she opened the doors, the garden lit up in a shimmer of radiance that haloed the trees, sparkled on the surface of the pond, and spilled, golden, across the pathways and grasses.

Dominic walked out along the central, curved and cobbled pathway like a man in a dream, turning in circles to take it all in. "This is amazing. This is . . . I knew places like this existed in New York, but I had no idea. I mean, I've seen pictures of some of the rooftop gardens along Fifth Avenue, but this . . . This outdoes them all. How did you ever manage this?"

"I have connections," she said, and elaborated no further. If she indulged herself in this folly, if she let herself love Dominic Amado (was it love?), she would find herself constantly saying such vague, meaningless things.

"This is probably just the power of suggestion, but I'd swear it's warmer here than it is down on the street. A lot warmer."

"Heat rises," she said. "And I had radiant heat installed under the flagstones and in the koi pond. I can't let my fishies freeze. Come see?"

She held out her hand and he crossed the cobbled walk to take it. She led him to the pond with its raised, mossy banks. They sat side by side on a stone bench and looked down into the artfully lit water. The koi were real. There were six of them, in shades of black and gold and bright fiery orange and combinations of all three. They swam to where Lucinda sat and lined up in a ragged, shifting row.

"Worshipful little things, aren't they?"

"I feed them," Lucinda said. "They'd better worship me."

He laughed.

She was still holding his hand. It was warm. Real. Human. She raised it to her cheek. "Mariel." She said it the way her mother had, with the stress on the last syllable—with the emphasis on God.

He grew very still and his hand trembled, conveying his sudden, visceral tension to Lucinda through her skin. She let the charge of sensual information wash through her, savoring it.

"My . . . the name my mother gave me is Mariel. And this"—she glanced around the garden—"is my sacred place. My little paradise."

He raised his other hand to her face. "Thank you, Mariel," he whispered, and then he kissed her.

She gave herself over to the kiss with abandon, letting it flood every centimeter of her senses. She felt the rising tide of passion between them and swam deeper into it, reaching up to tangle her fingers in his hair. She thought about making it warm enough here for them to make love on the mossy bank of the pond, but wasn't sure how she would explain that away with technology. So, when he broke away from her to look into her eyes, still framing her face between his hands, she took his hands in her own and rose, pulling him up after her.

She led him back inside, bringing a fire to life in the fireplace with a thought; it was roaring when they entered the living room. He granted it barely a glance as she turned and slid his jacket from his shoulders.

"Lucinda . . ." he murmured.

"Mariel," she corrected him. "Call me Mariel. And tell me you love me."

He caught her face between his hands again, brushing the pads of his thumbs over her lips, whisper-soft. "I *do* love you. I've loved you from the moment you thought you broke my camera . . . Mariel."

That name on his lips broke her. She reached for him with millennia of loneliness, need and unspent love welling up to swamp any modicum of sense or reason or self-preservation. She kissed him with every ounce of passion that she possessed and felt him respond, fire for fire. He pressed against her, his hands sliding beneath her sweater to caress her bare skin. She felt as if she might burst into flame, so unexpected and wild were the sensations flooding her, and almost wished the sweater gone before she caught herself.

Nick withdrew suddenly, pulling his hands away and unwinding hers from his neck.

"What?" she murmured, feeling drunk, or half drowned, or electrified—she wasn't sure which. "What's wrong?"

"This is. This is getting out of control."

She smiled. "That was the general idea. I find I want to be out of control with you, Dominic Amado."

"I know this is going to sound incredibly unfashionable and Victorian, but I can't do this."

She put a hand to his chest—could feel his heart pounding, his breath coming too quickly. She could feel the heat of his desire.

"You want me. You said you loved me."

"I do. Both. But my beliefs . . ." He paused. Exhaled sharply. Then looked into her eyes, letting her see all the way to his soul. "This is going to sound impossibly weird to you, but my beliefs aren't just something I put on and take off like a shirt or a pair of shoes. It's a covenant between me and God. I've broken faith with Him"—he took a deep breath—"in terrible ways. But this covenant, I want to keep. What that means is that for me, 'casual sex' is an oxymoron."

"I don't feel casual about this, do you?"

"I don't know how you feel. You haven't told me."

She hadn't. She'd been all about taking his love and his desire and devouring it, uncertain if she could give him anything in return.

Selfish, like my father.

She shook her head. "I don't know what I feel. I've never felt this—whatever it is. It's like . . ."

She pulled away from him completely and retreated to the sofa. He stood in the center of the room, so beautiful, it brought her almost physical pain. She looked away from him toward the fire.

"At the restaurant tonight," she said, "you made me laugh and feel . . . real joy. That's the first time I've experienced joy in another person's company since I was a child, I think. I didn't want it to end. I wanted to just be talking to you—laughing with you—until the world stopped. And I thought . . . I wondered, 'Is this love?'"

She sounded pathetic to her own ears. Her millennia of life experience, her vast, encyclopedic knowledge, her skills, her talents, her powers—all of it dissolved like a sand castle beneath a wave. Dominic Amado—gift of God or Trojan horse—had reached a part of her that she had kept sealed even from herself. He had opened a room in her home she hadn't known existed. That shouldn't exist. She couldn't let it exist. He was a danger to her—and she, even more of a danger to him.

This has to stop. She opened her mouth to say it, to send him away, when he answered her plea.

"It's what *I* feel," he said simply, "and I'd call it love."

She felt the tears running down her cheeks and barely remembered what they were. She'd cried when Lucifer had first taken her from her mother. After a while, the tears had stopped and she had assumed they were dried up forever. She raised a hand to her face and caught the tears on her fingertips, marveling at them.

Dominic came to his knees next to the sofa, his arms around her before she could frame a response. He held her for uncounted minutes as she wept. It registered somewhere in the back of her mind that it had begun to rain outside; she dimly wondered if she were causing it somehow.

"Who did this to you?" he asked her at length.

She shook her head, unable to stop the tears. *Stupid. Weak.*

"Mariel, hasn't anyone ever told you they loved you?"

His voice was so gentle it brought her fresh agony. She gasped at a long-buried memory—seeing her mother searching frantically for her in the clearing where she'd been playing, finding only the pictures she had drawn with a stick. Animals mostly.

"My mother. My mother loved me. My . . . I guess you'd call him my stepfather. He loved me."

"But not your father." His voice was stony—cold.

She rocked her head against his shoulder. "It's not in him to love anyone, I think."

"Is he . . . abusive?"

"No. Not exactly. Lucien wasn't—isn't—abusive in the way your dad was. Not physically. At least, not to me. It's not what he does to me that hurts. It's what I see him do to other people."

She felt him nodding. "When I was little," he told her, "my dad would shut me in my room before he beat Mom. As I got older—more likely to come out and get in his face—he'd lock me in a closet. I had to listen to him . . ." He took a deep breath. "Mom would let me out later—after."

He held her out at arm's length and looked into her eyes. She was stunned by the way her pulse quickened, by the sheer depth of what she saw in him—and the depth of her reaction to it.

"Lucinda . . . Mariel. Listen to me. Whether he's physically or emotionally abusive, you need to consider getting away from him. You're an adult—he can have no claim on you legally. None. You need to escape from him while you still have your soul. Before you've let him push you . . . into a corner."

She caught something dark and shifting beneath his words. He was speaking from experience now.

"Is that what your father did, Nick? Push you into a corner?"

He shook his head. "What my father did isn't the issue. It's what your father is doing to you. I don't want you to go through what I did. I don't want you to feel that much hatred for anyone . . . ever. Or that much despair."

She raised a hand to his face. "I'm sorry. I'm sorry you had to go through that." *Especially since I suspect that my father ultimately had a hand in it, one way or another.* "But it's not that simple with me, Nick. I can't leave."

"Why?"

Why, indeed? "It's . . . very, very complicated. It's not about me. It's about all the other people Lucien hurts."

"You can't stop that."

"Sometimes, yes, I can."

"I don't understand."

She relaxed against the sofa cushions and let her eyes go unfocused to the flames leaping in the fireplace. "He schemes. Big schemes. Little schemes. Business ventures. Politics. Social manipulation. He buys things. People. He twists people until they think they want what he wants. I can sometimes fix it so that he doesn't win."

"Doing God's work," he said, and she almost laughed.

She wasn't fit to do God's work. She was a ruined thing. Lucifer had seen to that. She did what she did because she loved humanity, hated what her father had done, and hoped that her work might make whatever corner of Hell she inherited a little less horrific.

"Just . . . trying to make rights out of wrongs. It's hard to explain."

He smiled crookedly. "That makes you an angel in my book—in God's book, too, I'm pretty sure."

She put her fingertips over his lips. "No! Don't say that! I'm no angel. Believe me, Dominic, I am not at all what I seem." *And you can't know me.*

He took her hand, brushed away the last of her tears, and kissed her again, gently, just as he had the first time on the street outside her shop. "I know you're not what you seem. You can *seem* distant and all business and worldly-wise. But that's not you, is it? That's just your . . . disguise."

She gasped aloud. "How do you do that? How do you read me like that? No one else can do it. Not even *him*—or maybe especially not him." *For which I should be grateful.*

Dominic's face darkened. "Him. Your father."

She nodded.

"You won't leave?"

"No. I can't. There are people I need to protect."

"Who protects *you?*"

She gave him a wry smile. "I've done a pretty good job of protecting myself, lo, these many years."

"And you never need help? A friend? A shoulder to irrigate?" He patted at the wet patch she'd left on his shirt.

She laughed.

"There, see. I serve a useful purpose. I make you laugh." He rose from the sofa and retrieved his jacket. "I should go," he told her, "but I'm not going to stay away. I promise. I'll see you tomorrow . . . and the next day and the day after that. And whenever you're feeling trapped or frustrated, remember"—he grinned—"the 'A' is for Adeodatus."

He leaned over to kiss her cheek and she reached up to touch his face, knowing she could get him to stay with her, to make love with her . . . and knowing she wouldn't. She would not manipulate him as she had been manipulated, would not steal his faith from him as hers had been stolen from her.

"God bless you," she told him.

CHAPTER EIGHTEEN

Rowdy Collins tried not to inhale the bacon and eggs he'd piled on his plate. He had half an hour for breakfast; might as well take advantage of it. The food—even if it wasn't as good as what came out of his mom's kitchen—was hot and familiar. Not that he didn't appreciate the spicy, alien flavors of Kuwaiti fare, but for his day-in and day-out food, he preferred the simple, homey tastes that came out of the post canteen. He guessed he was just a "meat and potatoes" kind of guy.

"Mind if I have a seat?"

Rowdy looked up to see another Marine—a corporal—standing across from him with a tray of food. He gave the other soldier a friendly smile. "Not at all. Help yourself."

The corporal pulled out a chair and sat himself down, depositing at least as many plates as Rowdy had brought to the table. Then he stuck out his hand for Rowdy to shake. "Thanks. I'm Gene Marcello."

Marcello took a moment to settle himself in, grab a bite of his bacon, and make the obligatory bacon grin.

Rowdy nodded. "Good, huh?"

"Hey, it's hard to screw up bacon." A couple of mouthfuls later, Marcello said, "I heard about your mom from Sergeant Martinez. That's tough."

Rowdy's heart clenched. He'd been quiet about his situation himself, but he knew how fast the military grapevine worked. "Yeah. I wish I'd been there for her."

"Well, you're *here* for her, aren't you?" Marcello asked. "I mean you're here to defend the interests of her country, right? So, you're doing your job, I figure."

Rowdy considered that. "Yeah. Thanks, Corporal. I think I needed to hear that."

"Call me Gene. And you go by Rowdy, right?"

"Yeah."

"So, what's your real name? I mean, your mom didn't name you Rowdy, right?"

"Randall. But I guess I was a handful when I was little, so—Rowdy."

"Well, Rowdy Randall, I got a message for you from a mutual friend."

Rowdy looked up from his plate. "You what?"

Marcello pulled his dog tags out of the collar of his shirt and showed them to Rowdy. There were three—two normal government issue and a third that looked like the one McLeod had shown him, set in a brass bezel.

Rowdy's heart kicked up a beat. "You're . . . you're a friend of—"

"Andy. Yeah. He wanted me to ask you if you'd gather some information for him about that person of interest you discussed."

Rowdy felt his ears go hot. "Can we talk about this here?"

"You think anyone can overhear us in this zoo?"

Rowdy looked around. Soldiers from several different arms of the military—from a number of countries—milled around the chow line, sat at tables eating and talking, bussed their trays with a clatter of plates and flatware. The guy had a point. The noisy, busy canteen probably afforded more privacy than quieter places where voices would carry.

"Probably not."

"Then here's the deal. Andy wants you to get him all the intel you can on Mr. S's social and political campaigns. Specifically, he wants to know if the gentleman is planning any policy moves or covert action against minority groups. *Any* minority groups."

Rowdy relaxed. "Okay. That's easy enough. I'm with him most of the time when I'm assigned to his detail. Even public bathrooms."

Marcello snorted. "Sounds like fun. There's a bit more. Andy wants the guy's schedule for the next two weeks."

"Why?" The question popped out reflexively.

"Need to know, Lance Corporal. But in general, Andy is in this to protect vital US interests. And your man represents a vital US interest."

Rowdy was pretty sure he represented the Devil, too, but he didn't say it aloud. "How do I deliver this intel?"

"Through me or through Private Glen—I'll introduce you. Glen's attached to another official."

"How will I get in touch with you?"

Marcello grinned at him. "Cell phone, maybe?"

"Uh . . . really?"

"Yeah. If you need to get an urgent message to me, anyway. Other than that—hey, you and I are going to be good buddies. People will get used to seeing us together. Won't think a thing of it. Pool work isn't all cloak and dagger."

Rowdy relaxed some more. "Okay. Okay. If intel is what . . . Andy needs, I'll get him intel."

"Good man." Marcello grinned, then tucked back into his breakfast.

By the end of the week, Rowdy had delivered several pieces of intel for "Andy." He'd passed on the cabinet minister's schedule for the week and added a summary on his political aims that Rowdy really wished he didn't know. He'd extracted some of it from documents Salim had no idea he could read, and even more from conversations Salim had no idea he could understand.

It had taken every ounce of stoicism Rowdy could muster to stand at attention in the same room with a man who spoke so bloodlessly about using "harsher measures" to keep the *bidoon jinsaya* from becoming a worse problem.

Why don't you just make them citizens, he wanted to shout. *Then you won't have to expend time and money trying to "deal" with them.*

He didn't understand it. What purpose was served by keeping the Bidoon around as second-class citizens? It became more inexplicable when he discovered that the Bidoon were also Muslims—mostly from the majority Sunni sect. That sectarian difference was something else he found difficult to wrap his head around. Sure, there'd been something like that in Christianity, too—the Orthodox and the Catholic, the Catholic and the Protestant, the intolerance between some Protestant sects—but among Sunnis and Shi'as there didn't seem to be deep doctrinal differences. At least not any deeper differences than seemed to exist between the myriad schools of Islamic thought.

Yet, there it was in Sheikh Salim's personal dogma and in his official workings—the perception that these minority groups must be suspected of being "other" in their goals and aspirations. That their aims must be seen as undermining the security of the larger society.

Rowdy decided he'd be glad when this gig was over—or at least his attachment to Sheikh Salim's guard. Apparently, the presence of American sharpshooters was something the Kuwaiti emir and prime minister had requested of the US government when Sheikh Salim's policy positions had inflamed Bidoon activists. Though their protests were largely peaceful, Rowdy gathered that some hotheads had made threats.

There were five other soldiers in the guard—two Kuwaitis, two Americans, and a Frenchman. The Frenchman, like Rowdy, was assigned to stay in close proximity to the parliamentarian during his workday. They went everywhere with him and his two Kuwaiti watchdogs. The other two Americans rode in a separate car directly behind the minister's limo and watched him from a bit farther away.

Tonight, Rowdy and Gene were dining together at a restaurant on Arabian Gulf Street. He had fresh details on the special events the minister was to attend over the next several weeks, plus his schedule for regular assembly sessions. As Gene had asked, Rowdy put the information on a whimsical, elephant-shaped thumb drive that looked like a key chain fob. Gene had given it to him two days before at breakfast. Rowdy flipped it nonchalantly across their shared table in the restaurant—an American-based chain.

"Cute, huh?" Rowdy said. "I figured Mom would like it."

Gene looked the drive over, pretending to admire it, then palmed it and flipped back an identical one.

"I'm sure she'll love it. You better check it and make sure you didn't leave any porn on it, though."

"Yeah."

"Seriously. Check it when you get back tonight."

Understood. "What, you put porn on it for me?"

Gene chuckled and leaned back in his chair with a careless ease that Rowdy envied. Rowdy might look and sound casual, but inside he was uncertain, out of his depth.

"Something like that," Gene said. "I'm sure you'll find it instructive."

They ordered, Rowdy speaking Arabic to the server, who seemed to appreciate the courtesy.

"You speak the language well," Gene observed. "I can see why Andy chose you."

"It's a beautiful language."

Gene made a wry face. "You think so, huh? Makes me want to shoot something. These towel heads are supposed to speak English here. Make 'em do it. It's good for them."

Rowdy stifled a tickle of anger and ignored the remark. He didn't dislike his new "good buddy," but he didn't like him either. Yeah, Gene was a funny guy. The kind of guy Rowdy'd liked well enough in school. Class clown, Rowdy would bet. But then he'd say stuff like that crack about "towel heads" and set Rowdy's teeth on edge. His speech was threaded through with veiled insults of Kuwaitis—often to their faces. Plus, raunchy crap about women—any women, but especially Kuwaiti women who wore traditional dress.

On the street in front of the restaurant, he'd made a snide remark about a quite beautiful young woman in a vividly dyed silk head scarf that was draped across her shoulders with a fringe that fell almost to her waist.

"Bet she's a freakin' cow under that thing. Or has tits the size of my little sister's."

Rowdy hadn't been able to control his tongue. "You know, Gene, I bet you'd be madder'n hell if you thought some guy was talking that way about what your little sister had going on under her clothes."

"Damn straight," Gene said, apparently missing the connection.

Rowdy went on doggedly, nodding toward the girl, who was walking ahead of them up the street, in company with an older woman. "Well, *she's* probably someone's little sister, too."

"Yeah. She's some *Arab's* little sister. Who gives a crap?"

Rowdy decided that trying to squeeze a sense of shared humanity out of Gene Marcello was futile. He shut up, and determined to keep things between him and his buddy light and casual.

The thumb drive was another kettle of fish, as his grandmother had liked to say. There wasn't porn on it, of course; there were—as Gene had hinted—instructions. He was supposed to check the pocket of his dress uniform for an item. No indication of what it was.

Sitting on his bunk in the barracks, surrounded by the members of his unit, he frowned and looked up from his laptop toward the shared closet in which he and his bunkmates stowed their gear and clothing. He was wearing a T-shirt and khakis—had taken off his jacket and boots. He set the laptop aside, went to the closet, and found his dress uniform. It took him a moment to pat down the pockets and find the item. It was in the inside breast pocket and fortunately was small enough to hide in the palm of his hand. There was a tiny thumb drive with it—roughly the size of a piece of chewing gum.

Rowdy palmed those and snagged a sweatshirt from the hanger next to the dress jacket and pulled it on before taking a detour to the latrine. There was no one else in there, but he slipped into a stall, closed the door, and sat down on the edge of the toilet to inspect what he'd gotten. It was round, metallic, and had some sort of magnetic disk on one side. There was an LED embedded in the center of the opposite side. Rowdy was pretty sure it was some sort of tracking device. He pocketed it and left the latrine to return to his laptop, where he inserted the drive and opened the lone file on it.

The instructions were simple. Rowdy was to place the tracking device on the Sheikh's vehicle. It was described as a "precaution." There was some concern, a terse note from Andy McLeod said, that a Bidoon insurgent group might try to kidnap Salim or that a mole in his entourage might possibly "detour" the vehicle somewhere they might booby-trap it with explosives. They wanted to know where the minister's car was every moment.

It seemed a sensible precaution. He wondered, though, why it couldn't go through channels. The answer to that internal query was chilling: it more than hinted that there might be a mole in either Salim's support group or in the American ambassadorial corps.

Rowdy erased the drive and hid the tracking device carefully until such time as he could plant it.

CHAPTER NINETEEN

Lucinda dreamed. She often dreamed, for her body and brain were human, after all, and dreaming was part of the human reality. She did not often remember her dreams as vividly as she did this one, but when she did remember them, she paid attention.

In her dream, she stood on the street outside Dominic's church, watching a red Mercedes hurtle toward him down the street. The car left a blurred afterimage behind so that it seemed a red serpent uncoiled between the buildings, homing in on the man. The scene repeated in a series of frozen moments: Nick looking up and recognizing the danger, his dark eyes widening in sudden fear. Lucinda desperately flipping the vehicle through the air. The sense of malice that roared as loudly as the Mercedes' engine. Her surprise that the driver of the car was fully human and as puzzled and appalled by the incident as anyone on the street.

It was as if her spirit were trying to provoke her to action she had not been ready to take. She had made a number of assumptions about the real force behind what she now saw as an attempt on Dominic Amado's life, but she could not be certain, and in her uncertainty, she had hesitated to do more than ward Dominic from harm. It was a ward, however, that a clever supernatural enemy might be able to circumvent, given enough time and opportunity.

Wards were words, just like any kinetic commandment. When God had begun this Universe, He had willed it into existence by "uttering" the word "Be" and then commanded, "Let there be light." Those words had not only set in motion the laws governing the physics of light, but had set the stage for the human acquisition of spiritual light: knowledge.

All words had power, but they could also be exploited, twisted, slipped between by someone with enough motive and ingenuity. That fact, ultimately, was what decided Lucinda on a course of action.

The dream fresh in her mind, she appeared at the pawnshop somewhat earlier than usual and casually summoned Vorden. The succubus's full lips were set in a mutinous pout when she shimmered into physical being in the small, neat kitchen at the rear of the store. She was wearing a slinky purple dress that seemed to defy physics in the way it accentuated her breasts and buttocks.

She looked, Lucinda thought, like she'd just stepped out of a comic book.

"You are before time," Vorden complained, her voice somehow sultry and whining at once. "Why are you before time? I was feeding."

Lucinda had brewed herself a cup of tea and held it close to her face, savoring the scent. She regarded the succubus archly through the steam. "I really don't care about your dietary habits, demon."

Vorden smiled, slowly, vilely. "He was delicious. I chose him because he looked much like your Dominic. I was pretending he *was* your Dominic. Is your Dominic delicious?"

Lucinda ignored the questions and the provocation. "Actually, it's Dominic I wanted to talk to you about."

"Oh! Will you let me have him? He is so . . . *vital.* I think he should be a feast."

Lucinda turned and fixed the succubus with a look that made her blink and cower and take a step in retreat. "I command thee, Vorden," Lucinda said, "to have no contact with Dominic Amado in either world. Nor in the Between."

Vorden remained cowed in the face of the ritual words, but pouted nonetheless. "You did not need to bind me with words, Mistress. You are my lord's daughter; a request would have been sufficient."

"I didn't care to risk it. You would ruin Nick Amado and I don't like ruined things. I need you to answer some questions."

Vorden put a hand to her gravity-defying cleavage. "I? You wish to ask *me* questions? What can I know that you do not?"

"Let's find out, shall we? Saturday, I went out with Dominic. You remember, I'm sure."

Vorden nodded. Her eyes were wary.

"You like Dominic, don't you, Vorden?"

"Of course. He is beautiful. I like beauty."

You like to devour beauty and pollute it, Lucinda thought, but said aloud, "Yes, he is beautiful. Did you follow us so you could watch him?"

Vorden squirmed. She didn't want to answer.

Lucinda spoke more ritual words: "I command thee, Vorden, to speak words of truth."

The succubus covered her ears with her hands and mewed miserably. "You are so cruel to Vorden. Fine. Yes, I followed. Until you went into that *place.* Then I stopped, because I knew that when you came out you would smell of holiness and candle wax. I hate both."

"You followed us only as far as the church? You weren't there when we came out?"

"No, Mistress. I was not."

That could not be a lie. "Did anyone else watch us?"

The succubus blinked. "Anyone else?" She couldn't lie, but she could dodge and duck and evade.

Lucinda set down her teacup on the tiles of the countertop. The sharp sound made Vorden jump. "Did Rey watch us, too? Was he with you?"

"He wanted to watch. He does not like your Dominic much. He does not like the thought that your Dominic gets things from you that he does not. He asked me to help him watch you."

"He *asked* you? Since when do you do favors for Rey without payback?"

Vorden shrugged and wound a strand of her gingery hair around her finger. "We made a deal. I use my powers to let him watch you with your Dominic and he lets me feed on him. This is nothing to him. He is all but immortal. Did you know that anger is an aphrodisiac?"

"Rey was angry, was he?"

Vorden's eyes glittered with remembered pleasure. "Enraged beyond human capacity. I am glad Rey is an immortal with human appetites. I'm also glad that he was even more enraged last night."

All of Lucinda's senses went on point. "He was angry last night—why?"

"Because you took your Dominic into your home and shut yourselves away from Rey. Even I could not pry my way into your private box."

So, Rey had been monitoring her time with Nick, insofar as Vorden's demonic powers allowed him. "You lied to me just a minute ago, didn't you? About a lover that looked like Dominic. You were with Rey. Is he likely to be late for work this morning?"

Vorden grinned like the Cheshire cat. "He is still *somewhat* human."

"You said you stopped watching us when Nick and I went into the church. That means that Rey had to stop watching us, too."

"Yes. Of course. He came back to himself here, in the shop, and I went to amuse myself elsewhere. Why so many questions?"

Lucinda studied Vorden long enough to make the succubus uncomfortable. How might she capitalize on the demon's circumstance? "Someone tried to kill my Dominic that day."

"You thought it was *me*?" The wave of distress that Vorden broadcast seemed entirely genuine. "I would never extinguish such a light. A man like that should be savored, not snuffed out as if his life essence was of no value."

"And Rey?"

"Rey has not the power to do such a thing. Nor would I help him to do it."

No, but someone else might. "Listen to me, Vorden. If you become aware of anyone wanting to harm Nick, I want to know."

"Yes, Mistress. But why? You are not like me."

Lucinda stared at the beautiful demon. Her words held no arrogance, no sense of superiority she claimed to feel because she was completely supernatural and Lucinda only partly so. She sounded . . . wistful.

"No," Lucinda told her. "I am not like you. I am half human and I have human hungers. I'm sure you understand why I might choose Dominic Amado to feed them."

Vorden nodded, and Lucinda dismissed her. Taking up her teacup, she moved to open the shop, her mind mulling over Vorden's answers to her questions. If Vorden had not helped Rey to continue spying on Lucinda and Nick, had someone else?

She turned her thoughts to Nathaniel. As often happened, that was all it took to bring him to her. She felt the opening of the gate between the Formed and Unformed and the peculiar sense of his presence. It was a presence that, as long as she'd known him, she'd never been able to put a finger on.

"You are early here today," he said, stepping from the ether into the center of the shop. "Is there something amiss?"

"Yes, there is. I think someone attempted to kill Dominic. They aimed a Mercedes-Benz at him. Or maybe I was the target. I'm not completely certain. Whoever it was, was full of malice and spite."

For the first time in her experience of him, Lucinda saw a flicker of *something* in the angel's eyes.

"Do you want me to help you determine who that might be?"

Lucinda felt, suddenly, as if she were engaged in a game of high-stakes chess. What was her next move?

"I was going to ask if perhaps *you* had something to do with it."

He seemed to freeze for an instant, and she wondered if she would have to resort to ritual with him, as she had with Vorden.

"I would not, Shaliah," he said simply, his face giving away nothing. "I am not . . . sanguine about your increasing closeness to this mortal. However, were he to die, you would feel loss, would you not?"

It was Lucinda's turn to shrink from a question. She could hardly admit to this fallen creature the depth of her growing emotional attachment to Nick Amado or her fear for his safety. She was not supposed to feel love, only desire.

"I would be displeased, of course," she said, finally. "I am enjoying him."

His gaze seemed to penetrate to her bones. "You would be more than displeased, I think, Shaliah. I am not blind."

Would that you were. "Yet, you claim you had nothing to do with the attack on us?"

"I would do nothing to harm you."

She smiled grimly. "It's not as if I can die, Nathaniel."

"But your human body can sustain damage that would cause you pain, and your spirit might be . . . compromised."

"Guarding Lucifer's jewels, are you?"

"No. Guarding *you*, Shaliah. *Whoever* offers you threat, I will protect you from them."

She gave him a searching look. What a remarkable thing to say. "You don't see Dominic as a threat?"

"I am unsure. I can't see the future. It isn't permitted. It is one of the things I left behind."

Lucinda's curiosity spiked. She had always wondered how Nathaniel had fallen, but had not considered it her right to ask. "Why did you leave it behind, Nathaniel? What caused you to exchange service to God for service to His Adversary?"

Again, there was a slight stirring of the fallen angel's spirit. She could see it in his eyes. Extraordinary. He seemed to be struggling with the answer.

"I cannot lie to you, Shaliah. Hence, I would rather not be required to answer."

"What? Can you have committed an act so heinous that Satan's own daughter cannot hear it? I can't imagine what that could be."

Nathaniel regarded her solemnly for a moment, then glanced up toward the door of the shop. "Amado is here," he said, and stepped back into the Between.

⁜

"Reynard, you are one of God's nastiest pieces of work, and your angst is enough to wake the dead."

Rey Granger all but leapt out of his skin at the sound of Lucifer's voice so close behind him. He felt like last night's leftovers, and had been concentrating so hard on fumbling a coffee cartridge into his single-cup machine that he'd had no inkling he was receiving a visit from the Boss. He turned to find the Lord of Demons, in his favorite human form, sitting cross-legged on the raised hearth of the gas fireplace in his apartment, like some black hole Buddha. Like a black hole, Lucifer seemed to suck all the warmth out of the room and the oxygen with it.

Rey managed to get his breathing under control enough to respond. "Lord, I expected you to summon me to the Between. I never imagined that you'd come to my place."

"You were distracting me. I sense you have something important to tell me. If you can still remember what it is. May I say that you look like Hell?"

Rey ran a shaking hand through his hair. "Yeah. I had a night."

"You had Vorden. Or, rather, she had you. If you weren't effectively immortal, you'd be dead. I, too, had a night. It took me far afield. What did I miss?"

"*He* was with her last night."

The memory of watching Lucinda and Dominic walk hand in hand into her warded apartment was still galling. Rey had sat in his car staring at the building for several minutes, telling himself he would sit there until Dominic came out again so he could run him down. Or shoot him. Or stab him to death. It hardly mattered—it would look like a mugging gone wrong, and any fingerprints Rey Granger left behind would appear in no database that law enforcement would even consider checking. Who'd expect a guy who'd gone MIA in 'Nam in the '70s to commit a murder in present-day Manhattan?

"By 'he,' I assume you mean the journalist and by 'her,' I assume you mean my daughter. What of it? She can indulge her appetites in any way she sees fit. It's not as if I can pretend moral superiority here."

"I thought you wanted her to be with *me*. I thought you wanted me to get her pregnant."

Lucifer stood, his movements liquid and languid. The strange, tilted eyes lit with a mocking gleam. "Right on both counts."

"Then why don't you let me try to kill him again? Why did you make me give up after one try?"

The golden eyes flashed warning. "I didn't 'give up,' Rey. I paused to consider my approach to this. Perhaps you failed to notice her reaction to his 'near death' experience."

"No, sir. No, I did not fail to notice. She saved his precious ass."

"Precisely. She's enamored of him. I have never known her to indulge in lust before. Never. Not in the millennia I've been grooming her."

The mention of Lucinda, lust, and Dominic Amado in the same breath made Rey's head fill with a hot, red rage. He'd felt like this before. Once too often. It was what had almost gotten him killed in Vietnam. He fought the blast furnace emotions under control.

"Pardon me, Lord, but isn't the idea that she lust after *me*?"

"Yes, it is, but what she's doing with Amado benefits you. He's awakened her desire, aroused her deep passions." Lucifer was watching Rey with a smile playing around his lips and darting in his eyes. "I can feel the rage in you from here. I felt it in the Between. Your rage is a powerful thing, Rey Granger. More powerful than your reason, your conscience—stronger, even, than your sense of self-preservation. I heard Vorden tell Lucinda mere moments ago that rage is an aphrodisiac."

"What's that got to do with—"

Lucifer raised a hand and Rey shut his mouth. His flesh felt hot, his eyes, as if they wanted to burst from his head. And yes, he was aroused. Aroused at the thought of rage and lust and Lucinda.

"My daughter, for her own reasons, has formed an attachment to her human pet. Killing him will not serve your cause. It will only make her angry. At you, if she discovers that you had a hand in trying to run him down in the street. You need to channel that wonderful passion that you feel into seducing her."

"She doesn't want me to seduce her, Lord. She says it's because she respects me—values our 'friendship.' That's bull, of course. She doesn't want me because she's the king's daughter and I'm just his flunky. She's not hot to shag the hired help."

"I agree."

"You . . . you do?"

"Completely." Lucifer moved to the kitchen counter and slid gracefully onto one of the tall, leather-upholstered stools. "Which is why I wish to offer you a bit of help with my stubborn offspring." He held out one hand, palm open. An object appeared in it—shiny, reddish-brown, and familiar.

"A *chestnut?*"

"That, my lustful friend, is not a chestnut. It is a Seed from the tree that gave humanity its first real 'taste' of the difference between good and evil. Take it."

Rey had handled almost every artifact in Lucinda's shop. He enjoyed handling them—savored the strong, even violent emotions they evoked, especially the rage and the fear and the passion. Human-manufactured porn was nothing compared to that. But this completely organic memento from the beginning of human consciousness was so laden with spiritual weakness—jealousy, rage, desire, and resentment—that the chaos tide flooded Rey's consciousness and left him breathless and shaking. He set the evil chestnut down on the counter and rubbed his sweating palms on his pants.

"Why is it so powerful?"

Lucifer smiled. "You don't need the details, but suffice it to say that this is a memento of Lucinda's creation. It is, perhaps, the only talisman on Earth that could affect her. Keep it with you—at least when you're with her."

Rey stared at the thing lying on his kitchen counter. It seemed so ordinary, so innocuous, but he could feel the power of the divine in it, coupled with the collected debris of human frailty—beginning with Lucinda's own parents. It was a perfect storm. A poison pill tailored for the Devil's daughter.

"What will it do to her?"

Lucifer touched the Seed with the tip of one finger. "That's a good question. When she was very young, it drew her into my arms. As she grew older, I like to think it made her susceptible to my mentoring, made her crave my approval, made her my willing apprentice. Whatever it does, it should serve your purposes well enough."

"Thank you, Lord," Rey said and quickly popped the talisman into his pants pocket where he could feel it, burning, against his upper thigh. "There is one other thing I'd like to ask. If it's even possible for you to do it."

Lucifer stood, looking down at him, sleek otter-brown eyebrows raised. "What do you imagine I can't do?"

Now, that was a loaded question. The list of what the Lord of Evil *couldn't* do was longer than Rey's Christmas list. Chiefly, he couldn't directly manipulate human beings. He had to use words to bend their free will—something that had not been lost on this apprentice.

"You've made me more or less immortal, but you haven't given me any immortal abilities. I can't enter the Between on my own. I can't cast wards or make glamours or any of that stuff. All I can do is, you know, chameleon into the background, project a little bit, convince mortals I am what I'm not."

"You want to be able to make glamours?"

"Mostly, I'd like to be able to come and go to the Between without a chaperone. In fact, glamours might not be a bad idea if I'm going to take advantage of the Bad Seed, here. I mean, what if she *sees* it?"

"She has no idea what it is. She doesn't even know it exists." The Lord of Demons seemed to go within himself for a moment, then looked directly at Rey in a way that made his insides squirm. "Very well. You may translate yourself to the Between as you wish and travel within it. You may also create palpable illusions. A word of advice: control yourself. Yes, I know that's a bit like telling a shark not to bite the soft, tasty, bleeding swimmer, but you are a human being and you have the ability to control your impulses . . . despite all evidence to the contrary."

Rey swallowed, barely able to believe how easy that had been after decades of hinting that he wanted more autonomy. "That's it? Just like that? Wow. *Thank you, Lord.* Really—thank you. I'm more grateful than you can know."

"I doubt that. However, something you said earlier is quite true: Lucinda might not respect a being that must depend on others to even function in her real world—a being so obviously inferior. Perhaps granting these powers to you will make you seem less a cowering fool to her. "

"Can I ask something?" Rey ventured.

"You may *ask*."

"Why don't you just tell Lucinda you want her to play mommy to the Antichrist and anoint me as the father figure?"

"That is not how our game is played. She is my daughter—a daughter whose tiny acts of rebellion are the sincerest form of flattery. She is also human. She needs to choose this of her own free will."

In other words, Rey translated, *you can't make her do anything she doesn't want to.*

"Free will, huh?" Rey patted the pocket that held the shiny Seed.

"It cannot manipulate her, it can only provide the proper atmosphere. In that, it is no different than any other artifact. It is simply much older and more primal, and therefore more potent."

"How do I, you know, go between here and there?" He gestured at the empty air.

"You simply step through. You can have Lucinda teach you how to do glamours . . . or Vorden, if you prefer."

Then he was gone, just like that, stepping into nowhere and leaving Rey to contemplate his new autonomy.

Lucinda pivoted toward the front door of the shop as it opened with the tinkle of the little bell. Dominic came in, bearing a bag from Gramercy Star and a cardboard tray with two steaming cups of coffee. His smile, when he saw her, was tentative.

"Morning. I brought scones and coffee . . ." He hesitated, searching her face. "You okay?"

"I'm fine," she said. "Why wouldn't I be?"

He came further into the shop to set the breakfast offering down on the table in the reading alcove. "It's just . . . last night, when I left, you were still a little . . . rocky."

Lucinda was suddenly hyperaware of the many eyes that could be watching—the ears that could be listening. She took a deep breath, fighting the sense of suffocation that evoked.

"Rocky? Is that what you'd call it? I was maudlin. Playing the poor-pitiful-me card and trying to push your protective buttons."

He hesitated, suddenly wary. "Playing?"

Lucinda hung for a moment, suspended between truth and lie. She could protect him best by sending him away, she knew, and all she needed to do was pretend that last night had been an act aimed at getting a pious man into her bed.

She made her decision, stupid as it was. She crossed the room to stand in front of him and look up into his face, putting a tight ward around them as she went. Only God would know what they said.

"Not when it came to . . . to what I said, to what I felt. When I said I thought I loved you, Dominic, that was me trying to be truthful."

He brushed a lock of hair back from her face. "Mariel . . ."

She put her fingers to his lips. "Call me El. I'm Lucinda to everyone here— to *him*. I don't want him—or anyone else—to know I shared that with you. He wouldn't understand. It would make him angry. I don't really want to deal with his anger."

"El, then."

He kissed her gently, then turned and opened the bag, pulling out napkins, scones, and little packets of cream for their coffee. She let the silence wards drop and sat down kitty-corner to him to share their meal. They talked about everything from koi to his stories to what sort of architecture they each liked in a house. He liked Prairie School; she favored Moorish influences. They agreed on the genius of Antoni Gaudí and Frank Lloyd Wright.

Lucinda had finished her scone and was sipping the last of her coffee when Rey Granger stepped out of the thin air behind the counter. Dominic, seeing the startled expression on her face, turned to look over his shoulder.

Rey offered a smile and a wave, though Lucinda saw something dark and brooding behind the smile.

"Hey," Nick said, then gathered up the remains of their breakfast and stuffed it back into the bag. "I guess it's probably time for me to get out of your hair and let you get your workday started." He glanced up at Rey, who was still smiling at them, made a tentative gesture toward Lucinda, then pulled his hand back. "I've got that new story I need to get started on. I'll call you later."

She nodded, not trusting herself to speak. They exchanged a look that told her he was as reluctant to let Rey see intimacy between them as she was, and he left, stepping out into the morning sunlight after sketching Rey a salute.

Lucinda stood, crossed her arms over her chest, and leaned a hip against the table. "So, tell me, Rey, how long have you been able to translate between realms?"

"For about five minutes. Literally. Took me a couple of tries to get the hang of it. But, ta-da! Here I am." He looked sheepish. "Sorry I'm late, I—"

"Yes," Lucinda said archly. "Vorden told me." She straightened and glanced down at her almost empty coffee cup, then made it disappear with a wave of her hand. "Let's get the day started, shall we? I've got some new items for you to catalogue."

Rey came out from behind the counter, rubbing his hands together. "Great. Where are they?"

She studied him for a moment; there was something different about him today. Physically, he seemed . . . softer somehow, more relaxed. The darkness she'd read in him before was gone. He was dressed differently, too, she realized. Gone was the usual three-piece suit. He wore a dark blue shirt with gray pants and a matching suit coat, but the collar of his shirt was open and he wore no tie. His hair was different, too. He'd allowed it to fall across his forehead rather than slicking it back with gel as he usually did.

"That's a new look for you," Lucinda told him as she moved to bring out the new artifacts. "More casual. Frankly, it suits you better. You've never seemed like the three-piece suit type to me." *More of a pinstripe suit type.*

"May I take that as a compliment?"

"Indeed, you may."

She lifted a large, finely carved wooden chest to the top of the counter. It was the size of a small coffee table and would have been impossible for a normal woman to lift. Lucinda felt the weight no more than she did the cold of the autumn wind. She opened it and began setting objects out on the large velvet pad assigned to that purpose. She wasn't thinking about the artifacts, though. She was thinking about how to proceed with Rey—did she confront him, or simply keep an eye on him? She trusted Nathaniel to do that in the course of protecting her.

Rey came around the counter, too, and passed behind her to the opposite side of the velvet pad. As he did, he brushed her arm ever so gently. She felt a strange, quivering heat flow through her, as if someone had poured warm liquid down her back. It penetrated to her bones and sinews—to her core.

She shivered and glanced aside at Rey. He had picked up the first of the new artifacts—a tall, brass and silver candlestick worked with Moroccan motifs—and begun to study it, his hands caressing the gleaming metal. She found herself noticing how neat his hands were, how his dark blue shirt contrasted with his fair complexion, the way sunlight falling through the front window gave his skin and hair a warm glow, the fact that he was wearing a small pentacle on a fine golden chain, and that the tiny charm lay in the hollow of his throat.

He looked up at her, his hair falling over one brow. Had it always had that glint of gold? His eyes were a warm gray and they seemed to be smiling at her.

"What?" he said, his lips curving upward. "Did I cut myself shaving or something?"

"No," she said, and turned her attention quickly to the artifacts in the box—which was, itself, one of her talismans. "*Can* you cut yourself shaving?" she asked to cover her own confusion.

He only chuckled and went back to assessing the artifacts, while Lucinda withdrew into herself. What in the name of the sacred and profane was going on?

CHAPTER TWENTY

It had been surprisingly easy to install the tracker on Sheikh Salim's limo. No one questioned that Rowdy, a member of the Sheikh's bodyguard, would want access to his vehicle to give it a security and safety check. It was a weird feeling, working for three masters—Sheikh Salim, the US military, and Blackpool. He tried to tell himself that it was just like Andy McLeod had said—it ultimately came down to working for US interests. But he still felt as if he were coddling a criminal, despite the Sheikh's high position in government.

Politicians were politicians, he guessed, no matter what part of the world they hailed from. They had a constituency that expected to be placed at the top of the pecking order when it came to making policy. Salim was no different; his constituency drove his policy. But Salim was an activist (Rowdy would have called him an extremist), and the policies he pursued not only benefitted his constituents, they hurt the people who weren't part of that group.

Rowdy hated being part of Salim's personal bodyguard. Only the sense that he was serving a higher purpose made it palatable, but he chafed at it anyway and occasionally let it show in front of Gene, whose response was to tease.

"Don't get your panties in a twist, Rowdy-boy," he said during one of their "off-campus" forays into the Souq al-Mubarakiya. "The time's coming when you won't have to protect that towel head. After that, you'll get to pick your assignments. And you'll get one of these."

He held up the Blackpool dog tag, which, Rowdy had learned, was more than just a company ID; it was an award for having completed your first major assignment.

They wandered a few yards more among the colorful stalls and shops when Gene chuckled as if at some secret joke.

"What's funny?" Rowdy asked.

"I don't get you, Collins."

"What don't you get?"

"I don't get why you give a rat's ass about these A-rabs. I mean, you hate the sheikh."

Rowdy felt his face grow warm. He wished he'd never voiced his distaste for Salim's politics in front of Gene—or anyone else, come to think of it. It hadn't escaped his notice that Andy had known he disliked being part of the cabinet minister's detail before their first meeting. Which means they'd been watching him pretty closely for some time.

"I don't hate him. I just don't like his politics."

"Yeah, yeah, I know. The Spittoons. I really don't get that. Why's that bunch of towel heads any different than any other?"

Rowdy cringed. The words *Father, forgive them* popped into his head. "It's *Bidoon*. And they *are* different. Don't you pay attention to anything, Gene? They're like third-class citizens here."

"Why do you care?"

Why did he care? He cared because it was what his mom had brought him up to do. "I care because I'm a Christian and because that's the way my parents brought me up—to do to others as I'd have them do to me."

Gene shrugged. "Whatever blows your skirt up. But these people aren't Christians, Rowdy. They're *Mooslims*."

"You ever hear the story of the Good Samaritan?" Rowdy asked.

"Yeah. I kind of remember it from Sunday school. That's the one about the Jew who falls off his mule or something and this Samaritan guy comes and helps him out, right?"

"He was set upon by robbers and left for dead. Other Jews passed him by and didn't bother to help him. Even Jewish holy men didn't want to touch him. But the Samaritan stopped and picked him up and took him to his house and took care of him. Jews and Samaritans were kind of like Hatfields and McCoys—didn't get along. The Jews looked down on the Samaritans. So when Jesus said we were supposed to love our neighbors as we love ourselves, his definition of 'neighbor' was pretty broad. He didn't leave a lot of wiggle room. So, the Bidoon, they're my neighbors, too. I just don't like what some people have in mind for them."

Gene gave him a slap on the shoulder. "You're a funny dude, Rowdy Randall. But I can see why Andy picked you."

"What—because I care about the locals?"

Gene shot him a laughing glance out of the corner of his eye. "No. Because you can suck it up and put your best effort into guarding a guy you don't like."

Rowdy had to admit, too, that the more intel he gathered about Sheikh Malik al-Salim the less he liked him. Salim actively resisted the movement spearheaded by Shi'a parliamentarians to enfranchise the Bidoon—to offer them health care, make them part of the existing welfare system, allow them to avail themselves of higher education, work in professional capacities and government jobs. He had introduced legislation that would have made Bidoon protests illegal and pro-Bidoon activism essentially a criminal act. The fact that the Bidoon's greatest advocates within the Kuwaiti government were Shi'a only contributed to sectarian tension with the majority Sunni.

Rowdy was developing a growing admiration for Ibrahim Darzi—a Shi'a attorney and minority MP who was an outspoken advocate for Bidoon inclusion. He would have been proud to guard a man like that.

Well, it is what it is, he told himself, and waited for the "time" Gene Marcello had promised him when his tour of duty as part of Sheikh Salim's detail would end.

A little over a week after he'd put the tracker on Salim's car, Rowdy was having breakfast with Gene in the canteen. Between bites of oatmeal, Gene said, "By the way, Andy's in town and wants us to get together for dinner tonight. You up for it?"

"Oh. Yeah, sure," Rowdy said.

As if he could say anything else. It wasn't as if it was the social get-together that Gene made it sound. Still, Rowdy found he was excited by the prospect of maybe getting to take on a real assignment. Something besides being a messenger boy and guard dog.

So it was with great anticipation that Rowdy put aside his uniform and went out with Gene for a Sabbath supper at a restaurant of Andy's choosing. It was a thoroughly Western place from food to decor to clientele. They dined in a private corner of an outdoor patio that overlooked the sea. The sound of waves provided natural soundproofing for their conversation, which didn't get serious until they'd finished their meals and sat over coffee.

Andy McLeod opened the business end of the conversation. "Gene tells me you're chomping at the bit for a major assignment."

"Well, yes sir, I suppose that's a good way to put it."

"Then what I'm about to tell you will come as good news. Our asset has run afoul of the wrong people and they've decided to eliminate him."

Rowdy felt as if someone had hit him with a cattle prod. "Eliminate? Have you informed my commanding officer?"

His two companions exchanged a look, then Andy said: "This is sub-rosa, Rowdy. No one knows but us."

"So . . . you're telling me it's up to us to stop it?"

"No. I'm not going to tell you that. I know how much this guy chafes you. Here's the way it's going to go down. As you know, the asset is scheduled for a series of special legislative sessions on the Bidoon problem. On the day of the event, his motorcade will arrive at the National Assembly complex at 0600 hours. That early in the morning, it will still be dark. At a predetermined point en route, the last car in the procession will be replaced by a vehicle with a special operative in it—a Bidoon. The motorcade will pull into the plaza in front of the assembly building. When the asset leaves his vehicle, the operative will exit his vehicle and shoot him."

Rowdy felt hot and cold at once. "You want me to—what—to neutralize the operative?"

"No. You are to let him complete his assignment. Then you are to eliminate him."

Rowdy didn't think he could possibly have heard that right. "Eliminate him? You want me to *shoot* the assassin? Don't you want him captured if possible, to find out who—"

"Rowdy," said Andy wryly, "we know who's behind the assassination. Our job is to make certain that the Bidoon operative succeeds and that he is not captured."

This could not be real. Rowdy glanced from one man to the other, a thousand questions clamoring for release. What came out first was: "Why?"

Gene laughed. "Why? You never shut up about why. If you think you don't like this guy, let me tell you, there are people who have a whole hell of a lot more reason to hate him than you do. Like the Bidoon who's going to do the deed."

"The man you want me to *kill*?" Rowdy heard the panic in his voice, felt it with every beat of his heart.

Andy regarded him soberly for a moment. "He wants to be a martyr, Rowdy. This is his key to Heaven. Who knows? It may be yours, too."

⊹

Janine made herself walk slowly across the millpond causeway, trailing a group of late-season tourists. She ignored their happy chatter, instead counting her footsteps and reciting the Twenty-Third Psalm in rhythm with her steps. She now had it completely memorized. In her hands, she held a single white rose.

She had made this pilgrimage every Sunday since Stevie's drowning, dropping rose petals in the water near the waterwheel. That was where they had found Stevie's body, not on the shallow side of the pond where she had fallen when Janine had warded her away. Janine knew that she had died trying to retrieve the Book of Shadows. That was two people whose deaths the book had cost.

Janine wondered if she came here in part because the spirit of the book called her to come. Standing at the rail every Sunday, she could feel it pulling at her, hear its dark whispers in her head. It was as if it was trying to pull her down to the depths, too, but she'd found she could shut the whispers out if she kept her mind on her scriptural lifeline. She'd made up a melody to go with the words, so that the psalm became an anthem that she used to block out the book's insistent voice.

The tourist family spent several minutes oohing and aahing over the mill wheel, which was now turning slowly in the current generated by the open floodgates beneath the causeway. Then they wandered off toward the manor house.

Standing on the spot where the wooden causeway met the pea gravel of the mill yard, Janine took a deep breath, steeling herself, then stepped up to the rail, the rose quivering in her hands. She heard the rush of the water, the creaking of the wheel, the coarse voices of crows . . . and nothing else. There were no whispers in her inner ear, nothing dark and sticky tugged at her soul.

Quaking with disbelief, Janine stared down into the water. She started to allow herself to feel relief, then quashed it. This made no sense. It was not as if she had felt the vigor of the book declining over the weeks. Its voracious pull had been as strong last Sunday as it had been the first. That left only one conclusion: somehow, Morgan le Fay's Book of Shadows was no longer at the bottom of the Sleepy Hollow millpond. No matter how hard she tried to tell herself that was a good thing, Janine couldn't make herself believe it.

She tossed her rose into the water with a murmured prayer for Stevie's soul and ran, shivering, back across the causeway. She didn't stop running until she was home.

CHAPTER TWENTY-ONE

Lucinda had retreated to her garden to think, to plan, to wash her Self clean of Rey or whatever he had brought with him into the pawnshop. She tried not to think about that now, but she knew she would have to confront it at some point. Clearly Lucifer had given his pet human a set of powers usually reserved for the supernatural denizens of his realm. The question was, what powers? Why had he granted them? Rey claimed they'd been bestowed after the attempt on Nick's life, but that hardly meant it was true.

Lucinda shook herself free of the quandary and moved to sit on the bench at the edge of the koi pond. It was, at the moment, the only part of the garden that Dominic would have recognized were he here. Lucinda had brought the trappings of her Between space here, hoping they would give her a sense of peace and clarity. The little pool of water with its tiny waterfall now sat at the edge of her corn-field in a swathe of emerald-green grass. The maples and chestnuts were bright plumes of flaming foliage and the air was that same perfect combination of cool and warm that permeated Lucinda's October garden in the Between. Outside her bubble of autumn, the chill sky of earthly October spilled tiny flakes of early snow that melted to soft rain before they reached the street.

The scarecrow was present, too, but here in this warded place, Lucifer could not inhabit him. Still, Lucinda felt as if she were watched. Only God could look down upon her here—was that something to hope for or something to dread? She decided it didn't matter. She did what she did for humanity, not for hope of reward or fear of damnation. According to her father, she was damned already . . . which meant she had nothing to lose.

She leaned forward and waved a hand over the still waters of the pool and, in an instant, the fish were obscured by a view of Ibrahim Darzi's private office, with the ibn Rušd Qur'án at the center of things. It was that Qur'án—that talisman—that enabled Lucinda to be able to see its environs. Darzi had placed it in a sealed display case, its pages open to *Al-Mâ'ûn*—Small Kindnesses, the *surah* he had read from in Lucinda's shop in the souq.

That was hopeful, but not conclusive. Darzi was still a question mark: Would he fall into Lucifer's camp, or hers? There was no way to know; she was no more allowed to peer into the future than Nathaniel was. She waved her hand over the water again and found herself peering into a prison cell. Dan Collins still had the watch—there was little or no hope for him. Her hopes were for his wife and step-son, whose lives were now free of the watch's pernicious effects. She knew that Brittany Anders was pursuing action against her unscrupulous former employer and client. Brittany had chosen her "side" in this ongoing battle between good and evil. She was connected to Lucinda by bonds she could not see.

That left the would-be witch, Janine. Lucinda knew that Janine had attempted to destroy le Fay's Book of Shadows. The girl had no way of knowing that an artifact that powerful could not be destroyed by simply dumping it into deep water, though with no human soul to seduce, the book was, at least, safely out of circulation. Because Janine had touched le Fay's book, Lucinda could still peek into her life across the miles, and did so now, calling Janine's image to her scrying pond.

She saw immediately that the girl was deeply upset, and in a different way than she had been upon the death of her friend, Stephanie. She had withdrawn to her room, curled herself around a pillow, and rocked back and forth. A Bible lay beside her on her bed. She had been memorizing passages from it. Lucinda could hear the echoes in her mind. The girl considered the verses a form of ward, but a ward against what?

Lucinda felt a gentle tug at her spirit. Nathaniel. She considered denying him access, but saw the impulse for what it was—stubbornness. She opened her wards and let the Fallen through. He materialized on the cobbled pathway that wound through her October garden, wearing his current "uniform"—jeans and a black shirt.

"Shaliah," he said before she could speak, "I have some news you may find of interest." He glanced at the scrying pool. "Ah, but perhaps you already know."

Lucinda rose from the pond's verge and gestured at the water. "Know what? Do you know what's distressing this girl?"

"Have you located the Book of Shadows?" he asked in return.

Lucinda frowned. "Locate it? The witch threw it into the millpond."

Some shift in the angel's expression caused Lucinda to shiver. She turned back to the pond, wiped away the image of Janine Sorentino's bedroom, and called to the book, but the surface of the pond did not change. It remained a swirling, misty gray, revealing nothing.

Lucinda turned back to Nathaniel. "It's gone. The book is no longer on Earth. Do you know where it is?"

"It has entered the Between," the Fallen said. "I am not certain how."

"A human is how. A human agency would have to have removed it from the millpond."

Nathaniel's sleek brows rose. "A human with access to the Between? Besides you, there is only one other."

"You knew of that—that my father granted Rey the power of translation?"

"It became obvious. Rey has been practicing."

Was it her imagination, or was that a glint of humor in the angel's eyes?

"What other powers has Lucifer granted him, I wonder," Lucinda murmured. "And why?"

"It is said that God moves in mysterious ways," Nathaniel observed. "The same is true of His spirit sons."

Typical of the Fallen—a nonanswer.

"Fingerprints," Lucinda said.

Nathaniel looked at her quizzically.

"My dear father has left his fingerprints on a number of things. le Fay's book, the attempt on Dominic's life."

Nathaniel's brows rose again. "I had never thought of Rey Granger as a fingerprint, but he seems to be the common thread in at least these two things."

Lucinda frowned at the blank scrying pool. A common thread, indeed. She recalled the role she was supposed to be playing and gave Nathaniel a smiling glance out of the corner of her eye.

"My father is a devious creature. He's testing me, I think. Or challenging me, perhaps, to see if I can divine his intent for the Book of Shadows. Shall I see if I can?"

Nathaniel gave her one of his long, studious looks, then said, "You test him also, do you not? Perhaps to see if he has divined your intent for the Qur'án?"

Lucinda froze, her mind frantically parsing the words for meaning. Had she slipped? Had she said too much or too little? Had distraction made her careless? Had she allowed her real emotions to glide too near the surface of her mind where the angel could read them?

"What might my intent be, but to help Lucifer foment discord in the heart of the Arab world?"

"What, indeed?" Nathaniel asked and then was simply no longer there.

Lucinda spent several moments steadying her very human nerves. She was becoming more and more alarmed by the prospect that the fallen angel had learned to read her, and was close to realizing her real purpose—not just with the Qur'án, but with the other "projects" she had undertaken in Lucifer's name. He had said he was loyal to her, personally, and would protect her from any threat, but when all was said and done, he was her father's dark angel. If he became certain that she had pitted herself against Lucifer, what would he do?

It was ironic, Lucinda thought grimly, that Nathaniel himself had played a significant role in her transformation from malleable child to rebellious adult by planting in her mind curiosity about her own personal genesis. In a sense, Nathaniel had been the catalyst for her rebellion. She doubted he would appreciate that knowledge.

She wanted to call Dominic, to beg him to drop whatever he was doing and come with her *somewhere*, anywhere. She wanted to just exist with him somewhere she could be simply a human woman. She wanted to see him, to hear what he was thinking. She shook the longing away. She wasn't human. She was a changeling pretending at being human. And she had work to do.

She left her rooftop garden and stepped into its mirror image in the Between. The two places differed in the way that a photograph and a painting of the same place differ. In the Between, Lucinda could see her brushstrokes more clearly. She seated herself on the stone bench by the portal that mirrored her scrying pond in the Real. Then she sent a mental invitation to Rey to join her. He appeared in her domain almost immediately, looking relaxed and elegant in a maroon sweater that colored his eyes a deep slate gray.

His relaxation was only on the surface. Beneath that was a nervous watchfulness underpinned with a coiled lust that made Lucinda want to retreat. She didn't retreat; she smiled at him and let her eyes invite him to sit opposite her on the stone bench.

"I have a question for you," she said when he settled next to her.

It was not her imagination that he withdrew from her slightly—not physically, but within. "A question for me? Really? I'm all ears."

"You remember the le Fay Book of Shadows."

"Oh, yeah. It made quite an impression on me."

It had, she realized, probing him gently. She could almost *smell* le Fay's sorcerous fragrance on him—which made sense if he had been the one to retrieve it from its watery holding cell.

"Do you know what happened to it? It's not where the little witch left it."

He met her eyes; she could almost hear the gears in his head turning. Lie or truth or . . .

He smiled. "What's in it for me? I mean, if I tell you, what do I get out of it?"

Had his eyes always had that hint of blue? Had his smile always been so warm? Certainly, he had never broadcast that aura of vitality. Lucinda felt, suddenly, unexpectedly, like Alice falling down her rabbit hole.

The words "What would you like?" hovered on her lips, but deep down in her soul she knew she could never say them. She knew what he wanted. There was only one conclusion she could draw—Lucifer had given Rey Granger more than just the ability to navigate the Between on his own. He was employing a glamour.

Her very knowledge of that fact allowed Lucinda to strip the illusions away. The effect was like looking at the same picture through a translucent filter. He looked no different, just less shiny; his smile was as predatory as she remembered, and his eyes were merely gray.

Seeing through the glamour did nothing to lessen the primal pull that was making her body shift toward him, even as her spirit recoiled in revulsion. She felt from him, in that moment, something of what must have made him fit for Hell—a deep, visceral emotion that was equal parts lust, greed, jealousy, and rage.

"That's the wrong question," she told him, keeping her voice cool and her roiling energies lidded. "The question is, what will it cost you if you *don't* tell me?"

He uttered a short bark of laughter and backed off, but only a bit. "Sorry, I guess I got a bit ahead of myself there. Yeah, I know where it is. Your old man has it—and, no, I don't know what he's going to do with it."

"He's given you powers. Why?"

Rey shrugged and brushed a lock of hair from his forehead. Against her will, Lucinda followed the motion with her eyes, wanting to reach up and touch—

"He felt I deserved a little perk for my faithful service," Rey said. "I'm a good little soldier in the Army of Darkness."

His tone was wry and self-deprecatory and Lucinda wanted to pity him.

"So, translation to the Between and glamours?" she guessed. "What else?"

"That's pretty much it."

"Nothing that would have allowed you to possess another person and make him try to kill Nick?"

A visible jolt ran through Rey's body, but he only shook his head. "Nothing like that. Though I can't say I'd be heartbroken if Nick wasn't in the picture. I don't like him. I don't like the effect he has on you. He makes you . . . less than you are. Or maybe you make yourself less *for* him. Makes sense. He can never know the real you. He can only know the cartoon version."

She ignored that observation and asked, point-blank, "You didn't try to run us down in front of Nick's church using a random human agent?"

He laughed. "Where would I get the chops to do that?"

"My father?"

"Your father would never trust me with that sort of power."

"If not you, then who?"

"I don't know—maybe one of your daddy's demons. He's got a million of 'em. Maybe it was Diabolus or Hellion or even Apollyon? He's the destructo demon, after all."

He was lying, of course, but because he was human she could not compel him with ritual words of power the way she could Vorden or Nathaniel. Yet, knowing he was lying made no impression on her human brain and body. Those felt pulled to Rey Granger as if he were a magnet and she a coarse sliver of iron.

She did the only thing that had any chance of stopping the assault on her senses; she thought of Dominic, bringing him to mind as fully and sensibly as she could. She visualized him standing on the cobbled path of her October garden, smiling, eyes warm and caressing. She remembered the passion he'd raised in her—a passion profoundly different than this bizarre, animal pull she felt from Rey. She focused her entire attention on Dominic, and pulled her gaze free of Rey's.

He frowned, then turned to see what she was staring at so intently. "Sonuvabitch!" he exclaimed, then shot to his feet and vanished in a ragged swirl of ether, leaving behind a wavering afterimage.

Lucinda let go of the phantom Dominic she'd imagined; it went to vapor. Simultaneously, she sent herself back into the *real* October garden. She had no more than returned than Nathaniel once more asked admittance. She dropped the wards for him before she'd had time to steady herself. He found her quivering by the koi pond—which was just a koi pond once more.

The angel was beside her literally in a heartbeat, laying a hand on her arm. "Shaliah, you are unwell?"

Lucinda took a deep breath and struggled to walk her words down a tightrope. "Father has given Rey a power I can't fathom. It . . . has a profoundly disturbing effect on me."

"It has disorganized your thoughts and emotions," the Fallen observed.

"It has, indeed. It felt as if something were pulling at me. Trying to . . . to sap my will."

Nathaniel seemed to withdraw ever so slightly. "What could have such an effect on you? You are the meeting of spirit and form, of mortal and immortal. You are daughter to an archangel."

Breathe. "I don't know, Nathaniel, but for my continued sanity, I think I must find out."

"You will stay away from Rey."

Lucinda gave the Fallen a sharp look. The words had come out sounding like a command.

"Will you not?" he added quickly. "If he discomposes you so . . ."

"Yes. Yes, I will stay away from him now. Or at least, I'll try."

Lucinda's cell phone went off then, playing a snatch of Vivaldi. It startled her in a way that the silent, spirit summons of Lucifer and his underlings did not. She knew who it was before she pulled it from her pocket and answered it.

"El?" Dominic's voice came to her through the device, warm, calming, and tinged with concern. "El, is everything . . . Are you all right?"

"I . . . what makes you ask?"

"You're going to laugh at me, I know, but I just had the strangest feeling that you . . . that there was something wrong."

Lucinda's breath stopped in her throat. She wanted to say that, yes, there was something wrong and that the mere thought of him had saved her from it, but Nathaniel was still . . .

She glanced up; Nathaniel had vanished. She dared to breathe again.

"Where are you?" she asked Nick.

"At home, working on an exposé. Where are you? I'll come—"

"Can I come to you?"

He hesitated, and the moment of silence felt like an eternity and hurt like a wound. "El, what's wrong? What's happened?"

"I'm not sure I can explain. Please. May I come over to your place?"

"Do you need me to come and get you?"

"No, I'll be there in . . ."—she did a hasty calculation of real-time travel by cab—"I'll be there in ten minutes."

She changed her clothes so that nothing she'd been wearing when she was with Rey was still on her person. Somehow the thought of going to Nick with Rey's spiritual scent on her was nauseating. Then she stepped through the Between to the community garden across the street from Nick's apartment, warding the garden as she stepped back into the Real. In the twilight shadows of the trees, she warded his apartment building, too, then walked across the street to the front doors, just in case he was watching for her.

He was, and had buzzed her in before she could even ring for him. He met her on the second-floor landing. She went into his arms and just stayed there for several minutes, absorbing his warmth and concern. He didn't press her to tell him what had caused her to reach out to him as she had, but she knew she'd have to tell him *something*, and that something couldn't be the truth.

Catch-22: How do I lie to a man I can't lie to?

He took her into his home—a renovated one-bedroom apartment with dark wood floors and crisp white walls—and sat her at a small bistro-style table just off the kitchen while he made tea. She felt as if he were trying to keep her where he could see her, and she was perfectly content with that, since she wanted him where she could see him as well.

He didn't speak until she was curled up on a love seat in front of a tiny gas fireplace, sipping tea. Then he asked only, "Can you talk about it?"

"I'm being a drama queen, I know, but . . ."

"Was it your father?"

She felt the darkness wash out from him that seemed always to come with the mention of her father—or his. She shook her head and told the half-truth she'd settled on.

"No. It was a stupid argument I got into with Rey. I lost my temper with him and now I think he's afraid he's going to lose his job."

Nick's gaze was on the contents of his teacup. "El, I think it was more than that. When I called you just now, you sounded . . . scared."

She had been scared, she realized. She was still scared. Whatever power Rey had been granted, she had no counter for. The physics of the supernatural world was no different than that of the natural world. You couldn't block an attack if you had no idea what weapon was being used. Of Rey's new, disturbing talent, she had no experience. She only knew that it was powerful. Truth to tell, she'd had no inkling that there was any ability that Lucifer could bestow that would have that power over her. Just recalling the effects of that power—just pondering the implications of it—made her want to hide.

You can't hide, Mariel, daughter of Eve, she told herself. *You have too much to do, with too much at stake.*

"El, look at me."

She did, and immediately wanted to tell him her truth—her entire truth. She couldn't. Not now, not ever.

"If you can't or don't want to tell me what really happened, that's fine. I just want to be sure that you're not in any danger. From anyone. Tell me that you're not in danger, then tell me what you want me to do."

I am in danger! she cried silently. Aloud she said, "I can't explain all of it. It's too complicated. All I can say is that something happened between me and Rey. I realized that he had expectations for a relationship between him and me that I . . ." She shook her head. "I knew he had kind of a *thing* for me. A crush or an infatuation or whatever, but it turned out to be more than that." That, at least, had the virtue of being true.

"So, he came on to you and frightened you? Is that what happened?"

She nodded. "I let him know that I didn't welcome his affections and he left. He was pretty upset."

"Are you afraid he might harm you?" Nick's eyes glittered with potential violence.

I'm afraid he might harm you! she wanted to say, and couldn't.

He must have seen something of that in her eyes, because he said, slowly, "You're afraid he'll confront *me* over this?"

She closed her eyes and lied. "No! Not that. It's just . . . my father favors Rey. He recently gave him a promotion in the organization. He's never said anything to me about it, but I've gotten the sense lately that he'd like to see Rey and me as a couple."

Nick frowned. "I thought Rey had a girlfriend—Vorden."

"She and Rey have a sort of casual relationship, but it's entirely physical. There's no emotional bond between them at all."

Nick sat back. "Ah. I see. Now I understand what happened in the store the other day. It wasn't Vorden Rey was jealous of. It was you."

Lucinda rolled her head back on the sofa cushions. "Yes."

"You came here. You were in trouble, and the place you wanted to be was here."

Lucinda sat up and opened her eyes. "No. I was in trouble and the person I wanted to be with was you."

He took the teacup out of her hands and carefully set it on the coffee table before kissing her. She put every scrap of herself into that kiss and knew that he was doing the same. She let his emotions wash over and around her and mingled hers in the returning tide. She had never, in her long, careful life felt anything like this. It was Heaven. It was Hell. It was life. It was death.

It was unimaginably dangerous to both of them.

They were both trembling when their lips finally parted. Nick raised his head and pointed at the windows that looked out over the turtle pond.

"I can see my church from that window," he said, his voice husky with emotion. "I'm just saying."

Lucinda laughed and, for a precious time, forgot what waited for her outside Dominic Amado's home.

CHAPTER TWENTY-TWO

Nathaniel had no problem locating his master. In the nether realms, Lucifer was like a lightless beacon. He broadcast energies that a human might describe as cold, dark, alien, bottomless, abyssal. Some human beings could even sense them, and might react with a sudden shiver, an insistent sense of dread, a heaviness around the heart, or that certain feeling that prompted them to say, "Someone just walked over my grave."

In a sense, those hypersensitive souls were right. Because Lucifer's thoughts and words gave birth to things that were neither beings nor strictly energies, but something in the twilight area between the two. Those things were—one and all—purposed to aid mankind in digging its collective grave. If those souls could see with Nathaniel's "eyes," they would behold vast hordes of these stray satanic thoughts and be horror-struck by how often they passed through them, as a jetliner passes through clouds on its way to sunlight.

To Nathaniel, Lucifer's beacon thoughts were a constant pull, an ethereal tether he was aware of every moment . . . except when he was in Lucinda's warded sanctum. He was as invisible there as she was.

He was visible now, and his lord called to him. He appeared instantaneously in the darkly mirrored place the Lord of Demons preferred, and where he wore his fleshly costume simply because he thought it beautiful. The Devil stood on the steps that led up to his obsidian altar. The altar held a book—*the* book, le Fay's Book of Shadows.

Lucifer had laid his hands on the book, palms pressed against the open pages as if he were absorbing the energies in it . . . or infusing it with some of his own. He wasn't looking at the book, though. He was staring at his own image in the black, shining walls.

Nathaniel had the impression of a feedback loop having formed. The Devil fed upon his own sinister beauty and funneled those energies into the Book of Shadows, which cast them back again. Nathaniel sharpened his gaze, and could see the symbols and runes Lucifer's fingers caressed on the gleaming pages gliding beneath the golden flesh of his face.

The Fallen did not interrupt this feeding, but simply waited for Lucifer to deign to notice his presence.

"My daughter has cut herself off from me again," the Devil said. "You have been with her recently, I perceive."

"Yes, Lord."

"What is her mood?"

"She is disturbed by your recent favors to Rey Granger and wishes to understand his new powers and the genesis of those powers."

Lucifer smiled. "She questions my choice?"

"Yes. She does. And she distrusts it. She thinks perhaps you have done this to . . . to test her, she said. Have you?"

The Devil canted his beautiful head to one side and smiled at the Fallen through his tilted eyes. "Nathaniel, you, who are so little below me in rank, should know that I was *written* to test the human spirit. My daughter is like me—at least in part." A peculiar expression rippled across his face. "She is the meeting of the sacred and the profane. My creation. Flesh of my flesh, bone of my bone, et cetera, et cetera."

"Yet you have neither, fortunately," Nathaniel observed.

"Yes, fortunately. Flesh is weak and prone to rage and lust and jealousy and error."

"You were asking about Lucinda," Nathaniel prompted.

"She is perplexed, you said. Annoyed? Angry? Intrigued?"

"Possibly all those things. Certainly, her curiosity knows no bounds. She is unable to fathom what power you have given Rey Granger that allows him to seduce her."

Lucifer's eyes lit with unholy enjoyment. "So she sequesters herself in that warded box of hers and what—tries to discover what that power is without falling to it?"

Nathaniel inclined his head slightly as if in agreement.

Lucifer turned to face the angel fully, throwing his arms wide. "She will never discover it, because it does not exist."

"I don't understand, my lord."

"No, of course you don't. Appreciate the complexity and simplicity of this test. There is no such power."

Lucifer descended the steps of the black altar and stopped in front of the angel, who was present only as a field of roiling multihued light.

"Show me your form," Nathaniel's lord demanded. "The one you show her."

The angel obeyed, becoming the tall, dark-haired, hazel-eyed man that Lucinda knew.

Lucifer made a wry face. "Perhaps I should have given *you* the Gift," he said, then shook his head. "Impossible, of course, but she might have fallen more easily to you. She trusts you. She knows you. You know her best, as well. Perhaps, in some ways, better than I do."

"The Gift?" A Gift it was impossible for him to have given Nathaniel? Meaning, what?

Lucifer made a dismissive gesture, but he was smiling, secretly enjoying something. "Tailor-made," he said. "Tailor-made to give this world what it deserves."

"I don't—"

"You don't understand. I know. But you will. And *He* will."

"God, you mean?"

"Soon—in less than a week's time, by human reckoning—the world of man will begin to unravel. I will relish watching the pulling of that first thread."

Nathaniel kept silent and waited for Lucifer to say more. He did, speaking in a low, fervent voice, slowly circling the black altar, his footfalls striking a rhythmic cadence on the ersatz stone of the steps.

"Have you ever considered the irony and ambiguity of God's gifts, Nathaniel? He gave mortals these marvelous acquisitive minds that they have used to bind their world ever more tightly together with threads of interdependence, struggling toward unity even as they struggled *with* it. Amazing technologies—each more miraculous than the magics of previous ages—have blossomed and grown and covered the face of the Earth to such a degree that mankind has the capacity to unify the species, to beat their swords into plowshares and enter a time of one fold and one shepherd."

He paused in his pacing and faced Nathaniel across the tall, obsidian altar; his face seemed to float above the glowing pages of le Fay's book.

"These technologies—the technologies that God purposed for the unification of His inane creatures—are the very things I shall use to split them into a million warring camps."

"I am astonished, my lord. When will this happen, and where will you pull the first thread?"

Lucifer's eyes took on the aspect of fire, burning and radiant in his golden face. "Oh, not I. I am not permitted to pull at the threads of existence. But I will certainly be there—on the ground, as they say—to watch them being pulled. My daughter—my beautiful, bright, and far-seeing daughter—has given me this gift. I only hope she appreciates my gift to her as much."

"Your gift to her, Lord?"

"That's for a future time," Lucifer said, then, "You said Lucinda was intrigued by Rey's seductive powers. Do you think she might allow herself to be seduced?"

"She does not share her deepest feelings with me, my lord. I observed that she was . . . deeply affected by Rey's presence. That she was drawn to him, almost against her will."

Lucifer met Nathaniel's gaze with a long, searching one of his own. "Never that," the Devil said. "Never, *ever* that."

No, for to directly force Lucinda's free human will to his own desires would cost Lucifer everything he had built.

"We must tread carefully with your daughter," Nathaniel said, "as we always have."

Lucifer didn't answer, but merely disappeared from his sanctum. Nathaniel took it as a tacit dismissal. The Fallen returned to Lucinda's place in the Between and asked admittance to her earthly garden. But she didn't answer his call, nor could he find her. That left two possibilities: either she was in her warded home and refusing to answer him, or she was in some other warded place. The first made no sense; she would surely expect him to bring her some report about Rey's new powers.

So, the Fallen sought her in the human environments she favored, and found a strange anomaly at the place where Dominic Amado lived. Lucinda had warded it so strongly and so carefully that he could not penetrate it, even to make his presence known to her. It stood to reason that she was there.

Nathaniel could wait. Time meant little to him. In the meantime, he would locate Rey Granger and try to get a sense of his "Gift."

✧

"Sonuvabitch! I *hate* it when you do that!" Rey Granger sat down hard on the reading table in the pawnshop, nearly upsetting it and dumping the neatly sorted contents onto the floor. "Damn it, Nathaniel, would you at least *try* to remember that I can't sense when you guys are gonna come out of nowhere like that?"

Except that he *could* sense them now—at least a bit. It was one of the new perks that Lucifer had given him, but it didn't seem to work consistently, or maybe he didn't understand how to use it. He'd been able to sense Vorden when she'd translated into the shop last, but Nathaniel didn't seem to make as much "noise." Maybe that was because the fallen angel wasn't one of Lucifer's "spin-offs."

"I shall try," the angel said imperturbably. "You're doing inventory? I thought you had finished that."

Rey glanced at the table. "Yeah, well, I had a less than satisfactory tête-à-tête with Her Ladyship, so I thought I'd work out my frustrations here. I like doing inventory. I find the spirits . . . energizing."

"Energizing?" Nathaniel gestured at a leather-bound copy of the 1797 edition of de Sade's *La Nouvelle Justine*. "You find them arousing."

Rey snorted. "So would you if you had an ounce of real blood in your veins, or real skin or real cojones. You know, I've always wondered: you come in here looking like a freaking demigod—are you anatomically correct?"

"Do I have male organs, you mean? I have what I need to fulfill my role—whatever that happens to be. As you just pointed out, none of this is real."

He gestured at himself . . . at his inhumanly beautiful self, and Rey felt a tickle of jealousy.

"So tell me, Nat, what do you need to fulfill your role with Lucinda, hmm?"

"Only what you see before you. I am not an incubus. I do not serve her in that way."

Rey shook his head. "I'll bet you want to, though, huh?"

The angel looked at him with imperturbable calm. "You're mistaken, Rey. Unlike you, I have no sexual desires."

"Yeah, I know. But *she* does. Maybe she wants you—ever think of that?"

"No."

"Nat, you're a disappointment. Don't you want to know if she's got the hots for you? Hey, maybe I can learn to cast a glamour that'll make me look like you so I can find out. I can do that now, you know."

"Lucifer told me as much. Congratulations. He has important plans for you."

Rey grinned. "He told you that, did he? I have to say, I was damn surprised when he sprung it on me. It was like the best Christmas a guy could imagine. I get what I've always wanted; he gets what he's always wanted. From where I stand that's a win-win."

He patted the cover of the de Sade novel. He wasn't much of a reader, but the engravings were cool, and the energies the old marquis had put into his little book were exquisite.

"He mentioned that he gave you a special Gift." Nathaniel said the last two words as if they weighed more than the others. "I must congratulate you on that, as well. I believe that makes you unique in Lucifer's service. The Gift is certainly unique."

The angel bowed then—actually *bowed*. Rey's grin was soul deep. He put his hand in his pants pocket, pulled out the Chestnut of Evil, and balanced it on his palm. It felt good in his hand now, like a hot, slick ember. It warmed him and filled him with a buzz of chaotic desire.

"Unique is one word for it. Trivial is another. I mean, just look at the damned thing. To look at it, you sure wouldn't think it was some big powerful nugget of bad juju."

When the angel didn't say anything, Rey glanced up at him. He seemed frozen, his eyes locked on the Seed, as if . . .

Rey shoved the thing back into his pocket. "Sorry, bucko, this little beauty is mine. You go find your own talisman. So, did you need something from me?"

"Only to offer my services—that is, if you need research on the provenance of any of the new pieces."

I'll just bet, Rey thought. *I saw the way you looked at the Bad Seed.*

Aloud, he said, "I get it. His nibs sent you to get a report on my progress with his charming daughter. Tell him I'm working on it. I'm getting through to her, but her *thing* for Amado isn't going to go away overnight. She's a stubborn little vixen, but then he knows that."

"Indeed. I will leave you to your studies, then," the angel said with a last glance at the de Sade novel. Then he was gone, like the last fizzle of a fireworks display.

Rey stood for a moment, looking at the spot where the fallen angel had been and wishing for the thirty-thousandth time that he could shape-shift. He gave some serious thought to how far his new ability to cast glamours might take him if he put on the right illusion.

Could be worth a shot, he thought, and sat down with his table full of cursed artifacts.

⁂

Lucinda could not talk Dominic out of driving her home. His car was already warded, so she thought it safe enough. When they emerged from his apartment building onto the street, though, she felt a momentary sense of being observed, but it lifted almost as soon as she'd felt it. There had been no malevolence in the awareness; in fact, there had been no emotion at all that she could detect.

Nathaniel, she thought. *Nathaniel, the blank page, the opaque window, the closed door.* Most of her father's "generals" were fallen angels. Besides Nathaniel, she was most familiar with Apollyon the Golden, Angel of Destruction, because of his inclusion in her father's inner circle. He was a being of cold, implacable ruin, who did not—as the saying went—play well with others. Apollyon was an unambiguous and impartial destroyer; Nathaniel was an enigma.

Dominic insisted on walking her to the front door of her building, where he kissed her good-night, resisted her invitation to come up to her apartment, and saw her inside with the lobby doors closed and locked before he went back to his car. She watched him drive away, feeling as if she were attached to him by a silver thread that unreeled from her heart as the miles separated them. He could go to the other side of the planet and that thread would still connect them, she realized, staring out through the glass doors at the front of the building. It was an extraordinary feeling.

She sensed the subtle shift of energies in the ether around her before Nathaniel took form between her and a potted fir tree in the lobby.

"Someday," she told him, "you're going to do that in the wrong place at the wrong time and I will have to give some poor, pathetic human a 'lost time' experience that will almost certainly cause them to imagine they've been abducted by aliens."

"I would never translate with mortals present," he said. He sounded disappointed that she thought he might.

She pointed to the ceiling to their left. "Security cameras."

"I was careful to appear in a blind spot."

So he had. "Well, come on up, why don't you." She turned and headed for the elevator. They rode up in silence.

"Why are you here?" she asked once they were in the safety of her apartment.

"I spoke to your father about his plans."

"His plans for Rey?"

"Indirectly, yes, but that is not what I came—"

"Did he tell you by what power Rey is able to—" She couldn't say it. Couldn't talk about the way Rey made her feel.

The angel moved to stand beside the hearth and lit the fire with an absent gesture. "He says that no power such as you describe exists."

"That's it? It's a power that doesn't exist?"

"He says not. I have never heard of it. And were he to force your will—"

She nodded. "He'd break the Law and his reign would be over." *We'd all be over.*

Sometimes she wondered if the best course of action would be to push her father into doing something that would violate the Law so that God would simply end him. Ironic, she thought, given that Lucifer was striving to drive mankind to the same fatal error.

But if Rey's newfound talent for sexual persuasion was not a power that Lucifer had bestowed . . . what, exactly?

Lucinda felt the angel's quiet gaze on her. "Do you get a sense of what it might be?" She felt Nathaniel's hesitation and glanced at him sharply. "What?"

"Your father and Rey both referred to it as a Gift." He laid subtle stress on the word.

"A gift that's not a *power?* What does that mean?" Lucinda strove to keep her voice light—to seem merely curious, rather than alarmed. "Rey seems different to me. You don't think Lucifer might have—I don't know—killed him and somehow made an incubus out of what was left?"

"No. Rey is still completely human, despite his new abilities. But, Shaliah, that is not what I came to tell you. Your father wishes to thank you for giving him what he has long desired. He referred to it as a thread that, once pulled, would begin the unraveling of the world. He said that technology would aid in this. I assume he was speaking of the Internet and social media. He said he would be there—on the ground, as he put it—where he could watch it begin to happen. I thought, perhaps, you would also wish to be there."

"Did he say when?"

"Soon. In less than a week's time."

Lucinda sank slowly to her sofa. This was happening too quickly. In less than a week, her father would go to Kuwait, expecting to watch the world begin to collapse in a paroxysm of violence. Perhaps only Ibrahim Darzi was in a position to prove him wrong.

"Yes," she said, her voice airless, "you're absolutely right, Nathaniel. I do want be there. Keep me informed."

"Always," the Fallen said. He inclined his head and vanished into the Between.

The room was dark. A mortal man would have been blind in it. Nathaniel was not a mortal man. He was not a man at all, while Rey Granger was, despite his new talents. Those apparently did not run to warding his apartment.

Having seen it, and recognized it for what it was, having felt its urgent promptings through the filter of Rey's humanity, Nathaniel was drawn directly to Rey's talisman. It was in a small velvet pouch on the nightstand. While Rey slept, the Fallen replaced Lucifer's Seed with a chestnut he had found in Central Park and infused with a bit of the energies from several pawnshop artifacts that Rey had a special fondness for—including *La Nouvelle Justine*, and a fairy tale clock.

What are you doing, Fallen? Vorden stood on the opposite side of the bed in vague corporeal form, watching Nathaniel through glowing eyes that saw beyond the physical.

The angel was taken aback. He had been so focused on his task that he had not read the succubus's presence in the room. A mistake. He should have suspected she would be with Rey. To a man like Rey, Vorden was a drug.

I am intervening in a matter that does not concern you.

Will it harm Rey? she wanted to know.

Do you care?

I would not like Rey to be harmed . . . too much.

214

Nathaniel considered his next thoughts carefully. Succubi were extremely focused creatures and this one was especially so.

My intervention may, indeed, save Rey's life . . . and put Lucinda forever out of his reach.

For a long moment, the demon and the angel stood silently, while the mortal slept, blissfully ignorant, between them. Then Vorden simply lowered her head and shimmered out of the Real and back to the realm of the Unformed, leaving Nathaniel to complete his task.

The Fallen followed her into the Between, already considering where he might "lose" the Seed. He knew of a perfect place for it, but getting it there unnoticed might be difficult.

CHAPTER TWENTY-THREE

Rowdy had not prayed—had not sincerely, deeply, and self-consciously prayed—for some time. Yes, he had gone to church and participated in congregational prayer, and he had sent God those brief, glancing prayers asking for this, apologizing for that, giving thanks for a favor, large or small. But he had not gotten down on his knees and beseeched the Lord to guide him—to give him some inkling of what to do.

If he'd had a Bible handy, he would have done something that Dan, ironically, had taught him to do long ago: when in doubt, hold the Good Book in one hand and rest the binding on the other, then let it fall open.

"You see, Rowdy?" his stepdad had said. "Your answer is right here, somewhere on these open pages."

It seemed a simplistic and superstitious thing to do, but it had never failed to provide an answer. He wondered if it had failed Dan. Or if Dan, himself, had failed.

Can I fail?

He had no Bible. So, he cast around in his mind for something in his memory of his faith that bore on what he was being asked to do. Andy was a colonel—or had been. The people he worked for were engaged in protecting the vital interests of the United States government and its citizens. Apparently, Andy—or his superiors—felt that included eliminating Sheikh Malik al-Salim in a very particular way. Rowdy knew the reason for the layers of deceit must be political in nature—must be connected to the Bidoon-Sunni-Shi'a dynamic—but he didn't know enough to understand those connections.

His insides squirmed at the thought of his part in this: to stand by while an anonymous assassin took out a man he was supposed to be protecting, then engage only to take out the assassin. Martyr him, as Andy had said.

For what cause?

Rowdy had asked, only to be told that the cause was just and dictated by what Blackpool and CIA intel had told them about Salim's ultimate agenda, which was far more extensive and draconian than even his public policies hinted at—at least according to Andy McLeod.

Rowdy thought about going to his commander, but Andy had already told him his commander knew only that he was working on a Blackpool mission. If he blabbed about the details, wouldn't that make him a traitor?

Of course it would. He was being asked to undertake a dangerous and difficult mission. He hadn't joined the Marines because it was easy. He'd joined because it was hard. He'd joined because he'd had something to prove.

What did I have to prove? Who did I have to prove it to? Not Mom. Dan? Was I trying to prove something to Dan?

The thought made him dizzy, even lying flat on his back. He decided it didn't matter, because regardless of why he'd walked into that recruitment office, he was proud to be a US Marine, and perfectly capable of handling a morally ambiguous mission. That was life, in or out of the military. The Bible was full of stories that were morally ambiguous. Hebrews killing foreign women and children, taking the land their bodies fell upon. They had followed orders. His job was to follow orders, too, regardless of his personal doubts and weaknesses. He needed to accept that and find a way to be okay with it.

He remembered the Lord's Prayer and murmured it under his breath in the darkness of the barracks. He remembered the Twenty-Third Psalm, memorized all those years ago in Sunday school, and recited that mentally as well. That finally allowed him to sleep, endlessly running words from the final stanza of the psalm through his head: *Surely, goodness and mercy shall follow me all the days of my life . . .*

✦

"This is fantastic, Nick," Brittany said, looking up from her reading of the piece he'd done on the relationship between Brant Redmon and his corporate lawyers. "This is going to blow the lid off this insider trading case. We just have to decide where to send it first. Who gets us the most exposure if we give them an exclusive? Do you have any thoughts on that?"

They sat in her office—she behind her desk, he in the conference chair on the opposite side of it. Paper wrappings from the sandwiches she'd had Terry bring in were scattered across the desktop.

Nick looked up at her over the top of his coffee cup. "I take it you had no luck with the DA?"

She made a rude noise. "It was about what I expected. When I mentioned that I had something on DC&P, he said he didn't even want to see me, and wasn't about to listen to anything I had to say. I was just a disgruntled employee."

"Did you tell him that you weren't fired—that you quit?"

"Uh-huh, and he said that he was tired of dealing with Aaron Price's 'situations.' He thought I was going to cry sexual harassment. When I said the words 'insider trading,' he hung up on me."

"So, we go to the press, then?"

She nodded. "It warms the cockles of my heart to hear you say 'we.' What do you think, Nick. I'm leaning toward the *Times*."

"Good call. Happens I know a good investigative reporter there. But I'd be ready to go into shotgun mode if that doesn't pan out. Send it to as many outlets as we can. *ProPublica, HuffPo* maybe." He gave her a 'look,' his face scarily solemn. "They're going to come after us, Brittany. After *you*. They're going to try to tear your story to shreds."

She shifted uneasily. She thought she'd factored that in, but to hear him say it . . .

"They who?" she asked.

"Everybody."

✦

At first, Rey was just jazzed that he could almost literally be a fly on the wall in that idiot lawyer's new office. He wasn't a fly—he couldn't shape-shift—but he could teleport there. Well, at least he thought of it as teleporting. *Translating*, the demon hordes called it. To them it was like walking to the corner store. Ho-hum. To him it was new and exhilarating. Once where he wanted to be, he could either watch and listen through a very tiny "hole" in the membrane between realms or he could enter the Real unseen, cloaked by a glamour.

He wasn't quite as good at glamours as Lucifer and his spirit crew—he left a bit of a waver or wobble in the fabric of the Real when he did it. So, in this case, he'd just gone into the Between and poked a hole through which he could eavesdrop on Amado and his lady friend. He wondered what would happen if he hinted to Lucinda that there was more going on between the two of them than she knew. Worth a try, he supposed, though he was disappointed that there so obviously *wasn't* something going on. Made him wonder what was wrong with these two. Anders was a knockout and Amado was what he supposed most women would call a stud. Rey failed to understand why they weren't going at it right there on the desk.

His own arousal at the thought almost blinded him to the real value of what he was witnessing. The Little Lawyer Babe and Tall Dark and Annoying were potentially on the verge of disrupting one of Lucifer's pet pipelines for the dirty money that fed unrest and excess around the globe. It was one of the many pieces of infernal infrastructure that the Great Deceiver had put centuries of effort into creating. Adam Clinton's pen was only the most recent artifact to contribute to it. Over a century before, Brant Redmon's grandpa had acquired a certain something that his grandson never went anywhere without—some Hindu demon thingie with a lot of arms and sharp teeth. If there were a more ironically fitting "good luck charm" for the Redmon clan, Rey couldn't conceive of it.

Now, Brittany Anders and Nick Amado were preparing to put the kibosh on the whole thing.

The meeting Rey had been monitoring concluded and the journalist left. Rey scrapped his plan to follow his "rival," instead opting to beg an audience with the Boss. This intel had to be worth some brownie points. It might even persuade his lord and master to let him try again to frag Nick Amado. He'd be able to do it on his own this time, with no ridiculous circus theatrics.

Rey's audience was granted. He found Lucifer in conference with two of his demons—a nasty piece of work named Diabolus, and Apollyon the Destructor. Rey knew better than to interrupt their communications, which were taking place at a level that he couldn't hear, even with his augmented ears.

To Rey's eyes, the three forms seemed to blur at the edges, with Lucifer's subsuming the other two. It was like a supernatural football huddle in which the quarterback was a blob so immense that he dwarfed and melted around his defenders. That was saying a lot—even in their "spirit form," the demon and angel were hulking specimens. Diabolus was a color that registered as red on the human eye; Apollyon was silvery-white running to charcoal gray. Rey had no idea if the colors signified anything other than personal preference.

Between one blink and the next, Diabolus and Apollyon were gone and Rey was looking "up" at Lucifer—the Demon Lord towered over him and made him tremble with a fear so deep it was almost sexual. He quailed, trying to make himself smaller.

"You have information for me." It was a statement, not a question.

"Yeah. Yes. I do. I . . . uh, it's about Amado and that Anders woman."

"Sometimes, Rey, I think you may be more fascinated by Dominic Amado than my daughter is."

"No, sir. 'Fascinated' is not the word. I hate his guts. But here's the deal: he and the lawyer are getting ready to out her ex-bosses and your favorite Mideast moneyman."

The darkness around Lucifer's bizarre Between form eddied and shifted, and his golden face swam more sharply into focus.

Thought that would get your attention.

"I am persuaded," Lucifer said, "that both of these idiot humans have a death wish."

"Hey, if you want, I'd be happy to grant Amado's wish any time."

"No. My daughter would be discomposed."

"So?"

Lucifer's eyes were like bright chips of magma. "She is my daughter and my heir. My most able general. I do not want her to be discomposed. Especially not now, as we move toward this key juncture. Continue to shadow Amado and report his movements to me. I will speak to Lucinda about the problem her lover poses. I'll let her take care of it."

As if she would, Rey thought. Aloud he said, "You might want to warn her about letting him have lunch dates with Little Lawyer Girl. Those two getting their heads together is bad on *so* many levels."

"An interesting spin on their association. I'll remark on it. This evening," Lucifer added, "there is a full moon. The female body and emotions are most susceptible at this time. Now, go to my daughter and seduce her."

Rey did not tell the Father of Misogyny that his seducing of Lucinda hadn't gone well so far, but he had faith in the artifact Lucifer had given him. He put his hand over it, feeling the heat of its sensual charge. It was only a matter of time . . .

✧

It annoyed the Lord of Hell to have to beg admittance to his daughter's domain as if she were his equal, but she had the full use of her powers and he could not take them away or limit them without her acquiescence—that, because she was human and must be given the exercise of her free will. He could ask her to let him sense her through her wards, but he could not force his way through. It was beneath him to ask or even demand, so he didn't.

He regretted, sometimes, what he had wrought by trying to show the All-Father that he, too, could create life. He had spawned a being that was neither mortal nor supernatural, and yet both. Her humanity made her ungovernable by direct means, while her powers made her a formidable ally. They could also make her a formidable opponent if she so chose. She was, in many ways, his equal. He wondered sometimes if he had been completely successful in hiding that from her.

Lucifer thought of Granger with his sensuality-soaked artifact and knew a moment of pause. Giving his mortal lackey the Seed was treading dangerously close to the line between influence and manipulation. He flattered himself that putting the thing in Rey Granger's hands distanced him enough from the Seed that God—who had also bound Himself to their covenant—would not intercede.

Lucifer became aware of Lucinda's presence in the street outside her apartment building. Ah, good. He would not be forced to ask leave to see her. She headed for the pawnshop, so he met her in the compact kitchen at the rear of the store. She had described it as cozy. It seemed claustrophobic to Lucifer when he confined his senses to the human body he wore.

"Father," she said coolly when she saw him. "To what do I owe the honor of your presence?"

"This is a brief visit to bring a confidence and a request."

She smiled. She had a beautiful smile. It reminded him of her mother. Her long-dead mother.

"A confidence!" she repeated. "How delightful. Please do tell."

"Rey has proven an estimable asset to me with his new powers. I would have given them to him before if I'd known just how valuable he could be. He tells me that your lover has been in repeated tête à têtes with the lady lawyer we tried and failed to recruit."

Lucinda straightened and crossed her arms across her breasts in a quaint human gesture of emotional self-defense. "Really."

"That displeases you."

"Why should it? He's only a man."

"A man you have claimed. Am I right?"

She inclined her head. "I suppose I have, at that. Are you telling me he's dissatisfied with *me*?"

He laughed, because the thought of any man being seduced away from Lucinda by a mere mortal was absurd. She was no succubus, but her beauty and charisma were quite literally supernatural.

"No. Perhaps that is the construction that Rey prefers to put on things. His concern, and mine, is that they're hatching a plot between them to bring down Redmon Industries and the woman's old legal firm."

Lucinda's coppery brows rose in graceful arcs. "That would be a rather significant inconvenience."

"Inconvenience? It would enrage me, Daughter. I have taken decades and longer to set up that financial pipeline and the edifice of corruption that supports it. This late in the process, I have only so much patience, and this network is key to many of our projects."

Lucifer admired the keen intelligence in Lucinda's face as she processed the information. Her bright gaze snapped back to meet his.

"What would you like me to do about this?"

"Persuade Dominic Amado that his interest in Brant Redmon's dealings is not healthy for him or for his lawyer friend. Redmon has . . . shall we say, defensive capabilities most businessmen do not. If he were to become aware of their plotting . . ." He shrugged. "I know you don't care about the woman. In fact, you may want her out of the way. But I'm sure you would prefer your human not suffer. He *will* suffer if Redmon's resources get to him."

"Resources that are practically your puppets."

Her eyes challenged him—something he suddenly disliked. He speared her with a glance. "Don't let him run afoul of me, Lucinda, or Brant Redmon will receive an anonymous tip that Dominic Amado is close to bringing him down. Your powers do not run to resurrection."

Her jaw set and she tossed her head in a momentary display of fire. By the time she spoke, any hint of fury had left her eyes. "Fine. I will speak to him about it."

Lucifer studied her for a moment. She was so cool, so controlled. He had long wanted to see the cracking of that careful facade, to witness her in rages when she indulged in only brief sulks—to see her in battle, instead of ninja-like subterfuge.

"You are a cold-blooded thing, aren't you? I think, when you smile, how much like your mother you are, but you are not much like her at all. Eve was a woman of warmth—an open creature."

Lucinda laughed, her eyes darkening and becoming extraordinarily green. "Were I a warm and open creature, Father, I would not survive long around you. I survive you because I am like you. You would neither trust nor respect me if I were not."

True enough, he had to allow. He kissed her cheek, and returned to the Between.

⊕

Lucinda stood for several long moments in the kitchenette, thankful to be alone. Lately, her interactions with Lucifer and his cohorts left her feeling drained of energy, both physical and spiritual. She felt drained now. She wished her powers ran to speeding up time or traveling forward in it, instead of only backward. If they did, she would fast-forward the day to the time when she would be with Dominic.

Yes, but when she saw him, what would she say? How could she persuade him not to pursue his collaboration with Brittany Anders? Did she want him to be persuaded? One of the things she loved about Nick—yes, *loved*—was his devotion to the principle of doing what was right and good, whether or not he derived personal benefit from it. In this case, she knew, what he was doing was both brave and foolhardy. But it was something he had not shared with her.

Even if he were to share it, she thought wryly, she could hardly tell him that he needed to back off or *Satan* would anonymously tip off Brant Redmon. She'd get him to tell her about the exposé, she decided, and she would do it without "turning on the charm." She had never done that with Nick and she vowed she wouldn't start now. He would either trust her, or he would not.

Sometime later, as she worked in the back of the shop laying out the artifacts Lucifer had chosen for several new targets, she was still trying to work out what to say to Dominic. It would be closing time soon, and she was counting the minutes until she would meet him for dinner. Maybe she would just let the situation dictate what she said.

The little bell on the front door rang, announcing someone was entering the shop. Lucinda cursed her distraction and sent questing tendrils of sense outward to test the energies there.

Odd. Her senses told a confused story of eagerness and anticipation, of nervousness and resolve. She peeked into the room through the Between; she would plan her own appearance based on what she could observe about her customer.

It wasn't a customer; it was Dominic, appearing like the answer to an unspoken prayer. Smiling, she hurried to the front of the shop. She greeted him with honest pleasure, moving to put her arms around him, lifting her face for his kiss.

"You're early. I thought we were going to meet at the restaurant."

Before their lips met, she knew something was wrong. He was cloaked in some way, yet abuzz with electric, sensual energy. It was energy that covered the surface of him and there was nothing beneath or beyond it. Only quaking desire. Only blazing sexual heat. Only . . .

She pushed away from him. He held her fast, his hands tightening painfully on her arms—digging into her flesh. His eyes seared her.

"Don't pull away from me, Lucinda. I want you so damn much."

Lucinda? She broke from him violently, took a step back, and smote him with a ball of fevered energy that lifted him from his feet and flung him against the bookcase to the left of the front door. He slid to the floor in a rain of cursed volumes.

"Damn you, Rey Granger! *Damn you to Hell!*"

His illusion evaporated as if vacuumed away, leaving behind a dazed Rey who could only wave his arms defensively. "No . . . Lucinda . . . no . . ."

"*To Hell!*" she repeated. "And don't think I can't, or won't. Don't you *ever* try to trick me or manipulate me again. Do you understand me? I will *end* you, if you *ever* do something like this again!"

The shrill cat-scream of her voice flayed her ears. She meant it. By all the Powers, she *meant* it, and it sickened her. She doubled over, in spiritual agony, tears pressing for release.

Rey stirred out of his pile of books, struggling to rise. "Lucinda, I'm sorry. I just—"

She thrust out a hand to check his words. The gesture hurled him back against the shelf; his head struck sharply and he cried out in pain. Lucinda covered her ears with her hands and leapt into the Between.

She went to the Gramercy Star, taking form in the darkness beneath an awning and stepping into the light of the windows. She peered through into the restaurant. She was too early; Nick wasn't there yet. Where would he be? She cast her net of sense wide for him—his apartment, el Paraiso, the streets between there and here.

She found him in his church and translated herself there so swiftly, she almost gave herself away to a group of parishioners who'd just entered the narthex through the street door. They gave her a startled glance as she rushed past them. She slipped into the sanctuary, heedless of that sense of intense regard she always got in houses of worship.

Nick was in the first pew on the right side of the altar, his head lowered in prayer. The sight of him there like that—so caught up in his connection with his God—gave Lucinda a moment of bereavement and loss. She had not experienced that connection since she was too young to remember it as more than a faded whisper of warmth and innocence.

She swallowed the bereavement and made her way swiftly up the aisle. She didn't speak to Nick or call out to him, as much as she wanted to, but only slid into the pew next to him, trying not to look at the painted Christ and apostles that stared out at her from the gold frame behind the altar.

She felt Nick sense her presence—felt it as a soft, warm, electric current in the air that wrapped around her and reached down into her soul. He reached out physically as well, and took her hand, though he kept his eyes closed in prayer. A smile curved the corners of his mouth. She wanted to kiss the smile, to put the tips of her fingers to it, to make sure it was real—that he was real. Instead, she sat beside him in this alien place and pretended to be praying, too. Perhaps she could not pray, but she could question.

Do You hear me? she asked God. *When I'm here, do You hear me—feel me? Do I disgust You? Does my presence anger You?*

Lucifer said it did.

She hung on that thought. Lucifer, the Great Deceiver, said, "God does not hear your prayers, little girl." But he'd also told her he lied. He lied about so many things, why should she trust this one?

I don't hate You, she told the silent God. *Do You hate me? Am I damned?*

She waited for an answer, but there was no answer. She'd long given up any expectation that she might receive one.

Beside her, Nick stirred and squeezed her hand. She glanced aside at him. His eyes were open and smiling at her. He mouthed the words *Let's go,* and stood, drawing her up off the pew and into the circle of his arm. He walked her back up the central aisle, smiling and nodding at the parishioners who'd nearly seen Lucinda translate into the foyer of their church. They smiled back, their affection for Dominic clear on their faces—as was their assessment of her.

No, she thought at them, *I'm not good enough for him. I'm the worst thing in the world for him. The worst thing in the Universe.*

He left his arm around her shoulders as they strolled across el Paraiso toward Fifth Street. "You came out without a coat again, El," he observed. "And you're an hour early for dinner and in the wrong place. What's happened?"

She couldn't exactly tell him that Rey had masqueraded as him and assaulted her. "My father happened. It's nothing, really, but it upset me. That's all."

"Can I ask you something?"

"Of course."

"Does your father know about me? That we're . . . seeing each other?"

"Yes."

"Hmm. And would this thing that's upset you have anything to do with that?"

She shook her head. "How do you do that? It's like you're psychic or something."

"Yeah. Or something. You're dodging, El."

He'd offered her an explanation as to why she was so obviously upset. She took it. "Yes. The argument was about you. I told you—he'd like to see me with Rey." She couldn't suppress a shiver at the memory of that scene in the pawnshop.

"What would you like to see?"

She looked up at him in the deep twilight. The full moon floated above the rooftops, lighting his face with pale radiance. "I like what I'm seeing right now."

"Don't flirt with me, El. I'm pretty sure we're past that. Aren't we?" He stopped walking just shy of the Fifth Street gate and turned her to face him.

"Yes. We are. Way past it."

They kissed, but even as the kiss warmed and elevated her, she thought of watching "eyes" and shivered again.

"You're cold," he said. "Let's go inside. Tell you what—let's eat in tonight. We'll get something delivered. What do you want?"

They decided on Italian from the little restaurant around the block. He made cappuccinos; she teased him about quitting his day job to pursue a career as a barista. After dinner, they sat on the floor in front of his little gas fire, her head on his shoulder, their fingers entwined, listening to a radio drama. Just like a normal human couple. She thought of the shop, of her father's plot coming to fruition in Kuwait, of dead teenaged witches and men facing trial because of it, of the Book of Shadow, and of returning to the Between. She thought of her life up until this moment and knew a desire to stay right here with this perfectly imperfect human man, and live. She could have almost anything in any of the worlds of creation, but this one thing she wanted more than any other, she could not have. She wanted it so much, she almost thought she'd said it aloud.

I want this.

Dominic murmured in her ear. "I love you. You know that, right?"

She drew in a sharp breath. "I *do* know it. It boggles the mind, truly."

He chuckled. "Not so much. You're beautiful, smart, kind, brave."

She mock-scowled at him. "Materialist. You said 'beautiful' first."

"I wasn't just talking about your face or your body. You know that."

She did know that. "Impressions lie."

"Not these." He turned so that they were eye to eye. "Marry me."

"What? Nick, we've known each other—"

"Long enough. My mom and stepdad knew each other for whole week. They're great together."

"You don't know me—"

"Yes, I do."

She shook her head. "Dominic, there are things about me—about my . . . my family, my life, that I'm not sure—"

"Yeah, and there are things about me that I'm not sure." He looked away from her at the little flames in the fireplace. "I guess we're both people with dark holes in our lives. That's okay." He looked back, met her eyes.

No, it's not okay! She wanted to scream the words. *You can't even imagine my dark holes. You wouldn't* believe *my dark holes.*

That wasn't the worst thing. The worst thing—the most horrible thing—was that he could spend the rest of his life with her, but she could not spend the rest of her life with him. He would age and sicken and die and she would go on. Alone.

But I could pretend. I could pretend to age.

Yes, and watch him age, for real—watch him die and pass beyond the Veil that she could never, *ever* penetrate. Heaven could never be hers and Nick would be lost to her just as her mother and father—her human father—were lost to her.

As painful as that was, the idea of walking away from this—of *not* having even that much of a life with Nick, of immortality in that sterile existence—made Lucinda want to beg God to let Azrael take her. Death would be a kindness.

Nick was watching her face, which made her want to hide, though she knew no intuitions he might have would come close to what she was really thinking.

"Mariel Amado," she said. "Works for me."

He drew in a long breath. "You don't have to change your name—"

"I know. I want to. I've wanted to for a long time."

"Ah. So I'm merely a convenience. You could just go do that at the DMV, you know."

"I'm not in love with the DMV."

He smiled. She drank the warmth of his smile and the kiss that followed—savored the human connection that she had denied herself for thousands of years. Later, she'd consider what she'd just covenanted to do, but she would not back out.

Though they were now unofficially engaged, he still did not take her to bed. She thought that quaint, but frustrating. She wanted him as she'd never wanted anything in her life. Every square inch of her flesh and every corner of her soul ached with desire for him.

During the drive back to her apartment, she remembered that she'd meant to ask him something. She forced words to her lips. "So, how's that exposé you've been working on? Do you have the goods on the expos-*ee*?"

He took a deep breath and exhaled before saying, "Yeah. I think we do."

"You and that lawyer friend of yours."

"Brittany. Yes." He glanced sidewise at her. "You are *not* jealous of Brittany."

"Is that an order, Mr. Amado?"

"Yeah."

"Yes, sir. I am not jealous of Brittany . . . really. I'm not. So, who's the target?" When he hesitated, she added, "Are you going to keep secrets from me after we're married?"

He shot her a startled glance and she saw that pall of darkness slip behind his eyes again, cutting her off.

"I . . . It's Brittany's old law firm, and one of the corporations they do business with. Insider trading. Possibly some shady dealings overseas. The DA took a pass. We're going to the press with it."

She let her good humor slip away on an honest tremor of fear for him. "Nick, that's dangerous, isn't it? I mean, what if those people decide to come after you legally or . . . or in some other way?"

He smiled crookedly. "I'm counting on you to protect me. You're pretty fierce."

"Dominic, this isn't funny. My father does business with that crowd. Some of them are . . . are like Mafia dons. Brant Redmon, for one, is—" She cut off on his exclamation of surprise. "What?"

"Brant Redmon is one of the people involved in the story Brittany and I are working on."

She twisted sideways in the passenger seat to look at him. "Dominic, Brant Redmon is a dangerous man. My father has warned me about him in particular. Is it too late for you to—I don't know—take your name off the piece?"

"I can't do that, El. It would be cowardly."

She lowered her forehead to his shoulder. "I know. And you're not a coward. I guess I'm just going to have to protect you—and Brittany."

He laughed, but Lucinda was already thinking about how she could make good on that promise without Lucifer finding out.

CHAPTER TWENTY-FOUR

In many ways the communication "system" employed by the immortals was more like a spider's web than it was like the mortals' Internet. It vibrated, or perhaps resonated, when things were about to occur where its strands met. It was doing that now, in a way that captured Nathaniel's complete attention. If human eyes could perceive it, they might see a multilayered spiderweb made of lightning and auroras. If their ears could hear it, it would sound like a billion buzzing bees, or like the sizzle of static electricity.

Nathaniel wasn't certain whether humanity's blindness and deafness to the supernal realm was a blessing or a curse to them. Mostly a curse, he thought, else they might understand that everything they thought, said, and did added strand after strand to the web or plucked it or severed bits of it. Human beings, the angel knew, were a dense lot for the most part. Each one existing at what they thought of as the center of the Universe and yet imagining that they were independent beings, unconnected to anyone or anything else—least of all to the consequences of their own actions.

No, least of all to the God who pervaded and supported All.

The strands of energy that converged on Kuwait were both carefully woven and accidental. Some were Lucifer's, some were Lucinda's, some were added by human beings. Some—in fact, many—spun off chaotically from the intersections of other threads. They were all telling the same story at this moment: something was about to happen. The threads connected to Aaron Price's pen, to Brant Redmon's golden idol, to Dan Collins' watch, to Darzi's Qur'án were all aglow and aquiver.

Nathaniel marked the timing. Critical. His lord would be focused on Kuwait City very soon. He translated himself into the Between and asked admittance to Lucinda's earthly domain, the Seed of Knowledge he had stolen from Rey Granger wrapped carefully in a kernel of thought.

She did not answer him immediately, and when she admitted him to her garden, she seemed . . . different. She was the same on the outside—cool, detached, in control. She was always that. But beneath that there was something the Fallen could not quite read. That he felt it at all was testament to the strength of whatever emotion it was.

"Are you quite well?" he asked her tentatively.

She actually paused to consider the question, tilting her head to one side. Her hair rippled sleekly with the movement. "I am . . . better than I have ever been," she said at last.

"Because of Kuwait?"

She glanced at him sharply. "Kuwait?"

Her eyes seemed to look far off over the rooftops of Manhattan, and Nathaniel fancied he could see the great web of fey threads reflected in them. She turned her gaze to the koi pond, then, and waved one graceful hand over it. Whatever she saw in the reflective surface seemed to affect her in some way that, again, the angel was unable to read. His task had never been an easy one; keeping watch over Lucinda required every talent and power he possessed. Lately, it had seemed exponentially more difficult.

She was frowning when she turned back to him. "The dominoes are falling."

"Yes."

She nodded. "We'll go, then. Give me a moment." She rose from the side of the pond, which was just a pond once more, then entered the apartment, closing the French doors behind her.

Nathaniel let his gaze wander the garden. It was still dressed in its October finery—the corn, the crows, the jack o' lanterns whose flames never went out, the scarecrow whose smile never faded. Surrounding all, like nodding sentinels, were a diverse variety of trees. One of them was a chestnut that was artfully losing its leaves, laying down a carpet of vivid flame. Mixed among the riot of reds and oranges and yellows were hundreds of small, reddish-brown nuts.

The angel moved to stand beneath the tree and gaze up into its branches, through which he could see the brilliant face of the full moon. He removed the infernal Seed from the pocket of his shirt, still wrapped in its own pocket of energetic ether, and dropped it on the grass where it was quickly lost among its fellows. Then he went back to the cobbled path to wait for Lucinda.

⚜

Rowdy was sweating bullets beneath his fatigues. It was actually pretty chilly in the predawn sea air, and he felt every degree of the cold, but the sweating wouldn't stop. He was sitting in the rear-facing passenger seat of the sheikh's stretch limo, next to a Brit—Lieutenant Archie Bingley. For reasons of his own, Sheikh Salim liked surrounding himself with a multinational crew. The two bodyguards sitting to either side of the politician were Kuwaiti, but the driver and the soldier occupying the front passenger seat were a Saudi and a Frenchman, respectively.

From where he sat, Rowdy could see clearly through the bulletproof rear window of the car. The headlights of the vehicle behind them were clearly visible, as were the lights of the rearmost car in the motorcade. There were six vehicles in the cortege all together; three of them carried Kuwaiti or Saudi dignitaries to the morning's parliamentary session.

Rowdy focused on the lights in the rear window until his eyes blurred and watered. He blinked, trying to clear his vision, then reached up to rub one eye. Had the lights of the rear car wobbled? Were they further back than they'd been a moment ago?

"Allergies, Lance Corporal?" asked Salim in his musically accented English.

"No, sir. Just something in my eye, sir."

Salim reached beneath the folds of his *jellaba* and produced a handkerchief. He handed it to Rowdy. "You may keep it. I have many."

Rowdy swallowed convulsively, taking the proffered tissue. "Uh, thank you, sir."

He wiped his eyes, then returned his gaze to the rear, poking the handkerchief into his uniform's breast pocket. Surreal, that's what this was. Freaking surreal. He had to be dreaming. *Had* to be. He'd wake up in his bunk in the barracks and this whole last six weeks would be gone.

Please, God. Please let this be a dream, a nightmare, a test of some sort. Let this not be real.

But it *was* real and he knew it. He wiped sweat from his upper lip as the motorcade pulled into the National Assembly complex and up to the front steps of the home of Kuwait's legislative body. The car stopped and the Frenchman in the front seat got out and came back to open the rear doors.

Heart pounding, breathing fast and shallow, Rowdy got out and brought his weapon to combat ready. He moved away from the car and trotted several steps up the staircase that led to the assembly building to give himself a better vantage point. Then he turned toward the rear of the motorcade, his eyes on the last vehicle. A single man got out. Armed.

Rowdy licked suddenly dry lips and sweated more.

Sheikh Salim exited his car and crossed to the marble steps, his Kuwaiti bodyguards on either side. Before and behind, car doors were opening and men were getting out, some in uniform, some in the flowing *jellabas* that many Kuwaiti men wore over their tailored suits.

Rowdy ignored them all; his gaze was trained on the man from the last car. He was walking toward the steps, toward Rowdy, toward Salim. Even from this distance—roughly thirty feet—he could see that the man's eyes were trained on the sheikh and that they burned with passion. Before he could decide to act, he saw the rear door of the car just behind Salim's swing open and a robed diplomat get out. Without hesitation, the man stepped into the would-be assassin's path and laid a hand on his arm.

Rowdy clutched his rifle tighter. *What the hell?*

The two Kuwaitis locked eyes. Rowdy heard their voices in muffled but animated conversation. He couldn't make out any words. He stole a glance back over his shoulder at Salim, who was climbing the steps of the assembly building slowly, engaged in conversation with a tall, regal man in flowing white robes.

What do I do, Lord? What do I do? My duty to government, or my duty to You?

"Render unto Caesar what is Caesar's and unto God what is God's," Jesus had said. But what of Rowdy Collins was Caesar's and what was God's?

"Rowdy," said a soft feminine voice almost in his ear. "Rowdy, you could never let me down. I have faith in you."

Mom?

Could this nightmare get any worse? Rowdy spun toward the source of the voice and found himself looking at his reflection in the limo's dark windows. He saw his mother's face looking back at him, too, as if—*Jesus, Lord*—as if she were standing right behind him. He whirled back toward the assassin. The man had shaken off the diplomat and was walking swiftly toward the steps and his target.

⊹

The Between offered its supernatural denizens their choice of perspectives. Lucinda and Nathaniel had chosen an elevated one, as if they hovered above the National Assembly plaza looking down on the cars and people clustered before the main building.

Her senses extended, Lucinda tasted of the energies here, and knew four things immediately: She knew the assassin was the man now striding toward Sheikh Salim's car. She knew the man who stepped into his path was Ibrahim Darzi, but she could not read his intentions in the chaos of his spirit; her glance into the koi pond had told her only that he had not touched the Qur'án for over a week. She knew Rowdy Collins was terrified and teetering on the edge of choice. And she knew the man who engaged Salim in conversation on the steps of the assembly building was not a man at all.

The dominoes are falling, observed Nathaniel from beside her.

Yes, and which way would they fall? This was a nexus—a point in time that, like the events in Nazi Germany so long ago, would reverberate around the world.

Salim's death, were it accomplished, could lead to sectarian violence and to the breaking of ties between the United States and its Arab allies.

The dominoes were falling.

Lucinda tasted the essence of the thing she had brought with her from her domain—one of the twenty dollar bills with which Mona Collins had lovingly paid for her husband's cursed watch. She could feel the mortal woman's energies on the crushed and wrinkled paper—the love, the concern, the quiet dignity. She beheld her father among the mortals below, skating so close to the razor edge of God's Law, shaping history even as he did nothing more than exchange pleasantries with an Arab diplomat.

Well, by the sacred and profane, *she* also knew how to skate.

At the speed of thought, she had wrapped herself in a glamour, stepped into the material realm, and spoken eleven potent words into Rowdy Collins' ear: "You could never let me down. I have faith in you."

She felt his soul decide its fate as her eyes locked with his in the reflection in a car window. He turned to face the assassin, backing up the stairs toward Salim and shouting, "Security breach! Clear the steps! Clear the steps!"

Then, there was chaos.

⟡

Stumbling backward up the steps, Rowdy kept his eyes on the would-be assassin. Around him there was suddenly a frenzy of activity—men shouted and ran, car doors slammed, questions and orders flew in a half-dozen languages.

The assassin, eyes still focused on Salim, brought his rifle up. Rowdy raised his own gun and fired, even as he made a final lunge backward, colliding with Salim. The assassin's weapon discharged and Rowdy heard Salim cry out in pain, felt his body jerk, felt him fall.

Damn it! No!

The assassin went down as well, blood pooling around him on the stones of the plaza. Rowdy turned back to Salim in time to see his two Kuwaiti bodyguards lift him from the steps and hustle him the rest of the way up to the National Assembly building. The tall man he'd been talking to was nowhere in sight. Salim seemed to be conscious, but a bright patch of red marred the pristine fabric of his *jellaba* at the shoulder.

Rowdy followed him, sidling up the stairs, rifle ready, watching the flurry of motion below. Once Salim and his men were inside the building, he trotted back down the steps to where the shooter had fallen. Was the man dead?

He'd just reached the body when he heard a series of gunshots and felt something strike his left arm just below the shoulder. His rifle slipped from his grasp and his vision blurred in a sudden tide of pain and darkness, then went black. When he could sense things again, he was being dragged across even ground and his arm hurt like hell. He couldn't see, though he was pretty sure his eyes were open. There was something over his head.

Pain exploded through him as he was literally thrown into a confined space. He smelled vinyl and oil. A vehicle of some sort. It rocked as another person climbed in beside him. There were two loud thumps and the vehicle jerked forward. He knew the sound of the engine—a Humvee.

"You, Rowdy-boy," said Gene Marcello's voice near his ear, "are a sorry excuse for a patriot. Not to mention a real disappointment to Blackpool. Thanks to you, our little Spittoon couldn't get off a clean shot. Salim's got a hole in him, but they're saying he's not dead. That's your damned fault."

He punctuated his words with a punch to Rowdy's wounded arm. Rowdy passed out again. When he came to, the vehicle was slowing. He heard the crunch of sand under the tires, felt the slight skid as it slewed to a stop. The rear door was opened and he was rolled out onto the sand. He grunted in pain, but fought the blackness that tried to take him.

"Get him over here!" Marcello again. "Let's get this over with."

Rowdy knew that "this" was him. They had brought him somewhere to shoot him for screwing up the mission. He wasn't sorry about that, he realized. He was only sorry that he'd ever let himself get caught up in the scheme to begin with.

God, forgive me. Mom, I'm so sorry.

Two men lifted him and dragged him away from the vehicle, where they dumped him, again, on the sand.

"Well, Rowdy-boy," said Gene. "I guess you're never gonna get your mission dog tag. I'll have one made up for you posthumously out of *this* bullet."

There was the unmistakable sound of a pistol slide being pulled back, but the shot, when it was fired, sounded more distant. In the darkness of the hood, Rowdy could see nothing, but he heard shouting, machine gun fire, the sound of a Humvee engine firing up and tires shredding sand, then more machine gun fire that seemed to come from directly over his head. The sound was deafening and Rowdy roared aloud in confusion and fear.

The silence, when it came, was sudden and nearly as terrifying as the earlier barrage of sound. Rowdy cut off his own hoarse cries and listened, extending every sense he possessed. Someone drew near and crouched or knelt near him. Then the hood was pulled from his head and he found himself looking up into the face of an Arab man he did not know, but who seemed somehow familiar. He was peripherally aware of a vehicle on fire, of bodies strewn across the sand near him; the closest was Gene Marcello's.

The Kuwaiti man spoke in softly accented English. "I am sorry, young man, for what has befallen you. My part in it is something it is best you not know fully. Suffice it to say that I regret it. I have proved false to you and to my God. I will try to get you back to your people, but it may take time."

Rowdy found his voice. "You were in the motorcade. You spoke to the shooter."

The man nodded. "I did. To no effect. I was unable to stop what I had set in motion. You did it—and with great bravery. I thank you for saving Salim's life and for saving me from my own devices."

"I'm glad I could save your friend's life, sir," Rowdy said, barely hanging onto consciousness now. "But I don't feel very brave."

The Kuwaiti official smiled wryly. "Oh, Malik al-Salim is not my friend. He is my enemy. At least, that is what I conceived him to be. Now . . . now, I am not sure what he is. Perhaps only God knows. I owe him and the man I sent to kill him both a great debt. I pray Allah that I will be able to repay it."

The Kuwaiti rose from the sand and gestured toward a group of armed men. They hurried to where Rowdy lay and lifted him carefully from the ground. He lost consciousness with the peculiar sensation that he was dreaming.

⊹

Nick dreamed. It was a familiar dream, but one he had not had recently. He had hoped never to have it again.

He was rushing to get home for dinner on time. He was late, and the setting sun turned the sidewalks to copper and the asphalt of the streets to bronze. Windows along his street glittered like gems. He had his camera with him.

Why did he have his camera with him?

Oh, yes—there'd been a photography club meeting. That was why he was late from school. He stopped to take pictures anyway, trying to capture the atmosphere of the street. It was like those imaginative illustrations of heaven that some Bibles had of roads made of precious stones and garden paths of beaten gold . . . that was, if you overlooked the trash blowing across the sidewalks and the dead leaves in the gutters and the overflowing trash bins between some of the buildings.

He took his last picture of the front of his own family's apartment building. When he looked at it in the camera's view finder, he saw a face in the glass of the lobby's front window. It was a face he knew. A face that should not have been there.

He ran. Or maybe he flew. One moment he was rooted to the sidewalk in front of his building, the next he was in the lobby. He was alone. The owner of that face was gone.

The elevator! It was going up. Second floor, third . . .

He took the stairs, vaulting up two at a time—or perhaps flying here, as well. The landings seemed to soar by and he didn't feel the weight of his backpack. He reached the fifth floor just as the elevator did, and took several steps down the hall toward his parents' flat. Then, he turned back toward the staircase and elevator core, slipped his backpack from his shoulders . . . and waited.

The elevator doors opened so slowly, it made Nick want to scream with impatience. A man stepped out, glanced at something in his hand—a piece of paper— then turned his gaze up the hall toward Nick.

Their eyes met and locked. Like his, the man's eyes were dark brown.

Nick was aware of his heart beating heavily in his chest, of his breath coming in shallow gasps, of his fists clenching at his sides. He was aware of something else, too, as the man came slowly toward him up the hall. Their eyes were on a level now. The last time Dominic Amado had faced his father, he'd had to look up at him. The last time he had faced him, it had taken weeks for the bruises to fade.

"Out of my way, son."

"Get out of here. You don't belong here."

"Don't talk to me that way. I'm your father—"

"Not anymore. You gave that up. Joe's my father now. You're—you're dead to me. To us."

"*Joe.*" Emilio Pavia sneered the name. "Your mother makes herself a whore for him. She's still mine. *You're* still mine."

"No. We're not. We—"

"You're mine and you will always be mine. You understand, Nicky? If I can't have you—have *her*—no one can. That's the way it is."

Slow motion, now. Time measured in breaths and heartbeats. Nick's father reached for something in a back pocket or waistband. There was a glint of metal. A gun, silvery and lethal.

Nick threw the backpack in his father's face, then followed it, launching himself through the air as if he were Superman—as if he thought he really might fly. Emilio Pavia caught the backpack and the full weight of Nick's attack. The moment they touched, the dream world flew apart.

I don't remember. I can't remember.

But he *did* remember. He remembered shrieking over and over: "Leave us alone! Leave. Us. Alone! I won't *let* you hurt her!"

He remembered the gleaming gun flying off down the hallway to land at the top of the stairs. He remembered the backpack between them, each trying to rip it from the other's grasp. He remembered the deafening sounds of their shouting.

He remembered the sudden silence.

It was the silence that always woke him. It woke him now, covered in a cold sweat and gasping, eyes open wide and staring at the moonlit ceiling. The dream always stopped there, but his memory didn't. He had told the police that he had dropped the backpack at the top of the staircase and that Emilio Pavia had tripped over it as he tried to flee. That was not what his memory told him.

They had struggled with the backpack between them. Nick's father had tried to work his way back to the gun, pulling Nick along as much as Nick was pushing him. It was when his father bent to pick up the gun that Nick let go of the back-pack and shoved.

In the silence that came after, he had staggered to the stairwell and looked down to see Emilio Pavia sprawled on the fourth-floor landing, his head against the wall, his neck at an impossible angle. The backpack huddled atop him like a malev-olent predator. The gun lay next to him on the landing.

Nick's mother had called to him as he clung to the bannister, his insides filling up with the enormity of what he'd done.

"Dominic! What is it? What's happened?"

He'd had no words then. He had spoken only when the police arrived and he'd told his story—his made-up story—of how Emilio Pavia had died. Everyone believed him because he was the only living witness, and because Emilio Pavia was a known abuser in violation of a restraining order. God knew, but God was silent, waiting for Nick to tell the truth: Emilio Pavia had not tripped over a backpack; his fourteen-year-old son had murdered him, and had never confessed it to anyone.

Dominic closed his eyes, knowing that the time for confession had come. Knowing that he could not marry Mariel Trompe until he told her the truth. It might cost him her love, but he knew that he could not marry her with this dark-ness clinging to his soul.

⚜

"I would be interested," Lucifer said, "in knowing what you were doing in Kuwait City at the nexus."

Lucinda faced him across the glassy, black altar in his sanctum. The le Fay Book of Shadows sat atop it, its cover closed, its evil muted by that and by the enormity and powers of this "place." She could still feel the wild spirit that was connected with it and tried not to be distracted by her questions about why Lucifer had sent Rey to dredge it up from its watery cell.

"Why should I not have been there?" she asked her father. "I had every bit as much influence in that situation as you did. Had just as much riding on it. Was just as engaged by it."

"It did not go as planned."

"No. Salim lives. But his would-be assassin is dead."

"So are several valuable Blackpool assets."

Lucinda shrugged. "You can always make more of those."

"I saw you," he said, drawing near to her. He was wearing his mortal disguise and, as he often did, was watching himself in the reflective surfaces that surrounded them.

Narcissist.

"And I saw you."

"I saw you swoop down to talk to the Collins boy."

"I saw you talking to Salim. Slowing him down. Making him vulnerable."

"What did you say to Collins and why?"

"He was indecisive. Weakening. I set him straight."

Lucifer made himself look suddenly vaster and brighter. "He foiled the assassination."

She laughed aloud, making herself of equal dimension, but never raising her voice. "Don't try to intimidate me, Father. I'm not some nitwit human you can impress with your beauty and glory, or bludgeon with your egotistical rages. I dealt with his fear—which was that he would be caught and court-martialed. He found a way to get Salim shot and kill the assassin while still seeming the hero. That is a trick worthy of you, is it not?"

He drew back and studied her. "You have never spoken to me so."

"Perhaps I should have, because you have always treated me so. Keeping me at arm's length, weaving your plots around me as if I were one of your human stooges. Did you imagine that I would not see what you were doing with Rey? That I would not detect your touch in his sudden new charisma?"

He shuttered himself behind his tilted golden eyes and turned away to circle the altar. "So, you think I have underestimated you?"

She moved to follow him, circling him as he circled the altar—a satellite, but not for much longer. She had come to a fork in the road she had been treading.

"I think you have forever tried to manipulate me. Treading oh-so-carefully around your covenant with the All-Father. A push here, a pull there, a word, a knowing look . . ." She peered up into his face. "You thought yourself clever, I warrant. Imagining, perhaps, that my humanity made me dense. I have spent millennia trying to discover who and what I am. Trying to get what I want. You tell me I'm your able general, your lieutenant, your daughter. But you treat me as if I were a pet, a minion, a servant."

He looked at her as if just seeing her for the first time, and she saw a strange combination of anger and respect dawn in his eyes. "I am merely careful. Can you blame me?"

"Blame you? I blame you, Father, for everything. But most recently, I blame you for trying to pair me with your sick human flunky. I don't know what Rey Granger did in the killing fields of Vietnam, but I *feel* what he did. I *feel* his lust for that stupid succubus you've tied to him and I can guess the nature of his sins. That is what you wish for your daughter? Well, it is not what I wish for myself. I am half human, *Lord*, and *I* choose."

Now, to rebel without seeming to rebel completely. She made a show of climbing to the step on which the altar sat and orbited it once, coming back to look down into Lucifer's falsely human face.

"I choose to wed myself to Dominic Amado. I will marry him in his church and I will live with him as a human woman in the Real, while in the Between, *I SHALL BE QUEEN.*" She raised her voice on these last words and they rang throughout Lucifer's great hall.

They stood like that—eye to eye—while time passed. Then Lucifer said, smiling, "Just like that—you shall be queen?"

"Just. Like. That. I have spent centuries under your mentorship. I am done with it." She smiled back at him. "I rebel against my father, just as you rebelled against yours."

She saw the war behind his eyes—felt it roiling his spirit. Resentment. Fury. Astonishment. Awe. Respect, however grudging. Pride. And one more thing: uncertainty.

He shook his head. "But to bind yourself to a mortal . . . If you want a mortal, Rey will last you far longer than this man."

"Yes, but Dominic is *mine*—body, heart, and soul. Rey is yours and always will be. Besides, why shouldn't I bind myself to a mortal? You did it yourself, after a fashion."

Now he laughed, but his laughter had violence in it. "Clever girl. Clever, clever Lucinda. Fine. Take your human. Bear his children. Eat him alive, for all I care. What of the shop—the artifacts?"

"It is mine and they are mine. I will use them as I see fit. And if my plans and yours converge, I may consider us allies. As of this moment, I consider us *equals*."

"Meaning what, exactly?"

She shrugged. "I suppose you will find out."

His laughter followed her back to her earthly sanctum, where she tightened her wards, huddled before her fire, and wept.

CHAPTER TWENTY-FIVE

Nathaniel was not surprised to be summoned to Lucifer's presence, though he was surprised at the environment his lord had created for the audience and by the other attendees. Lucifer sat in a huge, gleaming throne that seemed fashioned of liquid metal and shards of obsidian, while below him—seemingly on a glistening floor of pure hematite—were Apollyon the Golden and Rey Granger. Diabolus and Hellion were conspicuously absent; Nathaniel thought it telling that Lucifer—himself a fallen archangel—placed more trust in two other of the Fallen than he did the demons he had fashioned.

"You were with Lucinda in Kuwait, were you not?" the Demon Lord asked Nathaniel.

"You know I was."

"Did you find her behavior there . . . odd?"

Nathaniel considered his response. "You speak of her interaction with the Collins boy. No. She attempted to salvage the situation by means I assume she thought necessary. It seemed the young Marine might turn coward."

"What of her marriage to this human?"

Rey's head jerked up. "What? What marriage?"

"Shut up, Rey," Lucifer said softly.

The human subsided, though Nathaniel could feel rage pumping from him with every beat of his heart.

Again, the Fallen considered his words with care. "My lord, Lucinda has long felt that you have . . . held her back. You have underestimated her, kept her in the dark about the intent and shape of your plans, forced her to guess, to pry out your intentions by stealth and stubbornness."

Lucifer made a sweeping gesture with one elegant hand. "Yes, and that has made her quick and able. She is superior to any of my demons and above any fallen angel."

Nathaniel felt Apollyon's hostility uncoil beneath his golden facade. Nathaniel, personally, felt no slight. Of course Lucinda was superior. She was unique in all the Universe at present—an avatar that was at once human and otherworldly. Only a handful of beings throughout history had carried the essence of both worlds.

"She has long recognized her own qualities, I think," Nathaniel said, "and chafed at not being trusted to employ them fully. She plans to do that now."

Lucifer's eyes burned into the angel's spirit. "You will stay close to her."

"If she allows me to, yes. And I believe she will. She will need a lieutenant and she already entrusts me with much."

Lucifer turned to Apollyon next. "You are elevated. I will need you to fill the gaps that my daughter's absence in my court leaves."

"Lord," said Apollyon, and bowed his golden head in acquiescence.

"What about me, Lord?" Rey asked. "You had plans for me, I thought."

"I still do. Just not the ones you most wanted."

"You're not going to let her mate with this *human*."

Lucifer laughed. "You were fine with the idea of her mating with you."

"Yeah, but this guy—this guy's like some sort of religious nut. Pure as the driven snow and all that nonsense."

The Lord of Hell shook his head. "No. He is not. And that, mortal, gives me an 'in.' If my daughter will not desire a man I control, then I will control the man she desires . . . and the child they produce."

That, Nathaniel thought as the Devil dismissed them to their duties, would be a marriage made in Hell.

Rey had been at the point of zapping himself to a bar over on Lexington when Lucifer wrapped a tentacle of thought around him and pinned him to the throne room floor. He hated that aspect of their bargain. At least as a fully independent human, he had the capacity to say no to summonses from Demonland—if not the will. But having signed away that birthright in return for a pass on judgment, Rey Granger was as powerless before Lucifer as Diabolus or Vorden or the tiniest, most insignificant imp in the nether realms.

"What do you need from me, Lord?" Rey asked, feigning humility in spite of his inner rage.

"I need you to control your anger. It will not serve you here . . . or with her."

Rey uttered a bark of laughter. "Nothing will serve me with her. She hates me now. The last time I saw her, she said she'd *end* me if I ever tried to manipulate her again."

"So, don't try to manipulate her." Lucifer rose from his throne and descended the black steps slowly, the heels of his stovepipe boots clicking on the obsidian surface.

Rey would have rolled his eyes at the sheer theater of it if he didn't know that the darkness that hovered around the seemingly physical construct was real and always hungry. "Don't worry," he said. "I have no intention of trying."

"Do you still want her? Eventually? The man will die sooner or later."

Sooner, if I have anything to say about it.

The Lord of Demons sometimes let Rey pretend to have private thoughts. Now was not one of those times. "You have nothing to say about it," Lucifer told him, making him squirm. "Let her be. Let her have her toy. She'll tire of it, you'll see. She's not that human. Not really."

Rey tried to banish the image from his mind of Lucinda and Nick *together*.

Lucifer stopped two steps above him and chuckled, his voice low and sensual and infuriating. "I think it's clear that even were you the last man alive, she would never view you as more than a means of passing the time."

"Yeah, I get that. Fine. So, what if she gets above herself and gets in your way? You got a nuclear option?"

Lucifer looked at him searchingly. "Lucinda is immortal. Indestructible. She can be wounded, but not killed. What sort of nuclear option might I have? I planted the seed that gave her life, but God granted her a human soul and only God can take it back again."

"What if she blasphemes?"

Now he had the Devil's entire attention. "You know that as well as I do. A human who blasphemes dies. Body and soul. But Lucinda is too intelligent to blaspheme. She lives at the edges of the covenant, just as I do, but she would not cross over. Also, she is not quite human."

"Something less than blasphemy, then. You put a bit of demon spirit in her, right? So, theoretically, you could take it out of her. What would happen if you did that?"

Lucifer stared at him with something like fascination on his beautiful face. "Assuming I do, I can't imagine what would make me share that knowledge with *you*."

"Then what did you keep me here for?"

"I want you to go to her and grovel. Be repentant. Be subservient. Be useful. Show her none of your calculated lust. In fact, give me the Seed." He held out his hand.

Rey felt as if his head was going to explode. So much for the "promotion." He took the Chestnut of Doom out of his pocket and put it in Lucifer's hand. Lucifer stared at the thing as if it had done something unexpected and rude.

"What?" Rey asked. "Did I break it?"

"This is not the Seed from Eden. This is something else. What have you done with the real Seed?"

Rey felt panic rise up to swamp his rage. "Nothing. I did nothing with it. I keep it with me all the time. In my pocket or in a little pouch on my bedside table. What do you mean, it—"

Lucifer raised his hand to Rey's head and simply invaded his mind, spirit, and soul, scouring them and turning them inside out.

"It seems," the Devil's voice said as if from a great distance, "that you're telling the truth."

Rey came back to himself lying on the floor of his apartment, feeling as if his internal organs had been replaced with glacial ice. He was shaking with cold and abject terror that morphed swiftly into a rage so complete and boundless that he thought he would literally burst into flame.

Lucinda wasn't the only one sick of Lucifer's manipulation. Rey decided then that if he could not have Lucinda, no other man would either. Before, he had wanted to simply murder Dominic Amado, but he had learned much from his master. Subtlety—that was the key. He was certain, in his heart of hearts, that Lucinda was not as indestructible as her father insisted. He was also certain that while killing Dominic Amado might only enrage Lucinda, destroying *her* would devastate her human lover . . . and possibly even put a dent in Satan's armor.

Lucifer, Rey Granger thought, was not the only world-class schemer in the nether realms.

⊕

It took Lucinda several seconds to realize that someone was buzzing her from the lobby of her building. She looked at the clock by her bed. 3:00 A.M. She sent feelers of sense outward, downward.

Dominic! Even from here, she could feel the desperation in him. She leapt straight to the entryway of her apartment and opened the intercom.

"Nick, what's wrong?"

"I need to see you. Please. I . . . I have something I need to tell you."

"Of course. Come on up."

She turned away from the door, lit a fire with a thought, and fabricated a soft night robe out of the atoms around her. Floor-length, long-sleeved, but not too chaste. She was nervous. Worried. What could be wrong?

Again, she considered the human condition—the uncertainty, the frailty. It was awful. It was wonderful.

She let him into the entry and led him down the steps into the living room, where she put him in front of the fire. "Now look who's gone out without a coat," she teased gently, rubbing her hands up and down his arms. "It's threatening to snow again. Or hadn't you noticed?"

He captured her hands—his were freezing—and held them still. There it was: Nick's personal darkness, pouring out of him through his eyes.

"Nick, what's wrong?" she asked again, more sharply.

"I am, El. *I'm* wrong. I need you to know something about the man you've said you're going to marry."

246

"I know everything I need to—"

"No. No, you don't. Sit down. Please."

She sat on the raised hearth and looked up at him, while he stared at the floor, repeatedly raking his fingers through his long hair. He took several deep breaths as if he were preparing to dive into the sea, and she sensed suddenly, clearly, that that was what he was doing, in essence—diving into an unknown place. Her heart bled for him and she wanted to comfort him, though she had no idea why he needed to be comforted. She considered—for just a moment—reaching into his soul to understand, but she had made promises. If she broke them now, what guarantee was there that it would not become habit?

So, she waited.

"I told you about my dad," he said at length. His voice was low and tight and quivering.

She nodded. "Yes."

"I told you he died when I was fourteen."

"Yes."

He closed his eyes. "I did it. I killed him."

She frowned, reaching out to him—sensing him. "What do you mean, you killed him? How did—"

He opened his eyes and met her gaze straight on. His words came out in a torrent. "He came to the apartment—to where Joe and Mom and I were living. There was a restraining order against him, but he came anyway, and I saw him and I met him in the hall at the top of the staircase and he pulled a gun and I . . . I shoved him down a flight of stairs. He broke his neck. I told the police he tripped and fell, but he didn't trip. I pushed him."

He let out a breath and all but collapsed in front of her, coming to his knees before the hearth an arm's length away. She was speechless with the irony of it. How could he imagine that his secret was so very terrible?

May you never know mine.

"I've never confessed that to anyone," he murmured after a moment. "Not to the police. Not to my parents. Not to my priest."

"You confessed to God, though, right?"

"I didn't need to. He saw it happen. But, yes. I've talked it out with God many times over the years."

"And you've done penance for it every day since, haven't you?"

He shook his head. "How do you do penance for . . . for murdering your own father?"

She went to her knees on the floor in front of him, framing his face with her hands. "Nick, you didn't murder him. He pulled a gun; you defended yourself and your family. If you hadn't, he might have killed you all. If you hadn't . . ." It struck her hard. "I might never have known you."

"I should have told someone—the police, at least. But I was afraid of what it might mean to Mom and Joe if I ended up in prison . . ."

"That would never have happened." Lucinda looked up into his face. "Why are you confessing this to me?"

"I needed you to know it. So that if it made a difference—"

"Idiot," she called him, and cut off whatever he'd been going to say with a kiss.

When she finally let him raise his head, he blinked a couple of times as if clearing his eyes, then gave her a deeply penetrating look. "El, when I got here just now and rang, how did you know it was me?"

Oh. Was that what her life would be like from now on? Watching her words and behaviors, trying to catch the thousand little habits she'd developed? Well, one thing she knew of herself: she was very good at keeping secrets—though perhaps not from someone as keenly observant of her as Nick Amado.

⊹

She met Nick's mom and dad (he pointedly did not refer to Joe Amado as his stepfather) the day before the wedding. They had dinner together at an uptown restaurant. They were everything a child could ask for in a parent—loving, laughing, proud. She liked them on sight. Meeting Nick's mother, Natalia, she saw where he had gotten his height and dark beauty. And Joe—Joe was solid and bearlike and funny. They asked her a thousand questions even their son hadn't asked, and she answered each one carefully from her endless, made-up backstory. She had not known this sense of family since she was a small child.

She and Nick were married in the San Ysidro y San Leandro Orthodox Catholic Church of the Hispanic Rite. It was something that gave Lucinda horrible moments of angst that she couldn't completely hide—at least not from Nathaniel. As she readied herself for the wedding with the help of Nick's mother and Isolde Rendón, he appeared in his guise as the pawnshop's buyer. He was, she told her family-to-be, the closest friend she had in Manhattan.

She only just managed to get a moment alone with him in her garden.

"I sense that the prospect of partaking of a sacrament in a church is daunting to you," he said as they strolled the autumn pathways.

"I'm sure you can imagine."

"You don't have to marry him."

248

She sighed. "As far as he's concerned, if I'm going to have him, I do have to marry him. And I *will* have him."

"Then," said the Fallen, reasonably, "the ceremony is for appearances only and the marriage should satisfy Dominic and God's sensibilities. I don't think the All-Father would consider it blasphemous as long as you—how do they put it?—stick to the program."

She laughed and stretched up to kiss his cheek. "You are a good friend to me, Nathaniel."

Something Lucinda would have called wistfulness in anyone else's expression flickered in the angel's usually unreadable eyes.

All he said was, "Am I? I'm pleased you think so."

He sat with her in the car on the way to the church, she in a gown of white satin covered in seed pearls, her bright hair covered with a mantilla of frothy lace borrowed from Natalia Amado. She made the walk down the aisle on Nathaniel's arm. He, she thought, was every bit as beautiful as she was—something she could see confirmed in every female eye in the sanctuary.

Yet even Nathaniel, with his supernatural loveliness, was not equal to Dominic Adeodatus Amado. When Lucinda first saw him standing next to Alberto Rendón at the altar, she thought that perhaps he had tricked her, and that he was as much an archangel as her father had been—Michael, maybe, or Gabriel. And not Fallen. Never Fallen.

The ceremony itself was simple, and their memorized vows passages Dominic had chosen from a letter of Saint Paul to the Corinthians. They stood facing each other before the smiling priest and spoke words that made Lucinda want to weep.

Nick began: "Though I speak with the tongues of men and of angels, but have not love, I have become sounding brass or a clanging cymbal. And though I have the gift of prophecy, and understand all mysteries and all knowledge, and though I have all faith, so that I could remove mountains, but have not love, I am nothing. And though I bestow all my goods to feed the poor, and though I give my body to be burned, but have not love, it profits me nothing."

"Love suffers long and is kind," Lucinda responded, her voice husky with emotions she had never expected to experience. "Love does not envy; love does not parade itself, is not puffed up; does not behave rudely, does not seek its own, is not provoked, thinks no evil; does not rejoice in iniquity, but rejoices in the truth; bears all things, believes all things, hopes all things, endures all things."

"Love never fails," said Nick.

"When I was a child," murmured Lucinda, trying not to feel all the eyes on her, "I spoke as a child, I understood as a child, I thought as a child; but when I became a woman, I put away childish things. For now we see in a mirror, dimly, but then, face to face. Now I know in part, but then I shall know, just as I also am known."

There was a moment of silence in which Lucinda saw only Dominic—her mortal husband, Dominic—and heard only the slightest, breathless whispers and sighs from the guests. If her father was among them, he hid himself.

Then the priest, his face beaming, pronounced the final passage. "And now abide faith, hope, love, these three; but the greatest of these is love. Dominic, Lucinda, I pronounce you husband and wife."

A blur. It was a blur, after that, of smiling faces, and hugs, and congratulations. Then they were alone in her—no, *their*—apartment. Tomorrow, there would be a jet to Barcelona; tonight she would know even as she was known.

And though the webs of light and shadow and the human Internet and every television feed vibrated with the disturbing news out of Kuwait of an attempt on a Kuwaiti official's life by a Bidoon assassin, of a feared spike in sectarian violence, of the fact that the American Marine who had saved the diplomat's life was missing, the Devil's daughter ignored it all and gave herself over to being Mariel Amado.

She discovered that the laws of physics were not friendly to creatures like herself. It had taken her mere seconds to unbind her hair and remove her wedding dress, but she was then faced by the reality that no human woman could have done it that swiftly. Trying to at least *pretend* to be human, she had spent a torturous five minutes—all she could stand—running the water in the sink and chafing at the need to obey the laws of time.

When she felt it was safe to emerge from her cocoon, she found the bedroom empty and Dominic's tuxedo coat and shirt on the chaise in her reading nook. She went out into the living room to find the fire lit and a bottle of wine and two glasses sitting on the hearth. Nick stood at the French doors gazing out into the rooftop garden, wearing only his tuxedo pants.

Lucinda savored the hot rush of desire that burned its way up through her core. She moved quietly toward him, her bare feet cat-silent on the ebony floor, wishing she could just translate herself across the space between them.

"Dominic?" She savored his name, too, her voice husky with want.

He shifted, but continued to gaze out the window. "El, when did . . . how is there a cornfield and a scarecrow on your roof?"

She halted just in front of the fireplace, cursing her carelessness. Time for some improv. "Do you really care about that at this precise moment?"

He turned to look at her, and she let her dressing gown slide from her shoulders with classic movie grace. He seemed to forget about the garden completely.